FROM THE PAGES OF THE *CONFESSIONS*

Yet, my god, my life, my holy joy, what is this that I have said? What can any man say when he speaks of you? But woe to them that keep silence—since even those who say most are dumb.   (pages 4–5)

I believe, and therefore I speak.   (page 5)

Look down, lord god, and see patiently, as you are accustomed to do, how diligently the sons of men observe the conventional rules of letters and syllables, taught them by those who learned their letters beforehand, while they neglect the eternal rules of everlasting salvation taught by you.   (page 17)

These things I declare and confess to you, my god. I was applauded by those whom I then thought it my whole duty to please, for I did not perceive the gulf of infamy wherein I was cast away from your eyes.
                                                                  (page 17)

We carried off a huge load of pears, not to eat ourselves, but to dump out to the hogs, after barely tasting some of them ourselves. Doing this pleased us all the more because it was forbidden. Such was my heart, god, such was my heart—which you pitied even in that bottomless pit.
                                                                  (page 23)

Let me learn from you, who are truth, and put the ear of my heart to your mouth, so that you may tell me why weeping should be so sweet to the unhappy. Have you—though omnipresent—dismissed our miseries from your concern? You abide in yourself while we are tossed by trial after trial. Yet unless we wept in your ears, there would be no hope left for us. How does it happen that such sweet fruit is plucked from the bitterness of life, from groans, tears, sighs, and lamentations? Is it the hope that you will hear us that sweetens it?   (page 45)

I snatched it up, opened it, and in silence read the paragraph on which my eyes first fell: "Not in rioting and drunkenness, not in chambering and wantonness, not in strife and envying, but put on the lord Jesus

Christ, and make no provision for the flesh to fulfill the lusts thereof." I wanted to read no further, nor did I need to. For instantly, as the sentence ended, there was infused in my heart something like the light of full certainty and all the gloom of doubt vanished away. (page 126)

And while we were thus speaking and straining after it, we just barely touched it with the whole effort of our hearts. Then with a sigh, leaving the first fruits of the spirit bound to that ecstasy, we returned to the sounds of our own tongue, where the spoken word had both beginning and end. But what is like to your word, our lord, which remains in itself without becoming old, and makes all things new? (page 141)

My heart is deeply stirred, lord, when in this poor life of mine the words of your holy scripture strike upon it. This is why the poverty of the human intellect expresses itself in an abundance of language. Inquiry is more loquacious than discovery. Demanding takes longer than obtaining and the hand that knocks is more active than the hand that receives.
(page 207)

What man will teach men to understand this? And what angel will teach the angels? Or what angels will teach men? We must ask it of you; we must seek it in you; we must knock for it at your door. Only thus shall we receive; only thus shall we find; only thus shall your door be opened.
(page 260)

JB

BARNES & NOBLE CLASSICS

NEW YORK

Published by Barnes & Noble Books
122 Fifth Avenue
New York, NY 10011

www.barnesandnoble.com/classics

Augustine wrote his *Confessions* between 397 and 398.
Albert C. Outler's translation was first published in 1955, and it
appears here thoroughly revised by Mark Vessey.

Published in 2007 by Barnes & Noble Classics with new Introduction,
Notes, Biography, Chronology, Inspired By, Comments & Questions,
and For Further Reading.

Introduction, Notes, and For Further Reading
Copyright © 2007 by Mark Vessey.

Note on Augustine, The World of Augustine and the *Confessions*,
Inspired by Augustine and the *Confessions*, and Comments & Questions
Copyright © 2007 by Barnes & Noble, Inc.

Confessions
ISBN-13: 978-1-59308-259-8
ISBN-10: 1-59308-259-2
LC Control Number 2006939104

Produced and published in conjunction with:
Fine Creative Media, Inc.
322 Eighth Avenue
New York, NY 10001

Michael J. Fine, President and Publisher

Printed in the United States of America

QM

7 9 10 8

CONFESSIONS

Saint Augustine

Translated by Albert C. Outler

Translation revised throughout by Mark Vessey

*With an Introduction and Notes
by Mark Vessey*

George Stade
Consulting Editorial Director

BARNES & NOBLE CLASSICS
NEW YORK

AUGUSTINE

The most seminal Christian thinker after Saint Paul, of whom he would be an influential interpreter, Augustine of Hippo was born Aurelius Augustinus on November 13, 354, in Thagaste, a small town in the province of Numidia in what was then Roman North Africa (today Souk Ahras, Algeria). His mother, Monica, was a devout Christian; his father, Patricius, was a "pagan" who converted to Christianity on his deathbed. With financial help from a local grandee, his parents saw to it that he got the best possible education, culminating in study at Carthage, the regional metropolis. While at Carthage, Augustine began a longstanding and apparently monogamous relationship with a woman with whom he fathered a son, Adeodatus. He also joined the Manicheans, an outlawed Christian sect whose complex dualistic cosmology must have appealed to a brilliant young man in search of answers to difficult questions about the world and his place in it.

From 375 to 386 Augustine taught grammar and rhetoric in Thagaste, Carthage, Rome, and Milan, building a career that promised to carry him to the pinnacle of secular distinction. Once exposed to the Neoplatonist philosophy of writers like Plotinus, however, he quickly became weary with the Manicheans. Other, more specifically Christian influences also began to bear on him in Milan, including—as he would later recall—the preaching and example of Ambrose, the impressive and austere bishop of that city. Augustine was baptized by Ambrose at Easter 387, and in 389 moved back to Thagaste to set up a small community of Christian philosophers committed to the contemplative life as "servants of god."

During a visit to the nearby African city of Hippo in 391, Augustine was ordained as a presbyter, reportedly in response to popular demand. Then, in 395 or 396, he became bishop. Aside from travel to neighboring episcopal sees, he would remain in Hippo and its diocese for the rest of his life, heavily involved in the affairs of the locality at all levels—preaching and advising on spiritual matters, settling disputes, intervening with higher authorities to save prisoners from torture and execution, using church funds for the relief of orphans and the poor or to buy freedom for slaves. After the "Catholic" church in North Africa had received imperial endorsement against the rival party of "Donatist" Christians in the region, Augustine used all means at his disposal—including the civil arm—to enforce unity. He was no less tireless in controversy with those who were judged to be "heretics," such as the followers of Pelagius. As the letters and books that he wrote on these and a range of other doctrinal and disciplinary topics increasingly found an audience beyond the confines of his diocese, he became one of the best-known Christian intellectuals of his age.

From Augustine's enormous literary output (some 100 books and many more letters and sermons), a handful of works notably transcend the original circumstances of their composition. Around the year 400, Augustine published the *Confessions*, a soliloquy addressed to an almighty and all-knowing god, made to be heard as well by the author's fellow men and women, and full of curious and intimate detail about himself. In another idiom altogether, his treatise *On the Trinity* is a soaring synthesis of philosophy and biblical exegesis, without equal in Western theology down to his time or for long afterward. Between earth and heaven, *The City of God* ransacks the library of "classical" or "pagan" intellectual culture to reaffirm an understanding of the created order based on the Christian scriptures from Genesis to Revelation. Both these other works were long in the writing and were finished only in the late 420s. Seeing how much he had written by that date, and how closely some of it was being read, Augustine then began his *Retractationes* (*Revisions*), a self-critical review of all his works, designed to guide future readers. On August 28, 430, while Hippo was under siege by the Vandals, and before he could extend this annotated catalog to his letters and sermons, Augustine died of a fever. Western Christianity—and Western culture more generally—has been taking stock ever since of his extraordinary written legacy.

TABLE OF CONTENTS

The World of Augustine and the *Confessions* ix

Introduction by Mark Vessey xv

CONFESSIONS 1

Endnotes 261

Inspired by Augustine and the *Confessions* 293

Comments & Questions 297

For Further Reading 303

THE WORLD OF AUGUSTINE
AND THE *CONFESSIONS*

313   Emperors Constantine and Licinius agree on a policy of religious freedom for the whole Roman Empire: The Edict of Milan marks the end of the period of intermittent state persecution of Christians. In Africa, there is growing schism between Christians who continue to identify strongly with the tradition of the martyrs, and those who take a less heroic view of how the church should henceforth define itself. The hardliners, as followers of Donatus, bishop of Carthage, will be known as Donatists.

325   A council of bishops summoned by Constantine at Nicea draws up a rule of faith (the Nicene Creed) designed to exclude Arianism, a theological position that denies the full divinity of the second person of the Trinity. Controversy on this issue will nonetheless continue to divide the church within the empire for several decades. Around this time, Eusebius, bishop of Caesarea, publishes an expanded version of his *Ecclesiastical History*, recounting the history of Christianity from the Apostolic period to the present.

335   Constantine establishes a new capital of the Roman Empire at Byzantium on the Bosphorus: Constantinople.

337   Constantine dies. Eusebius of Caesarea publishes his *Life of Constantine*.

354   Aurelius Augustinus is born on November 13 in Thagaste, a small North African town in the Roman province of Numidia (Souk Ahras in today's Algeria). Augustine's mother, Monica, is a devout Christian who will eventually become the patron saint of mothers, wives, and abuse victims; Augustine himself will credit her with considerable influence on his spiritual development. His father, Patricius, is a "pagan" who will be baptized into Christianity on his deathbed. Socially respectable but not especially well-off, Augustine's parents are keen for him to succeed in the world. As a boy, he is sent first to the local school to study Latin and Greek language and literature, then to Madaura, a town 20 miles south of Thagaste reputed for its teachers. There he will move on to the study of rhetoric, a skill essential for anyone who wishes to succeed in a public career under the Roman Empire.

356   Antony, believed to be the first Christian hermit, dies in Egypt. The contemporary *Life of Antony*, by Athanasius, bishop of Alexandria, spreads his fame abroad and inspires many other Christians to experiment with monastic styles of life.

361   Julian rules as emperor. Though raised as a Christian, he has repudiated that faith and strives as emperor to restore traditional polytheistic cult practices, thereby earning the title "Apostate" from future ecclesiastical historians. He will die in battle against the Persians in 363.

364   Valentinian I becomes emperor in the West, reestablishing tolerance for Christians. He is the last emperor to subscribe to Arianism. He delegates his brother, Valens, also an Arian, as emperor of the East.

371   With financial help from a family friend, Augustine's parents send him to Carthage, the metropolis of Roman Africa, to complete his education in the language arts.

372   Augustine's father dies a convert. Augustine begins a relationship with a woman who will remain with him for more than a decade. She soon bears him a son, Adeodatus ("God-given").

373   Augustine reads Cicero's *Hortensius* (now lost), about the rewards of studying philosophy, and is spellbound. Not long afterward he becomes a "Hearer" among the Manicheans, an outlawed Christian sect that promises its adherents special insights into the order of the universe.

374   Aspiring Christian intellectual Eusebius Hieronymus (one day to be venerated as Saint Jerome) takes up the ascetic life; later he will claim to have spent time as a monk in the Syrian desert. Ambrose becomes bishop of Milan.

375   Augustine returns home to Thagaste to earn his living as a teacher.

376   Augustine opens a school of rhetoric in Carthage. Valens allows the Goths to settle within the empire.

378   The Goths defeat an army led by Valens at Adrianople; the emperor is killed. The battle is widely seen as a catastrophe for the empire.

379   Theodosius I becomes emperor in the East.

380   Theodosius establishes orthodox Christianity as the official state religion. All subjects are required to accept the Nicene

Creed, formulated at the Council of Nicea in 325, endorsed in a revised form by the Council of Constantinople in 381, and still in use today as an expression of Catholic Trinitarian theology.

382   Jerome goes to Rome, where he joins the entourage of Pope Damasus and cultivates a coterie of aristocratic Christian women. In due course he will claim a papal commission for his revised Latin version of the New Testament.

383   Seeking better-behaved students and with an eye to other prospects as well, Augustine goes to Rome to teach rhetoric but is disheartened when his pupils fail to pay their fees. His main companions, outside his immediate household, are still his fellow Manicheans.

384   Symmachus, prefect of Rome, appoints Augustine professor of rhetoric in Milan, one of two seats of imperial government in the West (the other is at Trier on the Rhine frontier), where the thirteen-year-old emperor Valentinian II now holds court. New contacts lead Augustine to new intellectual interests, including (probably) study of the works of Plotinus (A.D. 205–270), a Platonist philosopher who taught that the human soul could be united with the divine One through a process of progressive purification and spiritual ascent. Augustine also hears Bishop Ambrose preach; his commitment to Manichean doctrine begins to waver. Symmachus lobbies Valentinian II for the restoration of the traditional privileges of "pagan" religion at Rome but is fiercely opposed by Ambrose.

385   In Milan, Monica arranges a marriage for Augustine with a woman from a good family, to further his career. The marriage cannot take place until the girl is older. Meanwhile, Augustine's partner of many years and mother of his son is packed off home to Africa. He is devastated by the loss but quickly finds another woman for his bed.

386   Augustine resigns from his job and retires with a group of friends to the country estate of Cassiciacum outside Milan, where he composes a series of Christian philosophical dialogues, ostensibly based on conversations held at the time.

387   Augustine, his friend Alypius, and his son, Adeodatus, are baptized by Bishop Ambrose at Easter. Augustine and his household set off to return to Africa; his mother, Monica, dies while they are in Ostia, waiting to board ship. Augustine goes back to Rome for several months, where he begins the first of several treatises directed against the Manicheans.

389 Augustine returns to Africa with Adeodatus and establishes a community of "servants of god," living ascetically on his family property at Thagaste.

390 Adeodatus dies, to Augustine's deep distress. In Rome, a former soldier in the army of the Emperor Julian, Ammianus Marcellinus, completes a history of the Roman Empire for the period A.D. 96–378; the last large-scale Roman history written in Latin from a non-Christian viewpoint, it will be largely ignored until the Renaissance. In the meantime, Latin history-writing will mainly follow the model of the *Chronicle* of Jerome (based on an earlier work by Eusebius of Caesarea), an annalistic "universal history" stretching from the Hebrew patriarch Abraham to the battle of Adrianople in 378.

391 With a view to setting up a monastery there, Augustine visits the coastal city of Hippo Regius in the Roman province of Africa Proconsularis (now Annaba, in Algeria). At Mass one day, the congregation pleads with him to accept ordination, and he is made a presbyter. The emperor Theodosius orders the closing of pagan temples and an end to all "pagan" ceremonies.

393 At the invitation of Aurelius, the newly consecrated bishop of Carthage, Augustine delivers a lecture, *On the Faith and the Creed*, to a council of bishops held in Hippo. Jerome publishes *On Famous Men*, a catalog of (mainly) Christian writers from the New Testament to the present, the first work to offer a continuous account of a Christian literary tradition.

395 Emperor Theodosius dies. The empire will now be ruled by his sons Arcadius (in the East) and Honorius (in the West).

395/6 Augustine is ordained bishop of Hippo—in defiance of canon law, as there is already an elderly incumbent in the see. (The date is still debated by scholars.) His friend Alypius is already bishop of Thagaste. Soon Augustine begins drafting a guide to the interpretation of the Bible, entitled *On Christian Teaching*, possibly at the request of Bishop Aurelius. In Gaul, Sulpicius Severus composes a biography of Martin, monk and bishop of Tours, whose cult as a "saint" spreads rapidly after his death the following year.

397 Ambrose dies in Milan on April 4. Augustine breaks off the writing of *Christian Teaching*, which he will not finish until the late

420s. Apparently during a period of enforced idleness due to illness, he begins his *Confessions*, a prose-poem that praises the god
of the Christian scriptures, presents the author himself, and is designed to be overheard by readers. In Bethlehem, Jerome pursues
his self-appointed task of revising the Latin versions of the Old
Testament, despite doubts that Augustine has already expressed
to him about the wisdom of retranslating directly from the Hebrew originals. The fruits of Jerome's labors will be gathered into
the Latin Bible later to be called "the Vulgate."

406 The Vandals, who are Arian Christians, invade and overrun the
Roman provinces of Gaul, then continue into Spain.

410 In August an army of Goths under Alaric sacks Rome, burning
parts of the city. Aristocratic refugees flee to their overseas estates
in North Africa, accompanied by their hangers-on. Among the latter is Pelagius, a British monk, who, unlike Augustine, believes that
human beings have the ability to obey the divine commandments
in the Bible without special divine help.

411 At a conference of bishops in Carthage the imperial commissioner,
Count Marcellinus, gives judgment against the Donatists. An imperial edict will follow. Augustine and his fellow "Catholic" bishops in
North Africa can now take possession of their rivals' churches. Augustine is alerted to the teachings of Pelagius and his associates,
which are taking hold in Carthage. Having spent much of his energy since becoming a bishop arguing against the Donatists, he
will now embark on a long campaign against Pelagius and his sym-
pathizers, working out the consequences of the "fall" of Adam
and Eve in terms that will prove both influential and highly controversial in western Christianity.

413 Augustine begins writing *The City of God*, partly in response to
those who allege that the recent sack of Rome was punishment
for the abandonment of traditional ("pagan") religious cults. The
work, dedicated initially to Count Marcellinus, will not be completed for many years; it contains an elaborate demonstration of
the superiority of the Christian worldview (books 1–10) and a syn-
opsis of world history from the Creation to the end of time (books
11–22).

416 A pirated version of Augustine's treatise *On the Trinity* goes into
circulation; when issued in the 420s in its final authorial form, in
fifteen books, it will be the most philosophically ambitious account
of the Christian doctrine of the godhead yet produced by a Latin

theologian. Unusually for a doctrinal work by Augustine, it is not written in response to any immediate "heretical" challenge.

417   The teachings of Pelagius are condemned by successive popes; he and his supporters are subsequently banished from Rome.

418   Augustine leads more than 200 bishops at the Council of Carthage, which pronounces Pelagianism heretical. Honorius makes a treaty with Alaric's Goths and grants them a legal domain in Aquitaine, on the Atlantic coast of France; they make Toulouse their capital.

420   Jerome dies at Bethlehem on September 30.

425   Valentinian III becomes emperor in the West.

427   Augustine completes *The City of God*. He names Heraclius as his successor in Hippo and delegates to him many of the routine tasks of the bishop. In time spared from other pressing literary tasks, Augustine begins his *Retractationes* (*Revisions*), an annotated catalog of his writings that charts the progress of his thinking and identifies points he would, in hindsight, have treated differently.

429   The Vandals, led by Geiseric, invade Africa from Spain.

430   The Vandals ravage the North African coastal provinces of Mauretania and Numidia, burning Catholic churches as they go. Hippo, a fortified city, becomes a haven for refugees. Augustine prays with his congregants, while for several months a Vandal fleet stands off the coast. In the third month of the siege, on August 28, Augustine dies of a fever. Though Hippo is partly burned when the city falls, the library of Augustine's works—some 100 books (all but the last few of them listed in the *Revisions*), an extensive correspondence, several hundred sermons—is preserved. A disciple of his, Bishop Possidius of Calama, will compose a *Life of Augustine*, in which he carefully avoids duplicating material in the *Confessions*; he will annex to it an itemized bibliography of Augustine, thereby assuring this writer's texts a safer transmission in later ages than could normally be counted on before the invention of printing.

INTRODUCTION

The *Confessions* stands in a unique relationship to the Western idea of the literary classic. Augustine's most famous work challenges one of the supreme classics of ancient Latin literature, Virgil's *Aeneid*, the epic of Rome's imperial destiny. It contends against that sacred Roman model in an idiom derived from the Jewish and Christian scriptures, texts with their own strong claim to normative status in cultures of the ancient, medieval, and modern worlds. In the *Confessions* we witness the collision of two mighty traditions of storytelling, alike devoted to the long-term dealing of god(s) with human beings and societies. This alone would guarantee the work's historic interest. What makes it startling, even now, is Augustine's attempt to tell a story of the entire human race throughout all time, *in the first person singular*. The example of Roman epic encouraged narrative ambition. The Hebrew psalms provided an alternative dramatic voice. To say much more than that is to say more than we can know for certain about the genesis of this strange and utterly original creation. For a long while after Augustine's death, no one knew what to make of the *Confessions*. By the time we find readers responding to it with real excitement, between the twelfth and fourteenth centuries of the Christian era, they already resemble the modern selves we call our own.

–I–

"To Carthage then I came / Burning burning burning burning." The mood and movement are Augustine's, at the beginning of book 3 of the *Confessions*. As a Roman citizen of the late Empire, Augustine spoke and wrote in Latin. The English lines occur in a modern classic, T. S. Eliot's *The Waste Land* (1922), arguably the most influential English-language literary work of the twentieth century. (Its nearest competitor would be James Joyce's *Ulysses*, published in the same year, another composition that plays on a long tradition of poetry and myth from Homer forward.) In the explanatory notes that he added to his poem, Eliot acknowledged Augustine as a source, quoting the *Confessions* in the first translation ever made of it in English, by Tobie Matthew

(1620). "To Carthage then I came" was Matthew's rendering of Augustine's "Veni Carthaginem."

The Latin phrase had a special resonance for Augustine's readers in the early fifth century. In the far-off days of the Roman Republic, Carthage had been Rome's great enemy. A Carthaginian army under Hannibal once encamped beneath the walls of the city itself. "Carthage must be destroyed!" That was the famous refrain of the Roman statesman Cato in his speeches to the Senate. Ancient Punic Carthage *was* destroyed, politically and physically. The city razed, its territories became Roman possessions. But the rivalry lingered in historical and mythological accounts of the rise of Roman power.

In the time of Augustus Caesar, the first Roman emperor, the poet Virgil devised a prophetic storyline in which the Trojan refugee Aeneas, making his way to Italy under the gods' direction to found the future nation of Rome, was hospitably received at Carthage by Queen Dido. Aeneas' tale of the fall of Troy, told to Dido and her entourage in books 2 and 3 of the *Aeneid*, is the leading first-person narrative in Roman literature. Augustine, who composed mock speeches based on episodes in the *Aeneid* as a schoolboy and taught the poem to his own students for years afterward, would have known it by heart. After relating the wearisome journey of himself and his fellows down to the moment of his father's death in Sicily, before the storm at sea that cast them on the shore of Dido's kingdom, Aeneas comes to a stop. Having come to Carthage, he has no more to tell in his own person, and reverts to being the third-person subject of a poet's tale. In the inner time of the poem, meanwhile, Dido has fallen fatally in love with her storytelling guest. *Fatally*, because the fate or destiny of Rome and Aeneas is against her. The hero will go on his god-driven way, leaving Carthage and its queen behind without so much as a word of parting. Abandoned and betrayed, Dido takes her own life. As the Trojans sail over the horizon, they look back and see the city lit up by her funeral pyre. It is also the reader's last sight of Carthage in the poem, burning.

When T. S. Eliot was asked to give a lecture on Virgil in wartime London—another city lit by fire—he made his subject the question "What Is a Classic?" (1944). He answered it by claiming Virgil as the universal classic of European literature, and the *Aeneid* as the poem par excellence of European civilization. For Eliot, the Roman destiny of Aeneas already prefigured the Christian destiny of the Western nations after Rome. The idea was not altogether original; like others who appealed to Virgil as guardian spirit of "the West" during the dark years of the mid-twentieth century, Eliot was deeply indebted to Dante, the Christian poet who, in the *Commedia* (*Divine Comedy*) had taken the pagan Virgil as guide for part of *his* journey. Central to Eliot's vision of the literary classic is a scene of poignant separation that is also a promise for the future. There are only two moments in "What Is a Classic?" when he refers to a specific place in a literary text. The first is when he remembers how the shade of Dido refused to speak to Aeneas on his visit to the nether world. That passage in book 6 of the *Aeneid* Eliot calls "one of the most civilized . . . in poetry," because of the assurance that he found in it—in his own intuition of what Aeneas must have felt—that Virgil's hero possessed a "consciousness and conscience" suitable to the forerunner of European civilization. The second moment occurs at the very end of the lecture when Eliot quotes the lines spoken by the figure of Virgil as he takes his leave of Dante in the *Commedia*, having, says Eliot, "led Europe towards the Christian culture which he [Virgil] could never know." These twin scenes of Virgilian wayfaring provided Eliot in 1944 with the emotional grounds for a joint definition of the literary classic and of the Christian destiny of the West, one that appealed at the time to audiences on both sides of the Atlantic and whose echo has not yet died away. Neither scene, however, could have appeared in such a light without the intervention, between the pagan Virgil and the Christian Dante, of the wayfarer of Augustine's *Confessions*. Augustine, not Virgil, created the plot of the "divine comedy" onto which Eliot and other post-Romantic readers of Dante would one day graft their personal histories of the West. And that is perhaps the best reason for rating this work a classic in the twenty-first century. To read the *Confessions* is to go back to a place in memory from which the most expansive projections of Western civilization have been made—the place that Augustine, like Virgil before and Eliot after him, calls "Carthage."

−2−

The *Confessions* never had an introduction. When it began to circulate in lands of the Roman Mediterranean 1,600 years ago, the book carried only the barest of clues to its contents: a title, the author's name, a beginning ("You are great, lord . . ."). Some modern translations add chapter titles and subheadings; such devices were known to Augustine, but he did not use them here. He divided the *Confessions* into a number of "books," which we can now think of as chapters.* The older term "book" recalls a time not long before Augustine's when literary works were copied on papyrus rolls ("volumes") and all but the shortest of them filled several rolls or books each. The *Confessions*, however, was produced using the alternative technology of the codex or block-book. Anyone who found this work of Augustine's lying on a table would have picked up a single, spine-hinged object of the kind we are still familiar with today, only with parchment or papyrus pages and a text that had been hand-copied by a scribe from beginning to end. Apart from the division into books, the text would have consisted of a continuous series of Latin characters, without paragraph breaks or spacing between words, and with only the lightest punctuation. There would be no initial capitals for proper names or other key terms. Not even the words for "god" (*deus*) and "lord" (*dominus*) would be capitalized, though they might on occasion be abbreviated. The familiar "God" of centuries-old, settled monotheism takes for granted too much of what Augustine was still trying to make possible for his readers to conceptualize, and for that reason has been avoided here too. With such a book, skimming was not an option. Opening at random would yield only cryptic text-bites. Turning straight to the end of the codex, a prospective reader came upon the last line written by the scribe: "Here ends the thirteenth book of Augustine's *Confessions*." Thirteen sections in total—an odd number on most counts, one more than the "epic" number of twelve established by Virgil's *Aeneid*.

    That was all a prospective reader could know at first glance. If an introduction to the *Confessions* serves any purpose now, it will give us pause to realize how unlike a "classic" this book would have seemed to our counterparts in the ancient world, as they took it curiously in hand.

−3−

Who was Augustine, the author of this book? He was not then a saint in the sense now presumed by the title "Saint Augustine." Such titles are acquired posthumously. He was not even an especially well-known person by the standards of ancient, let alone modern, celebrity. Around the year 400, when the *Confessions* became available to read, only a handful

---

* The standard method of referring to parts of the *Confessions* is by book number followed by two further numbers derived from two originally separate (non-authorial) divisions into paragraphs.

of his nearest acquaintances could have filled in the salient points of his biography. To recognize the kind of literary event—or non-event—this work would then have been, we should begin by making a blank of the information in the chronology prefixed to this introduction, and ask what we could reasonably have known at the time.

What, for example, was the author's occupation? He could not have been just a writer. The only professional writers of his time were scribes who copied books and legal documents. The sons (and some daughters) of better-off families learned to compose poetry and artistic prose, but not in order to become poets or "authors" in the modern sense. As in other societies, so also under the Roman Empire, advanced literacy was both a status-marker and a prerequisite for the occupations of elite males. Literary creativity outside the schoolroom was essentially an amateur affair, the hobby of aristocrats and gentlemen. There was one major exception to this rule: the performance of highly wrought speeches praising emperors or top state officials. Such orations constituted a vital public relations medium for the imperial government, combining the functions of press conference and political broadcast. Some of the finest talents—including at one time Augustine's—were retained for the purpose.

The man behind the *Confessions* was still in fact a kind of civil servant, employed in a sector that was fast becoming as indispensable to the smooth operation of Roman society as the army and government bureaucracy. Augustine held the post of bishop in Hippo Regius, a coastal city in the Roman province of Africa Proconsularis (now Annaba in Algeria). It was a place of some economic importance, the second-largest port—after Carthage, the hub of the region—for the shipment of African grain and other staples to Italy and the city of Rome.

Rome, the Eternal City of imperial myth, was by this time no longer the political center of the Empire. Its functions had been taken over by the new eastern Roman capital of Constantinople, founded by the emperor Constantine in 330, and by the other regional capitals from which the emperors—as members, now, of a self-renewing imperial college—administered the realm and guarded its borders against incursions by neighboring peoples. Yet despite these changes the Eternal City retained its prestige as the historic focus of Roman civilization, and nowhere more so than in the eyes of well-educated, ambitious male citizens of the "Western," Latin-speaking provinces, including North Africa. Along with its grain and olive oil, Africa had traditionally sent its brightest and best to Italy to further their careers—as teachers, in the legal and medical professions, in government. Many of these metropolitan Africans returned home with high honors. Their statues with inscriptions proclaiming their achievements could be seen in the forum of every town. The pattern is familiar from other colonial histories. Augustine had very nearly conformed to it—but now he was a bishop in Hippo.

A bishop (literally "overseer") was chief executive of the local branch of an organization known as the "church" (translating the Greek *ekklesia*, "assembly"). Relatively unimportant before, this organization had increased dramatically in wealth and influence since the emperor Constantine (died 337) began the practice of enacting laws favorable to the establishment of the Christ cult, a breakaway version of messianic Judaism that, over three centuries, had won support in areas far beyond its ethnic and geographical roots in Roman Palestine. Having become sympathetic to the cult, which he eventually joined, Constantine overturned the policy of previous emperors, which had been either to tolerate the "Christians" as one visible minority among many or, for reasons of state, now and again to require them on pain of punishment—even, in rare cases, death—to perform the customary ceremonies of emperor worship. Just as every town council had until lately appointed an official to maintain the cult of the divine emperor, so the bishop in each community was manager of the ceremonies by which the Christ cult was kept up. In the more familiar language of ancient Mediterranean and Near Eastern religion, the bishop was a priest. Like other cult organizations, the Christians had a rite of initiation (which they called baptism) and a ritual meal (the eucharist or mass). Besides officiating at such events, the bishop was responsible for instructing Christian initiates in the special formulas and oracles of their community, beginning with the articles of the apostolic (or baptismal) creed. He was responsible for seeing that the rules of the community were observed, and that those who infringed them underwent a process of public correction (penance). In virtue of recent imperial laws, he also acted within his territory or diocese as judge of first instance in cases of civil law. Much of his time was spent settling disputes.

Not all bishops filled these roles effectively. A bishop's authority could be challenged, and many of Augustine's colleagues were men of modest origins and limited education, vulnerable to browbeating by local potentates. Still, a hard-working bishop could exercise significant influence both within and beyond his diocese. He would have few opportunities, however, to make his presence felt as a writer, even among the minority of the public who could read for themselves. The writerly functions of the Roman episcopate were above all administrative. When bishops met in council to discuss policy, they would typically produce memoranda of their decisions; in an emergency, they might delegate someone to provide written clarification of a doubtful point of discipline or doctrine. Like all persons of rank and responsibility, they were used to dictating and receiving letters and other business documents. For most of them, that would be the full extent of their literary labors. Augustine, author of the *Confessions* and many other works besides, was one of the exceptions.

Augustine had been ordained bishop of Hippo in 395—somewhat irregularly, since the man he was supposed to succeed was still alive and active in the job at the time. Even after this man's death, Augustine was not the only bishop in town. There was a rival claimant with his own basilica and congregation a few blocks away. It was a situation repeated in towns across North Africa. Members of the rival faction, called Donatists after a former leader, considered that the African Christian party to which Augustine now belonged had betrayed the name of Christ by capitulating to imperial pressure decades earlier, back in the days when it could still be dangerous to call oneself a Christian. Augustine's associates rejected this interpretation of events, declaring themselves the only "catholic" or universally recognized Christian community in the region. All of this was common knowledge in and around Hippo.

Many of Augustine's congregation would also have known that his family came from Thagaste, a town two days' ride inland, and that the bishop there, Alypius, was an old friend of his. Some would doubtless have heard stories about the life that Alypius, Augustine, and several other Africans had led together in Italy, in the 380s. When visitors to Hippo commented that the "catholic" bishop preached better sermons than they were used to hearing back home, well-informed locals could tell them that their preacher had formerly taught Latin literature and public speaking—that he had once, briefly, held a public appointment as professor of rhetoric in Milan, one of the two seats of imperial government in the West. A few may have known that he had delivered speeches in praise of the divine emperor. To them, the opening phrases of the *Confessions*, addressed as if to some almighty figure within earshot, would perhaps have carried echoes of court ceremonial: "You are great, lord, and greatly to be praised; great is your power, and infinite is your wisdom." Less knowledgeable readers would have had to make their own sense of such an emphatic, even abrupt, beginning. The title *Confessions* would not take them far. Lists exist of generic titles used by ancient Greek and Latin authors; "confessions" is not among them. The modern sense of "confessions" as a literary genre dates only from Rousseau in the eighteenth century, who took his cue directly from Augustine.

–4–

So what kind of a book *was* this, if not an imperial eulogy?

Augustine himself was no stranger to bibliographical puzzles. We know that he wrestled with one around the time that he began composing the *Confessions*. By watching him turn a quizzical eye on a book that then came into his hands, we may begin to grasp what was at issue in the one that has now come as far as ours.

In 397, after presiding at the festivities of Easter, Augustine left Hippo and traveled overland to Carthage. He stayed there until late summer, as was his habit. Carthage was the center of commerce, culture, government, and church for all the region. The bishop there, Aurelius, was an energetic propagandist for the self-proclaimed catholic party in Roman Africa, well on his way to turning its corps of bishops into the best organized brigade in the Empire-wide church. (Two decades later, when questions of divine grace and human free will were being debated by Latin churchmen, these African bishops would sway the opinion of the Bishop of Rome.) Augustine had been co-opted by Aurelius soon after his return from Italy. In 393, while Augustine was still a presbyter (the rank below bishop), Aurelius had booked him to deliver the keynote speech at a council-meeting of bishops in Hippo, an opportunity that he had happily seized. August 397 would see another council in Carthage, but that was not to be Augustine's only vacation business. That summer, at Aurelius' invitation, he preached more than thirty sermons in the city's basilicas, finishing in September with a series for the feast of Cyprian, bishop of Carthage, who had died a martyr's death in 258 and was revered as a local saint. For the preacher, the time away from Hippo provided a welcome change of scene, the pleasures of more cosmopolitan society, a chance to hear news of the Roman world beyond North Africa. Carthage, moreover, had always been a good place to pick up new books from abroad. It was there, in the summer of 397, that Augustine picked up the "Epitaph."

Was that really the book's title, as someone (a certain "brother" in the Christian faith) had told him? He had no immediate way of knowing, since the first page in his copy was missing. The work consisted of short, catalog-style notices on Christian authors and their books from the New

Testament to the present—without any mention of Augustine. An odd thing to call "Epitaph," especially as some of these writers were still alive! Also troubling was the inclusion of writers whose published opinions were not quite doctrinally correct or "orthodox" by current standards. The consensus on Christian dogmas—above all, on the mysteriously triple godhead of father, son, and holy spirit (the trinity)—had become narrower in recent decades. In 381 the emperors finally promulgated a definition of the faith based on a formula originally devised by a council of bishops summoned by Constantine at Nicaea in Asia Minor in 325 (the Nicene Creed). Surely the compiler of this new catalog should have pointed out that some Christian writers of earlier centuries failed to anticipate later norms. What was the use of the work, if it did not give an up-to-date account of the state of Christian knowledge? These were issues raised by Augustine in a letter that he lost no time in sending to the book's author, an individual whose identity he could determine even in the absence of a cover page, seeing that the last notice of the catalog was devoted to him.

That notice, the 134th after Saint Peter in the overall sequence, provided minimal biographical data—father's name, place of birth—and a full listing of the works of the best-known Christian freelance writer of the day. He was a presbyter named Jerome, who for the last decade had been living as a monk in Bethlehem, a town already firmly planted on the maps of Christian tourists to the Holy Land. There Jerome was toiling away on a new, improved Latin translation of the Old Testament (part of what would become the Vulgate Bible) and on a series of scholarly commentaries on its prophetic books. The culminating notice in the catalog began with words "I, Jerome." In some early copies it ended: "[I have also composed] an epitaph." This epitaph survives. It was a letter commemorating a departed friend of Jerome's—but a first-time browser of the catalog could not have known that. Anxious to discover what kind of book he had just picked up, lacking the advantage of a title page, such a person could easily have assumed that it was itself the "Epitaph," Jerome's latest composition, so named because it was a collective tribute to writers, most of them long dead, who had produced works on Christian subjects over the past four centuries. If someone in Carthage had made that mistaken inference, it would explain Augustine's bafflement.

When Jerome wrote "I, Jerome . . ." and gave an account of his life's work to date, he broke new ground. Concise as it was, and almost entirely *biblio*graphical, this act of self-presentation was virtually unprecedented in his culture. The point is not simply that there were hardly any ancient Greek or Roman *auto*biographies as such. There was not even any tradition of *bio*graphy of the living. To be the subject of a biography in classical antiquity, whether one wrote it oneself or not, one had normally to be dead. There was a rich record of "lives" of the famous dead, and not only of political or military leaders. Poets, philosophers, orators, and prose writers across a range of genres were also routinely commemorated, singly or in collective works. When Augustine queried the title "Epitaph," Jerome referred him to all the works on "famous men" that he must have read. Did he not see that this new bibliography was another of those, only now devoted to church writers? (*On Famous Men*—in Latin, *De viris illustribus*—is the title by which this work of Jerome's is generally known.) The point was a shrewd one, and more than a little disingenuous. Jerome knew that it was the rule of such bio-bibliographical collections to exclude living persons. "Lives," like epitaphs, were strictly for the dead. Conscious of stretching a genre, he even alluded in the preface to *Famous Men* to the example of Cicero, who had included living persons (and himself) in the history of Roman oratory narrated in one of his dialogues. Although still a powerful presence in Roman classrooms and courtrooms of the late Empire, Cicero had been dead for more than four hundred years. In Jerome's day, the only living persons who regularly received full biographical treatment were reigning emperors, whose life stories were retold with mythological embellishments in the set speeches or panegyrics that were regularly pronounced in their honor. But not even the divine emperor could escape the natural limitations of life, death, and "Lives." Although the preeminent example of a "Life" from the first half of the century, a Greek biography of Constantine by Eusebius, bishop of Caesarea in Palestine, possibly incorporates material from panegyrics given while the emperor was alive, its final form is posthumous.

As the last example suggests, the fourth-century rise of Christianity did not bring about any sudden change in the regime of biography. Rather, it reinforced it. The primary model for Christian biography, as for Christian living, was the life of Christ presented in the gospels; that life acquired its final significance from the physical death that it transcended— a death that had therefore to be recalled in as much circumstantial detail as possible. To lead a truly apostolic Christian life was to be willing like the first apostles to *die* for Christ. To die for Christ was to claim his promise of eternal life. These were the beliefs that fortified the victims of anti-Christian purges in the pre-Constantinian era, when the declaration "I am a Christian," made stubbornly to an imperial official, could bring down a capital sentence. As the church after Constantine began to flourish as never before, the memory of the martyrs was kept alive by special observances. Their death days became feast days, celebrations of Christian rebirth into eternal life. We have seen Augustine preaching for the feast of Saint Cyprian at Carthage in 397; he delivered many such sermons for saints' days every year in Hippo. Christian biography as a late-ancient literary genre is a by-product of the liturgical celebration of the martyrs. For ancient Greek and Roman biographers, the hero's death was a technical prerequisite. For Christians of Augustine's time, it was the very making of a "Life." *Auto*biography should still have been as difficult as ever.

-5-

And yet Jerome's "I, Jerome . . ." was more than just the narcissistic reflex of an exceptionally self-regarding Christian writer. Jerome spoke for a long and lengthening generation of Christians—those who had grown up since the outbreak of the Constantinian "peace" of the church. (The anti-Christian campaign of the "apostate" emperor Julian in the early 360s, although it made a good story, had little lasting impact.) The age of the martyrs was past. Christ's prophesied return to earth as judge of the living and the dead lay somewhere in the future. Meanwhile, thousands of Roman Christians were expiring in their beds at a ripe old age. For a cult that had set such a premium on death, this new abundance of life began to pose a problem. How were conscientious Christians of the present generation to sustain a sense of continuity with the martyrs of blessed memory? The author of the miscalled "Epitaph" exemplifies one possible response to the fourth-century crisis of Christian collective identity. Augustine's *Confessions* reinterprets the problem, in language that would prove even more beguiling in the long term.

Jerome's response was to *play* dead. As a young man, he became a monk. Although contemporary stories like the *Life of Antony* placed the first hermits further back in time, the ideology of Christian monasticism was forged in the decades after Constantine. The monks were functional successors to the martyrs. They defied the norms of human biological and social existence, skimping on basic creature comforts (food, shelter, clothing, sleep, sex) and living at the margins of civilization. Many took up residence in caves and deserted places, either as solitaries or in communities under the guidance of an abbot. Those who remained in the towns, like Jerome and his associates in Bethlehem, carefully secluded themselves.

The economics of monasticism varied. Some monks farmed, others sold craft goods, others again (such as Jerome) existed mainly on alms. In every case, the decision to "die" socially reflected a desire to move closer to the life of the angels and saints in heaven. The chosen means to that end was usually some combination of prayer, meditation on sacred texts, psalmody, and liturgy. For members of the Roman social elite, monastic observance was frequently affected by ideals of the contemplative life derived from ancient philosophical traditions. Platonism was a potent influence, especially in the mystical-theological version recently developed by the Greek philosopher Plotinus (who taught at Rome in the third century) and his disciple Porphyry. Ultimately, however, the only true "philosophy" for Christians was that taught by Christ and enshrined in texts that had become normative for his cult, those of the Old and New Testaments.

The mainstreaming of the Bible in Roman Christian life was another essentially fourth-century development, in which Jerome played a leading role. His *Famous Men* was a manifesto for Bible-centered Christianity, presented as a viable cultural alternative to the Greco-Roman tradition of literature and philosophy. Some years before compiling it, Jerome had made a name for himself with a pamphlet explaining how to lead the monastic life, addressed to a young noblewoman named Eustochium. In an autobiographical digression, he told her how in his own early days as a monk he had once almost died from a fever. His friends were ready to bury him. Suddenly in his delirium he saw himself dragged before a judge, who ordered him to account for himself. "I am a Christian," he confessed, echoing the martyrs of a bygone age. "Liar," retorted the judge, "you are a Ciceronian!" Jerome's deeply felt love of the classics of Latin literature had damned him before an imaginary grand inquisitor who doubled the roles of Christ-as-judge and Roman examining magistrate. After a severe flogging, he was released on the strength of a promise never to read "secular books" again, whereupon he came back to his senses and his grieving friends—and survived to tell the tale! With this graphic story of a near-death experience, Jerome announced his own, singularly *literary* monastic profession. Henceforth he would confine himself to "divine studies," murdering his passion for Cicero in order to share in the passion of Christ. In the days of the martyrs, a person who persisted in his or her Christian allegiance under judicial torture, but did not in the end suffer death for it, earned the honorable title of "confessor." In his letter to Eustochium, Jerome staged such a confession in reverse. Eager to emulate the martyrs as a monk, he was forced to confess another, non-Christian allegiance. His labors as a translator and interpreter of the Bible would be a penance for past sins of reading. He would die to the world—and to worldly books—in the hope of being recognized by Christ on the day of general resurrection.

Socially and culturally, Jerome and Augustine were more or less two of a kind. Both were sons of provincial families with the means to pay for a good schooling, even if Augustine's parents needed some help from a rich neighbor. Both had been drilled in the literary texts and rhetorical exercises of the Latin curriculum. Cicero was their exemplar of Latin eloquence, Virgil their poet of Rome's civilizing mission. A training in the verbal arts had fitted them for public service, and their talents had given early promise of future distinction. In the event, they distinguished themselves in unexpected ways. Jerome barely set foot on the ladder of advancement before renouncing secular ambition to become a monk. (We know this because he tells the story, or sketches its plot, in autobiographical digressions like the one recounted in the previous paragraph.) Augustine continued for much longer in the course of an ordinary Roman career before deciding to make a "profession" of Christ. The story of his change of direction is one of the chief intrigues of the work before us. The many-sided profession that he evokes and enacts in it can be readily broken down in terms of the history of Christianity already outlined. It is a cult profession, ritualized in the act of baptism and the adoption of a creed; a monastic profession, entailing a way of life radically different from that of the ordinary Roman citizen; a philosophical profession, visibly influenced by the author's Platonist readings; a biblical profession, marked at every turn by contact with the sacred and canonical texts of Christianity; and finally an episcopal profession, the self-declaration of an ordained Christian teacher and mystagogue.

If the work in question had been entitled "Professions of Augustine," we should be able to stop here. The actual title obliges us to go on. For it is hard to believe that Augustine's contemporaries, hearing of these *Confessions*, would not also have heard—or thought they heard—a strong hint of "confession" in the sense purposefully recalled by Jerome in the story of his near-martyrdom for Cicero. An African audience familiar with arguments between (so-called) catholics and Donatists about past acts of confession and betrayal would be especially alert to such reverberations. Was the catholic bishop of Hippo about to parade his credentials as a "confessor" and successor to the martyrs? A quick reading of the early sections of book 8 could encourage that suspicion. But it would be largely unjustified. For all their similarities, Augustine was no Jerome, and he was willing to go to impressive lengths to prove it. One thing that he was *not* willing to do was fake his own martyrdom. The only scene of the (future) author's near-demise in the *Confessions* is not even mock-heroic. Jerome had pushed the Christian genre of death-determined biography to the point where it tipped over into melodramatic monologue. Augustine in the *Confessions* cast a different, if no less passionate eye on life and death. In doing so, he may seem to have invented autobiography. It would not be the least, or last, of the many surprises sprung by a book that is almost as beset with accidents as human life itself.

–6–

The accidents of the *Confessions* are multi-dimensional. So far we have concentrated mainly on those of an external sort, arising from the general conditions under which the book found its first readers. An introduction cannot stray too far toward a book's more internal accidents—those experienced *by* its readers—without risk of ruining their effects. The risk is the greater when, as in this case, the author omitted to provide any formal introduction of his own. In many of his other works, Augustine provides some kind of preface, often in the form of a dedication to whoever had proposed the subject to him—but not here. Missing such a statement of authorial intention, scholars have endeavored to explain the genesis and nature of the work by looking outside it, hopeful that some circumstance, event, or document beyond the text might help account for the oddity of what we find within it. The best suggestion of this sort concerns a hypothetical, unwritten "Life" of Augustine's friend Alypius.

Although Augustine was a few years older than Alypius and from a less well-off family, the two nonetheless had much in common. They both grew up in Thagaste, received the same kind of education, and together became adherents of the outlawed sect of Manicheans. Mani was a third-century Persian sage who blended the teachings of Saint Paul with local ingredients to produce a cosmology and anthropology that accounted for every contingency of the universe and of each human life in terms of a constant struggle between primordial forces of light and darkness, good and evil. (The Manicheans rejected the Old Testament because its depiction of god struck them as incompatible with the idea of a divine being who was perfectly good and just.) To be a Manichean was to know that there were in fact *no* accidents in this world, that everything in nature could, so to speak, be scientifically explained. It was also to be confident that one's own life, as soon as one became a member of the "Elect" or superior Manichean cadre, was on the side of the light. This was a system of thought well-designed to appeal to idealistic and intelligent young men who had grown bored of outwitting their schoolteachers. For years it captivated Alypius and Augustine, though they never advanced beyond the status of novice Manicheans (known as "Hearers") and finally renounced their membership of the sect in favor of the mainstream Christianity with which both had been familiar from boyhood. They were baptized by Bishop Ambrose in Milan at Easter 387. We know this from the narrative of the *Confessions*, where Alypius receives fuller treatment than any character besides Augustine, his mother, and his god—if his god can truly be called a character. There are even moments in book 6 when the story seems to be as much about Alypius as it is about Augustine.

This curious internal feature of the work can be linked to another external circumstance. In 395 Alypius, by now a bishop back in his native Africa, began corresponding with a well-connected Christian in Italy, named Paulinus, to whom he made a gift of five works that Augustine had recently written to refute the system of the Manicheans. In return, Alypius asked Paulinus to send him a copy of the *Chronicle*, a synoptic history of the world from the time of the Old Testament patriarch Abraham to the present day, composed in Greek by Bishop Eusebius of Caesarea, author of the *Life of Constantine* and the first great historian of the Christian church after the writer of the Acts of the Apostles. The *Chronicle* had been expanded and translated into Latin by Jerome around 380. Granting his correspondent's request, Paulinus laid a fresh demand on him: In exchange for Eusebius' general history, would Alypius please send his own *personal* history? What was his background? How had he parted from his natural family and become a member of the family of the church? Had Bishop Ambrose of Milan, whom Paulinus knew, played any role in his life? (Paulinus was too tactful to refer to Alypius' Manichean past. If he had any doubts on that score, Augustine's works "against the Manichaeans" should have allayed them.)

This correspondence carries us back to an important threshold in the history of social relations. Men of Paulinus' and Alypius' class and culture, wherever they hailed from in the Roman Empire, had coded signals for recognizing each other. Besides their habits of dress and deportment, there was a common stock of references: books they had all read, history they shared, famous men whose lives they knew all about. A few deft allusions in spoken or written discourse were enough to reassure an interlocutor that he was in the presence of his equal or near-equal. (The male

pronouns signify fully. In the old Roman world, women's status—and
their own sense of it—depended on their menfolk. Gradually, Christianity would unsettle that situation, in ways that the *Confessions* can help us
partly to recapture.) Paulinus was a master of these exclusive social
codes. Yet without breaching the decorum of Roman epistolary conversation, he now invited a different kind of self-disclosure. His interest in
Alypius' life story was more than courtesy or curiosity. In the first place,
it was a modest deflection of the interest that Alypius had already shown
in Paulinus' life story. Paulinus was a contemporary Christian icon, a
wealthy aristocrat who had recently made his own sense of Christ's command to the rich man (Matthew 19:21) by dedicating all his considerable
financial and material assets to the service of god. With his wife, Therasia, he now lived a life of genteel asceticism at Nola in Campania, close to
the shrine of Saint Felix, a third-century confessor whose feast day he
honored every year with a Latin verse-panegyric. Paulinus was the most
dazzling representative, in the West, of a new class of Christian "con-
verts." These were men—and women—who turned, not from some other
cult to that of Christ, but from easygoing post-Constantinian Christianity
to the more demonstrative exercises of the ascetic and monastic way.
Paulinus and Therasia were the celebrity couple of the moment, models
of a radically Christian lifestyle that was firing the imaginations of people
all around the Mediterranean; Alypius and other African bishops allied
with Aurelius of Carthage had heard the stories about them. But what
was there to know about Alypius? By switching the biographical focus
back to his correspondent, Paulinus gave him an opportunity to consoli-
date a distinctively Christian collective identity. The reference to old and
new familial ties—underlined with allusions to Virgil and Saint Paul—
was heavily loaded. If Alypius would tell the story of his own life so far,
he could assist the mutual recognition of co-sharers in a "spiritual" ge-
nealogy.

It fell to Augustine to answer on behalf of his friend. Stricken with modesty but reluctant to disappoint Paulinus, Alypius asked the Bishop of
Hippo to recount his "history" for him. Augustine—he himself tells Paulinus in a letter—would gladly have done as much, if the man who was due
to carry the mail back to Italy from Africa had not been in such a hurry to
leave. That is the last we hear of a "Life of Alypius." Had it been written,
it could have been the first of its kind: the biography of a *living* Roman, and
a Christian, who was not an emperor. (It would have been closely contemporary with the Latin *Life* of Martin, monk and bishop of Tours, written by

Sulpicius Severus, another correspondent of Paulinus of Nola—a work that does in fact fit that description.) It is tempting to think that vestiges of a lost biography have survived in passages of the *Confessions* where Alypius is the main character, passages that are in any case remarkable for their vivid, almost novelistic portrayal of scenes from Roman civic life: a group of friends going to the gladiatorial show; a student preparing a class presentation; a petty larceny; a thwarted attempt at bribery in the tax department. Such realistic narrative is rare enough in Roman literature, and in Augustine's works, to lead one to think that there must have been a special stimulus for it. Most previous accounts of Christian lives, we have seen, had been rendered posthumously, in anticipation of god's final judgment. Augustine and Paulinus, by contrast, were interested in accounting for Christian lives still *in progress*, however provisionally. As a rhetorician whose job had once been to prepare his pupils for legal careers (Alypius had been one of them), Augustine knew how important it was for an advocate to get all the details straight in his initial summary of events relevant to a case. There is something of that forensic attention to detail in the (auto)biographical narrative of the *Confessions*, as if its author were pleading before the highest court.

−7−

While the traffic of letters and books between Alypius and Paulinus cannot begin to *explain* the *Confessions*, it does draw us further into the web of interests originally engaged by the work. It is worth noticing, for example, that the book for which a "Life of Alypius" was sought in exchange was Eusebius' *Chronicle*. This schematic account of a world history converging on the Roman imperial present had been extended as far as the year 378 by Jerome in his Latin adaptation of it. The need to keep updating Christian history was yet another reflection of the new reality of a Christian society in which it was possible to look beyond tomorrow and not see the apocalypse on the horizon. If the prophesied end of the world was still a way off, what sense could be made of world events in the meantime? Augustine would return to that question a decade and a half later in his *City of God*. We know that he was already giving it serious thought by the mid-390s. He was, after all, a highly literate Latin-thinking Roman citizen: Such men were accustomed to thinking about history and civilization on a grand scale.

Ever since the foundation of the Empire under Augustus four centuries

earlier, the Romans had maintained a strong conviction of their own manifest destiny. Even if the Greeks were the original masters of the finer arts
of humanity, fate had decreed that the Romans would impose the rule of
law—by force if necessary—and pacify the nations of the earth. That was
the vision proclaimed by Virgil's *Aeneid* and famously illustrated by the
scenes on Aeneas' divinely forged shield in book 8 of the poem. In the Virgilian expression of the myth, Jupiter, god-in-chief of the Roman pantheon,
had entrusted the Roman race with a mission of civilizing the world. An
everyday version of the same story held that successive emperors were em-
powered to discharge it. Divine foresight—in Latin, *providentia*—is one of
the qualities commonly attributed to emperors in fourth-century panegyrics and iconography. On the Arch of Constantine in Rome, that emperor is said to have triumphed over his enemies "by divine instinct." For
most Roman Christians after Constantine it was probably enough that
the emperors themselves were now followers of Christ. More restless
minds needed to be shown that Roman political history was still on the
side of divinity, and vice versa. The *Chronicle*, with its neat conflation of
biblical and non-biblical chronologies, was well made for the purpose. Yet
even the *Chronicle* left room for doubt. For what did the Bible have to
say about events of recent decades, some of them—such as major military
defeats at the hands of the Persians or the Goths—deeply troubling to the
Roman mind? What, indeed, did the Bible have to say about *anything*
that had happened since the time of Christ's apostles? The challenge of a
new Christian history mirrored the challenge of a new Christian biography: to tell a story as yet without end, but with full assurance of an end to
come.

Men like Augustine and Alypius who had felt the lure of the Manichean
theory of everything could hardly escape the fascination of such problems. They were accustomed, moreover, to looking for solutions in books.
The Manicheans were a bookish sect: They valued written knowledge
and venerated books as objects; some of their volumes were gorgeously
illustrated and decorated. Augustine's mature attitude to books appears
to have been profoundly utilitarian. Christian books in codex form were
now readily available to those who could afford to pay for copying or willing to act as their own scribes. Jerome's *Famous Men* catalogued a whole
virtual library. Some Christian books were recognized as more important
than others. On a cue from the Qur'an, we have grown used to thinking
of Christianity as a "religion of the book" or, even more pointedly, as a
religion of "the Book," meaning the Bible. We need to keep reminding

ourselves that the Christian Bible is an assemblage of texts of diverse dates, genres, and tendencies, which took centuries to acquire the kind of physical and conceptual stability *as a whole* that it can now appear to possess. By the end of the fourth century, there was broad agreement among Christian communities on the canons of the Old and New Testaments, and on the principle that the Old Testament (consisting of ancient Hebrew or Jewish texts) obtained its full meaning for Christians only in the light of the gospel teaching of the New. Lists of the canonical texts had begun to circulate. One of the most influential of these lists in the Latin-speaking West appeared in a letter addressed by Jerome to Paulinus around the time that Paulinus and Alypius were conducting the correspondence discussed above.

Jerome itemized the books from Genesis to Revelation and added quick hints on how to interpret them. Centuries later, his letter to Paulinus would be used as a preface to the Latin Bible as a whole. So far as we know, however, there were no Latin "Bibles" in the late fourth century to which it could have been prefixed. That is to say, there were no single-codex copies of all the canonical books together. There were sets of "biblical" books copied or bound within one pair of covers (for example, the Pentateuch, the Prophets, the Psalms, the Gospels, Paul's Epistles), and there was an emerging *idea* of a unified totality of divinely inspired writings, but there was no "Bible" as such that one could pick up. Augustine had no word for what Christians now call the Bible, nor did he ever set eyes on such a thing. He had known since childhood that Christians set special store by their "scriptures." His Manichean masters had taught him to look hard at certain texts, especially Paul's Epistles with their patterned contrasts between the law and the gospel, the letter and the spirit, the outer and the inner human being. These key Pauline figures of thought—which Augustine would help entrench in Western consciousness—were understood by Manicheans as further grounds for rejecting the "letter" of the Old Testament, beginning with the creation story in Genesis, which they could not reconcile with their own cosmology and anthropology. By the time he embarked on the *Confessions*, Augustine had more than once attempted to save Genesis from Manichean science. He had also seen Jerome's letter to Paulinus and knew about Jerome's projects as a biblical translator and interpreter. Whatever his instincts may formerly have been, he had now become convinced of the need to make *scriptural* teaching and preaching the mainstay of his pastorate. Possibly with the encouragement of Bishop Aurelius of

Carthage, he began to draft a handbook of biblical interpretation and exposition, entitled *De doctrina christiana* (*On Christian Teaching*), another first of its kind—at least on the scale on which he eventually finished it. (A Donatist named Tyconius had previously composed a booklet on the subject.)

However Augustine would eventually solve or reformulate the related problems of Christian cosmology and anthropology, history, and biography, one thing he already knew by the mid-390s: the beginning, middle, and end of the story as *he* told it would ring with the words of divine scripture. "You are great, lord, and greatly to be praised; great is your power, and infinite is your wisdom," says the speaker of the *Confessions*, slipping immediately into the language of the songs, or Psalms, of a certain David (Psalms 145:7, 147:5). Thirteen books later, the same speaker and his reader will close on a formula for "seeking" and "finding" spoken by Christ in one of the gospels (Matthew 7:7–8). Throughout the intervening pages, eye and ear are continually solicited by words, phrases, lines, and whole passages from the Christian sacred books.

Few, if any, of the scriptural elements embedded in the first ten books of Augustine's text would have been visibly signaled as quotations in the copies made by his scribes. To supply quotation marks and verse references for each and every one of them in a modern translation is impossible, and would be misleading even if it could be done. No two readers or hearers of the *Confessions*, in Augustine's time or any time since, have ever caught exactly the same set of quotations, near-quotations, distinct allusions, and fleeting reminiscences. Augustine has his favorite biblical places—the Psalms, Paul's Epistles, certain passages of the Gospels. In the closing books of the *Confessions* (11–13) he turns deliberately to the opening chapter of Genesis and begins a line-by-line exegesis. Not even the most precise scholarship, however, can track all the labyrinthine paths of his scriptural reference. Augustine had been trained from boyhood to remember and recycle culturally significant texts: That is how he knew his Virgil, and some Cicero. Having become a minister of the church, he began instead to stock his memory with the scriptures.

The analogy, however, is inexact, for the respective works of Virgil and Cicero remained *distinct* from each other in ways that the texts, say, of the psalmist David and the evangelist Matthew did not, for Augustine. The ultimate and sole author of *all* the scriptures—or "scripture" as Augustine also calls this notional ensemble—was god. Moses and the other named authors of the canonical books were merely his agents. In different voices and idioms, according to their own time and place and character, all spoke the same truth—now transparently, now more obscurely. It followed, then, that as coordinated expressions of a perfectly unified, endlessly capacious divine mind, every passage of scripture—no matter where in the canon it came from—had the potential to illuminate other passages of scripture in infinitely but consistently instructive ways. Thus conceived, "scripture" for Augustine and his contemporaries around the year 400 held something of the promise of the Internet for users around the year 2000. It was a new technology of knowledge, a lively and liberating new medium of thought and exchange, with power to change the world. For the time being, there was no universally agreed-upon set of user rules, only competing modes of expertise. Just how much could this scriptural technology be made to do in interpreting the cosmos, human history, and the lives of individual human beings? What were its practical and theoretical limits? What safety mechanisms needed to be put in place to ensure that the power of the biblical "word" was not abused? The biblical links in the *Confessions*, whether marked or unmarked in translation, are always worth following: The books of scripture are the implied supertext in relation to which Augustine's own text acquires its meanings. (We must bear in mind, however, that the Latin of Augustine's scriptures sometimes contained more or less than appears in English versions of the Bible.) The *Confessions* is the work of a brilliant pioneer of the "scripture-net," an independent experimenter who happened to engineer much of the system on which later users would run their programs for self- and world-understanding.

–8–

It is not quite true that Augustine failed to provide any introduction of his own to the *Confessions*. He may not have written a preface for the work when it first appeared, but he did compose a kind of postscript that medieval scribes and modern scholars have usually placed among the preliminaries of their editions. It takes the form of a short notice that he wrote while in the process of cataloguing and reevaluating his published writings for a work whose name and conception are interestingly parallel to those of the *Confessions*. The work is his *Retractationes*, best translated as *Revisions* or *Reconsiderations*. Apart from Jerome's concise

auto(bio)bibliography in *Famous Men*, there had never been anything
like this authorial self-assessment in Latin literature. Augustine lists
twenty-six major works that he wrote between resigning from his pro-
fessorial job at Milan in the late summer of 386 and becoming bishop of
Hippo in 395, and another sixty-seven that he had so far written as
bishop. As he explains in a preface, the titles follow one another in the
Revisions in the order of original composition, so that readers might see
clearly how the author's ideas developed "in the course of writing" and
thus follow his lead, "not in going wrong but in getting better." To assist
such progressive reading, Augustine made notes of the points in each
work which, on more mature judgment, he would wish to have handled
differently. It is on the strength of this chronological catalog that we are
now able to date the *Confessions*, or at least the beginning of its composition, to the year 397.

There are only two passages in the *Confessions* that Augustine saw the
need to retouch in the *Revisions*, neither of them of great significance (see
endnote 7 to book 4, and endnote 9 to book 13). More interesting is the
review that he gives of the work as a whole. He writes: "The thirteen
books of my *Confessions*, on both the goods and evils of myself, praise a
god who is just and good, and impel the mind and heart toward him—at
least, I can say that that is what they did for me while I was writing them
and what they do for me as I read them. What others think of them, they
must find out for themselves. I know, however, that these books have
given pleasure to many brothers [that is, in Christ] and that they continue
to do so." The insistent symmetry of these phrases is as characteristic of
the author as anything he wrote. To begin with, we seem to be pinned
with Augustine on a grid of paired and complementary terms: Augustine
is both good and evil, his god is exclusively just and good, his readers—if
they are like him and others known to him—will be intellectually and
emotionally moved by the *Confessions*. The structure of "self-review" is
implicitly coercive. Augustine is not saying only, "I can tell you from my
own experience how this work is likely to affect you," but also, "I can tell
you from the experience of others how it probably will." Faced with these
assurances, what kind of exception to the general rule will a non-
compliant reader dare to make?

On further consideration, however, we see that the circuit is not in
fact closed, nor the reader any more constrained than usual. For Augustine *does* acknowledge that other responses are possible. Literally,
what he says is, "Let others see for themselves what they think." The
idiom of "seeing" as "finding out" is native to Latin as it is to English.

Here it is used consequentially. As Augustine in this passage makes himself visible to us in the act of judging the effects of his own work, so, he suggests, we in turn shall become visible to ourselves as readers and judges of what he has written. This reflexive movement, modeled at length by the syntax of Augustine's self-scrutiny in the *Revisions*, is the master trope of the *Confessions*, the encompassing figure of speech, thought, and imagination that commands all the narrated and implicit turns or "conversions" of the work. More than any other literary production from Greek and Roman antiquity, the *Confessions* makes a spectacle of readers—and hence of *its* readers. Augustine's wariest and best readers, we may say, are supremely at risk of seeing and catching themselves in the act. At this imaginative level, the forensic drama of the *Confessions* faithfully recalls the earlier "confession" scenes of Jerome the guilty Ciceronian and his precursors, the Christian heroes who refused to give up their sacred books even when threatened with violence. Augustine cannot help writing in the afterlight of the martyrs, but he is more interested in the cognitive and moral psychology of reading than he is in parading lists of approved and prohibited books. The *Confessions*, like the *Revisions*, is a guide to the art of living through texts.

There is a little more in Augustine's notice on the *Confessions*. Having reported and modeled the effects of his work, he provides a precious sketch of its construction. "Books 1 to 10," he declares, "were written about me, and the remaining three about the holy scriptures—from where it is written 'In the beginning god made heaven and earth,' as far as the sabbath rest [Genesis 1:1–2:3]." He then mentions the two points where revision was needed, and closes the notice with a citation of the work's opening phrase, for the sake of scribes and other readers who might be stuck with a copy that lacked a cover page or was otherwise incomplete: "This work begins as follows: 'You are great, lord.'" One could hardly ask for a more succinct authorial guide. At a stroke, the subject of the work and the overall economy of its parts are accounted for. There are ten books on Augustine, followed by three more on the holy scriptures, beginning at the beginning of the book of Genesis and ending either at Genesis 2:3 or, if we take the writer's words less literally, with an evocation of the sabbath rest prophesied for the seventh "day" or age of world history as inferred by Augustine from a reading of the

Bible as a whole, from Genesis to Revelation. Whereas thirteen once seemed an odd number of books, it now appears as the sum of two standard "biblical" quotas (10+3), one of them also the number of the divine trinity.

On the basis of such information, we might expect there to be a shift of perspective at the beginning of book 11 of the *Confessions*. And so there is. At that point Augustine asks whether his god—whom, as always, he addresses out loud in writing—*needs* him to tell the tale of himself that he has been busily narrating in the previous books. Of course not, he concludes, since this god is outside time and knows everything inside it with perfect knowledge. Why, then, has Augustine been "confessing" all these things? He answers: "Certainly not in order to acquaint you with them through me; but, instead, so that through them I may stir up my own love and the love of my readers toward you, so that all may say [with the psalmist], 'Great is the lord and greatly to be praised.' " After ten books, the discourse of confession has come full circle. Yet there are still another three books to come, with no sign—at least none that we can now be sure of—that the author is departing from his original plan of the work, whatever that may have been.

If we grant, after glancing at the *Revisions*, that Augustine was a writer who advanced in understanding *as he wrote*, then we may allow that his understanding of his own acts of "confession" could have developed in the course of the composition of the work that he decided at some point to call his *Confessions*. The explanation given at the beginning of book 11 for the autobiographical narrative of books 1–10 is close enough to the one offered in the *Revisions* for us to recognize it as in some sense definitive for the writer himself. Reading backward, we also find it anticipated in earlier scenes and turns of phrase. Whatever the actual process of their composition, then, the earlier books of the *Confessions* do in fact answer the description that Augustine would later give of them. We should also observe, however, that as soon as we attempt to ascertain what *Confessions* as a book title could have meant to the first author ever to use it, almost all our proof-texts cluster at the beginning of book 11, at the beginning of book 10, and in the last pages of book 9. Book 10, the longest of the thirteen, is framed by Augustine's most explicit statements of intent. For anyone still in quest of an introduction to the *Confessions*, the best chance may finally be to read the work around that unfathomable book.

—*10*—

If a copy of the *Confessions* without cover page or books 10–13 came into our hands and we had to guess at the title, we might mistakenly call it "The Epitaph." At the end of book 9 Augustine buries his mother, Monica, and, with her, his father too. In other circumstances, the pair would have shared a funerary monument on the road out of Thagaste, perhaps with an inscription inviting passing travelers to pause long enough to utter the names of the departed and reflect on their own mortality. Roman tombs were sites for family gatherings and picnics in celebration of the dead. These feasts of remembrance were known as *parentalia*; an older contemporary of Augustine, the Latin poet Ausonius, composed a series of poems under that title in honor of his ancestors. As Christian beliefs about life and death became more prevalent, Roman commemorative practices assumed new forms and meanings. The tombs of the martyrs, considered as "relatives" in the larger family of Christ, became important places of resort and foci of collective memory. The Latin word for memory was used by Christians as a synonym for "tomb" or "monument." Early in the narrative of the *Confessions*, Augustine's mother spends a night at the memorial (*memoria*) of the martyr Cyprian in Carthage.

The only actual epitaph for Monica that has come to light—a block of stone inscribed with verses in which she is honored as Augustine's mother—was commissioned several decades after her death, apparently by a reader of the *Confessions* (see endnote 14 on book 9). Augustine himself gave no sign of wanting such a thing. Nor, needless to say, did he have the least idea of consecrating his mother as a saint. All he asks is that "readers of this book," the *Confessions*, remember her and her husband, Patricius, in their prayers in church. For all its seeming modesty, the sentence conveying this request is one of the most pregnant in the work. It brings Augustine's god, himself as a speaker and writer, his readers, including ourselves, the memory of his parents, and his book together in the prospect of a single, variably repeated performance that will also, wherever and whenever it occurs, be a sign of Christian devotion. Taken literally, the prayer into which Augustine transposes his mother's dying wish represents the ideal outcome of any reading of *Confessions* (1–9) as an act of worship or religious cult. To remember Monica at the altar is yet another way of saying or confessing, "You are great, lord." Artistically and conceptually, the logic of this imagined consummation is all but irresistible. Not until the moment of relating how he finally wept for Monica does Augustine speak both of confessing *in writing* and of his audience as *readers*. The full import of his *Confessions*—as a literary work with that title—thus first emerges clearly at the place in his text where he might otherwise have inscribed or quoted his mother's epitaph. Rhetorically speaking, Monica's grave is the birthplace of the *Confessions*.

Having begun book 1 with two impossible questions—How does god come into this discourse of mine? Where did I, the speaker, come from in the first place?—Augustine closes book 9 by calling his readers to a "confession" that takes its cue from the memory of the man and woman whose physical union brought him into the world. In the terms provided by one of Augustine's most acute twentieth-century readers, the philosopher Hannah Arendt, the memory of mortality serves in this case to underline the mystery of *natality*, the condition of having been born. With a renewed sense of urgency in book 11, Augustine will come to a story of the beginning of all human life, as told in Genesis. In the meantime, the recollection of what bound him to his own parents, encapsulated in the memory of the tears he wept for his mother, saves these *Confessions* from becoming just another Roman family memorial or, for that matter, just another Christian celebration of dying into eternity.

As a narrative of historical persons, places, and events—not that it is ever merely that—Augustine's discourse of himself ends with book 9. Ostia on the Tiber, where he buried his mother, was the port from which he would re-embark for Africa, there to remain for the rest of his life. Like Aeneas in book 3 of Virgil's epic, Augustine ends the story of his wayfaring at the last place on land before his latest landfall. Although counted by him among the autobiographical books of the *Confessions*, book 10 launches a new inquiry. Having retraced his past steps almost to the point of his return to Africa, the writer now ventures into the vast beyond of his own memory, forever in search of the twin objects of those impossible questions—Where is (my) god? Where am "I" from? Having come once more to Carthage, Augustine now asks whether remembering god is like returning in the mind to an image of that city. (The name of Carthage supplies almost the only concrete reference in a highly abstract book.) Platonic doctrines of the soul's power to recollect what it had learned in a prior existence provide a scaffold for part of the argument. Other ancient philosophical sources can be detected along the way. At bottom, however, the book is a daring improvisation. No Greek or Roman philosopher before Augustine had gone so far in accounting for what the mind could grasp—or what it ultimately failed to grasp and yet could still know. Summary balks at such a text. Only a reader can know its heights and depths. Here we can do no more than stop at the edge of it and ask ourselves how ever writer and reader came to this place of ultimate risk.

Augustine had a guide. He is the same one that Dante would rely upon centuries later in his *Commedia*, the Latin poet Virgil. As T. S. Eliot, C. S. Lewis, and others long ago recognized, and as more recent scholarly studies of imperial and colonial mythologies have rightly stressed, Virgil's *Aeneid* is the founding "classic" of the West, the plot and imaginative ground for most if not all subsequent narratives of the triumphal progress of Western civilization. Eliot's Dantean reflections on the nature and meaning of the Virgilian classic provided a starting point for this introduction. We can now complete the return to Augustine that this poet's reference to the *Confessions* in *The Waste Land* ("To Carthage then I came / Burning") already anticipates.

−*II*−

Aeneas and his band were refugees from the sacked city of Troy, whom the gods conspired to make the forefathers of a people or nation that would one day extend its sway throughout the lands of the Mediterranean and beyond. Such was the political teleology imbibed by young Roman males in schools throughout the Latin-speaking part of the Empire, as Augustine reminds us in book 1 of the *Confessions*. His own deep assimilation of Virgil's poem shines through at many points in the work, despite his professed mistrust of non-Christian myth and his regrets—perhaps inspired by Jerome's earlier confession—at having once wept needlessly for Dido. In the *Aeneid*, Aeneas sacrifices Dido for the higher cause of Rome. Now, belatedly, her compatriot Augustine tilts the balance of power back toward Carthage. The *Confessions* shows how a fully colonized African Roman could eventually reject the metropolitan-imperial attractions of Rome and Milan, and come home. Along with his "biblical" roles as prodigal son and latter-day psalmist, the anti-hero of the *Confessions* also plays African Aeneas-in-reverse.

Having defied Virgilian precedent by beginning his story at the historical beginning—his own birth—and going more or less steadily forward to the end of book 9, Augustine then seems to renounce narrative development in favor of other modes of exposition. We might infer that his unwriting and rewriting of the Virgilian myth of Roman national identity meant to go no further than this. To do so, however, would be to overlook the power of tears, and Augustine's desire to master it.

The *Aeneid* is a poem full of tears. Book 6, in which Aeneas descends to the underworld and obtains a vision of Rome's future greatness, begins with him weeping for his drowned helmsman, Palinurus, and ends in prophetic grief for a short-lived son of the Roman imperial family: When Virgil first recited this book, we are told, the sister of Augustus fainted at the lines about the young Marcellus. Book 10 of the *Confessions*, starting with a rule for measured weeping, announces Augustine's alternative to the Roman myth of sorrowfully manifest destiny. In the scheme proposed to Alypius by Paulinus, over a copy of Eusebius' and Jerome's *Chronicle* (see above, p. xxix), this is the point where autobiography rises to meet the challenge of universal history. Joining the author's retrospect on himself (books 1–9) to his projection of a biblical narrative of all times (books 11–13), book 10 may fairly be called the book of memory, as long as we understand memory as Augustine does—as comprehending past, present, *and* future. Virgil sent Aeneas to the underworld so that his poem might condense the whole destiny of Rome, to which Jupiter had set no boundary in time or space. Dante would later extend the journey to encompass all humanity as he saw it, and more. Augustine will, if he can, make such geographical and cosmographical detours unnecessary. No one goes anywhere in real space in book 10 of the *Confessions*. Instead, the reader—with Augustine as guide—experiences something like an inversion of the epic *katabasis* or descent to the underworld: a dizzying progress toward an unattainable place of inner knowledge, culminating but not concluding in a hymn of joy addressed to the god of the Christian scriptures. No Roman emperor had ever been praised like this, nor African martyr ever burned with such a love.

For centuries the *Aeneid* defined what it meant to be Roman. Augustine's *Confessions* is the first work to strike directly at the mythical foundations of that collective sense of identity, for the sake of a different—if by no means entirely separate—sense of personal belonging. The *Confessions* is also the oldest product of the Latin Christian imagination to be generally recognized in our own time as a classic. Whatever relation we posit between these two attributes of the work, we shall not fall into the trap of supposing that there was anything predictable, let alone inevitable or foreordained, about its long-term literary success. The initial history of the reception of the *Confessions* gave little hint of the exalted status it would one day enjoy. Augustine's own mention (in the *Revisions*) of his work's impact is nearly the only positive testimony we have for the first few generations. Other early readers were less enthusiastic, if not actually repelled. No wonder, perhaps, given the strange and sudden way this book begins.

Mark Vessey is Professor of English and holder of a Canada Research Chair in Literature / Christianity and Culture at the University of British Columbia. He is the author of *Latin Christian Authors in Late Antiquity and Their Texts* (2005) and co-editor of *Augustine and the Disciplines: Cassiciacum to "Confessions"* (2005). He has written extensively on the reception of early Christian Latin writings in the Renaissance and later periods.

CONFESSIONS

BOOK 1

[**1.1.1**] You are great, lord, and greatly to be praised; great is your power, and infinite is your wisdom.* And man desires to praise you, for he is a part of your creation; he bears his mortality about with him and carries the evidence of his sin and the proof that you resist the proud. Still he desires to praise you, this man who is only a small part of your creation. You have prompted him, that he should delight to praise you, for you have made us for yourself and restless is our heart until it comes to rest in you. Grant me, lord, to know and understand whether first to invoke you or to praise you; whether first to know you or call upon you. But who can invoke you, knowing you not? For one who knows you not may invoke you as another than you are. It may be that we should invoke you in order that we may come to know you. But how shall they call on him in whom they have not believed? Or how shall they believe without a preacher?† Now, they shall praise the lord who seek him, for those who seek shall find him, and, finding him, shall praise him. I will seek you, lord, and call upon you. I call upon you, lord, in my faith which you have given me, which you have inspired in me through the humanity of your son, and through the ministry of your preacher.

[**1.2.2**] And how shall I call upon my god—my god and my lord? For when I call on him I ask him to come into me. And what place is there in me into which my god can come? How could a god, the god who made both heaven and earth, come into me? Is there anything in me, lord my god, that can contain you? Do even the heaven and the earth, which you have made, and in which you made me, contain you? Is it possible that, since without you nothing would be which does exist, you made it so that whatever exists has some capacity to receive you? Why, then, do I ask you to come into me, since I also am and could not be if you were not in me? For I am not, after all, in hell—and yet you are there too, for "if I go down into hell, you are there."‡ Therefore I would not exist—I would simply not be at all—unless I exist in you, from whom and by whom and in whom all things are. So it is, lord; so it is. Where do I call you to, when I am

---

* Psalms 145:3, 147:5.
† Romans 10:14.
‡ Psalms 139:8.

already in you? Or from whence would you come into me? Where, beyond heaven and earth, could I go that there my god might come to me—he who has said, "I fill heaven and earth"?*

[1.3.3] Since, then, you fill the heaven and earth, do they contain you? Or, do you fill and overflow them, because they cannot contain you? And where do you pour out what remains of you after heaven and earth are full? Or, indeed, is there no need that you, who contain all things, should be contained by any, since those things which you do fill you fill by containing them? For the vessels which you do fill do not confine you, since even if they were broken, you would not be poured out. And, when you are poured out on us, you are not thereby brought down; rather, we are uplifted. You are not scattered; rather, you gather us together. But when you do fill all things, do you fill them with your whole being? Or, since not even all things together could contain you altogether, does any one thing contain a single part, and do all things contain that same part at the same time? Do singulars contain you singly? Do greater things contain more of you, and smaller things less? Or, is it not rather that you are wholly present everywhere, yet in such a way that nothing contains you wholly?

[1.4.4] What, therefore, is my god? What, I ask, but the lord god? "For who is lord but the lord himself, or who is god besides our god?"† Most high, most excellent, most potent, most omnipotent; most merciful and most just; most secret and most truly present; most beautiful and most strong; stable, yet not supported; unchangeable, yet changing all things; never new, never old; making all things new, yet bringing old age upon the proud, and they know it not; always working, ever at rest; gathering, yet needing nothing; sustaining, pervading, and protecting; creating, nourishing, and developing; seeking, and yet possessing all things. You love, but without passion; are jealous, yet free from care; repent, but without remorse; are angry, yet remain serene. You change your ways, leaving your plans unchanged; you recover what you have never really lost. You are never in need but still you rejoice at your gains; are never greedy, yet demand dividends. Men pay more than is required so that you become a debtor; yet who can possess anything at all which is not already yours? You owe men nothing, yet pay out to them as if in debt to your creature, and when you cancel debts you lose nothing thereby. Yet, my god, my life, my holy joy, what is this that I have

---

* Jeremiah 23:24.
† Psalms 18:31.

said? What can any man say when he speaks of you? But woe to them that keep silence—since even those who say most are dumb.

[1.5.5] Who shall bring me to rest in you? Who will send you into my heart so to overwhelm it that my sins shall be blotted out and I may embrace you, my only good? What are you to me? Have mercy that I may speak. What am I to you that you should command me to love you, and if I do it not, are angry and threaten vast misery? Is it, then, a trifling sorrow not to love you? It is not so to me. Tell me, by your mercy, lord, my god, what you are to me. Say to my soul, I am your salvation.* So speak that I may hear. Behold, the ears of my heart are before you, lord; open them and say to my soul, I am your salvation. I will hasten after that voice, and I will lay hold upon you. Hide not your face from me. Even if I die, let me see your face lest I die.

[1.5.6] The house of my soul is too narrow for you to come in to me; let it be enlarged by you. It is in ruins; restore it. There is much about it which must offend your eyes; I confess and know it. But who will cleanse it? Or, to whom shall I cry but to you? Cleanse me from my secret faults, lord, and keep back your servant from strange sins.† I believe, and therefore I speak. But you know, lord. Have I not confessed my transgressions to you, my god; and have you not put away the iniquity of my heart? I do not contend in judgment with you, who are truth itself; and I would not deceive myself, lest my iniquity lie even to itself. I do not, therefore, contend in judgment with you, for "if you, lord, should mark iniquities, lord, who shall stand?"‡

[1.6.7] Still, dust and ashes as I am, allow me to speak before your mercy. Allow me to speak, for, behold, it is to your mercy that I speak and not to a man who scorns me. Yet perhaps even you might scorn me; but when you turn and attend to me, you will have mercy upon me. For what do I wish to say, lord my god, but that I know not whence I came hither into this life-in-death. Or should I call it death-in-life? I do not know. And yet the consolations of your mercy have sustained me from the very beginning, as I have heard from my fleshly parents, from whom and in whom you formed me in time—for I cannot myself remember. Thus even though they sustained me by the consolation of woman's milk, neither my mother nor my nurses filled their own breasts but you, through them,

---

* Psalms 35:3.

† Psalms 19:12, 13.

‡ Psalms 130:3.

gave me the food of infancy according to your ordinance and your bounty which underlie all things. For it was you who caused me not to want more than you gave and it was you who gave to those who nourished me the will to give me what you gave them. And they, by an instinctive affection, were willing to give me what you had supplied abundantly. It was, indeed, good for them that my good should come through them, though, in truth, it was not from them but by them. For it is from you, god, that all good things come—and from my god is all my health. This is what I have since learned, as you have made it abundantly clear by all that I have seen you give, both to me and to those around me. For even at the very first I knew how to suck, to lie quiet when I was full, and to cry when in pain—nothing more.

[**1.6.8**] Afterward I began to laugh—at first in my sleep, then when waking. For this I have been told about myself and I believe it—though I cannot remember it—for I see the same things in other infants. Then, little by little, I realized where I was and wished to tell my wishes to those who might satisfy them, but I could not! For my wants were inside me, and they were outside, and they could not by any power of theirs come into my soul. And so I would fling my arms and legs about and cry, making the few and feeble gestures that I could, though indeed the signs were not much like what I inwardly desired and when I was not satisfied—either from not being understood or because what I got was not good for me—I grew indignant that my elders were not subject to me and that those on whom I actually had no claim did not wait on me as slaves—and I avenged myself on them by crying. That infants are like this, I have myself been able to learn by watching them; and they, though they knew me not, have shown me better what I was like than my own nurses who knew me.

[**1.6.9**] And, behold, my infancy died long ago, but I am still living. But you, lord, whose life is forever and in whom nothing dies—since before the world was, indeed, before all that can be called "before," you were, and you are the god and lord of all your creatures; and with you abide all the stable causes of all unstable things, the unchanging sources of all changeable things, and the eternal reasons of all non-rational and temporal things—tell me, your suppliant, god, tell me, merciful one, in pity tell a pitiful creature whether my infancy followed yet an earlier age of my life that had already passed away before it. Was it such another age which I spent in my mother's womb? For something of that sort has been suggested to me, and I have myself seen pregnant women. But what, god, my joy, preceded that period of life? Was I, indeed, anywhere, or anybody? No one can explain these things to me, neither father nor mother, nor the

experience of others, nor my own memory. Do you laugh at me for asking such things? Or do you command me to praise and confess to you
only what I know?

[**1.6.10**] I give thanks to you, lord of heaven and earth, giving praise to
you for that first being and my infancy of which I have no memory. For
you have granted to man that he should come to self-knowledge through
the knowledge of others, and that he should believe many things about
himself on the authority of the womenfolk. Now, clearly, I had life and
being; and, as my infancy closed, I was already learning signs by which my
feelings could be communicated to others.

Whence could such a creature come but from you, lord? Is any man
skillful enough to have fashioned himself? Or is there any other source
from which being and life could flow into us, save this, that you, lord, have
made us—you with whom being and life are one, since you yourself are
supreme being and supreme life both together. For you are infinite and in
you there is no change, nor an end to this present day—although there is
a sense in which it ends in you since all things are in you and there would
be no such thing as days passing away unless you sustained them. And
since your years shall have no end,* your years are an ever-present day.
And how many of ours and our fathers' days have passed through this
your day and have received from it what measure and fashion of being
they had? And all the days to come shall so receive and so pass away. But
you are the same! And all the things of tomorrow and the days yet to
come, and all of yesterday and the days that are past, you will gather into
this your day. What is it to me if someone does not understand this? Let
him still rejoice and continue to ask, "What is this?" Let him also rejoice
and prefer to seek you, even if he fails to find an answer, rather than to
seek an answer and not find you!

[**1.7.11**] "Hear me, god! Woe to the sins of men!" When a man cries
thus, you show him mercy, for you created the man but not the sin in him.
Who brings to remembrance the sins of my infancy? For in your sight
there is none free from sin, not even the infant who has lived but a day
upon this earth. Who brings this to my remembrance? Does not each little one, in whom I now observe what I no longer remember of myself? In
what ways, in that time, did I sin? Was it that I cried for the breast? If I
should now so cry—not indeed for the breast, but for food suitable to my
condition—I should be most justly laughed at and rebuked. What I did

---

* Psalms 102:27.

then deserved rebuke but, since I could not understand those who rebuked me, neither custom nor common sense permitted me to be rebuked. As we grow we root out and cast away from us such childish habits. Yet I have not seen anyone who is wise who cast away the good when trying to purge the bad. Nor was it good, even in that time, to strive to get by crying what, if it had been given me, would have been hurtful; or to be bitterly indignant at those who, because they were older—not slaves, either, but free—and wiser than I, would not indulge my capricious desires. Was it a good thing for me to try, by struggling as hard as I could, to harm them for not obeying me, even when it would have done me harm to have been obeyed? Thus, the infant's innocence lies in the weakness of his body and not in the infant mind. I have myself observed a baby to be jealous, though it could not speak; it was livid as it watched another infant at the breast.

Who is ignorant of this? Mothers and nurses tell us that they cure these things by I know not what remedies. But is this innocence, when the fountain of milk is flowing fresh and abundant, that another who needs it should not be allowed to share it, even though he requires such nourishment to sustain his life? Yet we look leniently on such things, not because they are not faults, or even small faults, but because they will vanish as the years pass. For, although we allow for such things in an infant, the same things could not be tolerated patiently in an adult.

[1.7.12] Therefore, lord my god, you who gave life to the infant, and a body which, as we see, you have furnished with senses, shaped with limbs, beautified with form, and endowed with all vital energies for its well-being and health—you command me to praise you for these things, to give thanks to the lord, and to sing praise to his name, most high. For you are god, omnipotent and good, even if you had done no more than these things, which no other but you can do—you alone who made all things fair and ordered everything according to your law.

I am loath to dwell on this part of my life of which, lord, I have no remembrance, about which I must trust the word of others and what I can surmise from observing other infants, even if such guesses are trustworthy. For it lies in the deep murk of my forgetfulness and thus is like the period which I passed in my mother's womb. But if "I was conceived in iniquity, and in sin my mother nourished me in her womb,"* where, I pray you, my god, where, lord, or when was I, your servant, ever innocent? But

---

* Psalms 51:5.

see now, I pass over that period, for what have I to do with a time from which I can recall no memories?

[1.8.13] Did I not, then, as I grew out of infancy, come next to boyhood, or rather did it not come to me and succeed my infancy? My infancy did not go away (for where would it go?). It was simply no longer present; and I was no longer an infant who could not speak, but now a chattering boy. I remember this, and I have since observed how I learned to speak. My elders did not teach me words by rote, as they taught me my letters afterward. But I myself, when I was unable to communicate all I wished to say to whomever I wished by means of whimperings and grunts and various gestures of my limbs (which I used to reinforce my demands), I myself repeated the sounds already stored in my memory by the mind which you, my god, had given me. When they called some thing by name and pointed it out while they spoke, I saw it and realized that the thing they wished to indicate was called by the name they then uttered. And what they meant was made plain by the gestures of their bodies, by a kind of natural language, common to all nations, which expresses itself through changes of countenance, glances of the eye, gestures and intonations which indicate a disposition and attitude—either to seek or to possess, to reject or to avoid. So it was that by frequently hearing words, in different phrases, I gradually identified the objects which the words stood for and, having formed my mouth to repeat these signs, I was thereby able to express my will. Thus I exchanged with those about me the verbal signs by which we express our wishes and advanced deeper into the stormy fellowship of human life, depending all the while upon the authority of my parents and the behest of my elders.

[1.9.14] God, my god! What miseries and mockeries did I then experience when it was impressed on me that obedience to my teachers was proper to my boyhood estate if I was to flourish in this world and distinguish myself in those tricks of speech which would gain honor for me among men, and deceitful riches! To this end I was sent to school to get learning, the value of which I knew not—wretch that I was. Yet if I was slow to learn, I was flogged. For this was deemed praiseworthy by our forefathers and many had passed before us in the same course, and thus had built up the precedent for the sorrowful road on which we too were compelled to travel, multiplying labor and sorrow upon the sons of Adam. About this time, lord, I observed men calling upon you, and I learned from them to conceive you—after my capacity for understanding as it was then—to be some great being, who, though not visible to our senses, was able to hear and help us. Thus as a boy I began to call upon you, my help and my refuge, and, in calling you, broke the bands of my tongue. Small as I was, I prayed with no slight earnestness that I might not be beaten at school. And when you did not heed me—for that would have been giving me over to my folly—my elders and even my parents too, who wished me no ill, treated my stripes as a joke, though they were then a great and grievous ill to me.[1]

[1.9.15] Is there anyone, lord, with a spirit so great, who cleaves to you with such steadfast affection (or is there even a kind of obtuseness that has the same effect)—is there any man who, by cleaving devoutly to you, is endowed with so great a courage that he can regard indifferently those racks and hooks and other torture weapons from which men throughout the world pray so fervently to be spared; and can they scorn those who so greatly fear these torments, just as my parents were amused at the torments with which our teachers punished us boys? For we were no less afraid of our pains, nor did we beseech you less to escape them. Yet, even so, we were sinning by writing or reading or studying less than our assigned lessons.

For I did not, lord, lack memory or capacity, for, by your will, I possessed enough for my age. However, my mind was absorbed only in play, and I was punished for this by those who were doing the same things themselves. But the idling of our elders is called business; the idling of boys, though quite like it, is punished by those same elders, and no one pities either the boys or the men. For will any common sense observer agree that I was rightly punished as a boy for playing ball—just because this hindered me from learning more quickly those lessons by means of which, as a man, I could play at more shameful games? And did he by whom I was beaten do anything different? When he was worsted in some small controversy with a fellow teacher, he was more tormented by anger and envy than I was when beaten by a playmate in the ball game.

[1.10.16] And yet I sinned, lord my god, ruler and creator of all natural things—but of sins only the ruler—I sinned, lord my god, in acting against the precepts of my parents and of those teachers. For this learning which they wished me to acquire—no matter what their motives were—I might have put to good account afterward. I disobeyed them, not because I had chosen a better way, but from a sheer love of play. I loved the vanity of victory, and I loved to have my ears tickled with lying fables, which made them itch even more ardently, and a similar curiosity glowed more and more in my eyes for the shows and sports of my elders. Yet those who put on such shows are held in such high repute that almost all desire the same for their children. They are therefore willing to have them beaten, if their childhood games keep them from the studies by which their parents desire them to grow up to be able to give such shows.[2] Look down on these things with mercy, lord, and deliver us who now call upon you; deliver those also who do not call upon you, so that they may call upon you, and you may deliver them.

[1.11.17] Even as a boy I had heard of eternal life promised to us through the humility of the lord our god, who came down to visit us in our pride, and I was signed with the sign of his cross, and was seasoned with his salt even from the womb of my mother, who greatly trusted in you.[3] You saw, lord, how, once, while I was still a child, I was suddenly seized with stomach pains and was at the point of death—you saw, my god, for even then you were my keeper, with what agitation and with what faith I solicited from the piety of my mother and from your church (which is the mother of us all) the baptism of your Christ, my lord and my god. The mother of my flesh was much perplexed, for, with a heart pure in your faith, she was always in deep travail for my eternal salvation. If I had not quickly recovered, she would have provided forthwith for my initiation and washing by your life-giving sacraments, confessing you, lord Jesus, for the forgiveness of sins. So my cleansing was deferred, as if it were inevitable that, were I to live, I would be further polluted; and, further, because the guilt contracted by sin after baptism would be still greater and more perilous.

Thus, at that time, I "believed" along with my mother and the whole household, except my father. But he did not overcome the influence of my mother's piety in me, nor did he prevent my believing in Christ, although he had not yet believed in him. For it was her desire, my god, that I should acknowledge you as my father rather than him. In this you helped her to overcome her husband, to whom, though his superior, she yielded obedience. In this way she also yielded obedience to you, who so command.

[1.11.18] I ask you, my god, for I would gladly know if it is your will, to what good end my baptism was deferred at that time? Was it indeed for my good that the reins were slackened, as it were, to encourage me in sin? Or, were they not slackened? If not, then why is it still dinned into our ears on all sides, "Let him alone, let him do as he pleases, for he is not yet baptized"? In the matter of bodily health, no one says, "Let him alone; let him be worse wounded; for he is not yet cured"! How much better, then, would it have been for me to have been cured at once—and if thereafter, through the diligent care of friends and myself, my soul's restored health had been kept safe in your keeping, who gave it in the first place! This would have been far better, in truth. But how many and great were the waves of temptation which appeared to hang over me as I grew out of childhood! These were foreseen by my mother, and she preferred that the unformed clay should be risked to them rather than the clay molded after Christ's image.

[1.12.19] But in this time of childhood—which was far less dreaded for me than my adolescence—I had no love of learning, and hated to be driven to it. Yet I was driven to it just the same, and good was done for me, even though I did not do it well, for I would not have learned if I had not been forced to it. For no man does well against his will, even if what he does is a good thing. Neither did they who forced me do well, but the good that was done me came from you, my god. For they did not care about the way in which I would use what they forced me to learn, and took it for granted that it was to satisfy the inordinate desires of a rich beggary and a shameful glory. But you, lord, by whom the hairs of our head are numbered,* made use for my good of the error of all who pushed me on to study: but my error in not being willing to learn you used for my punishment. And I—though so small a boy yet so great a sinner— was not punished without warrant. Thus by the instrumentality of those who did not do well, you did well for me; and by my own sin you justly punished me. For it is just as you have ordained: that every inordinate affection brings on its own punishment.

[1.13.20] But what were the causes for my strong dislike of Greek literature, which I studied from my boyhood? Even to this day I have not fully understood them. For Latin I loved exceedingly—not just the rudiments, but what the grammarians teach. For those beginner's lessons in reading, writing, and counting, I considered no less a burden and pain than Greek. Yet whence came this, unless from the sin and vanity of this life? For I was but flesh, a wind that passes away and does not come again.† Those first lessons were better, assuredly, because they were more certain, and through them I acquired, and still retain, the power of reading what I find written and of writing for myself what I will. In the other subjects, however, I was compelled to learn about the wanderings of a certain Aeneas, oblivious of my own wanderings, and to weep for Dido dead, who slew herself for love. And all this while I bore with dry eyes my own wretched self dying to you, god, my life, in the midst of these things.[4]

* Matthew 10:30.
† Psalms 78:39.

[1.13.21] For what can be more wretched than the wretch who has no pity upon himself, who sheds tears over Dido, dead for the love of Aeneas, but who sheds no tears for his own death in not loving you, god, light of my heart, and bread of the inner mouth of my soul, power that links together my mind with my inmost thoughts? I did not love you, and thus committed fornication against you.* Those around me, also sinning, cried out: "Well done! Well done!" The friendship of this world is fornication against you; and "Well done! Well done!" is cried until one feels ashamed not to show himself a man in this way. For my own condition I shed no tears, though I wept for Dido, who "sought death at the sword's point," while I myself was seeking the lowest rung of your creation, having forsaken you; earth sinking back to earth again. And, if I had been forbidden to read these poems, I would have grieved that I was not allowed to read what grieved me. This sort of madness is considered more honorable and more fruitful learning than the beginner's course in which I learned to read and write.

[1.13.22] But now, my god, cry to my soul, and let your truth say to me: "Not so, not so! That first learning was far better." For, obviously, I would rather forget the wanderings of Aeneas, and all such things, than forget how to write and read. Still, over the entrance of the grammar school there hangs a veil. This is not so much the sign of a covering for a mystery as a curtain for error. Let them exclaim against me—those I no longer fear—while I confess to you, my god, what my soul desires, and let me find some rest, for in blaming my own evil ways I may come to love your holy ways. Neither let those cry out against me who buy and sell the baubles of literature. For if I ask them if it is true, as the poet says, that Aeneas once came to Carthage, the unlearned will reply that they do not know and the learned will deny that it is true. But if I ask with what letters the name Aeneas is written, all who have ever learned this will answer correctly, in accordance with the conventional understanding men have agreed upon as to these signs. Again, if I should ask which would cause the greatest inconvenience in our life, if it were forgotten: reading and writing, or these poetical fictions, who does not see what everyone would answer who had not entirely lost his own memory? I erred, then, when as a boy I preferred those vain studies to these more profitable ones, or rather loved the one and hated the other. "One and one are two, two and two are four": this was then a truly hateful song to me. But the wooden horse full of its armed soldiers, and the

---

* Psalms 73:27.

holocaust of Troy, and the spectral image of Creusa were all a most delightful—and vain—show!

[1.14.23] But why, then, did I dislike Greek learning, which was full of such tales? For Homer was skillful in inventing such poetic fictions and is most sweetly wanton; yet when I was a boy, he was most disagreeable to me. I believe that Virgil would have the same effect on Greek boys as Homer did on me if they were forced to learn him. For the tedium of learning a foreign language mingled gall into the sweetness of those Grecian myths. For I did not understand a word of the language, and yet I was driven with threats and cruel punishments to learn it. There was also a time when, as an infant, I knew no Latin; but this I acquired without any fear or tormenting, but merely by being alert to the blandishments of my nurses, the jests of those who smiled on me, and the sportiveness of those who toyed with me. I learned all this, indeed, without being urged by any pressure of punishment, for my own heart urged me to bring forth its own fashioning, which I could not do except by learning words: not from those who taught me but those who talked to me, into whose ears I could pour forth whatever I could fashion. From this it is sufficiently clear that a free curiosity is more effective in learning than a discipline based on fear. Yet, by your ordinance, god, discipline is given to restrain the excesses of freedom; this ranges from the ferule of the schoolmaster to the trials of the martyr and has the effect of mingling for us a wholesome bitterness, which calls us back to you from the poisonous pleasures that first drew us from you.

[1.15.24] Hear my prayer, lord; let not my soul faint under your discipline, nor let me faint in confessing to you your mercies, whereby you have saved me from all my most wicked ways until you became sweet to me beyond all the allurements that I used to follow. Let me come to love you wholly, and grasp your hand with my whole heart so that you may deliver me from every temptation, until the very last. And thus, lord, my king and my god, may all things useful that I learned as a boy now be offered in your service—let it be for your service that I now speak and write and count. For when I was learning vain things, you imposed your discipline upon me: and you have forgiven me my sin of delighting in those vanities. In those studies I learned many a useful word, but these might have been learned in matters not so vain; and surely that is the safe way for youths to walk in.

[1.16.25] But woe to you, torrent of human custom! Who shall stay your course? When will you ever run dry? How long will you carry down the sons of Eve into that vast and hideous ocean, scarcely to be crossed even by those who have the wood of the cross for an ark? Do I not read in you the stories of Jove the thunderer—and the adulterer? How could he be both? But so it says, and the sham thunder served as a cloak for him to play at real adultery. Yet which of our gowned masters will give a civil hearing to a man trained in their own schools who cries out and says: "These were Homer's fictions; he transfers human things to the gods. I could have wished that he would transfer divine things to us." But it would have been more true if he said, "These are, indeed, his fictions, but he attributed divine attributes to sinful men, that crimes might not be accounted crimes, and that whoever committed such crimes might appear to imitate the celestial gods and not abandoned men."[5]

[1.16.26] And yet, torrent of hell, the sons of men are still cast into you, and they pay fees for learning all these things. And it is no small affair when this goes on in the forum under the auspices of laws which provide for a salary over and above the teacher's fees. And you beat against your rocky shore and roar: "Here words may be learned; here you can attain the eloquence which is so necessary to persuade people to your way of thinking; so helpful in unfolding your opinions." Indeed, they seem to argue that we should never have understood these words, "shower of gold," "bosom," "intrigue," "highest heavens," and others such, if Terence had not introduced a good-for-nothing youth upon the stage, setting up a picture of Jove as his example of lewdness and telling the tale

> *Of Jove's descending in a shower of gold*
> *Into Danae's bosom . . .*
> *With a woman to intrigue.*

See how he excites himself to lust, as if by a heavenly authority, when he says:

> *Great Jove,*
> *Who shakes the highest heavens with his thunder;*
> *Shall I, poor mortal man, not do the same?*
> *I've done it, and with all my heart, I'm glad.*[6]

These words are not learned one whit more easily because of this vileness, but through them the vileness is more boldly perpetrated. I do not blame the words, for they are, as it were, choice and precious vessels, but I do deplore the wine of error which was poured out to us by teachers already drunk. And, unless we also drank we were beaten, without liberty of appeal to a sober judge. And yet, my god, in whose presence I can now with security recall this, I learned these things willingly and with delight, and for it I was called a boy of good promise.

[1.17.27] Bear with me, my god, while I speak a little of those talents, your gifts, and of the follies on which I wasted them. For a lesson was given me that sufficiently disturbed my soul, for in it there was both hope of praise and fear of shame or stripes. The assignment was that I should declaim the words of Juno, as she raged and sorrowed that she could not "bar off Italy from all the approaches of the Teucrian king."[7] I had learned that Juno had never uttered these words. Yet we were compelled to stray in the footsteps of these poetic fictions, and to turn into prose what the poet had said in verse. In the declamation, the boy won most applause who most strikingly reproduced the passions of anger and sorrow according to the "character" of the persons presented and who clothed it all in the most suitable language. What is it now to me, my true life, my god, that my declaiming was applauded above that of many of my classmates and fellow students? Actually, was not all that smoke and wind? Besides, was there nothing else on which I could have exercised my wit and tongue? Your praise, lord, your praises might have propped up the tendrils of my heart by your scriptures; and it would not have been dragged away by these empty trifles, a shameful prey to the spirits of the air. For there is more than one way in which men sacrifice to the fallen angels.

[1.18.28] But it was no wonder that I was thus carried toward vanity and was estranged from you, my god, when men were held up as models to me who, when relating a deed of theirs—not in itself evil—were covered with confusion if found guilty of a barbarism or a solecism, but who could tell of their own licentiousness and be applauded for it, so long as they did it in a full and ornate oration of well-chosen words.[8] You see all this, lord, and keep silence—long-suffering, and plenteous in mercy and truth as you are. Will you keep silence forever? Even now you draw from that vast deep the soul that seeks you and thirsts after your delight, whose heart said to you, "I have sought your face; your face, lord, will I seek."* For I was far from your face in the dark shadows of passion. For it is not by our feet, nor by change of place, that we either turn from you or return to you. That younger son did not charter horses or chariots, or ships, or fly away on visible wings, or journey by walking so that in the far country he might prodigally waste all that you gave him when he set out.†[9]

---

* Psalms 27:8.
† Luke 15:11–32.

A kind father when you gave; and kinder still when he returned destitute! To be wanton, that is to say, to be darkened in heart—this is to be far from your face.

[**1.18.29**] Look down, lord god, and see patiently, as you are accustomed to do, how diligently the sons of men observe the conventional rules of letters and syllables, taught them by those who learned their letters beforehand, while they neglect the eternal rules of everlasting salvation taught by you. They carry it so far that if he who practices or teaches the established rules of pronunciation should speak, contrary to grammatical usage, without aspirating the first syllable of *hominem* [human being], he will offend his fellow human beings more than if he, a human being, were to hate another human being contrary to your commandments. It is as if he should feel that there is an enemy who could be more destructive to himself than that hatred which excites him against his fellow; or that he could destroy him whom he hates more completely than he destroys his own soul by this same hatred. Now, obviously, there is no knowledge of letters more innate than the writing of conscience—against doing to another what one would not have done to himself. How mysterious you are, who dwell on high in silence, the only great god, who by an unwearied law hurl down the penalty of blindness to unlawful desire! When a man seeking the reputation of eloquence stands before a human judge, while a thronging multitude surrounds him, and inveighs against his enemy with the most fierce hatred, he takes most vigilant heed that his tongue does not slip in a grammatical error, for example, and say *inter hominibus* [instead of *inter homines*], but he takes no heed lest, in the fury of his spirit, he cut someone off from his fellow human beings [*ex hominibus*].

[**1.18.30**] These were the customs in the midst of which I was cast, an unhappy boy. This was the wrestling arena in which I was more fearful of perpetrating a barbarism than, having done so, of envying those who had not. These things I declare and confess to you, my god. I was applauded by those whom I then thought it my whole duty to please, for I did not perceive the gulf of infamy wherein I was cast away from your eyes. For in your eyes, what was more infamous than I was already, since I displeased even my own kind and deceived, with endless lies, my tutor, my masters and parents—all from a love of play, a craving for frivolous spectacles, a stage-struck restlessness to imitate what I saw in these shows? I pilfered from my parents' cellar and table, sometimes driven by gluttony, sometimes just to have something to give to other boys in exchange for their baubles, which they were prepared to sell even though they liked them as well as I. Moreover, in this kind of play, I often sought dishonest victories, being myself conquered by the vain desire for pre-eminence. And what was I so unwilling to endure, and what was it that I censured so violently when I caught anyone, except the very things I did to others? And, when I was myself detected and censured, I preferred to quarrel rather than to yield. Is this the innocence of childhood? It is not, lord, it is not. I entreat your mercy, my god, for these same sins as we grow older are transferred from tutors and masters; they pass from nuts and balls and sparrows, to magistrates and kings, to gold and lands and slaves, just as the rod is succeeded by more severe chastisements. It was, then, the fact of humility in childhood that you, our king, approved as a symbol of humility when you said, "Of such is the kingdom of heaven."*

[1.19.31] However, lord, to you most excellent and most good, architect and governor of the universe, thanks would be due, our god, even if you had not willed that I should survive my boyhood. For I existed even then; I lived and felt and was solicitous about my own well-being—a trace of that most mysterious unity from whence I had my being. I kept watch, by my inner sense, over the integrity of my outer senses, and even in these trifles and also in my thoughts about trifles, I learned to take pleasure in truth. I was averse to being deceived; I had a vigorous memory; I was gifted with the power of speech, was softened by friendship, shunned sorrow, meanness, ignorance. Is not such an animated creature as this wonderful and praiseworthy? But all these are gifts of my god; I did not give them to myself. Moreover, they are good, and they all together constitute myself. Good, then, is he that made me, and he is my god; and before him will I rejoice exceedingly for every good gift which, even as a boy, I had. But herein lay my sin, that it was not in him, but in his creatures—myself and the rest—that I sought for pleasures, honors, and truths. And I fell thereby into sorrows, troubles, and errors. Thanks be to you, my joy, my pride, my confidence, my god—thanks be to you for your gifts; but I ask you to preserve them in me. For thus will you preserve me; and those things which you have given me shall be developed and perfected, and I myself shall be with you, for from you is my being.

---

* Matthew 19:14.

BOOK 2

[2.1.1] I wish now to review in memory my past wickedness and the carnal corruptions of my soul—not because I still love them, but that I may love you, my god. For love of your love I do this, recalling in the bitterness of self-examination my wicked ways, that you may grow sweet to me, you sweetness without deception! You sweetness happy and assured! Thus you may gather me up out of those fragments in which I was torn to pieces, while I turned away from you who are one, and lost myself among the many.[1] For as I became a youth, I longed to be satisfied with worldly things, and I dared to grow wild in a succession of various and shadowy loves. My form wasted away, and I became corrupt in your eyes, yet I was still pleasing to my own eyes—and eager to please the eyes of men.

[2.2.2] But what was it that delighted me except to love and to be loved? Still I did not keep the moderate way of the love of mind to mind—the bright path of friendship. Instead, the mists of passion steamed up out of the puddly concupiscence of the flesh, and the hot imagination of puberty, and they so obscured and overcast my heart that I was unable to distinguish pure affection from unholy desire. Both boiled confusedly within me, and dragged my unstable youth down over the cliffs of unchaste desires and plunged me into a gulf of infamy. Your anger had come upon me, and I knew it not. I had been deafened by the clanking of the chains of my mortality, the punishment for my soul's pride, and I wandered farther from you, and you permitted me to do so. I was tossed to and fro, and wasted, and poured out, and I boiled over in my fornications—and yet you held your peace, my tardy joy! You still held your peace, and I wandered still farther from you into more and yet more barren fields of sorrow, in proud dejection and restless lassitude.

[2.2.3] If only there had been someone to regulate my disorder and turn to my profit the fleeting beauties of the things around me, and to fix a bound to their sweetness, so that the tides of my youth might have spent themselves upon the shore of marriage! Then they might have been tranquilized and satisfied with having children, as your law prescribes, lord—you who form the offspring of our death and are able also with a tender hand to blunt the thorns which were excluded from your

19

paradise!* For your omnipotence is not far from us even when we are far from you. Now, on the other hand, I might have given more vigilant heed to the voice from the clouds: "Nevertheless, such shall have trouble in the flesh, but I spare you,"† and, "It is good for a man not to touch a woman,"‡ and, "He that is unmarried cares for the things that belong to the lord, how he may please the lord; but he that is married cares for the things that are of the world, how he may please his wife."§ I should have listened more attentively to these words, and, thus having been "made a eunuch for the kingdom of heaven's sake,"‖ I would have with greater happiness expected your embraces.

[2.2.4] But, fool that I was, I foamed in my wickedness as the sea and, abandoning you, followed the rushing of my own tide, and burst out of all your bounds. But I did not escape your lashes. For what mortal can do so? You were always by me, mercifully angry and flavoring all my unlawful pleasures with bitter discontent, in order that I might seek pleasures free from discontent. But where could I find such pleasure except in you, lord—except in you, who teach us by sorrow, who wound us to heal us, and kill us so that we may not die apart from you. Where was I, and how far was I exiled from the delights of your house, in that sixteenth year of the age of my flesh, when the madness of lust held full sway in me—that madness which grants indulgence to human shamelessness, even though it is forbidden by your laws—and I gave myself entirely to it? Meanwhile, my family took no care to save me from ruin by marriage, for their only care was that I should learn how to make a powerful speech and become a persuasive orator.

[2.3.5] Now, in that year my studies were interrupted. I had come back from Madauros, a neighboring city where I had gone to study grammar and rhetoric; and the money for a further term at Carthage was being got together for me. This project was more a matter of my father's ambition than of his means, for he was only a poor citizen of Thagaste.[2] To whom am I narrating all this? Not to you, my god, but to my own kind in your presence—to that small part of the human race who may chance to come upon these writings. And to what end? That I and all who read them may

---

* Genesis 3:18.

† 1 Corinthians 7:28.

‡ 1 Corinthians 7:1.

§ 1 Corinthians 7:32–33.

‖ Matthew 19:12.

understand what depths there are from which we are to cry to you.* For
what is more surely heard in your ear than a confessing heart and a faithful life? Who did not extol and praise my father, because he went quite
beyond his means to supply his son with the necessary expenses for a far
journey in the interest of his education? For many far richer citizens did
not do so much for their children. Still, this same father troubled himself
not at all as to how I was progressing toward you nor how chaste I was,
just so long as I was skillful in speaking—no matter how barren I was to
your tillage, god, who are the one true and good lord of my heart, which
is your field.

[2.3.6] During that sixteenth year of my age, I lived with my parents,
having a holiday from school for a time—this idleness imposed upon me
by my parents' straitened finances. The thornbushes of lust grew rank
about my head, and there was no hand to root them out. Indeed, when
my father saw me one day at the baths and perceived that I was becoming a man, and was showing the signs of adolescence, he joyfully told my
mother about it as if already looking forward to grandchildren, rejoicing
in that sort of inebriation in which the world so often forgets you, its creator, and falls in love with your creature instead of you—the inebriation
of that invisible wine of a perverted will which turns and bows down to
infamy. But in my mother's breast you had already begun to build your
temple and the foundation of your holy habitation—whereas my father
was only a catechumen, and that but recently. She was, therefore, startled
with a holy fear and trembling: for though I had not yet been baptized,
she feared those crooked ways in which they walk who turn their backs
to you and not their faces.

[2.3.7] Alas for me! Do I dare say that you held your peace, my god,
while I wandered farther away from you? Did you really then hold your
peace? Then whose words were they but yours which by my mother,
your faithful handmaid, you poured into my ears? None of them, however, sank into my heart to make me do anything. She was anxious—and,
as I remember, warned me privately with great solicitude—that I should
not commit fornication and above all things never defile another man's
wife. These appeared to me mere womanish counsels, which I would have
blushed to obey. Yet they were from you, and I knew it not. I thought that
you were silent and that it was only she who spoke. Yet it was through her
that you did not keep silence toward me; and in rejecting her counsel I

---

* Psalms 130:1.

was rejecting you—I, her son, "the son of your handmaid, your servant."* But I did not realize this, and rushed on headlong with such blindness that, among my friends, I was ashamed to be less shameless than they, when I heard them boasting of their disgraceful exploits—yes, and glorying all the more the worse their baseness was. What is worse, I took pleasure in such exploits, not for the pleasure's sake only but mostly for praise. What is worthy of vituperation except vice itself? Yet I made myself out worse than I was, in order that I might not go lacking for praise. And when in anything I had not sinned as the worst ones in the group, I would still say that I had done what I had not done, in order not to appear contemptible because I was more innocent than they; and not to drop in their esteem because I was more chaste.

[2.3.8] See with what companions I walked the streets of Babylon![3] I rolled in its mire and lolled about on it, as if on a bed of spices and precious ointments. And, drawing me more closely to the very center of that city, my invisible enemy trod me down and seduced me, for I was easy to seduce. My mother had already fled out of the midst of Babylon† and was progressing, albeit slowly, toward its outskirts. For in counseling me to chastity, she did not bear in mind what her husband had told her about me. And although she knew that my passions were destructive even then and dangerous for the future, she did not think they should be restrained by the bonds of conjugal affection—if, indeed, they could not be cut away to the quick. She took no heed of this, for she was afraid lest a wife should prove a hindrance and a burden to my hopes. These were not her hopes of the world to come, which my mother had in you, but the hope of learning, which both my parents were too anxious that I should acquire—my father, because he had little or no thought of you, and only vain thoughts for me; my mother, because she thought that the usual course of study would not only be no hindrance but actually a furtherance toward my eventual return to you. This much I conjecture, recalling as well as I can the temperaments of my parents. Meantime, the reins of discipline were slackened on me, so that without the restraint of due severity, I might play at whatsoever I fancied, even to the point of dissoluteness. And in all this there was that mist which shut out from my sight the brightness of your truth, my god; and my iniquity bulged out, as it were, with fatness!‡

---

* Psalms 116:16.

† Jeremiah 51:6.

‡ Psalms 73:7.

[2.4.9] Theft is punished by your law, lord, and by the law written in men's hearts, which not even ingrained wickedness can erase. For what thief will tolerate another thief stealing from him? Even a rich thief will not tolerate a poor thief who is driven to theft by want. Yet I had a desire to commit robbery, and did so, compelled to it by neither hunger nor poverty, but through a contempt for well-doing and a strong impulse to iniquity. For I pilfered something which I already had in sufficient measure, and of much better quality. I did not desire to enjoy what I stole, but only the theft and the sin itself. There was a pear tree close to our own vineyard, heavily laden with fruit, which was not tempting either for its color or for its flavor. Late one night—having prolonged our games in the streets until then, as our bad habit was—a group of young scoundrels, and I among them, went to shake and rob this tree. We carried off a huge load of pears, not to eat ourselves, but to dump out to the hogs, after barely tasting some of them ourselves. Doing this pleased us all the more because it was forbidden. Such was my heart, god, such was my heart—which you pitied even in that bottomless pit. See now, let my heart confess to you what it was seeking there, when I was being gratuitously wicked, having no inducement to evil but the evil itself. It was foul, and I loved it. I loved my own undoing. I loved my error—not that for which I erred but the error itself. A depraved soul, falling away from security in you to destruction in itself, seeking nothing from the shameful deed but shame itself.

[2.5.10] Now there is a splendor in all beautiful bodies, and in gold and silver and all things. The sense of touch has its own power to please and the other senses find their proper objects in physical sensation. Worldly honor also has its own glory, and so do the powers to command and to overcome: and from these there springs up the desire for revenge. Yet, in seeking these pleasures, we must not depart from you, lord, nor deviate from your law. The life which we live here has its own peculiar attractiveness because it has a certain measure of decorum of its own and a harmony with all these inferior values. The bond of human friendship has a sweetness of its own, binding many souls together as one. Yet because of these values, sin is committed, because we have an inordinate preference for these goods of a lower order and neglect the better and the higher good—neglecting you, our lord god, and your truth and your law. For these inferior values have their delights, but not at all equal to my god, who made them all. For in him do the righteous delight and he is the sweetness of the upright in heart.

[2.5.11] When, therefore, we inquire why a crime was committed, we

do not accept the explanation unless it appears that there was the desire
to obtain some of those values which we designate inferior, or else a fear
of losing them. For truly they are beautiful and decorous, though in comparison with the superior and celestial goods they are abject and contemptible. A man has murdered another man—what was his motive?
Either he desired his wife or his property or else he would steal to support himself; or else he was afraid of losing something to him; or else, having been injured, he was burning to be revenged. Would a man commit
murder without a motive, taking delight simply in the act of murder?
Who would believe such a thing? Even for that savage and brutal man, of
whom it was said that he was gratuitously wicked and cruel, there is still
a motive assigned to his deeds. "Lest through idleness," he says, "hand or
heart should grow inactive." And to what purpose? Why, namely this:
that, having once got possession of the city through his practice of his
wicked ways, he might gain honors, empire, and wealth, and thus be ex-
empt from the fear of the laws and from financial difficulties in supplying
the needs of his family—and from the consciousness of his own wickedness. So it seems that even Catiline himself loved not his own villainies,
but something else, and it was this that gave him the motive for his
crimes.[4]

[2.6.12] What was it in you, theft of mine, that I, poor wretch, doted
on—you deed of darkness—in that sixteenth year of my age? Beautiful
you were not, for you were a theft. But are you anything at all, so that I
could analyze the case with you? Those pears that we stole were fair to
the sight because they were your creation, beauty beyond compare, creator of all, you good god—god the highest good and my true good. Those
pears were truly pleasant to the sight, but it was not for them that my
miserable soul lusted, for I had an abundance of better pears. I stole
those simply that I might steal, for, having stolen them, I threw them
away. My sole gratification in them was my own sin, which I was pleased
to enjoy; for, if any one of these pears entered my mouth, the only good
flavor it had was my sin in eating it. And now, lord my god, I ask what it
was in that theft of mine that caused me such delight; for behold it had
no beauty of its own—certainly not the sort of beauty that exists in justice and wisdom, nor such as is in the mind, memory, senses, and the animal life of man; nor yet the kind that is the glory and beauty of the stars
in their courses; nor the beauty of the earth, or the sea—teeming with
spawning life, replacing in birth that which dies and decays. Indeed, it
did not have that false and shadowy beauty which attends the deceptions
of vice.

[2.6.13] For thus we see pride wearing the mask of high-spiritedness, although only you, god, are high above all. Ambition seeks honor and glory, whereas only you should be honored above all, and glorified forever. The powerful man seeks to be feared, because of his cruelty; but who ought really to be feared but god only? What can be forced away or withdrawn out of his power—when or where or whither or by whom? The enticements of the lustful claim the name of love; and yet nothing is more enticing than your love, nor is anything loved more healthfully than your truth, bright and beautiful above all. Curiosity prompts a desire for knowledge, whereas it is only you who know all things supremely. Indeed, ignorance and foolishness themselves go masked under the names of simplicity and innocence; yet there is no being that has true simplicity like yours, and none is innocent as you are. Thus it is that by a sinner's own deeds he is himself harmed. Human sloth pretends to long for rest, but what sure rest is there except in the lord? Luxury would like to be called plenty and abundance; but you are the fullness and unfailing abundance of unfading joy. Prodigality presents a show of liberality; but you are the most lavish giver of all good things. Covetousness desires to possess much; but you are already the possessor of all things. Envy contends that its aim is for excellence; but what is so excellent as you? Anger seeks revenge; but who avenges more justly than you? Fear recoils at the unfamiliar and the sudden changes which threaten things beloved, and is wary for its own security; but what can happen that is unfamiliar or sudden to you? Or who can deprive you of what you love? Where, really, is there unshaken security except with you? Grief languishes for things lost in which desire had taken delight, because it wishes to have nothing taken from it, just as nothing can be taken from you.

[2.6.14] Thus the soul commits fornication when she is turned from you, and seeks apart from you what she cannot find pure and untainted until she returns to you. All things thus imitate you—but pervertedly—when they separate themselves far from you and raise themselves up against you. But, even in this act of perverse imitation, they acknowledge you to be the creator of all nature, and recognize that there is no place where they can altogether separate themselves from you. What was it, then, that I loved in that theft? And how was I imitating my lord, even in a corrupted and perverted way? Did I wish, if only by gesture, to rebel against your law, even though I had no power to do so actually—so that, even as a captive, I might produce a sort of counterfeit liberty, by doing with impunity deeds that were forbidden, in a deluded sense of omnipotence? See this servant of yours, fleeing from his lord and following a shadow! What rottenness! What monstrousness of life and abyss of death! Could I find pleasure only in what was unlawful, and only because it was unlawful?

[**2.7.15**] What shall I render to the lord for the fact that while my memory recalls these things my soul no longer fears them? I will love you, lord, and thank you, and confess to your name, because you have put away from me such wicked and evil deeds. To your grace I attribute it and to your mercy, that you have melted away my sin as if it were ice. To your grace also I attribute whatever evil I did not commit—for what might I not have done, loving sin as I did, just for the sake of sinning? And I confess that all has been forgiven me, both those things which I committed willfully and those which, by your providence, I did not commit. What man is there who, when reflecting upon his own infirmity, dares to ascribe his chastity and innocence to his own powers, so that he should love you less—as if he were in less need of your mercy in which you forgive the transgressions of those who return to you? As for that man who, when called by you, obeyed your voice and shunned those things which he here reads of me as I recall and confess them of myself, let him not despise me—for I, who was sick, have been healed by the same physician by whose aid it was that he did not fall sick, or rather was less sick than I. And for this let him love you just as much—indeed, all the more—since he sees me restored from such a great weakness of sin by the same person by whom he sees himself preserved from such a weakness.

[**2.8.16**] What profit did I, a wretched one, receive from those things which, when I remember them now, cause me shame—above all, from that theft, which I loved only for the theft's sake? And, as the theft itself was nothing, I was all the more wretched in that I loved it so. Yet by myself alone I would not have done it—I still recall how I felt about this then—I could not have done it alone. I loved it then because of the companionship of my accomplices with whom I did it. I did not, therefore, love the theft alone—yet, indeed, it was only the theft that I loved, for the companionship was nothing. What is this paradox? Who is it that can explain it to me but god, who illumines my heart and searches out the dark corners thereof? What is it that has prompted my mind to inquire about it, to discuss and to reflect upon all this? For had I at that time loved the pears that I stole and wished to enjoy them, I might have done so alone, if I could have been satisfied with the mere act of theft by which my pleasure was served. Nor did I need to have that itching of my own passions inflamed by the encouragement of my accomplices. But since the pleasure

I got was not from the pears, it was in the crime itself, enhanced by the companionship of my fellow sinners.

[2.9.17] By what passion, then, was I animated? It was undoubtedly depraved and a great misfortune for me to feel it. But still, what was it? "Who can understand his errors?"* We laughed because our hearts were tickled at the thought of deceiving the owners, who had no idea of what we were doing and would have strenuously objected. Yet, again, why did I find such delight in doing this which I would not have done alone? Is it that no one readily laughs alone? No one does so readily; but still sometimes, when people are by themselves and no one else is about, a fit of laughter will overcome them when something very droll presents itself to their sense or mind. Yet alone I would not have done it—alone I could not have done it at all. See, my god, the lively review of my soul's career is laid bare before you. I would not have committed that theft alone. My pleasure in it was not what I stole but, rather, the act of stealing. Nor would I have enjoyed doing it alone—indeed I would not have done it! What an unfriendly friendship this is, and strange seduction of the soul, eager to make mischief from games and jokes, craving another's loss without any desire for profit or revenge of mine—only so that, when they say, "Let's go, let's do it," we are ashamed not to be shameless.

[2.10.18] Who can unravel such a twisted and tangled knottiness? It is unclean. I hate to reflect upon it. I hate to look on it. But I do long for you, righteousness and innocence, so beautiful and well-proportioned to all virtuous eyes—I long for you with an insatiable satiety. With you is perfect rest, and life unchanging. The one who enters into you enters into the joy of his lord, and shall have no fear and shall achieve excellence in the excellent one. I fell away from you, my god, and in my youth I wandered too far from you, my true support. And I became a wasteland to myself.[5]

---

* Job 10:15.

BOOK 3

[**3.1.1**] I came to Carthage, where a caldron of unholy loves was seething and bubbling all around me. I was not in love as yet, but I was in love with love; and, from a hidden hunger, I hated myself for not feeling more intensely a sense of hunger. I was looking for something to love, for I was in love with loving, and I hated security and a smooth way, free from snares. Within me I had a dearth of that inner food which is yourself, my god—although that dearth caused me no hunger. And I remained without any appetite for incorruptible food—not because I was already filled with it, but because the emptier I became the more I loathed it. Because of this my soul was unhealthy; and, full of sores, it exuded itself forth, itching to be scratched by scraping on the things of the senses. Yet, had these things no soul, they would certainly not inspire our love. To love and to be loved was sweet to me, and all the more when I gained the enjoyment of the body of the person I loved. Thus I polluted the spring of friendship with the filth of concupiscence and I dimmed its luster with the slime of lust. Yet, foul and unclean as I was, I still craved, in excessive vanity, to be thought elegant and urbane. And I did fall precipitately into the love I was longing for. My god, my mercy, with how much bitterness did you, out of your infinite goodness, flavor that sweetness for me! For I was loved in return and secretly forged a bond of pleasure; and yet I was joyfully bound with troublesome ties, so that I could be scourged with the burning iron rods of jealousy, suspicion, fear, anger, and strife.

[**3.2.2**] Stage plays also captivated me, with their sights full of the images of my own miseries: fuel for my own fire. Now, why does a man like to be made sad by viewing doleful and tragic scenes, which he himself could not by any means endure? Yet, as a spectator, he wishes to experience from them a sense of grief, and in this very sense of grief his pleasure consists. What is this but wretched madness? For a man is more affected by these actions the more he is spuriously involved in these affections. Now, if he should suffer them in his own person, it is the custom to call this misery. But when he suffers with another, then it is called compassion. But what kind of compassion is it that arises from viewing fictitious and unreal sufferings? The spectator is not expected to aid the sufferer but merely to grieve for him. And the more he grieves the more he applauds the actor of these fictions. If the misfortunes of the characters—whether historical or entirely imaginary—are

28

represented so as not to touch the feelings of the spectator, he goes away disgusted and complaining. But if his feelings are deeply touched, he sits it out attentively, and sheds tears of joy.

[3.2.3] Tears and sorrow, then, are loved. Surely every man desires to be joyful. And, though no one is willingly miserable, one may, nevertheless, be pleased to be merciful so that we love sorrows because without them we should have nothing to pity. This also springs from that same vein of friendship. But where does it go? In what direction does it flow? Why does it run into that torrent of pitch, those huge tides of loathsome lusts in which it is changed and altered past recognition, being diverted and corrupted from its celestial purity by its own will? Shall, then, compassion be repudiated? By no means! Let us, then, love the sorrows of others. But let us beware of uncleanness, my soul, under the protection of my god, the god of our fathers, who is to be praised and exalted—let us beware of uncleanness. I have not yet ceased to have compassion. But in those days in the theaters I sympathized with lovers when they sinfully enjoyed one another, although this was done fictitiously in the play. And when they lost one another, I grieved with them, as if pitying them, and yet had delight in both grief and pity. Nowadays I feel much more pity for one who delights in his wickedness than for one who counts himself unfortunate because he fails to obtain some harmful pleasure or suffers the loss of some miserable felicity. This, surely, is the truer compassion, but the sorrow I feel in it has no delight for me. For although he who grieves with the unhappy should be commended for his work of love, yet he who has the power of real compassion would still prefer that there be nothing for him to grieve about. For if good will were to be ill will—which it cannot be—only then could he who is truly and sincerely compassionate wish that there were some unhappy people so that he might commiserate them. Some grief may then be justified, but none of it loved. Thus it is that you act, lord god, for you love souls far more purely than we do and are more incorruptibly compassionate, although you are never wounded by any sorrow. "And who is sufficient for these things?"*

[3.2.4] But at that time, in my wretchedness, I loved to grieve; and I sought for things to grieve about. In another man's misery, even though it was feigned and impersonated on the stage, that performance of the actor pleased me best and attracted me most powerfully which moved me to tears. What marvel then was it that an unhappy sheep, straying from your

---

* 2 Corinthians 2:16.

flock and impatient of your care, I became infected with a foul disease? This is the reason for my love of griefs: that they would not probe into me too deeply (for I did not love to suffer in myself such things as I loved to look at), and they were the sort of grief which came from hearing those fictions, which affected only the surface of my emotion. Still, just as if they had been poisoned fingernails, their scratching was followed by inflammation, swelling, putrefaction, and corruption. Such was my life! But was it life, my god?

[3.3.5] And still your faithful mercy hovered over me from afar. In what unseemly iniquities did I wear myself out, following a sacrilegious curiosity, which, having deserted you, then began to drag me down into the treacherous abyss, into the beguiling obedience of devils, to whom I made offerings of my wicked deeds. And still in all this you did not fail to scourge me. I dared, even while your solemn rites were being celebrated inside the walls of your church, to indulge my lust and to plan a project which merited death as its fruit.[1] For this you chastised me with grievous punishments, but nothing in comparison with my fault, you my greatest mercy, my god, my refuge from those terrible dangers in which I wandered with stiff neck, receding farther from you, loving my own ways and not yours—loving a vagrant liberty!

[3.3.6] Those studies I was then pursuing, generally accounted as respectable, were aimed at distinction in the courts of law—to excel in which, the more crafty I was, the more I should be praised. Such is the blindness of men that they even glory in their blindness. And by this time I had become a master in the school of rhetoric, and I rejoiced proudly in this honor and became inflated with arrogance. Still I was relatively sedate, lord, as you know, and had no share in the wreckings of the Wreckers (for this stupid and diabolical name was regarded as the very badge of gallantry) among whom I lived with a sort of ashamed embarrassment that I was not even as they were. But I lived with them, and at times I was delighted with their friendship, even when I abhorred their acts (that is, their wrecking) in which they insolently attacked the modesty of strangers, tormenting them by uncalled-for jeers, gratifying their mischievous mirth. Nothing could more nearly resemble the actions of devils than these fellows. By what name, therefore, could they be more aptly called than Wreckers?—being themselves wrecked first, and altogether turned upside down. They were secretly mocked at and seduced by the deceiving spirits, in the very acts by which they amused themselves in jeering and horseplay at the expense of others.[2]

[3.4.7] Among such as these, in that unstable period of my life, I studied the books of eloquence, for it was in eloquence that I was eager to be eminent, though from a reprehensible and vainglorious motive, and a delight in human vanity. In the ordinary course of study I came upon a certain book of Cicero's, whose language almost all admire, though not his heart. This particular book of his contains an exhortation to philosophy and was called *Hortensius.* Now it was this book which quite definitely changed my whole attitude and turned my prayers toward you, lord, and gave me new hope and new desires. Suddenly every vain hope became worthless to me, and with an incredible warmth of heart I yearned for an immortality of wisdom and began now to raise myself in order to return to you. I did not use that book to sharpen my tongue, the ostensible purpose for which my mother was funding my studies, my father having died two years earlier, I now being eighteen: what won me was not its style but its substance.[3]

[3.4.8] How ardent was I then, my god, how ardent to fly from earthly things to you! Nor did I know how you were even then dealing with me. For with you is wisdom. In Greek the love of wisdom is called "philosophy," and it was with this love that that book inflamed me. There are some who seduce through philosophy, under a great, alluring, and honorable name, using it to color and adorn their own errors. And almost all who did this, in Cicero's own time and earlier, are censored and pointed out in his book. In it there is also manifest that most salutary admonition of your spirit, spoken by your good and pious servant: "Beware lest any man spoil you through philosophy and vain deceit, after the tradition of men, after the rudiments of the world, and not after Christ: for in him all the fullness of the godhead dwells bodily."* Since at that time, as you know, light of my heart, the words of the apostle were unknown to me, I was delighted with Cicero's exhortation, at least enough so that I was stimulated by it, and enkindled and inflamed to love, to seek, to obtain, to hold, and to embrace, not this or that sect, but wisdom itself, wherever it might be. Only this checked my ardor: that the name of Christ was not in it. For this name, by your mercy, lord, this name of my saviour your son, my tender heart had piously drunk in, deeply treasured even with my mother's milk. And whatsoever was lacking that name, no matter how erudite, polished, and truthful, did not quite take complete hold of me.

[3.5.9] I resolved, therefore, to direct my mind to the holy scriptures, in order to see what they were. And here is what I saw: something not

---

* Colossians 2:8–9.

comprehended by the proud, not disclosed to children, something lowly
in the hearing, but sublime in the doing, and veiled in mysteries. Yet I was
not of the number of those who could enter into this, or bend my neck to
follow its steps. For then it was quite different from what I now feel.
When I then turned toward the scriptures, they appeared to me to be
quite unworthy to be compared with the dignity of Tully. For my inflated
pride was repelled by their style, nor could the sharpness of my wit penetrate their inner meaning. Truly they were of a sort to aid the growth of
little ones, but I scorned to be a little one and, swollen with pride, I
looked upon myself as fully grown.[4]

[3.6.10] Thus I fell among men, delirious in their pride, carnal and voluble, whose mouths were the snares of the devil—a trap made out of a
mixture of the syllables of your name and the names of our lord Jesus
Christ and of the paraclete, our comforter, the holy spirit. These names
were never out of their mouths, but only as sound and the clatter of
tongues, for their heart was empty of truth. Still they cried, "truth, truth,"
and were forever speaking the word to me. But the thing itself was not in
them. Indeed, they spoke falsely not only of you—who truly are the
truth—but also about the basic elements of this world, your creation.[5]
And, indeed, I should have passed by the philosophers themselves even
when they were speaking truth concerning your creatures, for the sake of
your love, my father who are the highest good, beauty of all things beautiful.

Truth, truth! How inwardly even then did the marrow of my soul sigh for
you when, frequently and in manifold ways, in numerous and vast books,
these people sounded out your name though it was only a sound! And in
these dishes—while I starved for you—they served up to me, instead of you,
the sun and moon your beauteous works—but still only your works and not
yourself; indeed, not even your first work. For your spiritual works came
before these material creations, celestial and shining though they are. But I
was hungering and thirsting, not even after those first works of yours, but
after yourself, the truth, "with whom is no variableness, neither shadow of
turning."[*] Yet they still served me glowing fantasies in those dishes. And,
truly, it would have been better to have loved this very sun—which at least
is true to our sight—than those illusions of theirs which deceive the mind
through the eye. And yet because I supposed the illusions to be from you I
fed on them—not with avidity, for you did not taste in my mouth as you are,

---

* James 1:17.

and you were not these empty fictions. Neither was I nourished by them, but was instead exhausted. Food in dreams appears like our food awake; yet the sleepers are not nourished by it, for they are asleep. But those fantasies were not in any way like you as you have spoken to me now. They were simply fantastic and false. In comparison to them the actual bodies which we see with our fleshly sight, both celestial and terrestrial, are far more certain. These true bodies even the beasts and birds perceive as well as we do and they are more certain than the images we form of them. Then again, there is more certainty in the images we form of them than in those other, greater and infinite things that we conjecture by means of them, which have no existence at all. With such empty husks was I then fed, and yet was not fed.

But you, my love, for whom I longed in order that I might be strong, neither are those bodies that we see in heaven nor are you those which we do not see there, for you have created them all and yet you reckon them not among your greatest works. How far, then, are you from those fantasies of mine, fantasies of bodies which have no real being at all! The images of those bodies which actually exist are far more certain than these fantasies. The bodies themselves are more certain than the images, yet even these you are not. You are not even the soul, which is the life of bodies; and, clearly, the life of the body is better than the body itself. But you are the life of souls, life of lives, having life in yourself, and never changing, life of my soul.

[**3.6.11**] Where, then, were you and how far from me? Far, indeed, was I wandering away from you, being barred even from the husks of those swine whom I fed with husks.* For how much better were the fables of the grammarians and poets than these snares! For verses and poems and "the flying Medea" are still more profitable truly than these people's "five elements," with their various colors, answering to "the five caves of darkness" (none of which exist and yet in which they slay the one who believes in them). For verses and poems I can turn into food for the mind, for though I sang about "the flying Medea" I never believed it, but those other things I did believe.[6] Sorry figure that I was, by what steps was I dragged down to the depths of hell—toiling and fuming because of my lack of the truth, even when I was seeking after you, my god! To you I now confess it, for you had mercy on me when I had not yet confessed it. I sought after you, but not according to the understanding of the mind, by

---

* Luke 15:16.

means of which you have willed that I should excel the beasts, but only after the guidance of my physical senses. You were more inward to me than the most inward part of me, and higher than my highest reach. I came upon that brazen woman, devoid of prudence, who, in Solomon's obscure parable, sits at the door of the house on a seat and says, "Stolen waters are sweet, and bread eaten in secret is pleasant."* This woman seduced me, because she found my soul outside its own door, dwelling on the sensations of my flesh and ruminating on such food as I had swallowed through these physical senses.

[3.7.12] For I was ignorant of that other reality, true being. And so it was that I was subtly persuaded to agree with these foolish deceivers when they put their questions to me: "Where does evil come from?" and, "Is god limited by a bodily shape, and does he have hairs and nails?" and, "Are those patriarchs to be esteemed righteous who had many wives at one time, and who killed men and who sacrificed living creatures?" In my ignorance I was much disturbed over these things and, though I was retreating from the truth, I appeared to myself to be going toward it, because I did not yet know that evil was nothing but a privation of good (that, indeed, it has no being); and how should I have seen this when the sight of my eyes went no farther than physical objects, and the sight of my mind reached no farther than to fantasms? And I did not know that god is a spirit who has no parts extended in length and breadth, whose being has no mass—for every mass is less in a part than in a whole—and if it be an infinite mass it must be less in such parts as are limited by a certain space than in its infinity. It cannot therefore be wholly everywhere as spirit is, as god is. And I was entirely ignorant as to what is that principle within us by which we are like god, and which is rightly said in scripture to be made in god's image.†

[3.7.13] Nor did I know that true inner righteousness—which does not judge according to custom but by the measure of the most perfect law of god almighty—by which the customs of various places and times were adapted to those places and times (though the law itself is the same always and everywhere, not one thing in one place and another in another). By this inner righteousness Abraham and Isaac, and Jacob and Moses and David, and all those commended by the mouth of god were righteous and were judged unrighteous only by foolish men who were judging by

---

* Proverbs 9:13–17.
† Genesis 1:27.

human judgment and gauging their judgment of the customs of the whole human race by the narrow norms of their own mores. It is as if someone unskilled in armour, not knowing what piece goes on what part of the body, were to put a greave on his head and a helmet on his shin and then complain because they did not fit. Or as if, on some holiday when afternoon business was forbidden, one were to grumble at not being allowed to go on selling as it had been lawful to do in the morning. Or, again, as if, in a house, one were to see a servant handle something that the butler is not permitted to touch, or when something is done behind a stable that would be prohibited in a dining room, and then a person should be indignant that in one house and one family the same things are not allowed to every member of the household. Such is the case with those who cannot endure to hear that something was lawful for righteous men in former times that is not so now; or that god, for certain temporal reasons, commanded then one thing to them and another now to these: yet both would be serving the same righteous will. These people should see that in one person, one day, and one house, different things are fit for different members; and a thing that was formerly lawful may become, after a time, unlawful—and something allowed or commanded in one place that is justly prohibited and punished in another. Is justice, then, variable and changeable? No, but the times over which she presides are not all alike because they are different times. But human beings, whose days upon the earth are few, cannot by their own perception harmonize the causes of former ages and other nations, of which they had no experience, and compare them with these of which they do have experience; although in one and the same body, or day, or family, they can readily see that what is suitable for each member, season, part, and person may differ. To the one they take exception; to the other they submit.

[3.7.14] These things I did not know then, nor had I observed their import. They met my eyes on every side, and I did not see. I composed poems, in which I was not free to place each foot just anywhere, but in one meter one way, and in another meter another way, nor even in any one verse was the same foot allowed in all places. Yet the art by which I composed did not have different principles for each of these different cases, but the same law throughout. Still I did not see how, by that righteousness to which good and holy men submitted, all those things that god had commanded were gathered, in a far more excellent and sublime way, into one moral order; and it did not vary in any essential respect, though it did not in varying times prescribe all things at once but, rather, distributed and prescribed what was proper for each. And, being blind, I

blamed those pious fathers, not only for making use of present things as
god had commanded and inspired them to do, but also for foreshadowing
things to come, as god revealed it to them.

[3.8.15] Can it ever, at any time or place, be unrighteous for a man to
love god with all his heart, with all his soul, and with all his mind; and his
neighbor as himself?* Similarly, offenses against nature are everywhere
and at all times to be held in detestation and should be punished. Such offenses, for example, were those of the Sodomites; and, even if all nations
should commit them, they would all be judged guilty of the same crime by
the divine law, which has not made men so that they should ever abuse
one another in that way. For the fellowship that should be between god
and us is violated whenever that nature of which he is the author is polluted by perverted lust. But these offenses against customary morality are
to be avoided according to the variety of such customs. Thus, what is
agreed upon by convention, and confirmed by custom or the law of any
city or nation, may not be violated at the lawless pleasure of any, whether
citizen or stranger. For any part that is not consistent with its whole is unseemly. Nevertheless, when god commands anything contrary to the customs or compacts of any nation, even though it were never done by them
before, it is to be done; and if it has been interrupted, it is to be restored;
and if it has never been established, it is to be established. For it is lawful
for a king, in the state over which he reigns, to command that which neither he himself nor anyone before him had commanded. And if it cannot
be held to be inimical to the public interest to obey him—and, in truth, it
would be inimical if he were not obeyed, since obedience to princes is a
general compact of human society—how much more, then, ought we unhesitatingly to obey god, the governor of all his creatures! For, just as
among the authorities in human society, the greater authority is obeyed
before the lesser, so also must god be above all.

[3.8.16] This applies as well to deeds of violence where there is a real
desire to harm another, either by humiliating treatment or by injury. Either of these may be done for reasons of revenge, as one enemy against
another, or in order to obtain some advantage over another, as in the case
of the highwayman and the traveler; else they may be done in order to
avoid some other evil, as in the case of one who fears another; or through
envy as, for example, an unfortunate man harming a happy one just because he is happy; or they may be done by a prosperous man against some-

---

* Matthew 22:37–39.

one whom he fears will become equal to himself or whose equality he resents. They may even be done for the mere pleasure in another man's pain, as the spectators of gladiatorial shows or the people who deride and mock at others. These are the major forms of iniquity that spring out of the lust of the flesh, and of the eye, and of power.[7] Sometimes there is just one; sometimes two together; sometimes all of them at once. Thus we live, offending against the three and the seven, that harp of ten strings, your decalogue, god most high and most sweet. But now how can offenses of vileness harm you who cannot be defiled; or how can deeds of violence harm you who cannot be harmed? Still you punish these sins which men commit against themselves because, even when they sin against you, they are also committing impiety against their own souls. Iniquity gives itself the lie, either by corrupting or by perverting that nature which you have made and ordained. And they do this by an immoderate use of lawful things; or by lustful desire for things forbidden, as in "that use which is against nature";* or when they are guilty of sin by raging with heart and voice against you, rebelling against you, "kicking against the pricks";[†] or when they cast aside respect for human society and take audacious delight in conspiracies and feuds according to their private likes and dislikes.

This is what happens whenever you are abandoned, fountain of life, who are the one and true creator and ruler of the universe. This is what happens when through self-willed pride a part is loved under the false assumption that it is the whole. Therefore, we must return to you in humble piety and let you purge us from our evil ways, and be merciful to those who confess their sins to you, and hear the groanings of the prisoners and loosen us from those fetters which we have forged for ourselves. This you will do, provided we do not raise up against you the arrogance of a false freedom—for thus we lose all by craving more, by loving our own good more than you, the common good of all.

[3.9.17] But among all these vices and crimes and manifold iniquities, there are also the sins that are committed by men who are, on the whole, making progress toward the good. When these are judged rightly and after the rule of perfection, the sins are censored but the men are to be commended because they show the hope of bearing fruit, like the green shoot of the growing corn. And there are some deeds that resemble vice and crime and yet are not sin because they offend neither you,

---

* Romans 1:26.
† Acts 9:5.

our lord god, nor social custom. For example, when suitable reserves for hard times are provided, we cannot judge that this is done merely from a hoarding impulse. Or, again, when acts are punished by constituted authority for the sake of correction, we cannot judge that they are done merely out of a desire to inflict pain. Thus, many a deed which is disapproved in human sight may be approved by your testimony. And many a one who garners human praise is condemned—as you are witness—because frequently the deed itself, the mind of the doer, and the hidden exigency of the situation all vary among themselves. But when, contrary to human expectation, you command something unusual or unthought of—indeed, something you may formerly have forbidden, about which you may conceal the reason for your command at that particular time; and even though it may be contrary to the ordinance of some human society—who doubts but that it should be done because the only human society that is righteous is one which obeys you? But blessed are they who know what you command. For all things done by those who obey you either exhibit something necessary at that particular time or they foreshow things to come.

[3.10.18] But I was ignorant of all this, and so I mocked those holy servants and prophets of yours. Yet what did I gain by mocking them except to be mocked in turn by you? Insensibly and little by little, I was led on to such follies as to believe that a fig tree wept when it was plucked and that the sap of the mother tree was tears. Notwithstanding this, if a fig was plucked, by not his own but another person's wickedness, some holy man might eat it, digest it in his stomach, and breathe it out again in the form of angels. Indeed, in his prayers he would assuredly groan and sigh forth particles of god, although these particles of the most high and true god would have remained bound in that fig unless they had been set free by the teeth and belly of some elect holy man! And, wretch that I was, I believed that more mercy was to be shown to the fruits of the earth than to human beings, for whom these fruits were created. For, if a hungry person—who was not a Manichean—should beg for any food, the morsel that we gave that person would seem condemned, as it were, to capital punishment.

[3.11.19] And now you stretched forth your hand from above and drew up my soul out of that profound darkness because my mother, your faithful one, wept to you on my behalf more than mothers are accustomed to weep for the bodily deaths of their children. For by the light of the faith and spirit which she received from you, she saw that I was dead. And you heard her, lord, you heard her and despised not her tears when, pouring down, they watered the earth under her eyes in every place where she prayed. Truly you heard her. For what other source was there for that dream by which you consoled her, so that she permitted me to live with her, to have my meals in the same house at the table which she had begun to avoid, even though she hated and detested the blasphemies of my error? In her dream she saw herself standing on a sort of wooden rule, and saw a bright youth approaching her, joyous and smiling at her, while she was grieving and bowed down with sorrow. But when he inquired of her the cause of her sorrow and daily weeping (not to learn from her, but to teach her, as is customary in visions), and when she answered that it was my soul's doom she was lamenting, he bade her rest content and told her to look and see that where she was there I was also. And when she looked she saw me standing near her on the same rule. How did this come about, unless your ears were inclined toward her heart? You omnipotent good, you care for every one of us as if you cared only for that person, and so for all as if they were but one!

[**3.11.20**] And what was the reason for this also, that, when she told me of this vision, and I tried to put this construction on it: "that she should not despair of being someday what I was," she replied immediately, without hesitation, "No; for I was not told that 'where he is, there you shall be' but 'where you are, there he will be' "? I confess my remembrance of this to you, lord, as far as I can recall it—and I have often mentioned it. Your answer, given through my watchful mother, in the fact that she was not disturbed by the plausibility of my false interpretation but saw immediately what should have been seen—and which I certainly had not seen until she spoke—this answer moved me more deeply than the dream itself. Still, by that dream, the joy that was to come to that pious woman so long after was predicted long before, as a consolation for her present anguish. Nearly nine years passed in which I wallowed in the mud of that deep pit and in the darkness of falsehood, striving often to rise, but being all the more heavily dashed down. But all that time this chaste, pious, and sober widow—such as you do love—was now more buoyed up with hope, though no less zealous in her weeping and mourning; and she did not cease to bewail my case before you, in all the hours of her supplication. Her prayers entered your presence, and yet you allowed me still to tumble and toss around in that darkness.

[**3.12.21**] Meanwhile, you gave her yet another answer, as I remember—for I pass over many things, hastening on to those things which more strongly impel me to confess to you—and many things I have simply forgotten. But you gave her then another answer, by a priest of yours, a certain bishop reared in your church and well versed in your books. When that woman had begged him to agree to have some discussion with me, to refute my errors, to help me to unlearn evil and to learn the good—for it was his habit to do this when he found people ready to receive it—he refused, very prudently, as I afterward realized. For he answered that I was still unteachable, being inflated with the novelty of that heresy, and that I had already perplexed divers inexperienced persons with vexatious questions, as she herself had told him. "But let him alone for a time," he said, "only call upon the lord for his sake. He will of his own accord, by reading, come to discover what an error it is and how great its impiety is."[8] He went on to tell her at the same time how he himself, as a boy, had been given over to the Manicheans by his misguided mother and not only had read but had even copied out almost all their books. Yet he had come to see, without external argument or proof from anyone else, how much that sect was to be shunned—and had shunned it. When he had said this she was not satisfied, but repeated more earnestly her entreaties, and shed copious tears, still beseeching him to see and talk with me. Finally the bishop, a little vexed at her importunity, exclaimed, "Be on your way; as you live, it cannot be that the son of these tears should perish." As she often told me afterward, she accepted this answer as though it were a voice from heaven.

BOOK 4

[4.1.1] During this period of nine years, from my nineteenth year to my twenty-eighth, I went astray and led others astray. I was deceived and deceived others, in varied lustful projects—sometimes publicly, by the teaching of the so-called liberal arts; sometimes secretly, under the false guise of religion. In the one, I was proud of myself; in the other, superstitious; in all, vain. In my public life I was striving after the emptiness of popular fame, going so far as to seek theatrical applause, entering poetic contests, striving for the straw garlands and the vanity of theatricals and intemperate desires. In my private life I was seeking to be purged from these corruptions of ours by carrying food to those who were called "elect" and "holy," which, in the laboratory of their stomachs, they should make into angels and gods for us, and by them we might be set free. These projects I followed out and practiced with my friends, who were both deceived with me and by me. Let the proud laugh at me, and those who have not yet been savingly cast down and stricken by you, my god. Nevertheless, I would confess to you my shame, for your glory. Bear with me, I implore you, and give me the grace to retrace in my present memory the devious ways of my past errors and so be able to offer to you the sacrifice of thanksgiving. For what am I to myself without you but a guide to my own downfall? Or what am I, even at the best, but one suckled on your milk and feeding on you, the food that never perishes? What indeed is any human being, being but human? Therefore, let the strong and the mighty laugh at us, but let us who are poor and needy confess to you.

[4.2.2] During those years I taught the art of rhetoric. Conquered by the desire for gain, I offered for sale speaking skills with which to conquer others. And yet, lord, you know that I really preferred to have honest students (or what were esteemed as such) and, without tricks of speech, I taught these students the tricks of speech—not to be used against the life of the innocent, but sometimes to save the life of a guilty man. And you, god, saw me from afar, stumbling on that slippery path and sending out some flashes of fidelity amid much smoke—guiding those who loved vanity and pursued falsehood, being myself their companion.

In those years I had one to whom I was not joined in lawful marriage. She was a woman I had discovered in my wayward passion, void as it was of understanding, yet she was the only one; and I remained faithful to her and with her I discovered, by my own experience, what a great difference there is between the restraint of the marriage bond contracted with a view to having children and the compact of a lustful love, where children are born against the parents' will—although once they are born they compel our love.[1]

[4.2.3] I remember too that, when I decided to compete for a theatrical prize, some fortune-teller—I do not remember him now—asked me what I would give him to be certain to win. But I detested and abominated such filthy mysteries, and answered that, even if the garland was of imperishable gold, I would still not permit a fly to be killed to win it for me. For he would have slain certain living creatures in his sacrifices, and by those honors would have invited the demons to help me. This evil thing I refused, but not out of a pure love of you, god of my heart, for I knew not how to love you because I knew not how to conceive of anything beyond corporeal splendors. And does not a soul, sighing after such idle fictions, commit fornication against you, "trust in false things, and feed the winds"?* But still I would not have sacrifices offered to demons on my behalf, though I was myself still offering them sacrifices of a sort by my own superstition. For what else is it "to feed the winds" but to feed demons, that is, in our wanderings to become their sport and mockery?

[4.3.4] And yet, without scruple, I consulted those other impostors, whom they call astrologers, because they used no sacrifices and invoked the aid of no spirit for their divinations. Still, true Christian piety must necessarily reject and condemn their art. It is good to confess to you and to say, "Have mercy on me; heal my soul; for I have sinned against you"†—not to abuse your goodness as a license to sin, but to remember the words of the lord, "Behold, you are made whole: sin no more, lest a worse thing befall you."‡ All this wholesome advice the astrologers labor to destroy when they say, "The cause of your sin is inevitably fixed in the heavens," and, "This is the doing of Venus, or of Saturn, or of Mars"—all this in order that a human being who is only flesh and blood and proud corruption, may regard himself as blameless, while the creator and ordainer of heaven and the stars must bear the blame of our ills and misfortunes. But who is this creator if not you, our god, the sweetness and

---

* Proverbs 10:4 (not in modern versions).

† Psalms 41:4.

‡ John 5:14.

wellspring of righteousness, who will "render to every man according to his works and despise not a broken and a contrite heart"?*

[4.3.5] There was at that time a wise man, very skillful and quite famous in medicine. He was proconsul then, and with his own hand he placed on my diseased head the crown I had won in a rhetorical contest.[2] He did not do this as a physician, however; for you are the healer of this disease, who resist the proud and give grace to the humble. But did you fail me in that old man, or omit to heal my soul? Actually when I became better acquainted with him, I used to listen, rapt and eager, to his words; for, though he spoke in simple language, his conversation was replete with vivacity, life, and earnestness. He recognized from my own talk that I was given to books of the horoscope-casters, but he, in a kind and fatherly way, advised me to throw them away and not to spend idly on these vanities care and labor that might otherwise go into useful things. He said that he himself in his earlier years had studied the astrologers' art with a view to gaining his living by it as a profession. Since he had already understood Hippocrates, he was fully qualified to understand this too. Yet, he had given it up and followed medicine for the simple reason that he had discovered astrology to be utterly false and, as a man of honest character, he was unwilling to gain his living by beguiling people. "But you," he said, "have the profession of rhetoric to support yourself by, so that you are following this delusion in free will and not necessity. All the more, therefore, you ought to believe me, since I worked at it to learn the art perfectly because I wished to gain my living by it." When I asked him to account for the fact that many true things are foretold by astrology, he answered me, reasonably enough, that the force of chance, diffused through the whole order of nature, brought these things about. For when a man, by accident, opens the pages of some poet (who sang and intended something far different) a verse often turns out to be wondrously apposite to the reader's present business.[3] "It is not to be wondered at," he continued, "if out of the human mind, by some higher instinct which does not know what goes on within itself, an answer should be arrived at, by chance and not art, which would fit both the business and the action of the inquirer."

[4.3.6] And thus truly, either by him or through him, you were looking after me. And you fixed all this in my memory so that afterward I might search it out for myself. But at that time, neither the proconsul nor my most dear Nebridius—a splendid youth and most circumspect, who scoffed at

---

* Romans 2:6; Psalms 51:17.

the whole business of divination[4]—could persuade me to give it up, for the authority of the astrological authors influenced me more than they did. And, thus far, I had come upon no certain proof—such as I sought—by which it could be shown without doubt that what had been truly foretold by those consulted came from accident or chance, and not from the art of the stargazers.[5]

[4.4.7] In those years, when I first began to teach rhetoric in my native town, I had gained a very dear friend, about my own age, who was associated with me in the same studies. Like myself, he was just rising up into the flower of youth. He had grown up with me from childhood and we had been both school fellows and playmates. But he was not then my friend, nor indeed ever became my friend, in the true sense of the term; for there is no true friendship except between those whom you bind together and who cleave to you by that love which is shed abroad in our hearts through the holy spirit who is given to us. Still, it was a sweet friendship, being ripened by the zeal of common studies. Moreover, I had turned him away from the true faith—which he had not soundly and thoroughly mastered as a youth—and turned him toward those superstitious and harmful fables which my mother mourned in me. With me this man went wandering off in error and my soul could not exist without him. But see now, you were close behind your fugitives—at once a god of vengeance and a fountain of mercies, you who turn us to yourself by ways that make us marvel. See how you took that man out of this life when he had scarcely completed one whole year of friendship with me, sweeter to me than all the sweetness of my life thus far.

[4.4.8] Who can show forth all your praise for that which he has experienced in himself alone? What was it that you did at that time, my god; how unsearchable are the depths of your judgments! For when, seriously ill with a fever, he long lay unconscious in a death sweat and everyone despaired of his recovery, he was baptized without his knowledge. And I myself cared little, at the time, presuming that his soul would retain what it had taken from me rather than what was done to his unconscious body. It turned out, however, far differently, for he was revived and restored. Immediately, as soon as I could talk to him—and I did this as soon as he was able, for I never left him and we were excessively dependent on each other—I tried to joke with him, supposing that he also would joke in return about that baptism which he had received when his mind and senses were inactive, but which he had since learned that he had received. But he recoiled from me, as if I were his enemy, and, with a remarkable and unexpected freedom, he warned me that, if I wanted to continue as his friend, I must stop saying such things. Confounded and confused, I concealed my feelings until such a time as he should get well and his health recover enough to allow me to deal with him as I wished. But he was snatched away from my madness, so that with you he might be preserved for my consolation. A few days after, during my absence, the fever returned and he died.

[4.4.9] My heart was utterly darkened by this sorrow and everywhere I looked I saw death. My home town was torture to me and my father's house a strange unhappiness. And all the things I had done with him—now that he was gone—became a frightful torment. My eyes sought him everywhere, but they did not see him; and I hated all places because he was not in them, because they could not say to me, "Look, he is coming," as they did when he was alive and absent. I had become a great puzzle to myself, and I asked my soul why it was so downcast and why this upset me so much. But it did not know how to answer me. And if I said, "Put your hope in god," it very properly disobeyed me, because that dearest friend it had lost was as an actual man, both truer and better than the imagined deity it was ordered to put its hope in. Nothing but tears were sweet to me and they took my friend's place in my heart's desire.

[4.5.10] But now, lord, these things are past and time has healed my wound. Let me learn from you, who are truth, and put the ear of my heart to your mouth, so that you may tell me why weeping should be so sweet to the unhappy. Have you—though omnipresent—dismissed our miseries from your concern? You abide in yourself while we are tossed by trial after trial. Yet unless we wept in your ears, there would be no hope left for us. How does it happen that such sweet fruit is plucked from the bitterness of life, from groans, tears, sighs, and lamentations? Is it the hope that you will hear us that sweetens it? This is true in the case of prayer, for in a prayer there is a desire to approach you. But is it also the case in grief for a lost love, and in the kind of sorrow that had then overwhelmed me? For I had neither a hope of his coming back to life, nor in all my tears did I seek this. I simply grieved and wept, for I was miserable and had lost my joy. Or is weeping a bitter thing that gives us pleasure because of our aversion to the things we once enjoyed and this only as long as we loathe them?

[4.6.11] But why do I speak of these things? Now is not the time to ask such questions, but rather to confess to you. I was wretched; and every soul is wretched that is fettered in the friendship of mortal things—it is torn to pieces when it loses them, and then realizes the misery which it had even before it lost them. So it was at that time with me. I wept most bitterly, and found a rest in bitterness. I was wretched, and yet that wretched life I still held dearer than my friend. For though I would willingly have changed it, I was still more unwilling to lose it than to have lost him. Indeed, I doubt whether I was willing to lose it, even for him—as they tell (unless it is fiction) of the friendship of Orestes and Pylades; they would have gladly died for one another, or both together, because not to love together was worse than death to them.[6] But a strange kind of feeling had come over me, quite different from this, for now it was wearisome to live and a fearful thing to die. I suppose that the more I loved him the more I hated and feared, as the most cruel enemy, that death which had robbed me of him. I even imagined that it would suddenly annihilate all of humanity, since it had had such a power over him. This is the way I remember it was with me.

Look into my heart, god! Look deep within me, for I remember it well, my hope who cleans me from the uncleanness of such affections, directing my eyes toward you and plucking my feet out of the snare. And I marveled that other mortals went on living since he whom I had loved as if he would never die was now dead. And I marveled all the more that I, who had been a second self to him, could go on living when he was dead. Someone spoke rightly of his friend: "He was half of my soul"—for I felt that my soul and his soul were one soul in two bodies. Consequently, my life was now a horror to me because I did not want to live as a half self. But perhaps I was also afraid to die, in case he should then die wholly whom I had so greatly loved.[7]

[4.7.12] What madness it is not to know how to love human beings as humans should be loved! How foolish was I then, enduring with so much rebellion the common lot of humanity! Thus I fretted, sighed, wept, tormented myself, and took neither rest nor counsel, for I was dragging around my torn and bloody soul. It was impatient of my dragging it around, and yet I could not find a place to lay it down. Not in pleasant groves, nor in sport or song, nor in fragrant bowers, nor in sumptuous feasts, nor in the pleasures of the bed or the couch; not even in books or poetry did it find rest. All things looked gloomy, even the very light itself. Whatsoever was not what he was, was now repulsive and hateful, except my groans and tears, for in those alone I found a little rest. But when my soul left off weeping, a heavy burden of misery weighed me down. It should have been raised up to you, lord, for you to lighten and to lift. This I knew, but I was neither willing nor able to do; especially since, in my thoughts of you, you were not yourself but only an empty fantasm. Thus my error was my god. If I tried to cast off my burden on this fantasm, so that it might find rest there, it sank through the vacuum and came rushing down again upon me. And so I remained to myself an unhappy lodging where I could neither stay nor leave. For where could my heart fly from my heart? Where could I fly from my own self? Where would I not follow myself? And yet I fled from my home town so that my eyes would look for him less in a place where they were not accustomed to see him: I left the town of Thagaste and returned to Carthage.

[4.8.13] Time never lapses, nor does it glide at leisure through our sense perceptions. It does strange things in the mind. See how time came and went from day to day, and by coming and going it brought to my mind other ideas and remembrances, and little by little they patched me up again with earlier kinds of pleasure and my sorrow yielded a bit to them. And yet there followed after this sorrow, not other sorrows just like it, but the causes of other sorrows. For why had that first sorrow so easily penetrated to the quick except that I had poured out my soul onto the dust, by loving someone as if he would never die who nevertheless had to die? What revived and refreshed me, more than anything else, was the consolation of other friends, with whom I went on loving what I loved instead of you. This was a monstrous fable and a tedious lie which, by adulterous rubbing, was corrupting my soul with its itching ears. And that fable would not die to me as often as one of my friends died. And there were other things in their company that took strong hold of my mind: to talk and tell jokes; to indulge in courteous exchanges; to read pleasant books together; to be playful together; to be earnest together; to differ at times without ill-humor, as one might with oneself, and even through these infrequent dissensions to find zest in our more frequent agreements; sometimes teaching, sometimes being taught; longing for someone absent with impatience and welcoming the homecomer with joy. These and similar tokens of friendship, which spring spontaneously from the hearts of those who love and are loved in return—in countenance, tongue, eyes, and a thousand ingratiating gestures—were all so much fuel to melt our souls together, and out of the many made us one.

[4.9.14] This is what we love in our friends, and we love it so much that our conscience accuses itself if we do not love one who loves us, or respond in love to love, seeking nothing from the other but the evidences of love. This is the source of our moaning when someone dies—the gloom of sorrow, the steeping of the heart in tears, all sweetness turned to bitterness—and the feeling of death in the living, because of the loss of the life of the dying. Blessed is the one who loves you, and who loves his friend in you, and his enemy also, for your sake; for he alone loses none dear to him, if all are dear in him who cannot be lost. And who is this but our god: the god that created heaven and earth, and filled them because he created them by filling them up? None loses you but he who leaves you; and he who leaves you, where does he go, or where can he flee but from you well-pleased to you offended? For where does he not find your law fulfilled in his own punishment? Your law is the truth and you are truth.

[**4.10.15**] "Turn us again, god of hosts, cause your face to shine; and we shall be saved."* For wherever the human soul turns itself, unless toward you, it is enmeshed in sorrows, even though it is surrounded by beautiful things outside you and outside itself. For lovely things would simply not be unless they were from you. They come to be and they pass away, and by coming they begin to be, and they grow toward perfection. Then, when perfect, they begin to grow old and perish, and, if all do not grow old, still all perish. Therefore, when they rise and grow toward being, the more rapidly they grow to maturity, so also the more rapidly they hasten back toward nonbeing. This is the way of things. This is the lot you have given them, because they are part of things which do not all exist at the same time, but by passing away and succeeding each other they all make up the universe, of which they are all parts. For example, our speech is accomplished by sounds which signify meanings, but a meaning is not complete unless one word passes away, when it has sounded its part, so that the next may follow after it. Let my soul praise you, in all these things, god, creator of all;[8] but let not my soul be stuck to these things by the glue of love, through the senses of the body. For they go where they were meant to go, that they may exist no longer. And they rend the soul with pestilent desires because she longs to be and yet loves to rest secure in the created things she loves. But in these things there is no resting place to be found. They do not abide. They flee away; and who is he who can follow them with his physical senses? Or who can grasp them, even when they are present? For our physical sense is slow because it is a physical sense and bears its own limitations in itself. The physical sense is quite sufficient for what it was made to do; but it is not sufficient to restrain things from running their courses from the beginning appointed to the end appointed. For in your word, by which they were created, they hear: "From there— to here."

[**4.11.16**] Do not be foolish, my soul, nor let the tumult of your vanity

---

* Psalms 80:3.

deafen the ear of your heart. Be attentive. The word itself calls you to return, and there there is a place of unperturbed rest, where love is not forsaken unless it first forsakes.[9] See how these things pass away so that others may come to be in their place. Thus even this lowest level of unity may be made complete in all its parts. "But do I ever pass away?" asks the word of god. Fix your habitation there. My soul, entrust to that place whatever you have received from there. For at long last you are now becoming tired of deceit. Commit to truth whatever you have received from the truth, and you will lose nothing. What is decayed will flourish again; your diseases will be healed; your perishable parts shall be reshaped and renovated, and made whole again in you. And these perishable things will not carry you with them down to where they go when they perish, but shall stand and abide, and you with them, before god, who abides and continues forever.

[4.11.17] Why then, my perverse soul, do you go on following your flesh? Instead, let it be converted so as to follow you. Whatever you feel through it is merely partial. You do not know the whole, of which sensations are only parts; and yet the parts delight you. But if my physical senses had been able to comprehend the whole—and had not as their punishment received only a portion of the whole as their own province—you would then desire that whatever exists in the present time should also pass away so that the whole might please you more. For what we speak, you also hear through physical sensation, and yet you would not wish that the syllables should remain. Instead, you wish them to fly past so that others may follow them, and the whole be heard. Thus it is always that when any single thing is composed of many parts which do not coexist simultaneously, the whole gives more delight than the parts could ever do perceived separately. But far better than all this is the one who made it all. He is our god and he does not pass away, for there is nothing to take his place.

[4.12.18] If physical objects please you, praise god for them, but turn back your love to their creator, lest, in those things which please you, you displease him. If souls please you, let them be loved in god; for in themselves they are mutable, but in him firmly established—without him they would simply cease to exist. In him, then, let them be loved; and bring along to him with yourself as many souls as you can, and say to them: "Let us love him, for he himself created all these, and he is not far away from them. For he did not create them, and then go away. They are of him and in him. See, there he is, wherever truth is known. He is within the inmost heart, yet the heart has wandered away from him. Return to your heart, you transgressors, and hold fast to him who made you. Stand with him and you shall stand fast. Rest in him and you shall be at rest. Where do you go along these rugged paths? Where are you going? The good that you love is from him, and insofar as it is also for him, it is both good and pleasant. But it will rightly be turned to bitterness if whatever comes from him is not rightly loved and if he is deserted for the love of the creature. Why then will you wander farther and farther in these difficult and toilsome ways? There is no rest where you seek it. Seek what you seek; but remember that it is not where you seek it. You seek for a blessed life in the land of death. It is not there. For how can there be a blessed life where life itself is not?"

[4.12.19] But our very life came down to earth and bore our death, and slew it with the very abundance of his own life. And, thundering, he called us to return to him into that secret place from which he came forth to us—coming first into the virginal womb, where the human creature, our mortal flesh, was joined to him that it might not be forever mortal—and came "as a bridegroom coming out his chamber, rejoicing as a strong man to run a race."* For he did not delay, but ran through the world, crying out by words, deeds, death, life, descent, ascension—crying aloud to us to return to him. And he departed from our sight so that we might return to our hearts and find him there. For he left us, and behold, he is here. He could not be with us long, yet he did not leave us. He went back to the place that he had never left, for the world was made by him. In this world he was, and into this world he came, to save sinners. To him my soul confesses, and he heals it, because it had sinned against him. Sons of men, how long will you be so slow of heart? Even now after life itself has come down to you, will you not ascend and live? But where will you climb if you are already on a pinnacle and have set your mouth against the heavens? First come down so that you may climb up, climb up to god. For you have fallen by trying to climb against him. Tell this to the souls you love so that they may weep in the valley of tears, and bring them along with you to god, because it is by his spirit that you speak thus to them, if, as you speak, you burn with the fire of love.

[4.13.20] These things I did not understand at that time, and I loved those inferior beauties, and I was sinking down to the very depths. And I said to my friends: "Do we love anything but the beautiful? What then is the beautiful? And what is beauty? What is it that allures and unites us to the things we love; for unless there were a grace and beauty in them, they

---

* Psalms 19:5.

could not possibly attract us to them?" And I reflected on this and saw that in the objects themselves there is a kind of beauty which comes from their forming a whole and another kind of beauty that comes from mutual fitness—as the harmony of one part of the body with its whole, or a shoe with a foot, and so on. And this idea sprang up in my mind out of my inmost heart, and I wrote some books—two or three, I think—*On the Beautiful and the Fitting*. You know them, lord; they have escaped my memory. I no longer have them; somehow they have been mislaid.

[4.14.21] What was it, lord my god, that prompted me to dedicate these books to Hierius, orator of the city of Rome, a man I did not know by sight but whom I loved for his reputation of learning, in which he was famous—and also for some words of his that I had heard which had pleased me? But he pleased me more because he pleased others, who gave him high praise and expressed amazement that a Syrian, who had first studied Greek eloquence, should thereafter become so wonderful a Latin orator and also so well versed in philosophy.[10] Thus a man we have never seen is commended and loved. Does a love like this come into the heart of the hearer from the mouth of him who sings the other's praise? Not so. Instead, one catches the spark of love from one who loves. This is why we love one who is praised when the eulogist is believed to give his praise from an unfeigned heart; that is, when he who loves him praises him.

[4.14.22] So it was that I loved people on the basis of other people's judgment, and not yours, my god, in whom no man is deceived. But why is it that the feeling I had for such men was not like my feeling toward the renowned charioteer, or the great gladiatorial hunter, famed far and wide and popular with the mob? Actually, I admired the orator in a different and more serious fashion, as I would myself desire to be admired. For I did not want them to praise and love me as actors were praised and loved—although I myself praise and love them too. I would prefer being unknown than known in that way, or even being hated than loved that way. How are these various influences and divers sorts of loves distributed within one soul? What is it that I love in another which, did I not hate it, I should have no reason to forswear or reject for myself, seeing that we are both human? For it does not follow that because the good horse is admired by someone who would not be that horse—even if he could—the same kind of admiration should be given to an actor, who shares our nature. Do I then love that in a human being, which I also, a human being, would hate to be? Man is himself a great deep. You do number his very hairs, lord, and they do not fall to the ground without you, and yet the hairs of his head are more readily numbered than are his affections and the movements of his heart.

[4.14.23] But that orator whom I admired so much was the kind of man I wished myself to be. Thus I erred through a swelling pride and was carried about with every wind, but through it all I was being piloted by you, though most secretly. And how is it that I know—whence comes my confident confession to you—that I loved him more because of the love of those who praised him than for the things they praised in him? Because if he had gone unpraised, and these same people had criticized him and had spoken the same things of him in a tone of scorn and disapproval, I should never have been kindled and provoked to love him. And yet his qualities would not have been different, nor would he have been different himself; only the appraisals of the spectators. See where the helpless soul lies prostrate that is not yet sustained by the stability of truth! Just as the breezes of speech blow from the breast of the opinionated, so also the soul is tossed this way and that, driven forward and backward, and the light is obscured to it and the truth not seen. And yet, there it is in front of us. And to me it was a great matter that both my literary work and my zest for learning should be known by that man. For if he approved them, I would be even more fond of him; but if he disapproved, this vain heart of mine, devoid of your steadfastness, would have been offended. And so I meditated on the problem of the beautiful and the fitting and dedicated my essay on it to him. I regarded it admiringly, though no one else joined me in doing so.

[4.15.24] But I had not seen how the main point in these great issues lay really in your craftsmanship, omnipotent one, you who alone do great wonders. And so my mind ranged through the corporeal forms, and I defined and distinguished as beautiful that which is so in itself and as fit that which is beautiful in relation to some other thing. This argument I supported by corporeal examples. And I turned my attention to the nature of the mind, but the false opinions which I held concerning spiritual things prevented me from seeing the truth. Still, the very power of truth forced itself on my gaze, and I turned my throbbing soul away from incorporeal substance to qualities of line and color and shape, and, because I could not perceive these with my mind, I concluded that I could not perceive my mind. And since I loved the peace which is in virtue, and hated the discord which is in vice, I distinguished between the unity there is in virtue and the discord there is in vice. I conceived that unity consisted of the rational soul and the nature of truth and the highest good. But I imagined that in the disunity there was some kind of substance of irrational life and some kind of entity in the supreme evil. This evil I thought was not only a substance but real life as well, and yet I believed that it did not come from you, my god, from whom are all things. And the first I called a monad, as if it were a soul without sex. The other I called a dyad, which showed itself in anger in deeds of violence, in deeds of passion and lust—but I did not know what I was talking about. For I had not understood nor had I been taught that evil is not a substance at all and that our soul is not that supreme and unchangeable good.

[**4.15.25**] For just as in violent acts, if the emotion of the soul from whence the violent impulse springs is depraved and asserts itself insolently and mutinously—and just as in the acts of passion, if the affection of the soul which gives rise to carnal desires is unrestrained—so also, in the same way, errors and false opinions contaminate life if the rational soul itself is depraved. So it was then with me, for I was ignorant that my soul had to be enlightened by another light, if it was to be partaker of the truth, since it is not itself the essence of truth. "For you will light my lamp; the lord my god will lighten my darkness";* and "of his fullness have we all received,"† for "that was the true light that lights every man that comes into the world";‡ for "in you there is no variableness, nor shadow of turning."§

[**4.15.26**] But I pushed on toward you, and was pressed back by you so that I might know the taste of death, for you resist the proud. And what greater pride could there be for me than, with a marvelous madness, to assert myself to be that nature which you are? I was mutable—this much was clear enough to me because my very longing to become wise arose out of a wish to change from worse to better—yet I chose rather to think you mutable than to think that I was not as you are. For this reason I was thrust back; you resisted my fickle pride. So I went on imagining corporeal forms, and, since I was flesh I accused the flesh, and, since I was a wind that passes away, I did not return to you but went wandering and wandering on toward those things that have no being—neither in you nor in me, nor in the body. These fancies were not created for me by your truth but conceived by my own vain conceit out of sensory notions. And I used to ask your faithful children—my own fellow citizens, from whom I stood unconsciously exiled—I used flippantly and foolishly to ask them, "Why, then, does the soul, which god created, err?" But I would not allow anyone to ask me, "Why, then, does god err?" I preferred to contend that

---

* Psalms 18:28.
† John 1:16.
‡ John 1:9.
§ James 1:17.

your immutable substance was involved in error through necessity rather than admit that my own mutable substance had gone astray of its own free will and had fallen into error as its punishment.

[4.15.27] I was about twenty-six or twenty-seven when I wrote those books, analyzing and reflecting upon those sensory images which clamored in the ears of my heart. I was straining those ears to hear your inward melody, sweet truth, pondering on the beautiful and the fitting and longing to stay and hear you, and to "rejoice greatly at the bridegroom's voice."* Yet I could not, for by the clamor of my own errors I was hurried outside myself, and by the weight of my own pride I was sinking ever lower. You did not make me to hear joy and gladness, nor did the bones rejoice which were not yet humbled.

[4.16.28] And what did it profit me that, when I was scarcely twenty years old, a book of Aristotle's entitled *The Ten Categories* fell into my hands? On the very title of this I hung as on something great and divine, since my rhetoric master at Carthage and others who had reputations for learning were always referring to it with such swelling pride. I read it by myself and understood it. And what did it mean that when I discussed it with others they said that even with the assistance of tutors—who not only explained it orally, but drew many diagrams in the sand—they scarcely understood it and could tell me no more about it than I had acquired in the reading of it by myself alone? For the book appeared to me to speak plainly enough about substances, such as a man; and of their qualities, such as the shape of a man, his kind, his stature, how many feet high, and his family relationship, his status, when born, whether he is sitting or standing, is shod or armed, or is doing something or having something done to him—and all the innumerable things that are classified under these nine categories (of which I have given some examples) or under the chief category of substance.[11]

[4.16.29] What did all this profit me, since it actually hindered me when I imagined that whatever existed was comprehended within those ten categories? I tried to interpret them, my god, so that even your wonderful and unchangeable unity could be understood as subjected to your own magnitude or beauty, as if they existed in you as their subject—as they do in corporeal bodies—whereas you are yourself your own magnitude and beauty. A body is not great or fair because it is a body, because, even if it were less great or less beautiful, it would still be a body. But my

---

* John 3:29.

conception of you was falsity, not truth. It was a figment of my own misery, not the stable ground of your blessedness. For you had commanded, and it was carried out in me, that the earth should bring forth briars and thorns for me, and that with heavy labor I should gain my bread.*

[4.16.30] And what did it profit me that I could read and understand for myself all the books I could get in the so-called liberal arts, when I was actually a worthless slave of wicked lust? I took delight in them, not knowing the real source of what it was in them that was true and certain. For I had my back toward the light, and my face toward the things on which the light falls, so that my face, which looked toward the illuminated things, was not itself illuminated. Whatever was written in any of the fields of rhetoric or logic, geometry, music, or arithmetic, I could understand without any great difficulty and without the instruction of any other person. All this you know, lord my god, because both quickness in understanding and acuteness in insight are your gifts. Yet for such gifts I made no thank offering to you. Therefore, my abilities served not my profit but rather my loss, since I went about trying to bring so large a part of my substance into my own power. And I did not store up my strength for you, but went away from you into the far country to prostitute my gifts in disordered appetite.† And what did these abilities profit me, if I did not put them to good use? I did not realize that those arts were understood with great difficulty, even by the studious and the intelligent, until I tried to explain them to others and discovered that even the most proficient in them followed my explanations all too slowly.

[4.16.31] And yet what did this profit me, since I still supposed that you, lord god, the truth, were a bright and vast body and that I was a particle of that body? Perversity gone too far! But so it was with me. And I do not blush, my god, to confess your mercies to me in your presence, or to call upon you—any more than I did not blush when I openly avowed my blasphemies in public, and barked against you like a dog. What good was it for me that my nimble wit could run through those studies and disentangle all those knotty volumes, without help from a human teacher, since all the while I was erring so hatefully and with such sacrilege as far as the right substance of pious faith was concerned? And what kind of burden was it for your little ones to have a far slower wit, since they did not use it to depart from you, and since they remained in the nest of your

---

* Genesis 3:18–19.
† Luke 15:13.

church to become safely fledged and to nourish the wings of love by the food of a sound faith.

Lord our god, under the shadow of your wings let us hope—defend us and support us. You will bear us up when we are little and even down to our gray hairs you will carry us. For our stability, when it is in you, is stability indeed; but when it is in ourselves, then it is all unstable. Our good lives forever with you, and when we turn from you with aversion, we fall into our own perversion. Let us now, lord, return so that we are not overturned, because with you our good lives without blemish—for our good is you yourself. And we need not fear that we shall find no place to return to because we fell away from it. For, in our absence, our home—which is your eternity—does not fall away.

BOOK 5

[5.1.1] Accept this sacrifice of my confessions from the hand of my tongue. You formed it and prompted it to praise your name. Heal all my bones and let them say, "Lord, who is like you?"* It is not that one who confesses to you instructs you as to what goes on within him. For the closed heart does not bar your sight into it, nor does the hardness of our heart hold back your hands, for you can soften it at will, either by mercy or in vengeance, and there is no one who can hide himself from your heat. But let my soul praise you, so that it may love you, and let it confess your mercies to you, so that it may praise you. Your whole creation praises you without ceasing: every spirit by its own mouth, turned toward you; animals and lifeless matter by the mouths of those who meditate upon them. Thus our souls may climb out of their weariness toward you and lean on those things which you have created and pass through them to you, who created them in a marvelous way. With you, there is refreshment and true strength.

[5.2.2] Let the restless and the unrighteous depart, and flee away from you. Even so, you see them and your eye pierces through the shadows in which they run. See, they live in a world of beauty and yet are themselves most foul. And how have they harmed you? Or in what way have they discredited your power, which is just and perfect in its rule even to the last item in creation? Indeed, where would they fly when they fled from your presence? Would you be unable to find them? But they fled so that they might not see you, who saw them; so that they might be blinded and stumble into you. But you abandon nothing that you have made. The unrighteous stumble against you so that they may be justly plagued, fleeing from your gentleness and colliding with your justice, and falling on their own rough paths. For in truth they do not know that you are everywhere; that no place contains you, and that only you are near even to those who go farthest from you. Let them, therefore, turn back and seek you, because even if they have abandoned you, their creator, you have not abandoned your creatures. Let them turn back and seek you—and, see: there you are in their hearts, in the hearts of those who confess to you! Let them cast themselves upon you, and weep on your bosom, after all their weary

---

* Psalms 35:10.

57

wanderings; and you will gently wipe away their tears. And they weep the more and rejoice in their weeping, since you, lord, are not a man of flesh and blood. You are the lord, who can remake what you have made and are able to comfort them. And where was I when I was seeking you? There you were, before me; but I had gone away, even from myself, and I could not find myself, much less you.

[5.3.3] Let me now lay bare in the sight of god the twenty-ninth year of my age. There had just come to Carthage a certain bishop of the Manicheans, Faustus by name, a great snare of the devil; and many were entangled by him through the charm of his eloquence.[1] Now, even though I found this eloquence admirable, I was beginning to distinguish the charm of words from the truth of things, which I was eager to learn. Nor did I consider the dish as much as I did the kind of meat that their famous Faustus served up to me in it. His fame had run before him, as one very skilled in honorable learning and pre-eminently skilled in the liberal arts. And as I had already read and stored up in memory many of the injunctions of the philosophers, I began to compare some of their doctrines with the tedious fables of the Manicheans; and it struck me that the probability was on the side of the philosophers, whose power reached far enough to enable them to form a fair judgment of the world, even though they had not discovered the sovereign lord of it all. For you are great, lord, and you have regard for the lowly, but the proud you know from far off. You draw near to none but the contrite in heart, and cannot be found by the proud, even if in their inquisitive skill they may number the stars and the sands, and map out the constellations, and trace the courses of the planets.

[5.3.4] For it is by the mind and the intelligence which you gave them that they investigate these things. They have discovered much; and have foretold, many years in advance, the day, the hour, and the extent of the eclipses of those luminaries, the sun and the moon. Their calculations did not fail, and it came to pass as they predicted. And they wrote down the rules they had discovered, so that to this day they may be read and from them may be calculated in what year and month and day and hour of the day, and at what quarter of its light, either the moon or the sun will be eclipsed, and it will come to pass just as predicted. And those who are ignorant in these matters marvel and are amazed; and those who understand them exult and are exalted. Both, by an impious pride, withdraw from you and abandon your light. They foretell an eclipse of the sun before it happens, but they do not see their own eclipse which is even now occurring. For they do not ask, as religious persons should, what is the source of the intelligence by which they investigate these matters. Moreover, when they discover that you made them, they do not give themselves up to you so that you might preserve what you have made. Nor do they offer, as sacrifice to you, what they have made of themselves. For they do not slaughter their own pride—as they do the sacrificial fowls—nor their own curiosities by which, like the fishes of the sea, they wander through the unknown paths of the deep. Nor do they curb their own extravagances as they do those of the beasts of the field, so that you, lord, a consuming fire, may burn up their mortal cares and renew them to immortality.

[5.3.5] They do not know the way which is your word, by which you created all the things that are and also the men who measure them, and the senses by which they perceive what they measure, and the intelligence whereby they discern the patterns of measure. Hence they do not know that your wisdom is beyond measure. But the only-begotten has been "made to us wisdom, and righteousness, and sanctification"* and has been numbered among us and paid tribute to Caesar.† And they do not know this way by which they could descend from themselves to him in order to ascend through him to him. They did not know this way, and so they fancied themselves exalted to the stars and the shining heavens. And so they fell upon the earth, and their foolish heart was darkened. They say many true things about what has been created but they do not seek with true piety for the truth, the architect of creation, and hence they do not find him. Or, if they do find him, and know that he is god, they do not glorify him as god; neither are they thankful but become vain in their imagination, and say that they themselves are wise, and attribute to themselves what is yours. At the same time, with the most perverse blindness, they wish to attribute to you their own quality—so that they load their lies on you who are the truth, "changing the glory of the incorruptible god for an image of corruptible man, and birds, and four-footed beasts, and creeping things." They "exchanged your truth for a lie, and worshiped and served the creature rather than the creator."‡

[5.3.6] Yet I remembered many a true saying of the philosophers about the creation, and I saw the confirmation of their calculations in the orderly sequence of seasons and in the visible evidence of the stars. And I compared

---

* 1 Corinthians 1:30.
† Matthew 22:21.
‡ Romans 1:23, 25.

this with the doctrines of Mani, who in his voluminous folly wrote many books on these subjects. But I could not discover there any account, of either the solstices or the equinoxes, or the eclipses of the sun and moon, or anything of the sort that I had learned in the books of secular philosophy. But still I was ordered to believe, even where the ideas did not correspond with—even when they contradicted—the rational theories established by mathematics and my own eyes, but were very different.

[5.4.7] Yet, lord god of truth, is any man pleasing to you because he knows these things? No, for surely that man is unhappy who knows these things and does not know you. And that person is happy who knows you, even though he does not know these things. He who knows both you and these things is not the more blessed for his learning, for you alone are his blessing, if knowing you as god he glorifies you and gives thanks and does not become vain in his thoughts. For just as a person who knows how to possess a tree, and give thanks to you for the use of it—although he may not know how many feet high it is or how wide it spreads—is better than one who can measure it and count all its branches, but neither owns it nor knows or loves its creator: just so is a faithful person who possesses the world's wealth as though he had nothing, and possesses all things through his union through you, whom all things serve, even though he does not know the circlings of the Great Bear. Just so it is foolish to doubt that this faithful person may truly be better than one who can measure the heavens and number the stars and weigh the elements, but who is forgetful of you "who has set in order all things in number, weight, and measure."*

[5.5.8] And who ordered this Mani to write about these things, knowledge of which is not necessary to piety? For you have told human beings, "Behold, godliness is wisdom"†—and of this he might have been ignorant, however perfectly he may have known these other things. Yet, since he did not know even these other things, and most impudently dared to teach them, it is clear that he had no knowledge of piety. For, even when we have a knowledge of this worldly lore, it is folly to make a profession of it, when piety comes from confession to you. From piety, therefore, Mani had gone astray, and all his show of learning only enabled the truly learned to perceive, from his ignorance of what they knew, how little he was to be trusted to make plain these more really difficult matters. For he did not aim to be lightly esteemed, but went around trying to persuade

---

* Wisdom of Solomon 11:21.

† Job 28:28.

men that the holy spirit, the comforter and enricher of your faithful ones, was personally resident in him with full authority. And, therefore, when he was detected in manifest errors about the sky, the stars, the movements of the sun and moon, even though these things do not relate to religious doctrine, the impious presumption of the man became clearly evident; for he not only taught things about which he was ignorant but also perverted them, and this with pride so foolish and mad that he sought to claim that his own utterances were as if they had been those of a divine person.

[5.5.9] When I hear of a Christian brother, ignorant of these things, or in error concerning them, I can tolerate his uninformed opinion; and I do not see that any lack of knowledge as to the form or nature of this material creation can do him much harm, as long as he does not hold a belief in anything which is unworthy of you, lord, the creator of all. But if he thinks that his secular knowledge pertains to the essence of the doctrine of piety, or ventures to assert dogmatic opinions in matters in which he is ignorant—there lies the injury. And yet even a weakness such as this, in the infancy of our faith, is tolerated by mother charity until the new person can grow up "to a perfect man," and not be "carried away with every wind of doctrine."* But Mani had presumed to be at once the teacher, author, guide, and leader of all whom he could persuade to believe this, so that all who followed him believed that they were following not an ordinary man but your holy spirit. And who would not judge that such great madness, when it once stood convicted of false teaching, should then be abhorred and utterly rejected? But I had not yet clearly decided whether the alternation of day and night, and of longer and shorter days and nights, and the eclipses of sun and moon, and whatever else I read about in other books could be explained consistently with his theories. If they could have been so explained, there would still have remained a doubt in my mind whether the theories were right or wrong. Yet I was prepared, on the strength of his reputed godliness, to rest my faith on his authority.

[5.6.10] For almost the whole of the nine years that I listened with unsettled mind to the Manichean teaching I had been looking forward with unbounded eagerness to the arrival of this Faustus. For all the other members of the sect that I happened to meet, when they were unable to answer the questions I raised, always referred me to his coming. They promised that, in discussion with him, these and even greater difficulties,

---

* Ephesians 4:13–14.

if I had them, would be quite easily and amply cleared away. When at last
he did come, I found him to be a man of pleasant speech, who spoke of
the very same things they themselves did, although more fluently and in
a more agreeable style. But what profit was there to me in the elegance
of my cupbearer, since he could not offer me the more precious draught
for which I thirsted? My ears had already had their fill of such stuff, and
now it did not seem any better because it was better expressed nor more
true because it was dressed up in rhetoric; nor could I think the man's soul
necessarily wise because his face was handsome and his language eloquent. But they who extolled him to me were not competent judges. They
thought him able and wise because his eloquence delighted them. At the
same time I realized that there is another kind of person who is suspicious
even of truth itself, if it is expressed in smooth and flowing language. But
you, my god, had already taught me in wonderful and marvelous ways,
and therefore I believed—because it is true—that you taught me and that
beside you there is no other teacher of truth, wherever truth shines forth.
Already I had learned from you that because a thing is eloquently expressed it should not be taken to be as necessarily true; nor because it is
uttered with stammering lips should it be supposed false. Nor, again, is it
necessarily true because rudely uttered, nor untrue because the language
is brilliant. Wisdom and folly are like meats that are wholesome and un-
wholesome, and elegant or inelegant words are like town- or country-
style dishes—both kinds of food may be served in either.

[**5.6.11**] That eagerness, therefore, with which I had so long awaited this
man, was indeed delighted with his energy and feeling in argument, and
with the fluent and apt words with which he clothed his ideas. I was delighted, therefore, and I joined with others—and even exceeded them—in
exalting and praising him. Yet it was a source of annoyance to me that, in
his lecture room, I was not allowed to introduce and raise any of those
questions that troubled me, in a familiar exchange of discussion with him.
As soon as I found an opportunity for this, and gained his ear at a time
when it was not inconvenient for him to enter into a discussion with me
and my friends, I laid before him some of my doubts. I discovered at once
that he knew nothing of the liberal arts except grammar, and that only in
an ordinary way. He had, however, read some of Tully's orations, a very
few books of Seneca, and some of the poets,[2] and such few books of his
own sect as were written in good Latin. With this meager learning and his
daily practice in speaking, he had acquired a sort of eloquence which
proved the more delightful and enticing because it was under the direction
of a ready wit and a sort of native grace. Was this not exactly as I now

recall it, lord my god, judge of my conscience? My heart and my memory
are laid open before you, who were even then guiding me by the secret impulse of your providence and were setting my shameful errors before my
face so that I might see and hate them.

[5.7.12] For as soon as it became plain to me that Faustus was ignorant
in those arts in which I had believed him eminent, I began to despair of
his being able to clarify and explain all these perplexities that troubled
me—though I realized that such ignorance need not have affected the authenticity of his piety, if he had not been a Manichean. For their books are
full of long fables about the sky and the stars, the sun and the moon; and
I had ceased to believe him able to show me in any satisfactory fashion
what I so ardently desired: whether the explanations contained in the
Manichean books were better or at least as good as the mathematical explanations I had read elsewhere. But when I proposed that these subjects
should be considered and discussed, he quite modestly did not dare to undertake the task, for he was aware that he had no knowledge of these
things and was not ashamed to confess it. For he was not one of those
talkative people—from whom I had endured so much—who undertook
to teach me what I wanted to know, and then said nothing. Faustus had a
heart which, if not right toward you, was at least not altogether false toward himself; for he was not ignorant of his own ignorance, and he did
not choose to be entangled in a controversy from which he could not
draw back or retire gracefully. For this I liked him all the more. For the
modesty of an ingenious mind is a finer thing than the acquisition of that
knowledge I desired; and this I found to be his attitude toward all abstruse and difficult questions.

[5.7.13] Thus the zeal with which I had plunged into the Manichean
system was checked, and I despaired even more of their other teachers,
because Faustus who was so famous among them had turned out so
poorly in the various matters that puzzled me. And so I began to occupy
myself with him in the pursuit of his own passion, which was for the readings that I was already teaching as a professor of rhetoric among the
young Carthaginian students. With Faustus then I read whatever he himself wished to read, or what I judged suitable to his bent of mind. But all
my endeavors to make further progress in Manicheism came completely
to an end through my acquaintance with that man. I did not wholly separate myself from them, but as one who had not yet found anything better
I decided to content myself, for the time being, with what I had stumbled
upon one way or another, until by chance something more desirable
should present itself. And so that Faustus who had entrapped so many to

their death now began, unintentionally and unwittingly, to loosen the snare in which I had been caught. For your hands, my god, in the hidden design of your providence did not desert my soul; and out of the blood of my mother's heart, through the tears that she poured out by day and by night, there was a sacrifice offered to you for me, and by marvelous ways you dealt with me. For it was you, my god, who did it: for "the steps of a man are ordered by the lord, and he shall choose his way."* How shall we attain salvation without your hand remaking what you have already made?

[5.8.14] You so dealt with me, therefore, that I was persuaded to go to Rome and teach there what I had been teaching at Carthage. And how I was persuaded to do this I will not omit to confess to you, for in this also the profoundest workings of your wisdom and your constant mercy toward us must be pondered and acknowledged. I did not wish to go to Rome because of the richer fees and the higher dignity which my friends promised me there—though these considerations did affect my decision. My principal and almost sole motive was that I had been informed that the students there studied more quietly and were better kept under the control of stern discipline, so that they did not capriciously and impudently rush into the classroom of a teacher not their own—indeed, they were not admitted at all without the permission of the teacher. At Carthage, on the contrary, there was a shameful and intemperate license among the students. They burst in rudely and, with furious gestures, would disrupt the discipline which the teacher had established for the good of his pupils. Many outrages they perpetrated with astounding effrontery, things that would be punishable by law if they were not sustained by custom. Thus custom makes plain that such behavior is all the more worthless because it allows men to do what your eternal law never will allow. They think that they act thus with impunity, though the very blindness with which they act is their punishment, and they suffer far greater harm than they inflict. The manners that I would not adopt as a student I was compelled as a teacher to endure in others. And so I was glad to go where all who knew the situation assured me that such conduct was not allowed. But you, "my refuge and my portion in the land of the living,"† goaded me thus at Carthage so that I might thereby be pulled away from it and change my worldly habitation for the preservation of my

* Psalms 37:23–24.
† Psalms 142:5.

soul. At the same time, you offered me at Rome an enticement, through the agency of men enchanted with this death-in-life—by their insane conduct in the one place and their empty promises in the other. To correct my wandering footsteps, you secretly employed their perversity and my own. For those who disturbed my tranquillity were blinded by shameful madness and also those who allured me elsewhere had nothing better than the earth's cunning. And I who hated actual misery in the one place sought fictitious happiness in the other.

[5.8.15] You knew the cause of my going from one country to the other, god, but you did not disclose it either to me or to my mother, who grieved deeply over my departure and followed me down to the sea. She clasped me tight in her embrace, willing either to keep me back or to go with me, but I deceived her, pretending that I had a friend whom I could not leave until he had a favorable wind to set sail. Thus I lied to my mother—and such a mother!—and escaped. For this too you mercifully pardoned me—fool that I was—and preserved me from the waters of the sea for the water of your grace; so that, when I was purified by that, the fountain of my mother's eyes, from which she had daily watered the ground for me as she prayed to you, should be dried. And, since she refused to return without me, I persuaded her, with some difficulty, to remain that night in a place quite close to our ship, where there was a shrine in memory of the blessed Cyprian. That night I slipped away secretly, and she remained to pray and weep.[3] And what was it, lord, that she was asking of you in such a flood of tears but that you would not allow me to sail? But you, taking your own secret counsel and noting the real point to her desire, did not grant what she was then asking in order to grant to her the thing that she had always been asking. The wind blew and filled our sails, and the shore dropped out of sight. Wild with grief, she was there the next morning and filled your ears with complaints and groans which you disregarded, although, at the very same time, you were using my longings as a means and were hastening me on to the fulfillment of all longing. Thus the earthly part of her love to me was justly purged by the scourge of sorrow. Still, like all mothers—though even more than others—she loved to have me with her, and did not know what joy you were preparing for her through my going away. Not knowing this secret end, she wept and mourned and saw in her agony the inheritance of Eve—seeking in sorrow what she had brought forth in sorrow. And yet, after accusing me of perfidy and cruelty, she still continued her intercessions for me to you. She returned to her own home, and I went on to Rome.

There I was received by the scourge of bodily sickness; and I was very close to falling into hell, burdened with all the many and grievous sins I had committed against you, myself, and others—all over and above that fetter of original sin whereby we all die in Adam. For you had forgiven me none of these things in Christ, neither had he abolished by his cross the enmity that I had incurred from you through my sins. For how could he do so by the crucifixion of a phantom, which was all I supposed him to be? The death of my soul was as real then as the death of his flesh appeared to me unreal.[4] And the life of my soul was as false, because it was as unreal as the death of his flesh was real, though I believed it not. My fever increased, and I was on the verge of passing away and perishing; for, if I had passed away then, where should I have gone but into the fiery torment which my misdeeds deserved, measured by the truth of your rule? My mother knew nothing of this; yet, far away, she went on praying for me. And you, present everywhere, heard her where she was and had pity on me where I was, so that I regained my bodily health, although I was still disordered in my sacrilegious heart. For that peril of death did not make me wish to be baptized. I was even better when, as a lad, I appealed to my devout mother for baptism, as I have already related and confessed. But now I had increased in dishonor, and I madly scoffed at all the purposes of your medicine which would not have allowed me, though a sinner such as I was, to die a double death. Had my mother's heart been pierced with this wound, it never could have been cured, for I cannot adequately tell of the love she had for me, or how she still travailed for me in the spirit with a far keener anguish than when she bore me in the flesh.

[5.9.17] I cannot conceive, therefore, how she could have been healed if my death (still in my sins) had pierced her inmost love. Where, then, would have been all her earnest, frequent, and ceaseless prayers to you? Nowhere but with you. But could you, most merciful god, despise the contrite and humble heart of that pure and prudent widow, who was so constant in her alms, so gracious and attentive to your saints, never missing a visit to church twice a day, morning and evening—and this not for vain gossiping, nor old wives' fables, but in order that she might listen to you in your sermons, and you to her in her prayers? Could you, by whose gifts she was so inspired, despise and disregard the tears of such a one without coming to her aid—those tears by which she entreated you, not for gold or silver, and not for any changing or fleeting good, but for the salvation of the soul of her son? By no means, lord. It is certain that you were near and were hearing and were carrying out the plan by which you had predetermined it should be done. Far be it from you that you should have deluded her in those visions and the answers she had received from you—some of which I have mentioned, and others not—which she kept in her faithful heart, and, forever beseeching, urged them on you as if they had your own signature. For because your mercy endures forever, you have so condescended to those whose debts you have pardoned that you yourself become a debtor by your promises.

[5.10.18] You restored me then from that illness, and healed the son of your handmaid in his body, so that he might live for you and so that you might endow him with a better and more certain health. After this, at Rome, I again joined those deluding and deluded saints; and not their hearers only, such as the man was in whose house I had fallen sick, but also with those whom they called the elect. For it still seemed to me that it was not we who sinned, but some other nature that sinned in us. And it gratified my pride to be beyond blame, and when I did anything wrong not to have to confess that *I* had done wrong, so that you might heal my soul because *it* was sinning against you. I loved to excuse myself and to accuse something else inside me (I knew not what) but which was not I. But, assuredly, it was I, and it was my impiety that had divided me against myself. That sin then was all the more incurable because I did not deem myself a sinner. It was an execrable iniquity, omnipotent god, that I would have preferred to have you defeated in me, to my destruction, than to be defeated by you to my salvation. Not yet, therefore, had you set a watch upon my mouth and a door around my lips so that my heart might not incline to evil speech, to make excuse for sin with those who work iniquity. And, therefore, I continued still in the company of their elect. But now, hopeless of gaining any profit from that false doctrine, I began to hold more loosely and negligently even to those points which I had decided to rest content with, if I could find nothing better.

[5.10.19] I was now half inclined to believe that those philosophers whom they call Academics were wiser than the rest in holding that we ought to doubt everything, and in maintaining that humans do not have the power of comprehending any certain truth, for, although I had not yet understood their meaning, I was fully persuaded that they thought just as they are commonly reputed to do.[5] And I did not fail openly to dissuade my host from his confidence which I observed that he had in those fictions which fill the works of the Manicheans. For all this, I was still on terms of more intimate friendship with these people than with others who were not of their heresy. I did not indeed defend it with my former ardor; but my familiarity with that group—and there were many of them concealed in Rome at that time—made me slower to seek any other way. This was particularly easy since I had no hope of finding in your church the truth from which they had turned me aside, lord of heaven and earth, creator of all things visible and invisible. And it still seemed to me most unseemly to believe that you could have the form of human flesh and be bounded by the bodily shape of our limbs. And when I wished to meditate on my god, I did not know what to think of but a huge extended body—for what did not have bodily extension did not seem to me to exist—and this was the greatest and almost the sole cause of my unavoidable errors.

[5.10.20] And thus I also believed that evil was a similar kind of substance, and that it had its own hideous and deformed extended body—either in a dense form which they called the earth or in a thin and subtle form as, for example, the substance of the air, which they imagined as some malignant spirit penetrating that earth. And because my piety—such as it was—still compelled me to believe that the good god never created any evil substance, I formed the idea of two masses, one opposed to the other, both infinite but with the evil more contracted and the good more expansive. And from this diseased beginning, the other sacrileges followed after. For when my mind tried to turn back to the catholic faith, I was cast down, since the catholic faith was not what I judged it to be. And it seemed to me a greater piety to regard you, my god—to whom I make confession of your mercies—as infinite in all respects except that one: where the extended mass of evil stood opposed to you, where I was compelled to confess that you are finite—than if I should think that you could be confined by the form of a human body on every side. And it seemed better to me to believe that no evil had been created by you—for in my ignorance evil appeared not only to be some kind of substance but a corporeal one at that. This was because I had, thus far, no conception of mind, except as a subtle body diffused throughout local spaces. This seemed better than to believe that anything could emanate from you which had the character that I considered evil to be in its nature. And I believed that our saviour himself also—your only-begotten—had been brought forth, as it were, for our salvation out of the mass of your bright shining substance, so that I could believe nothing about him except what I was able to harmonize with these vain imaginations. I thought, therefore, that such a nature could not be born of the virgin Mary without being mingled with the flesh, and I could not see how the divine substance, as I had conceived it, could be mingled in this way without being contaminated. I was afraid, therefore, to believe that he had been born in the flesh, in case I should also be compelled to believe that he had been contaminated by the flesh. Now your spiritual ones will smile blandly and lovingly at me if they read these confessions. Yet such was I.

[5.11.21] Furthermore, the things they censured in your scriptures I thought impossible to be defended. And yet, occasionally, I wished to confer on various matters with someone well learned in those books, to test what he thought of them. For already the words of one Elpidius, who spoke and disputed face to face against these same Manicheans, had begun to impress me, even when I was at Carthage; because he brought forth things out of the scriptures that were not easily withstood, to which their answers appeared to me feeble. One of their answers they did not give forth publicly, but only to us in private—when they said that the writings of the New Testament had been tampered with by unknown persons who desired to ingraft the Jewish law into the Christian faith. But they themselves never brought forward any uncorrupted copies. Still thinking in corporeal categories and very much ensnared and to some extent stifled, I was borne down by those conceptions of bodily substance. I panted under this load for the air of your truth, but I was not able to breathe it pure and undefiled.

[5.12.22] I set about diligently to practice what I came to Rome to do—the teaching of rhetoric. First I brought together in my home a few people to whom and through whom I had begun to be known, whereupon I discovered that other offenses were committed in Rome which I had not had to bear in Africa. Just as I had been told, those riotous disruptions by young blackguards were not practiced here. Yet, now, my friends told me, many of the Roman students—breakers of faith, who, for the love of money, set a small value on justice—would conspire together and suddenly transfer to another teacher, to evade paying their master's fees. My heart hated such people, though not with a perfect hatred; for doubtless I hated them more because I was to suffer from them than on account of their own illicit acts. Still, such people are base indeed; they fornicate against you, for they love the transitory mockeries of temporal things and the filthy gain which begrimes the hand that grabs it; they embrace the fleeting world and scorn you, who abide and invite us to return to you and who pardon the prostituted human soul when it does return to you. Now I hate such crooked and perverse people, although I love them if they will be corrected and come to prefer the learning they obtain to money and, above all, to prefer you to such learning, god, the truth and fullness of our positive good, and our most pure peace. But then the wish was stronger in me for my own sake not to suffer evil from them than was my desire that they should become good for your sake.

[5.13.23] When, therefore, the officials of Milan sent to Rome, to the prefect of the city, to ask that he provide them with a teacher of rhetoric for their city and to send him at the public expense, I used the influence of those same persons, drunk with the Manichean vanities, to be freed from whom I was going away—though neither they nor I were aware of it at the time, to ensure that Symmachus, who was then prefect, after he had proved me by audition, should appoint me.[6] And to Milan I came, to Ambrose the bishop, famed through the whole world as one of the best of mortals, your devoted servant.[7] His eloquent discourse in those times abundantly provided your people with the flour of your wheat, the gladness of your oil, and the sober intoxication of your wine. To him I was led by you without my knowledge, so that by him I might be led to you in full knowledge. That man of god received me as a father would, and welcomed my coming as a good bishop should. And I began to love him, of course, not at the first as a teacher of the truth, for I had entirely despaired of finding that in your church—but as a friendly man. And I studiously listened to him—though not with the right motive—as he preached to the people. I was trying to discover whether his eloquence came up to his reputation, and whether it flowed fuller or thinner than others said it did. And thus I hung on his words intently, but, as to his subject matter, I was only a careless and contemptuous listener. I was delighted with the charm of his speech, which was more erudite, though less cheerful and soothing, than Faustus' style. As for subject matter, however, there could be no comparison, for the latter was wandering around in Manichean deceptions, while the former was teaching salvation most soundly. But salvation is far from the wicked, such as I was then when I stood before him. Yet I was drawing nearer, gradually and unconsciously.

[5.14.24] For, although I took no trouble to learn what he said, but only to hear how he said it—for this empty concern remained foremost with me as long as I despaired of finding a clear path to you—yet, along with the eloquence I prized, there also came into my mind the ideas which I ignored; for I could not separate them. And, while I opened my heart to acknowledge how skillfully he spoke, there also came an awareness of how truly he spoke—but only gradually. First of all, his ideas had already begun to appear to me defensible; and the catholic faith, for which I supposed that nothing could be said against the onslaught of the Manicheans, I now realized could be maintained without presumption. This was especially clear after I had heard one or two parts of the Old Testament explained allegorically—whereas before this, when I had interpreted them literally, they had killed me spiritually. However, when many of these passages in those books were expounded to me thus, I came to blame my own despair for having believed that no reply could be given to those who hated and scoffed at the Law and the Prophets. Yet I did not see that this was reason enough to follow the catholic way, just because it had learned advocates who could answer objections adequately and without absurdity. Nor could I see that what I had held to heretofore should now be condemned, because both sides were equally defensible. For the catholic way appeared to me unvanquished, without yet appearing victorious.

[5.14.25] But now I earnestly bent my mind to see if there was any possible way to prove the Manicheans guilty of falsehood. If I could have conceived of a spiritual substance, all their strongholds would have collapsed and been cast out of my mind. But I could not. Still, concerning the body of this world, nature as a whole—now that I was able to consider and compare such things more and more—I decided that the majority of the philosophers held the more probable views. So, in what I thought was the method of the Academics—doubting everything and fluctuating between all the options—I came to the conclusion that the Manicheans were to be abandoned. For I judged, even in that period of doubt, that I could not remain in a sect to which I preferred some of the philosophers. But I refused to commit the cure of my fainting soul to the philosophers, because they were without the saving name of Christ. I resolved, therefore, to become a catechumen in the catholic church—which my parents had so much urged upon me—until something certain shone forth by which I might guide my course.

BOOK 6

[6.1.1] Hope of mine from my youth onward, where were you to me and where had you gone? For had you not created me and differentiated me from the beasts of the field and the birds of the air, making me wiser than they? And yet I was wandering about in a dark and slippery way, seeking you outside myself and thus not finding the god of my heart. I had gone down into the depths of the sea and had lost faith, and had despaired of ever finding the truth.

By this time my mother had come to me, having mustered the courage of piety, following over sea and land, secure in you through all the perils of the journey. For in the dangers of the voyage she comforted the sailors—to whom the inexperienced voyagers, when alarmed, were accustomed to go for comfort—and assured them of a safe arrival because she had been so assured by you in a vision. She found me in deadly peril through my despair of ever finding the truth. But when I told her that I was now no longer a Manichean, though not yet a catholic Christian, she did not leap for joy as if this were unexpected; for she had already been reassured about that part of my misery for which she had mourned me as one dead, but also as one who would be raised to you. She had carried me out on the bier of her thoughts, so that you might say to the widow's son, "Young man, I say to you, arise!"* and then he would revive and begin to speak, and you would deliver him to his mother. Therefore, her heart was not agitated with any violent exultation when she heard that so great a part of what she daily entreated you to do had actually already been done—that, though I had not yet grasped the truth, I was rescued from falsehood. Instead, she was fully confident that you who had promised the whole would give her the rest, and thus most calmly, and with a fully confident heart, she replied to me that she believed, in Christ, that before she died she would see me a faithful catholic. And she said no more than this to me. But to you, fountain of mercy, she poured out still more frequent prayers and tears that you would hasten your aid and enlighten my darkness, and she hurried all the more zealously to the church and hung upon the words of Ambrose, praying for the fountain of water that

---

* Luke 7:14.

springs up into everlasting life.* For she loved that man as an angel of god, since she knew that it was by him that I had been brought thus far to that wavering state of agitation I was now in, through which she was fully persuaded I should pass from sickness to health, even though it would be after a still sharper convulsion which physicians call the crisis.

[6.2.2] So also my mother brought to certain oratories, erected in the memory of the saints, offerings of porridge, bread, and wine—as had been her custom in Africa—and she was forbidden to do so by the door-keeper. And as soon as she learned that it was the bishop who had forbidden it, she acquiesced so devoutly and obediently that I myself marveled how readily she could bring herself to turn critic of her own customs, rather than question his prohibition.[1] For her spirit was not possessed by a weakness for wine, nor did the love of wine stimulate her to hate the truth, as it does too many, both male and female, who turn as sick at a hymn to sobriety as drunkards do at a draught of water. When she had brought her basket with the festive gifts, which were to be first tasted and then given away, she would never allow herself more than one little cup of wine, diluted according to her own temperate palate, which she would taste out of courtesy. And, if there were many oratories of departed saints to be honored in the same way, she still carried around with her the same little cup, to be used everywhere. This became not only very much watered but also quite tepid with carrying it about. She would distribute it by small sips to those around, for she sought to stimulate their devotion, not pleasure.

But as soon as she found that this custom was forbidden by that famous preacher and most pious prelate, even to those who would use it in moderation, lest thereby it might be an occasion of gluttony for those who were already given to drink (and also because these funereal memorials were very much like some of the superstitious practices of the pagans), she most willingly abstained from it. And, in place of a basket filled with fruits of the earth, she had learned to bring to the oratories of the martyrs a heart full of purer petitions, and to give all that she could to the poor—so that the communion of the lord's body might be rightly celebrated in those places where, after the example of his passion, the martyrs had been sacrificed and crowned. But yet it seems to me, lord my god—and my heart thinks of it this way in your sight—that my mother would probably not have given way so easily to the rejection of this custom if it had

* John 4:14.

been forbidden by another, whom she did not love as she did Ambrose. For, out of her concern for my salvation, she loved him most dearly; and he loved her truly, on account of her faithful religious life, in which she frequented the church with good works, fervent in spirit. Thus he would, when he saw me, often burst forth into praise of her, congratulating me that I had such a mother—little knowing what a son she had in me, who was still a skeptic in all these matters and who could not conceive that the way of life could be found out.

[**6.3.3**] Nor had I come yet to groan in my prayers that you would help me. My mind was wholly intent on knowledge and eager for disputation. Ambrose himself I esteemed a happy man, as the world counted happiness, because great personages held him in honor. Only his celibacy appeared to me a painful burden.[2] But what hope he cherished, what struggles he had against the temptations that beset his high station, what solace in adversity, and what savory joys your bread possessed for the hidden mouth of his heart when feeding on it, I could neither conjecture nor experience. Nor did he know my own frustrations, nor the pit of my danger. For I could not request of him what I wanted as I wanted it, because I was debarred from hearing and speaking to him by crowds of busy people to whose infirmities he devoted himself. And when he was not engaged with them—which was never for long at a time—he was either refreshing his body with necessary food or his mind with reading.

Now, as he read, his eyes glanced over the pages and his heart searched out the sense, but his voice and tongue were silent. Often when we came to him—for no one was forbidden to enter, nor was it his custom that the arrival of visitors should be announced to him—we would see him thus reading to himself. After we had sat for a long time in silence—for who would dare interrupt one so intent?—we would then depart, realizing that he was unwilling to be distracted in the little time he could gain for the refreshment of his mind, free from the clamor of other men's business. Perhaps he was fearful lest, if the author he was studying should express himself vaguely, some doubtful and attentive hearer would ask him to expound it or discuss some of the more abstruse questions, so that he could not get through as much material as he wished, if his time was occupied with others. And an even truer reason for his reading to himself might have been the care for preserving his voice, which was very easily weakened. Whatever his motive was in so doing, it was doubtless, in such a man, a good one.[3]

[**6.3.4**] In any case, I could find no opportunity of putting the questions I desired to that holy oracle of yours, his heart, unless it was a matter which could be dealt with briefly. However, those surgings in me required that he should give me his full leisure so that I might pour them out to him; but I never found him so. I heard him, indeed, every Lord's Day, "rightly dividing the word of truth"* among the people. And I became all the more convinced that all those knots of crafty calumnies which those deceivers of ours had knit together against the divine books could be unraveled.

I soon understood that the statement that man was made after the image of him that created him† was not understood by your spiritual sons—whom you have regenerated through the catholic mother through grace—as if they believed and imagined that you were bounded by a human form, although what was the nature of a spiritual substance I had not the faintest or vaguest notion. Still rejoicing, I blushed that for so many years I had bayed, not against the catholic faith, but against the fables of fleshly imagination. For I had been both impious and rash in this, that I had condemned by pronouncement what I ought to have learned by inquiry. For you, most high, and most near, most secret, yet most present, who do not have limbs, some of which are larger and some smaller, but who are wholly everywhere and nowhere in space, and are not shaped by some corporeal form: you created humanity after your own image and, see, the human being dwells in space, both head and feet.

[6.4.5] Since I could not then understand how this image of yours could subsist, I should have knocked on the door and propounded the doubt as to how it was to be believed, and not have insultingly opposed it as if it were actually believed. Therefore, my anxiety as to what I could retain as certain gnawed all the more sharply into my soul, and I felt quite ashamed because during the long time I had been deluded and deceived by the promises of certainties, I had, with childish petulance, chattered of so many uncertainties as if they were certain. That they were falsehoods became apparent to me only afterward. It was certain, however, that they were uncertain and that I had once held them as if they were certain, when I accused your catholic church with a blind contentiousness. Even if I had not yet discovered that the church taught the truth, I now knew that it did not teach what I had so vehemently accused it of. In this respect, at least, I was confounded and converted; and I rejoiced, my god, that the one church, the body of your only son—in which the name of

---

* 2 Timothy 2:15.
† Genesis 1:26.

Christ had been sealed upon me as an infant—did not relish these childish trifles and did not maintain in its sound doctrine any tenet that would
involve pressing you, the creator of all, into space, which, however extended and immense, would still be bounded on all sides—like the shape
of a human body.

[6.4.6] I was also glad that the old scriptures of the Law and the
Prophets were laid before me to be read, not now with an eye to what had
seemed absurd in them when formerly I censured your holy ones for
thinking thus, when they actually did not think in that way. And I listened
with delight to Ambrose, in his sermons to the people, often recommending this text most diligently as a rule: "The letter kills, but the spirit
gives life,"*4 while at the same time he drew aside the mystic veil and
opened to view the spiritual meaning of what seemed to teach perverse
doctrine if it were taken according to the letter. I found nothing in his
teachings that offended me, though I could not yet know for certain
whether what he taught was true. For all this time I restrained my heart
from assenting to anything, fearing to fall headlong into error. Instead, by
this hanging in suspense, I was being strangled. For my desire was to be
as certain of invisible things as I was that seven and three are ten. I was
not so deranged as to believe that this could not be comprehended, but
my desire was to have other things as clear as this, whether they were
physical objects, which were not present to my senses, or spiritual objects,
which I did not know how to conceive of except in physical terms. If I
could have believed, I might have been cured, and, with the sight of my
soul cleared up, it might in some way have been directed toward your
truth, which always abides and fails in nothing. But, just as it happens that
a man who has tried a bad physician fears to trust himself with a good
one, so it was with the health of my soul, which could not be healed except by believing. But lest it should believe falsehoods, it refused to be
cured, resisting your hand, who have prepared for us the medicines of
faith and applied them to the maladies of the whole world, and endowed
them with such great efficacy.

[6.5.7] Still, from this time forward, I began to prefer the catholic doctrine. I felt that it was with moderation and honesty that it commanded
things to be believed that were not demonstrated—whether they could be
demonstrated, but not to everyone, or whether they could not be demonstrated at all. This was far better than the method of the Manicheans, in

---

* 2 Corinthians 3:6.

which our credulity was mocked by an audacious promise of knowledge and then many fabulous and absurd things were forced upon believers because they were incapable of demonstration. After that, lord, little by little, with a gentle and most merciful hand, drawing and calming my heart, you persuaded me that if I considered the innumerable things which I believed but which I had never seen nor been present for when they were enacted, as for example so many events of secular history, so many reports of places and cities which I had not seen, so many things I had heard from friends, or physicians, or from these or those persons (things we are bound to believe, unless we would do nothing at all in this life), and if, finally, I considered with what an unalterable assurance I believed which two people were my parents, though this was impossible for me to know otherwise than by hearsay—thus, I say, you persuaded me that it was not the ones who believed your books, which with so great authority you have established among nearly all nations, but those who did not believe them who were to be blamed. Moreover, those men were not to be heeded who would say to me, "How do you know that those scriptures were imparted to mankind by the spirit of the one and most true god?" For this was the point that was most of all to be believed, since no wranglings of blasphemous questions such as I had read in the books of the self-contradicting philosophers could once snatch from me the belief that you do exist—although what you are I did not know—and that to you belongs the governance of human affairs.

[6.5.8] This much I believed, some times more strongly than other times. But I always believed both that you are and that you have a care for us, although I was ignorant both as to what should be thought about your substance and as to which way led, or led back, to you. Thus, since we are too weak by unaided reason to find out truth, and since, because of this, we need the authority of the holy writings, I had now begun to believe that you would not, under any circumstances, have given such eminent authority to those scriptures throughout all lands if it had not been that through them your will may be believed in and that you might be sought.[5] For, as to those passages in the scripture which had heretofore appeared incongruous and offensive to me, now that I had heard several of them expounded reasonably, I could see that they were to be resolved by the mysteries of spiritual interpretation. The authority of scripture seemed to me all the more revered and worthy of devout belief because, although it was visible for all to read, it reserved the full majesty of its secret wisdom within its spiritual profundity. While it stooped to all in the great plainness of its language and simplicity of style, it yet required the closest attention

of the most serious-minded—so that it might receive all into its common
bosom, and direct some few through its narrow passages toward you, yet
many more than would have been the case had there not been in it such a
lofty authority, which nevertheless allured multitudes to its bosom of its
holy humility. I continued to reflect upon these things, and you were with
me. I sighed, and you heard me. I vacillated, and you guided me. I roamed
the broad way of the world, and you did not desert me.

[6.6.9] I was still eagerly aspiring to honors, money, and matrimony;
and you mocked me. In pursuit of these ambitions I endured the most bitter hardships, in which you were being the more gracious the less you
would allow anything that was not you to grow sweet to me. Look into my
heart, lord, whose prompting it is that I should recall all this, and confess
it to you. Now let my soul cleave to you, now that you have freed it from
that fast-sticking glue of death. How wretched it was! And you irritated
its sore wound so that it might abandon all else and turn to you—who are
above all and without whom all things would be nothing at all—so that it
should be converted and healed. How wretched I was at that time, and
how you dealt with me so as to make me aware of my wretchedness, I recall from the incident of the day on which I was preparing to recite a panegyric on the emperor.[6] In it I was to deliver many a lie, and the lying was
to be applauded by those who knew I was lying. My heart was agitated
with this sense of guilt and it seethed with the fever of my uneasiness. For,
while walking along one of the streets of Milan, I saw a poor beggar—
with what I believe was a full belly—joking and joyful. And I sighed and
spoke to the friends around me of the many sorrows that flowed from our
madness, because in spite of all our exertions—such as those I was then
laboring in, dragging the burden of my unhappiness under the spur of ambition, and, by dragging it, increasing it at the same time—still we aimed
only to attain that very happiness which this beggar had reached before
us; and there was a grim chance that we should never attain it. For what
he had obtained through a few coins, got by his begging, I was still schem-
ing for by many a wretched and tortuous turning—namely, the joy of a
passing happiness. He had not, indeed, gained true joy, but, at the same
time, with all my ambitions, I was seeking one still more untrue. Anyhow,
he was now joyous and I was anxious. He was free from care, and I was
full of alarms. Now, if anyone should inquire of me whether I should prefer to be cheerful or anxious, I would reply, "Cheerful." Again, if I had
been asked whether I should prefer to be as he was or as I myself then
was, I would have chosen to be myself; though I was beset with cares and
alarms. But would not this have been a false choice? Was the contrast

valid? Actually, I ought not to prefer myself to him because I happened to be more learned than he was; for I got no great pleasure from my learning, but sought, rather, to please people by its exhibition—and this not to instruct, but only to please. Thus you broke my bones with the rod of your correction.

[6.6.10] Let my soul take its leave of those who say: "It makes a difference as to the object from which a man derives his joy. The beggar rejoiced in drunkenness; you longed to rejoice in glory." What glory, lord? The kind that is not in you, for, just as his was no true joy, so was mine no true glory; but it turned my head all the more. He would get over his drunkenness that same night, but I had slept with mine many a night and risen again with it, and was to sleep again and rise again with it, I know not how many times. It does indeed make a difference what the object of one's joy is. I know this is so, and I know that the joy of a faithful hope is incomparably beyond such vanity. Yet, at the same time, this beggar was beyond me, for he truly was the happier man—not only because he was thoroughly steeped in his joy while I was torn to pieces with my cares, but because he had acquired his wine by giving good wishes to the passers-by while I was following after the ambition of my pride by lying. Much to this effect I said to my good companions, and I saw how readily they reacted much as I did. Thus I found that it went ill with me; and I fretted, and doubled that very ill. And if any prosperity smiled upon me, I loathed to seize it, for almost before I could grasp it, it would fly away.

[6.7.11] Those of us who were living like friends together used to bemoan our lot in our common talk; but I discussed it with Alypius and Nebridius more especially and in very familiar terms. Alypius had been born in the same town as I; his parents were of the highest rank there, but he was a bit younger than I.[7] He had studied under me when I first taught in our town, and then afterward at Carthage. He esteemed me highly because I appeared to him good and learned, and I esteemed him for his inborn love of virtue, which was uncommonly marked in a man so young. But the whirlpool of Carthaginian fashion—where frivolous spectacles are hotly followed—had sucked him into the madness of the gladiatorial games. While he was miserably tossing in this passion, I was teaching rhetoric there in a public school. At that time he was not attending my classes because of some ill feeling that had arisen between me and his father. I then came to discover how fatally he loved the circus, and I was deeply grieved, for he seemed likely to cast away his very great promise—if, indeed, he had not already done so. Yet I had no means of advising him, or any way of reclaiming him through restraint, either by the kindness of a friend or by the authority of a teacher. For I imagined that his feelings toward me were the same as his father's. But this turned out not to be the case. Indeed, disregarding his father's will in the matter, he began to be friendly and to visit my lecture room, to listen for a while and then depart.

[6.7.12] But it slipped my memory to try to deal with his problem, to prevent him from ruining his excellent mind in his blind and headstrong passion for frivolous sport. But you, lord, who hold the helm of all that you have created, you had not forgotten him who was one day to be numbered among your sons, a chief minister of your sacrament. And in order that his amendment might plainly be attributed to you, you brought it about through me while I knew nothing of it.

One day, when I was sitting in my accustomed place with my students before me, he came in, greeted me, sat himself down, and fixed his attention on the subject I was then discussing. It so happened that I had a passage in hand and, while I was interpreting it, a simile occurred to me, taken from the gladiatorial games. It struck me as relevant to make more pleasant and plain the point I wanted to convey by adding a biting gibe at those whom that madness had enthralled. You know, our god, that I had no thought at that time of curing Alypius of that plague. But he took it to himself and thought that I would not have said it but for his sake. And what any other would have taken as an occasion of offense against me, this worthy young man took as a reason for being offended at himself, and for loving me the more fervently. You had said it long ago and inserted it in your writings, "Rebuke a wise man, and he will love you."* Now I had not rebuked him; but you who can make use of everything, both what is intentional and what is not, and in the order which you yourself know to be best—and that order is right—you made my heart and tongue into burning coals with which you might cauterize and cure the hopeful mind thus languishing. Let him be silent in your praise who does not meditate on your mercy, which rises up in my inmost parts to confess to you. For after that speech Alypius rushed up out of that deep pit into which he had willfully plunged and in which he had been blinded by its miserable pleasures. And he roused his mind with a resolve to moderation. When he had done this, all the filth of the gladiatorial pleasures dropped away from him, and he went to them no more. Then he also prevailed upon his reluctant father to let him be my pupil. And, at the son's urging, the father at last consented. Thus Alypius began again to hear my

---

* Proverbs 9:8.

lectures and became involved with me in the same superstition, loving in the Manicheans that outward display of ascetic discipline which he believed was true and unfeigned. It was, however, a senseless and seducing continence, which ensnared precious souls who were not able as yet to reach the height of true virtue, and who were easily beguiled with the veneer of what was only a shadowy and feigned virtue.

[6.8.13] He had gone on to Rome before me to study law—which was the worldly way which his parents were forever urging him to pursue—and there he was carried away again with an incredible passion for the gladiatorial shows. For, although he had been utterly opposed to such spectacles and detested them, one day he met by chance a company of his acquaintances and fellow students returning from dinner; and, with a friendly violence, they drew him, resisting and objecting vehemently, into the amphitheater, on a day of those cruel and murderous shows. He protested to them: "Though you drag my body to that place and set me down there, you cannot force me to give my mind or lend my eyes to these shows. Thus I will be absent while present, and so overcome both you and them." When they heard this, they dragged him on in, probably interested to see whether he could do as he said. When they got to the arena, and had taken what seats they could get, the whole place became a tumult of inhuman frenzy. But Alypius kept his eyes closed and forbade his mind to roam abroad after such wickedness. If only he had shut his ears too! For when one of the combatants fell in the fight, a mighty cry from the whole audience stirred him so strongly that, overcome by curiosity and still prepared (as he thought) to despise and overcome whatever it was he saw, he opened his eyes and was struck with a deeper wound in his soul than the victim whom he desired to see had been in his body. Thus he fell more miserably than the one whose fall had raised that mighty clamor which had entered through his ears and unlocked his eyes to make way for the wounding and beating down of his soul, which was more audacious than truly valiant—also it was weaker because it presumed on its own strength when it ought to have depended on you. For, as soon as he saw the blood, he drank in with it a savage temper, and he did not turn away, but fixed his eyes on the bloody pastime, unwittingly drinking in the madness—delighted with the wicked contest and drunk with blood lust. He was now no longer the same man who came in, but was one of the mob he came into, a true companion of those who had brought him thither. Why need I say more? He looked, he shouted, he was excited, and he took away with him the madness that would stimulate him to come again: not only with those who first enticed him, but even without them; indeed, dragging in others besides. And yet from all this, with a most

powerful and most merciful hand, you plucked him and taught him not to
rest his confidence in himself but in you—but not till long after.

[6.9.14] But this was all being stored up in his memory as medicine for
the future. So also was that other incident when he was still studying under
me at Carthage and was meditating at noonday in the market place on
what he had to recite—as students usually have to do for practice—and
you allowed him to be arrested by the police officers in the market place
as a thief. I believe, my god, that you allowed this for no other reason than
that this man who was in the future to prove so great should now begin to
learn that, in making just decisions, a person should not readily be condemned by others with reckless credulity. For as he was walking up and
down alone before the judgment seat with his tablets and pen, a young
man—another one of the students, who was the real thief—secretly brought
a hatchet and, without Alypius seeing him, got as far as the lead gratings
which protected the silversmiths' shops from above and began to hack
away at the lead. But when the noise of the hatchet was heard the silversmiths below began to call to each other in whispers and sent men to ar-
rest whosoever they should find. The thief heard their voices and ran away,
leaving his hatchet because he was afraid to be caught with it. Now Alypius, who had not seen him come in, got a glimpse of him as he went out
and noticed that he went off in great haste. Being curious to know the reasons, he went up to the place, where he found the hatchet, and stood won-
dering and pondering—at which moment, those who had been sent caught
him alone, holding the hatchet which had made the noise which had startled them and brought them there. They seized him and dragged him
away, gathering the tenants of the market place about them and boasting
that they had caught a notorious thief. Thereupon he was led away to appear before the judge.

[6.9.15] But this is as far as his lesson was to go. For immediately, lord,
you came to the rescue of his innocence, of which you were the sole witness.
As he was being led off to prison or punishment, they were met by the master builder who had charge of the public buildings. The captors were especially glad to meet him because he had more than once suspected them of
stealing goods that had been lost out of the market place. Now, at last, they
thought they could convince him who it was that had committed the thefts.
But this man had often met Alypius at the house of a certain senator, whose
receptions he used to attend. He recognized him at once and, taking his
hand, led him apart from the throng, inquired the cause of all the trouble,
and learned what had occurred. He then commanded all the rabble still
around—and very uproarious and full of threatenings they were—to come

along with him, and they came to the house of the young man who had committed the deed. There, before the door, was a slave boy so young that he
was not restrained from telling the whole story by fear of harming his master. For he had followed his master to the market place. Alypius recognized
him, and whispered to the architect, who showed the boy the hatchet and
asked whose it was. "Ours," he answered directly. And, being further
questioned, he disclosed the whole affair. Thus the guilt was shifted to that
household and the rabble, who had begun to triumph over Alypius, were
shamed. And so he went away home, this man who was to be the future
steward of your word and judge of so many causes in your church—a wiser
and more experienced man.

[6.10.16] I found him at Rome, and he bound himself to me with the
strongest possible ties, and he went with me to Milan, in order that he
might not be separated from me, and also so that he might obtain some
law practice, for which he had qualified with a view to pleasing his parents more than himself. He had already sat three times as assessor, showing an integrity that seemed strange to many others, though he thought
them strange who could prefer gold to integrity. His character had also
been tested, not only by the bait of covetousness, but by the spur of fear.
At Rome he was assessor to the secretary of the Italian Treasury. There was
at that time a very powerful senator to whose favors many were indebted,
and of whom many stood in fear. In his usual highhanded way he demanded to have a favor granted him that was forbidden by the laws. This
Alypius resisted. A bribe was promised, but he scorned it with all his heart.
Threats were employed, but he trampled them underfoot—so that all men
marveled at so rare a spirit, which neither coveted the friendship nor feared
the enmity of a man at once so powerful and so widely known for the
countless ways he had of helping his friends and doing harm to his enemies.
Even the official whose counselor Alypius was—although he was unwilling
that the favor should be granted—would not openly refuse the request, but
passed the responsibility on to Alypius, alleging that he would not permit
him to give his assent. And the truth was that even if the judge had agreed,
Alypius would have simply left the court.

There was one matter, however, which appealed to his love of learning, in which he was very nearly led astray. He found out that he might
have books copied for himself at praetorian rates. But his sense of justice
prevailed, and he changed his mind for the better, thinking that the rule
that forbade him was still more profitable than the privilege that his office would have allowed him. These are little things, but "he that is faithful in a little matter is faithful also in a great one." Nor can that possibly

be void which was uttered by the mouth of your truth: "If, therefore, you have not been faithful in the unrighteous mammon, who will commit to your trust the true riches? And if you have not been faithful in that which is another man's, who shall give you that which is your own?"* Such a man was Alypius, who clung to me at that time and who wavered in his purpose, just as I did, as to what course of life to follow.

[6.10.17] Nebridius also had come to Milan for no other reason than that he might live with me in a most ardent search after truth and wisdom. He had left his native place near Carthage—and Carthage itself, where he usually lived—leaving behind his fine family estate, his house, and his mother, who would not follow him. Like me, he sighed; like me, he wavered; an ardent seeker after the true life and a most acute analyst of the most abstruse questions. So there were three begging mouths, sighing out their wants one to the other, and looking to you to "give them meat in due season."† And in all the vexations with which your mercy followed our worldly pursuits, we sought for the reason why we suffered so—and all was darkness. We turned away groaning and exclaiming, "How long shall these things be?" And this we often asked, yet for all our asking we did not relinquish them; for as yet we had not discovered anything certain which, when we gave those others up, we might grasp in their stead.

[6.11.18] And I especially puzzled and wondered when I remembered how long a time had passed since my nineteenth year, in which I had first fallen in love with wisdom and had determined as soon as I could find her to abandon the empty hopes and mad delusions of vain desires. I was now getting close to thirty, still stuck fast in the same mire, still greedy of enjoying present goods which fly away and distract me; and I was still saying, "Tomorrow I shall discover it; suddenly it will become plain, and I shall see it; Faustus will come and explain everything. You mighty Academics, is there no certainty that man can grasp for the guidance of his life? No, let us search the more diligently, and let us not despair. See, the things in the church's books that appeared so absurd to us before do not appear so now, and may be otherwise and honestly interpreted. I will set my feet upon that step where, as a child, my parents placed me, until the clear truth is discovered. But where and when shall it be sought? Ambrose has no leisure—we have no leisure to read. Where are we to find the books? How or where could I get hold of them? From whom could I borrow

---

* Luke 16:10–12.

† Psalms 145:15.

them? Let me set a schedule for my days and set apart certain hours for the health of the soul. A great hope has risen up in us, because the catholic faith does not teach what we thought it did, and vainly accused it of. Its teachers hold it as an abomination to believe that god is limited by the form of a human body. And do I doubt that I should knock in order for the rest also to be opened to me? My pupils take up the morning hours; what am I doing with the rest of the day? Why not do this? But, then, when am I to visit my influential friends, whose favors I need? When am I to prepare the orations that I sell to the class? When would I get some recreation and relax my mind from the strain of work?

[6.11.19] "Perish everything and let us dismiss these idle triflings. Let me devote myself solely to the search for truth. This life is unhappy, death uncertain. If it comes upon me suddenly, in what state shall I go hence and where shall I learn what here I have neglected? Should I not indeed suffer the punishment of my negligence here? But suppose death cuts off and finishes all care and feeling. This too is a question that calls for inquiry. God forbid that it should be so. It is not without reason, it is not in vain, that the stately authority of the Christian faith has spread over the entire world, and god would never have done such great things for us if the life of the soul perished with the death of the body. Why, therefore, do I delay in abandoning my hopes of this world and giving myself wholly to seek after god and the blessed life? But wait a moment. This life also is pleasant, and it has a sweetness of its own, not at all negligible. We must not abandon it lightly, for it would be shameful to lapse back into it again. See now, it is important to gain some post of honor. And what more should I desire? I have crowds of influential friends, if nothing else; and, if I push my claims, a governorship may be offered me, and a wife with some money, so that she would not be an added expense. This would be the height of my desire. Many men, who are great and worthy of imitation, have combined the pursuit of wisdom with married life."

[6.11.20] While I talked about these things, and the winds of opinions veered about and tossed my heart hither and thither, time was slipping away. I delayed my conversion to the lord; I postponed from day to day the life in you, but I could not postpone the daily death in myself. I was enamored of a happy life, but I still feared to seek it in its own abode, and so I fled from it while I sought it. I thought I should be miserable if I were deprived of the embraces of a woman, and I never gave a thought to the medicine that your mercy has provided for the healing of that infirmity, for I had never tried it. As for continence, I imagined that it depended on one's own strength, though I found no such strength in

myself, for in my folly I knew not what is written, "None can be continent unless you do grant it."* Certainly you would have given it, if I had
besieged your ears with heartfelt groaning, and if I had cast my care
upon you with firm faith.

[6.12.21] Actually, it was Alypius who prevented me from marrying,
urging that if I did so it would not be possible for us to live together and
to have as much undistracted leisure in the love of wisdom as we had
long desired. For he himself was so chaste that it was wonderful, all the
more because in his early youth he had entered upon the path of promis-
cuity, but had not continued in it. Instead, feeling sorrow and disgust at
it, he had lived from that time down to the present most continently. I
quoted against him the examples of men who had been married and still
lovers of wisdom, who had pleased god and had been loyal and affec-
tionate to their friends. I fell far short of them in greatness of soul, and,
enthralled with the disease of my carnality and its deadly sweetness, I
dragged my chain along, fearing to be loosed of it. Thus I rejected the
words of him who counseled me wisely, as if the hand that would have
loosed the chain only hurt my wound. Moreover, the serpent spoke to
Alypius himself by me, weaving and lying in his path, by my tongue to
catch him with pleasant snares in which his honorable and free feet
might be entangled.

[6.12.22] For he wondered that I, for whom he had such a great esteem, should be stuck so fast in the gluepot of pleasure as to maintain,
whenever we discussed the subject, that I could not possibly live a celibate life. And when I urged in my defense against his accusing questions
that the hasty and stolen delight, which he had tasted and now hardly
remembered, and therefore too easily disparaged, was not to be compared with a settled acquaintance with it; and that, if to this stable acquaintance were added the honorable name of marriage, he would not
then be astonished at my inability to give it up—when I spoke thus, then
he also began to wish to be married, not because he was overcome by
the lust for such pleasures, but out of curiosity. For, he said, he longed
to know what that could be without which my life, which he thought was
so happy, seemed to me to be no life at all, but a punishment. For he
who wore no chain was amazed at my slavery, and his amazement
awoke the desire for experience, and from that he would have gone on
to the experiment itself, and then perhaps he would have fallen into the

---

* Wisdom of Solomon 8:21.

very slavery that amazed him in me, since he was ready to enter into a pact with death, for "he that loves danger shall fall into it."*

Now, the question of conjugal honor in the ordering of a good married life and the bringing up of children was of only slight interest to us. What afflicted me most and what had made me already a slave to it was the habit of satisfying an insatiable lust; but Alypius was about to be enslaved by a merely curious wonder. This is the state we were in until you, most high, who never abandon our lowliness, took pity on our misery and came to our rescue in wonderful and secret ways.

[6.13.23] Active efforts were made to get me a wife. I wooed; I was engaged; and my mother took the greatest pains in the matter. For her hope was that, when I was once married, I might be washed clean in health-giving baptism for which I was being daily prepared, as she joyfully saw, taking note that her desires and promises were being fulfilled in my faith. Yet, when, at my request and on her own impulse, she called upon you daily with strong, heartfelt cries, that you would, by a vision, disclose to her something about my future marriage, you would not. She did, indeed, see certain vain and fantastic things, such as are conjured up by the strong preoccupation of the human spirit, and these she supposed had some reference to me. And she told me about them, but not with the confidence she usually had when you had shown her anything. For she always said that she could distinguish, by a certain feeling impossible to describe, between your revelations and the dreams of her own soul. Yet the matter was pressed forward, and proposals were made for a girl who was as yet some two years too young to marry. And because she pleased me, I agreed to wait for her.

[6.14.24] Many in my band of friends, consulting about and abhorring the turbulent vexations of human life, had often considered and were now almost determined to undertake a peaceful life, away from the crowds. This we thought could be obtained by bringing together what we severally owned and making of it a common household, so that in the sincerity of our friendship nothing should belong more to one than to the other; but all were to have one purse and the whole was to belong to each and to all. We thought that this group might consist of ten persons, some of whom were very rich—especially Romanianus, my fellow townsman, an intimate friend from childhood days.[8] He had been brought up to the court on grave business matters and he was the most earnest of us

---

* Ecclesiasticus 3:27.

all about the project and his voice was of great weight in commending it because his estate was far more ample than that of the others. We had resolved, also, that each year two of us should be managers and provide all that was necessary, while the rest were left undisturbed. But when we began to reflect whether this would be permitted by our wives, which some of us had already and others hoped to have, the whole plan, so excellently framed, collapsed in our hands and was utterly wrecked and cast aside. From this we fell again into sighs and groans, and our steps followed the broad and beaten ways of the world; for many thoughts were in our hearts, but "your counsel stands fast forever."* In your counsel you mocked ours, and prepared your own plan, for it was your purpose "to give us meat in due season, to open your hand, and to fill our souls with blessing."†

[6.15.25] Meanwhile my sins were being multiplied. The woman I was accustomed to sleeping with was torn from my side as an impediment to my marriage, and my heart which clung to her was cut and wounded till it bled. And she went back to Africa, vowing to you never to know any other man and leaving with me my natural son by her. But I, unhappy as I was, and weaker than a woman, could not bear the delay of the two years that should elapse before I could obtain the bride I sought. And so, since I was not a lover of wedlock so much as a slave of lust, I got hold of another woman — not as a wife, of course — so that, in bondage to a lasting habit, the disease of my soul might be nursed up and kept in its vigor or even increased until it reached the realm of matrimony. Nor indeed was the wound healed that had been caused by cutting away my former mistress; only it ceased to burn and throb, and began to fester, and was more dangerous because it was less painful.

[6.16.26] Yours be the praise; to you be the glory, fountain of mercies. I became more wretched and you came nearer. Your right hand was ever ready to pluck me out of the mire and to cleanse me, but I did not know it. Nor did anything call me back from a still deeper plunge into carnal pleasure except the fear of death and of your future judgment, which, amid all the waverings of my opinions, never faded from my breast. And I discussed with my friends, Alypius and Nebridius, the nature of good and evil, maintaining that, in my judgment, Epicurus would have carried off the palm if I had not believed what Epicurus would not believe: that

---

* Psalms 33:11.
† Psalms 145:15–16.

after death there remains a life for the soul, and places of recompense. And I demanded of them: "Suppose we are immortal and live in the enjoyment of perpetual bodily pleasure, and that without any fear of losing it—why, then, should we not be happy, or why should we search for anything else?" I did not know that this was in fact the root of my misery: that I was so fallen and blinded that I could not discern the light of virtue and of beauty which must be embraced for its own sake, which the eye of flesh cannot see, and only the inner vision can. Nor did I, wretch that I was, consider the reason why I found delight in discussing these very perplexities, shameful as they were, with my friends. For I could not be happy without friends, even according to the notions of happiness I had then, and no matter how rich the store of my carnal pleasures might be. Yet I loved my friends for their own sakes, and felt that they in turn loved me for my own sake.

Such crooked ways! Unhappy the audacious soul which hoped that by abandoning you it would find some better thing! It tossed and turned, upon back and side and belly—but the bed is hard, and you alone are rest. And here you are, to deliver us from our wretched wanderings and set us in your way, and you comfort us and say, "Run, I will carry you and I will lead you home, and there I will carry you."*

---

* Isaiah 46:4.

BOOK 7

[7.1.1] Dead now was that evil and shameful youth of mine, and I was passing into full adulthood. As I increased in years, the worse was my vanity. For I could not conceive of any substance but the sort I could see with my own eyes. I no longer thought of you, god, by the analogy of a human body. Ever since I inclined my ear to philosophy I had avoided this error—and the truth on this point I rejoiced to find in the faith of our spiritual mother, your catholic church. Yet I could not see how else to conceive you. And I, a man—and such a man!—sought to conceive you, the sovereign and only true god. In my inmost heart, I believed that you are incorruptible and inviolable and unchangeable, because—though I knew not how or why—I could still see plainly and without doubt that the corruptible is inferior to the incorruptible, the inviolable obviously superior to its opposite, and the unchangeable better than the changeable. My heart cried out violently against all fantasms, and with this one clear certainty I endeavored to brush away the swarm of unclean flies that swarmed around the eyes of my mind. But they were scarcely scattered before they gathered again, buzzed against my face, and beclouded my vision. I no longer thought of god in the analogy of a human body, yet I was constrained to conceive you to be some kind of body in space, either infused into the world, or infinitely diffused beyond the world—and this was the incorruptible, inviolable, unchangeable substance, which I thought was better than the corruptible, the violable, and the changeable. For whatever I conceived to be deprived of the dimensions of space appeared to me to be nothing, absolutely nothing; not even a void, for if a body is taken out of space, or if space is emptied of all its contents (of earth, water, air, or heaven), yet it remains an empty space—a spacious nothing, as it were.

[7.1.2] Being thus gross-hearted and not clear even to myself, I then held that whatever had neither length nor breadth nor density nor solidity, and did not or could not receive such dimensions, was absolutely nothing. For at that time my mind dwelt only with ideas, which resembled the forms with which my eyes are still familiar, nor could I see that the act of thought, by which I formed those ideas, was itself immaterial, and yet it could not have formed them if it were not itself a measurable entity. So also I thought about you, life of my life, as stretched out through infinite space, interpenetrating the whole mass of the world, reaching out beyond in all directions, to immensity without end; so that the earth should have you, the heaven have you, all things have you, and all of them be limited in you, while you are placed nowhere at all. As the body of the air above the earth does not bar the passage of the light of the sun, so that the light penetrates it, not by bursting nor dividing, but filling it entirely, so I imagined that the body of heaven and air and sea, and even of the earth, was all open to you and, in all its greatest parts as well as the smallest, was ready to receive your presence by a secret inspiration which, from within or without all, orders all things you have created. This was my conjecture, because I was unable to think of anything else; yet it was untrue. For in this way a greater part of the earth would contain a greater part of you; a smaller part, a smaller fraction of you. All things would be full of you in such a sense that there would be more of you in an elephant than in a sparrow, because one is larger than the other and fills a larger space. And this would make the portions of yourself present in the several portions of the world in fragments, great to the great, small to the small. But you are not such a one. But as yet you had not enlightened my darkness.

[7.2.3] But it was not sufficient for me, lord, to be able to oppose those deceived deceivers and those dumb orators—dumb because your word did not sound forth from them—to oppose them with the answer which, in the old Carthaginian days, Nebridius used to propound, shaking all of us who heard it: "What could this imaginary people of darkness, which the Manicheans usually set up as an army opposed to you, have done to you if you had declined the combat?" If they replied that it could have hurt you, they would then have made you violable and corruptible. If, on the other hand, the dark could have done you no harm, then there was no cause for any battle at all; there was less cause for a battle in which a part of you, one of your members, a child of your own substance, should be mixed up with opposing powers, not of your creation; and should be corrupted and deteriorated and changed by them from happiness into misery, so that it could not be delivered and cleansed without your help. This offspring of your substance was supposed to be the human soul to which your word—free, pure, and entire—could bring help when it was being enslaved, contaminated, and corrupted. But on their hypothesis that word was itself corruptible because it is one and the same substance as the soul. And therefore if they admitted that your nature—whatsoever you are—is incorruptible, then all these assertions of theirs are false and should be rejected with horror. But if your substance is corruptible, then this is self-evidently false and should be abhorred at first utterance. This line of argument, then, was enough against those deceivers who ought to be cast forth from a surfeited stomach—for out of this dilemma they could find no way of escape without dreadful sacrilege of mind and tongue, when they think and speak such things about you.

[7.3.4] But as yet, although I said and was firmly persuaded that you our lord, the true god, who made not only our souls but our bodies as well—and not only our souls and bodies but all creatures and all things— were free from stain and alteration and in no way mutable, yet I could not readily and clearly understand what was the cause of evil. Whatever it was, I realized that the question must be so analyzed as not to constrain me by any answer to believe that the immutable god was mutable, lest I should myself become the thing that I was seeking out. And so I pursued the search with a quiet mind, now in a confident feeling that what had been said by the Manicheans—and I shrank from them with my whole heart—could not be true. I now realized that when they asked what was the origin of evil their answer was dictated by a wicked pride, which would rather affirm that your nature is capable of suffering evil than that their own nature is capable of doing it.

[7.3.5] And I directed my attention to understand what I now was told, that free will is the cause of our doing evil and that your just judgment is the cause of our having to suffer from its consequences. But I could not see this clearly. So then, trying to draw the eye of my mind up out of that pit, I was plunged back into it again, and trying often was just as often plunged back down. But one thing lifted me up toward your light: it was that I had come to know that I had a will as certainly as I knew that I had life. When, therefore, I willed or was unwilling to do something, I was utterly certain that it was none but myself who willed or was unwilling—and immediately I realized that there was the cause of my sin. I could see that what I did against my will I suffered rather than did; and I did not regard such actions as faults, but rather as punishments in which I might quickly confess that I was not unjustly punished, since I believed you to be most just. But then I would say: Who was it that put this in me, and implanted in me the root of bitterness, in spite of the fact that I was altogether the handiwork of my most sweet god? If the devil is to blame, who made the devil himself? And if he was a good angel who by his own wicked will became the devil, how did there happen to be in him that wicked will by which he became a devil, since a good creator made him wholly a good angel?[1] By these reflections was I again cast down and stultified. Yet I was not plunged into that hell of error—where no man confesses to you—where I thought that you suffered evil, rather than that human beings do it.

[7.4.6] For in my struggle to solve the rest of my difficulties, I now assumed henceforth as settled truth that the incorruptible must be superior to the corruptible, and I acknowledged that you, whatever you are, are incorruptible. For there never yet was, nor will be, a soul able to conceive of anything better than you, who are the highest and best good. And since most truly and certainly the incorruptible is to be placed above the corruptible—as I now admit it—it followed that I could rise in my thoughts to something better than my god, if you were not incorruptible. When, therefore, I saw that the incorruptible was to be preferred to the corruptible, I saw then where I ought to seek you, and where I should look for the source of evil: that is, the corruption by which your substance can in no way be profaned. For it is obvious that corruption in no way injures our god, by no inclination, by no necessity, by no unforeseen chance—because he is our god, and what he wills is good, and he himself is that good. But to be corrupted is not good. Nor are you compelled to do anything against your will, since your will is not greater than your power. But it would have to be greater if you yourself were greater than yourself—for the will and power of god are god himself. And what can take you by surprise, since you know all, and there is no sort of nature but you know it? And what more should we say about why that substance which god is cannot be corrupted, because if this were so it could not be god?

[7.5.7] And I kept seeking for an answer to the question: Where does evil come from? And I sought it in an evil way, and I did not see the evil in my own search. I marshaled before the sight of my spirit all creation: all that we see of earth and sea and air and stars and trees and animals; and all that we do not see, the firmament of the sky above and all the angels and all spiritual things, for my imagination arranged these also, as if they were bodies, in this place or that. And I pictured to myself your creation as one vast mass, composed of various kinds of bodies—some of which were actually bodies, and some of which were the bodies I imagined spirits to be like. I pictured this mass as vast—of course not in its full dimensions, for these I could not know—but as large as I could possibly think, still only finite on every side. But you, lord, I imagined as environing the mass on every side and penetrating it, still infinite in every direction—as if there were a sea everywhere, and everywhere through measureless space nothing but an infinite sea; and it contained within itself some sort of sponge, huge but still finite, so that the sponge would in all its parts be filled from the immeasurable sea.

Thus I conceived your creation itself to be finite, and filled by you, the infinite. And I said: See, there is god and what god has created! God is good and most mightily and incomparably better than all his works. Yet he who is good has created them good; see how he encircles and fills them. Where, then, is evil, and whence does it come and how has it crept in? What is its root and what its seed? Has it no being at all? Why, then, do we fear and shun what has no being? Or if we fear it needlessly, then surely that fear is evil by which the heart is unnecessarily stabbed and tortured—and indeed a greater evil since we have nothing real to fear, and yet do fear. Therefore, either that is evil which we fear, or the act of fearing is in itself evil. But, then, whence does it come, since god who is good has made all these things good? Indeed, he is the greatest and chief good, and has created these lesser goods; but both creator and created are all good. Whence, then, is evil? Was there some evil matter out of which he made and formed and ordered things, of which he left some behind, that he did not convert into good? But why should this be? Was he powerless to change the whole lump so that no evil would remain in it, if he is omnipotent? Finally, why would he make anything at all out of such stuff? Why did he not, rather, annihilate it by his same almighty power? Could evil exist contrary to his will? And if it existed from eternity, why did he permit it to exist for unmeasured intervals of time in the past, and why, then, was he pleased to make something out of it after so long a time? Or, if he wished now all of a sudden to create something, would not an almighty being have chosen to annihilate this evil matter and live by himself—the perfect, true, sovereign, and infinite good? Or, if it were not good that he who was good should not also be the framer and creator of what was good, then why was that evil matter not removed and brought to nothing, so that he might form good matter, out of which he might then create all things? For he would not be omnipotent if he were not able to create something good without being assisted by that matter which had not been created by himself.

Such perplexities I revolved in my wretched breast, overwhelmed with gnawing cares lest I die before I discovered the truth. And still the faith of your Christ, our lord and saviour, as it was taught me by the catholic church, stuck fast in my heart. As yet it was unformed on many points and diverged from the rule of right doctrine, but my mind did not utterly lose it, and every day drank in more and more of it.

[7.6.8] By now I had also repudiated the lying divinations and impious absurdities of the astrologers. Let your mercies, out of the depth of my soul, confess this to you also, my god. For you, you only (for who else is it who calls us back from the death of all errors except the life which does not know how to die and the wisdom which gives light to minds that need it, although it itself has no need of light—by which the whole universe is governed, even to the fluttering leaves of the trees?), you provided someone to deal with that obstinacy of mine, the obstinacy with which I struggled against Vindicianus, a sagacious old man, and Nebridius, that remarkably talented young man, of whom the former declared vehemently and the latter frequently—though with some reservation—that no art existed by which we foresee future things but that human surmises often have the help of chance, and that out of many things foretold some come to pass unawares to the predictors, who light on the truth by making so many guesses. You provided a friend for me, who was not a negligent consulter of the astrologers even though he was not thoroughly skilled in the art either—as I said, one who consulted them out of curiosity. He knew a good deal about it, which, he said, he had heard from his father, and he never realized how far his ideas would help to overthrow my estimation of that art. His name was Firminus[2] and he had received a liberal education and was a cultivated rhetorician.

It so happened that he consulted me, as one very dear to him, as to what I thought about some affairs of his in which his worldly hopes had risen, viewed in the light of his so-called horoscope. Although I had now begun to lean in this matter toward Nebridius' opinion, I did not quite decline to speculate about the matter or to tell him what thoughts still came into my irresolute mind, although I did add that I was almost persuaded now that these were but empty and ridiculous follies. He then told me that his father had been very much interested in such books, and that he had a friend who was as much interested in them as he was himself. They, in combined study and consultation, fanned the flame of their affection for this folly, going so far as to observe the moment when the dumb animals which belonged to their household gave birth to young, and then observed the position of the heavens with regard to them, so as to gather fresh evidence for this so-called art. Moreover, Firminus reported that his father had told him that, at the same time his mother was about to give birth to him, a female slave of a friend of his father's was also pregnant. This could not be hidden from her master, who kept records with the most diligent exactness of the birth dates even of his dogs. And so it happened that—under the most careful observations, one for his wife and the other for his servant, with exact calculations of the days, hours, and minutes—both women were delivered at the same moment, so that both were compelled to cast the selfsame horoscope, down to the minute: the one for his son, the other for his young slave. For as soon as the women began to be in labor, they each sent word to the other as to what was happening in their respective houses and had messengers ready to dispatch to one another as soon as they had information of the actual birth—and each, of course, knew instantly the exact time. It turned out, he said, that the messengers from the respective houses met one another at a point equidistant from either house, so that neither of them could discern any difference either in the position of the stars or any other of the most minute points. And yet Firminus, born in a high estate in his parents' house, ran his course through the prosperous paths of this world, was increased in wealth, and elevated to honors. At the same time, the slave, the yoke of his condition being still unrelaxed, continued to serve his masters as Firminus, who knew him, was able to report.

[7.6.9] Upon hearing and believing these things related by so reliable a person all my resistance melted away. First, I endeavored to reclaim Firminus himself from his superstition by telling him that after inspecting his horoscope, I ought, if I could foretell truly, to have seen in it parents eminent among their neighbors, a noble family in its own city, a good birth, a proper education, and liberal learning. But if that servant had consulted me with the same horoscope, since he had the same one, I ought again to tell him likewise truly that I saw in it the lowliness of his origin, the abjectness of his condition, and everything else different and contrary to the former prediction. If, then, by casting up the same horoscopes I should, in order to speak the truth, make contrary analyses, or else speak falsely if I made identical readings, then surely it followed that whatever was truly foretold by the analysis of the horoscopes was not by art, but by chance. And whatever was said falsely was not from incompetence in the art, but from the error of chance.

[7.6.10] An opening being thus made in my darkness, I began to consider other implications involved here. Suppose that one of the fools— who followed such an occupation and whom I longed to assail, and to reduce to confusion—should urge against me that Firminus had given me false information, or that his father had informed him falsely. I then turned my thoughts to those that are born twins, who generally come out of the womb so near the one to the other that the short interval between them—whatever importance they may ascribe to it in the nature of things—cannot be noted by human observation or expressed in those tables which the astrologer uses to examine when he undertakes to pronounce the truth. But such pronouncements cannot be true. For looking into the same horoscopes, he must have foretold the same future for Esau and Jacob,* whereas the same future did not turn out for them. He must therefore speak falsely. If he is to speak truly, then he must read contrary predictions into the same horoscopes. But this would mean that it was not by art, but by chance, that he would speak truly.

For you, lord, most righteous ruler of the universe, work by a secret impulse—whether those who inquire or those inquired of know it or not—so that the inquirer may hear what, according to the secret merit of his soul, he ought to hear from the deeps of your righteous judgment. Therefore let no-one say to you, "What is this?" or, "Why is that?" Let no-one speak thus, for the inquirer is only human.

[7.7.11] By now, my helper, you had freed me from those fetters. But still I inquired, Whence is evil?—and found no answer. But you did not allow me to be carried away from the faith by these fluctuations of thought. I still believed both that you do exist and that your substance is immutable, and that you care for and will judge all human beings, and that in Christ, your son our lord, and the holy scriptures, which the authority of your catholic church pressed on me, you have planned the way of man's salvation to that life which is to come after this death. With these convictions safe and immovably settled in my mind, I eagerly inquired, Whence is evil? What torments did my travailing heart then endure! What sighs, my god! Yet even then your ears were open and I knew it not, and when in stillness I sought earnestly, those silent contritions of my soul were loud cries to your mercy. No man knew, but you knew what I endured. How little of it could I express in words to the ears of my dearest friends! How could the whole tumult of my soul, for which neither time nor speech was sufficient, come to them? Yet the whole of it went into your ears, all of which I bellowed out in the anguish of my heart. My desire was before you, and the light of my eyes was not with me; for it was within and I was without. Nor was that light in any place; but I still kept thinking only of things that are contained in a place, and could find among them no place to rest in. They did not receive me in such a way that I could say, "It is sufficient; it is well." Nor did they allow me to turn back to where it might be well enough with me. For I was higher than

---

* Genesis 25 ff.

they, though lower than you. You are my true joy if I depend upon you, and you had subjected to me what you created lower than I. And this was the true mean and middle way of salvation for me, to continue in your image and by serving you have dominion over the body. But when I lifted myself proudly against you, and "ran against the lord, even against his neck, with the thick bosses of my buckler,"* even the lower things were placed above me and pressed down on me, so that there was no respite or breathing space. They thrust on my sight on every side, in crowds and masses, and when I tried to think, the images of bodies obtruded themselves into my way back to you, as if they would say to me, "Where are you going, unworthy and unclean one?" And all these had sprung out of my wound, for you had humbled the haughty as one that is wounded. By my swelling pride I was separated from you, and my bloated cheeks blinded my eyes.

[7.8.12] But you, lord, are forever the same, yet you are not forever angry with us, for you have compassion on our dust and ashes. It was pleasing in your sight to reform my deformity, and by inward stings you disturbed me so that I was impatient until you were made clear to my inward sight. By the secret hand of your healing my swelling was lessened, the disordered and darkened eyesight of my mind was from day to day made whole by the stinging salve of wholesome grief.

[7.9.13] And first of all, willing to show me how you "resist the proud, but give grace to the humble,"† and how mercifully you have made known to men the way of humility in that your word "was made flesh and dwelt among men," you procured for me, through one inflated with the most monstrous pride, certain books of the Platonists, translated from Greek into Latin.[3] And there I found, not indeed in the same words, but to the very same effect, enforced by many and various reasons that "In the beginning was the word, and the word was with god, and the word was god. The same was in the beginning with god. All things were made by him; and without him was not anything made that was made." That which was made by him is "life, and the life was the light of men. And the light shined in darkness; and the darkness comprehended it not." Furthermore, I read that the soul of man, though it "bears witness to the light," yet itself "is not the light; but the word of god, being god, is that true light that lights every man who comes into the world." And further, that "he

---

* Job 15:26.
† James 4:6.

was in the world, and the world was made by him, and the world knew him not." But that "he came to his own, and his own received him not. And as many as received him, to them gave he power to become the sons of god, even to them that believed on his name"*—this I did not find there.

[7.9.14] Similarly, I read there that god the word was born "not of flesh nor of blood, nor of the will of man, nor the will of the flesh, but of god." But, that "the word was made flesh, and dwelt among us"†—I found this nowhere there. And I discovered in those books, expressed in many and various ways, that "the son was in the form of god and thought it not robbery to be equal in god,"‡ for he was naturally of the same substance. But, that "he emptied himself and took upon himself the form of a servant, and was made in the likeness of men: and being found in fashion as a man, he humbled himself, and became obedient to death, even the death of the cross. Wherefore god also has highly exalted him" from the dead, "and given him a name above every name; that at the name of Jesus every knee should bow, of things in heaven, and things in earth, and things under the earth; and that every tongue should confess that Jesus Christ is lord, to the glory of god the father"§—this those books have not. I read further in them that before all times and beyond all times, your only son remains unchangeably co-eternal with you, and that of his fullness all souls receive so that they may be blessed, and that by participation in that wisdom which abides in them, they are renewed so that they may be wise. But, that "in due time, Christ died for the ungodly" and that you "spared not your only son, but delivered him up for us all"‖—this is not there. "For you have hid these things from the wise and prudent, and have revealed them to babes," so that they "that labor and are heavy laden" might "come to him and he might refresh them" because he is "meek and lowly in heart."** "The meek will he guide in judgment; and the meek will he teach his way; beholding our lowliness and our trouble and forgiving all

---

* John 1:1–12.

† John 1:13–14.

‡ Philippians 2:6.

§ Philippians 2:7–11.

‖ Romans 5:6, 8:32.

Luke 10:21.

** Matthew 11:28–29.

our sins."* But those who strut in the high boots of what they deem to
be superior knowledge will not hear him who says, "Learn of me, for I
am meek and lowly in heart, and you shall find rest for your souls."†
Thus, though they know god, yet they do not glorify him as god, nor are
they thankful. Therefore, they "become vain in their imaginations; their
foolish heart is darkened, and professing themselves to be wise they become fools."‡

[7.9.15] And, moreover, I also read there how "they changed the glory
of your incorruptible nature into idols and various images—into an image
made like corruptible man and to birds and four-footed beasts, and creeping things":§ namely, into that Egyptian food for which Esau lost his
birthright;‖ so that your first-born people worshiped the head of a four-
footed beast instead of you, turning back in their hearts toward Egypt and
prostrating your image (their own soul) before the image of an ox that eats
grass.# These things I found there, but I fed not on them. For it pleased
you, lord, to take away the reproach of his minority from Jacob, so that the
elder should serve the younger and you might call the gentiles, and I had
sought strenuously after that gold which you did allow your people to take
from Egypt,** since wherever it was it was yours.[4] And you said to the
Athenians by the mouth of your apostle that in you "we live and move and
have our being," as one of their own poets had said.†† And truly these
books came from there. But I did not set my mind on the idols of Egypt
which they fashioned of gold, "changing the truth of god into a lie and
worshiping and serving the creature more than the creator."‡‡

[7.10.16] And being admonished by these books to return into myself,
I entered into my inward soul, guided by you. This I could do because you
were my helper. And I entered, and with the eye of my soul—such as it
was—saw above the same eye of my soul and above my mind the immutable light. It was not the common light, which all flesh can see; nor was
it simply a greater one of the same sort, as if the light of day were to grow

---

* Psalms 25:9, 18.
† Matthew 11:29.
‡ Romans 1:21–22.
§ Romans 1:23.
‖ Genesis 25:33 ff.
Exodus 32:1–6.
** Exodus 3:22, 11:2.
†† Acts 17:28.
‡‡ Romans 1:25.

brighter and brighter, and flood all space. It was not like that light, but different, very different from all earthly light whatever. Nor was it above my mind in the same way as oil is above water, or heaven above earth, but it was higher, because it made me, and I was below it, because I was made by it. He who knows the truth knows that light, and he who knows it knows eternity. Love knows it. Eternal truth and true love and beloved eternity! You are my god, to whom I sigh both night and day. When I first knew you, you lifted me up, so that I might see that there was something to be seen, though I was not yet fit to see it. And you beat back the weakness of my sight, shining forth upon me your dazzling beams of light, and I trembled with love and fear. I realized that I was far away from you in the land of unlikeness, as if I heard your voice from on high: "I am the food of strong men; grow and you shall feed on me; nor shall you change me, like the food of your flesh into yourself, but you shall be changed into my likeness." And I understood that "you chasten man for his iniquity, and make my soul to be eaten away as though by a spider."* And I said, "Is truth, therefore, nothing, because it is not diffused through space—neither finite nor infinite?" And you cried to me from afar, "I am that I am."† And I heard this, as things are heard in the heart, and there was no room for doubt. I should have more readily doubted that I am alive than that the truth exists—the truth which is "clearly seen, being understood by the things that are made."‡

[7.11.17] And I viewed all the other things that are beneath you, and I realized that they are neither wholly real nor wholly unreal. They are real in so far as they come from you; but they are unreal in so far as they are not what you are. For that is truly real which remains immutable. It is good, then, for me to hold fast to god, for if I do not remain in him, neither shall I abide in myself; but he, remaining in himself, renews all things. And you are the lord my god, since you stand in no need of my goodness.

[7.12.18] And it was made clear to me that all things are good even if they are corrupted. They could not be corrupted if they were supremely good; but unless they were good they could not be corrupted. If they were supremely good, they would be incorruptible; if they were not good at all, there would be nothing in them to be corrupted. For corruption harms; but unless it could diminish goodness, it could not harm. Either, then, corruption does not harm—which cannot be—or, as is certain, all that is corrupted is thereby deprived of good. But if they are deprived of all

---

* Psalms 39:11.

† Exodus 3:14.

‡ Romans 1:20.

good, they will cease to be. For if they are at all and cannot be at all corrupted, they will become better, because they will remain incorruptible. Now what can be more monstrous than to maintain that by losing all good they have become better? If, then, they are deprived of all good, they will cease to exist. So long as they are, therefore, they are good. Therefore, whatsoever is, is good. Evil, then, the origin of which I had been seeking, has no substance at all; for if it were a substance, it would be good. For either it would be an incorruptible substance and so a supreme good, or a corruptible substance, which could not be corrupted unless it were good. I understood, therefore, and it was made clear to me that you made all things good, nor is there any substance at all not made by you. And because all that you made is not equal, each by itself is good, and the sum of all of them is very good, for our god made "all things very good."*

[**7.13.19**] To you there is no such thing as evil, and even in your whole creation taken as a whole, there is not; because there is nothing from beyond it that can burst in and destroy the order which you have appointed for it. But in the parts of creation, some things, because they do not harmonize with others, are considered evil. Yet those same things harmonize with others and are good, and in themselves are good. And all these things which do not harmonize with each other still harmonize with the inferior part of creation which we call the earth, having its own cloudy and windy sky of like nature with itself. Far be it from me, then, to say, "These things should not be." For if I could see nothing but these, I should indeed desire something better—but still I ought to praise you, if only for these created things. For that you are to be praised is shown from the fact that "earth, dragons, and all deeps; fire, and hail, snow and vapors, stormy winds fulfilling your word; mountains, and all hills, fruitful trees, and all cedars; beasts and all cattle; creeping things, and flying fowl; things of the earth, and all people; princes, and all judges of the earth; both young men and maidens, old men and children"† praise your name! But seeing also that in heaven all your angels praise you, god, praise you in the heights, "and all your hosts, sun and moon, all stars and light, the heavens of heavens, and the waters that are above the heavens"‡ praise your name—seeing this, I say, I no longer desire a better world, because my thought ranged over all, and with a sounder judgment I reflected that

---

* Genesis 1:31.

† Psalms 148:7–12.

‡ Psalms 148:1–5.

the things above were better than those below, yet that all creation together was better than the higher things alone.

[7.14.20] There is no health in those who find fault with any part of your
creation; as there was no health in me when I found fault with so many of
your works. And, because my soul dared not be displeased with my god, it
would not allow that the things which displeased me were from you. Hence
it had wandered into the notion of two substances, and could find no rest,
but talked foolishly. And turning from that error, it had then made for itself
a god extended through infinite space; and it thought this was you and set
it up in its heart, and it became once more the temple of its own idol, an
abomination to you. But you soothed my brain, though I was unaware of
it, and closed my eyes lest they should behold vanity; and thus I ceased
from preoccupation with self by a little and my madness was lulled to sleep;
and I awoke in you, and beheld you as the infinite, but not in the way I had
thought—and this vision was not derived from the flesh.

[7.15.21] And I looked around at other things, and I saw that it was to
you that all of them owed their being, and that they were all finite in you;
yet they are in you not as in a space, but because you hold all things in the
hand of your truth, and because all things are true in so far as they are;
and because falsehood is nothing except the existence in thought of what
does not exist in fact. And I saw that all things harmonize, not only in
their places but also in their seasons. And I saw that you, who alone are
eternal, did not begin to work after unnumbered periods of time—because
all ages, both those which are past and those which shall pass, neither go
nor come except through your working and abiding.

[7.16.22] And I saw and found it no marvel that bread which is dis-
tasteful to an unhealthy palate is pleasant to a healthy one; or that the
light, which is painful to sore eyes, is a delight to sound ones. Your righteousness displeases the wicked, and they find even more fault with the
viper and the little worm, which you have created good, fitting in as they
do with the inferior parts of creation. The wicked themselves also fit in
here, and proportionately more so as they become unlike you—but they
harmonize with the higher creation proportionately as they become like
you. And I asked what wickedness was, and I found that it was no substance, but a perversion of the will bent aside from you, god, the supreme
substance, toward these lower things, casting away its inmost treasure and
becoming bloated with external good.

[7.17.23] And I marveled that I now loved you, and no fantasm in your
stead, and yet I was not stable enough to enjoy my god steadily. Instead I
was transported to you by your beauty, and then presently torn away from

you by my own weight, sinking with grief into these lower things. This weight was carnal habit. But your memory dwelt with me, and I never doubted in the least that there was one for me to cleave to; but I was not yet ready to cleave to you firmly. For the body which is corrupted presses down the soul, and the earthly dwelling weighs down the mind, which muses upon many things. My greatest certainty was that "the invisible things of yours from the creation of the world are clearly seen, being understood by the things that are made, even your eternal power and godhead."* For when I inquired how it was that I could appreciate the beauty of bodies, both celestial and terrestrial; and what it was that supported me in making correct judgments about things mutable; and when I concluded, "This ought to be thus; this ought not"—then when I inquired how it was that I could make such judgments (since I did, in fact, make them), I realized that I had found the unchangeable and true eternity of truth above my changeable mind.

And thus by degrees I was led upward from bodies to the soul which perceives them by means of the bodily senses, and from there on to the soul's inward faculty, to which the bodily senses report outward things— and this belongs even to the capacities of the beasts—and thence on up to the reasoning power, to whose judgment is referred the experience received from the bodily sense. And when this power of reason within me also found that it was changeable, it raised itself up to its own intellectual principle, and withdrew its thoughts from experience, abstracting itself from the contradictory throng of fantasms in order to seek for that light in which it was bathed. Then, without any doubting, it cried out that the unchangeable was better than the changeable. From this it follows that the mind somehow knew the unchangeable, for, unless it had known it in some fashion, it could have had no sure ground for preferring it to the changeable. And thus with the flash of a trembling glance, it arrived at that which is. And I saw "your invisible things understood by means of the things that are made."† But I was not able to sustain my gaze. My weakness was dashed back, and I lapsed again into my accustomed ways, carrying along with me nothing but a loving memory of my vision, and an appetite for what I had, as it were, smelled the odor of, but was not yet able to eat.[5]

[7.18.24] I sought, therefore, some way to acquire the strength sufficient to enjoy you; but I did not find it until I embraced that "mediator between god and man, the man Christ Jesus,"‡ "who is over all, god

---

* Romans 1:20.

† Romans 1:20.

‡ 1 Timothy 2:5.

blessed forever,"* who came calling and saying, "I am the way, the truth, and the life,"† and mingling with our fleshly humanity the heavenly food I was unable to receive. For "the word was made flesh"‡ in order that your wisdom, by which you created all things, might become milk for our infancy. And, as yet, I was not humble enough to hold the humble Jesus; nor did I understand what lesson his weakness was meant to teach us. For your word, the eternal truth, far exalted above even the higher parts of your creation, lifts his subjects up toward himself. But in this lower world, he built for himself a humble habitation of our own clay, so that he might pull down from themselves and win over to himself those whom he is to bring subject to him; lowering their pride and heightening their love, to the end that they might go on no farther in self-confidence—but rather should become weak, seeing at their feet the deity made weak by sharing our coats of skin—so that they might cast themselves, exhausted, upon him and be uplifted by his rising.

[7.19.25] But I thought otherwise. I saw in our lord Christ only a man of eminent wisdom to whom no other man could be compared—especially because he was miraculously born of a virgin—sent to set us an example of despising worldly things for the attainment of immortality, and thus exhibiting his divine care for us.[6] It was because of this, I held, that he had merited his great authority as leader. But concerning the mystery contained in "the word was made flesh," I could not even form a notion. From what I learned from what has been handed down to us in the books about him—that he ate, drank, slept, walked, rejoiced in spirit, was sad, and discoursed with his fellows—I realized that his flesh alone was not bound to your word, but also that there was a bond with the human soul and body. Everyone knows this who knows the unchangeableness of your word, and this I knew by now, as far as I was able, and I had no doubts at all about it. For at one time to move the limbs by an act of will, at another time not; at one time to feel some emotion, at another time not; at one time to speak intelligibly through verbal signs, at another, not—these are all properties of a soul and mind subject to change. And if these things were falsely written about him, all the rest would risk the imputation of falsehood, and there would remain in those books no saving faith for the human race.

---

* Romans 9:5.
† John 14:6.
‡ John 1:14.

Therefore, because they were written truthfully, I acknowledged a perfect man to be in Christ—not the body of a man only, nor, in the body, an animal soul without a rational one as well, but a true man. And this man I held to be superior to all others, not only because he was a form of the truth, but also because of the great excellence and perfection of his human nature, due to his participation in wisdom.

Alypius, on the other hand, supposed the catholics to believe that god was so clothed with flesh that besides god and the flesh there was no soul in Christ, and he did not think that a human mind was ascribed to him. And because he was fully persuaded that the actions recorded of him could not have been performed except by a living rational creature, he moved the more slowly toward Christian faith. But when he later learned that this was the error of the Apollinarian heretics, he rejoiced in the catholic faith and accepted it. For myself, I must confess that it was even later that I learned how in the sentence, "the word was made flesh," the catholic truth can be distinguished from the falsehood of Photinus. For the refutation of heretics makes the tenets of your church and sound doctrine to stand out boldly. "For there must also be heresies, so that those who are approved may be made manifest among the weak."*

[7.20.26] By having thus read the books of the Platonists, and having been taught by them to search for the incorporeal truth, I saw how your invisible things are understood through the things that are made. And, even when I was thrown back, I still sensed what it was that the dullness of my soul would not allow me to contemplate. I was assured that you were, and that you were infinite, though not diffused in finite space or infinity; that you truly are, who are ever the same, varying neither in part nor motion; and that all things are from you, as is proved by this sure cause alone: that they exist.

Of all this I was convinced, yet I was too weak to enjoy you. I chattered away as if I were an expert; but if I had not sought your way in Christ our saviour, my knowledge would have turned out to be not instruction but destruction. For now full of what was in fact my punishment, I had begun to desire to seem wise. I did not mourn my ignorance, but rather was puffed up with knowledge. For where was that love which builds upon the foundation of humility, which is Jesus Christ? Or, when would these books teach me this? I now believe that it was your pleasure that I should fall upon these books before I studied your scriptures, in order that it might

---

* 1 Corinthians 11:19.

be impressed on my memory how I was affected by them; and then afterward, when I was subdued by your scriptures and when my wounds were touched by your healing fingers, I might discern and distinguish what a difference there is between presumption and confession—between those who saw where they were to go even if they did not see the way, and the way which leads, not only to the observing, but also the inhabiting of the blessed country. For had I first been molded in your holy scriptures, and if you had grown sweet to me through my familiar use of them, and if then I had afterward fallen on those volumes, they might have pushed me off the solid ground of godliness—or if I had stood firm in that wholesome disposition which I had there acquired, I might have thought that wisdom could be attained by the study of those [Platonist] books alone.

[7.21.27] With great eagerness, then, I fastened upon the venerable writings of your spirit and principally upon the apostle Paul. I had thought that he sometimes contradicted himself and that the text of his teaching did not agree with the testimonies of the Law and the Prophets; but now all these doubts vanished away. And I saw that those pure words had but one face, and I learned to rejoice with trembling. So I began, and I found that whatever truth I had read [in the Platonists] was here combined with the exaltation of your grace. Thus, he who sees must not glory as if he had not received, not only the things that he sees, but the very power of sight—for "what does he have that he has not received?"* By this he is not only exhorted to see, but also to be cleansed, that he may grasp you, who are ever the same; and thus he who cannot see you afar off may yet enter upon the road that leads to reaching, seeing, and possessing you. For although a man may "delight in the law of god after the inward man," what shall he do with that other "law in his members which wars against the law of his mind, and brings him into captivity under the law of sin, which is in his members"?† You are righteous, lord; but we have sinned and committed iniquities, and have done wickedly. Your hand has grown heavy upon us, and we are justly delivered over to that ancient sinner, the lord of death. For he persuaded our wills to become like his will, by which he remained not in your truth. What shall "wretched man" do? "Who shall deliver him from the body of this death,"‡ except your grace through Jesus Christ our lord; whom you have begotten, coeternal with yourself, and created in the beginning of

---

* 1 Corinthians 4:7.

† Romans 7:22–23.

‡ Romans 7:24–25.

your ways—in whom the prince of this world found nothing worthy of death, yet he killed him—and so "the handwriting which was all against us was blotted out"?*

The books of the Platonists tell nothing of this. Their pages do not contain the expression of this kind of godliness—the tears of confession, your sacrifice, a troubled spirit, a broken and a contrite heart,[†] the salvation of your people, the espoused city,[‡] the earnest of the holy spirit,[§] the cup of our redemption. In them, no man sings: "Shall not my soul be subject to god, for from him comes my salvation? He is my god and my salvation, my defender; I shall no more be moved."[||] In them, no one hears him calling, "Come to me all you who labor."[#] They scorn to learn of him because he is meek and lowly of heart; for "you have hidden those things from the wise and prudent, and hast revealed them to babes."[**] For it is one thing to see the land of peace from a wooded mountaintop and fail to find the way thither—to attempt impassable ways in vain, opposed and waylaid by fugitives and deserters under their captain, the "lion" and "dragon";[††] but it is quite another thing to keep to the highway that leads thither, guarded by the hosts of the heavenly emperor, on which there are no deserters from the heavenly army to rob the passers-by, for they shun it as a torment. These thoughts sank wondrously into my heart, when I read that "least of your apostles"[‡‡] and when I had considered all your works and trembled.

---

* Colossians 2:14.
† Psalms 51:17.
‡ Revelation 21:1–5.
§ 2 Corinthians 5:5.
|| Psalms 62:1–2.
Matthew 11:28.
** Matthew 11:25.
†† Psalms 91:13.
‡‡ 1 Corinthians 15:9.

BOOK 8

[8.1.1] My god, let me remember with gratitude and confess to you your mercies toward me. Let my bones be bathed in your love, and let them say: "Lord, who is like you? You have broken my bonds asunder, I will offer to you the sacrifice of thanksgiving."* And how you broke them I will declare, and all who worship you shall say, when they hear these things: "Blessed be the lord in heaven and earth, great and wonderful is his name."† Your words had stuck fast in my breast, and I was hedged round about by you on every side. Of your eternal life I was now certain, although I had seen it "through a glass darkly."‡ And I had been relieved of all doubt that there is an incorruptible substance and that it is the source of every other substance. Nor did I any longer crave greater certainty about you, but rather greater steadfastness in you. But as for my temporal life, everything was uncertain, and my heart had to be purged of the old leaven. The way—the saviour himself—pleased me well, but as yet I was reluctant to pass through the strait gate. And you put it into my mind, and it seemed good in my own sight, to go to Simplicianus, who appeared to me a faithful servant of yours, and your grace shone forth in him. I had also been told that from his youth up he had lived in entire devotion to you. He was already an old man, and because of his great age, which he had passed in such a zealous discipleship in your way, he appeared to me likely to have gained much wisdom—and, indeed, he had. From all his experience, I desired him to tell me—setting before him all my agitations—which would be the most fitting way for one who felt as I did to walk in your way.[1]

[8.1.2] For I saw the church full, and one man was going this way and another that. Still, I could not be satisfied with the life I was living in the world. Now, indeed, my passions had ceased to excite me as of old with hopes of honor and wealth, and it was a grievous burden to go on in such servitude. For, compared with your sweetness and the beauty of your house—which I loved—those things delighted me no longer. But I was still tightly bound by a woman; nor did the apostle forbid me to marry,

---

* Psalms 35:10; 116:16–17.

† Psalms 8:1.

‡ 1 Corinthians 13:12.

109

although he exhorted me to something better, wishing earnestly that all
men were as he himself was. But I was weak and chose the easier way, and
for this single reason my whole life was one of inner turbulence and list-
less indecision, because from so many influences I was compelled—even
though unwilling—to agree to a married life which bound me hand and
foot. I had heard from the mouth of truth that "there are eunuchs who
have made themselves eunuchs for the kingdom of heaven's sake" but,
said he, "He that is able to receive it, let him receive it."* Of a certainty,
all men are vain who do not have the knowledge of god, or have not been
able, from the good things that are seen, to find him who is good. But I
was no longer fettered in that vanity. I had surmounted it, and from the
united testimony of your whole creation had found you, our creator, and
your word—god with you, and together with you and the holy spirit, one
god—by whom you have created all things. There is still another sort of
wicked men, who "when they knew god, they glorified him not as god,
neither were thankful."† Into this also I had fallen, but your right hand
held me up and bore me away, and you placed me where I might recover.
For you have said to men, "Behold the fear of the lord, this is wisdom,"‡
and, "Be not wise in your own eyes,"§ because "they that profess themselves to be wise become fools."‖ But I had now found the goodly pearl;
and I ought to have sold all that I had and bought it—yet I hesitated.

[8.2.3] I went, therefore, to Simplicianus, the spiritual father of Ambrose (then a bishop), whom Ambrose truly loved as a father. I recounted
to him all the mazes of my wanderings, but when I mentioned to him that
I had read certain books of the Platonists which Victorinus—formerly
professor of rhetoric at Rome, who died a Christian, as I had been told—
had translated into Latin, Simplicianus congratulated me that I had not
fallen upon the writings of other philosophers, which were full of fallacies
and deceit, "after the beggarly elements of this world,"# whereas in the
Platonists, at every turn, the pathway led to belief in god and his Word.
Then, to encourage me to copy the humility of Christ, which is hidden
from the wise and revealed to babes, he told me about Victorinus himself,

---

* Matthew 19:12.

† Romans 1:21.

‡ Job 28:28.

§ Proverbs 3:7.

‖ Romans 1:22.

Colossians 2:8.

whom he had known intimately at Rome. And I cannot refrain from repeating what he told me about him. For it contains a glorious proof of your grace, which ought to be confessed to you: how that old man, most learned, most skilled in all the liberal arts; who had read, criticized, and explained so many of the writings of the philosophers; the teacher of so many noble senators; one who, as a mark of his distinguished service in office had both merited and obtained a statue in the Roman Forum—which men of this world esteem a great honor—this man who, up to an advanced age, had been a worshiper of idols, a communicant in the sacrilegious rites to which almost all the nobility of Rome were wedded; and who had inspired the people with the love of Osiris and

> *The dog Anubis, and a medley crew*
> *Of monster gods who 'gainst Neptune stand in arms*
> *'Gainst Venus and Minerva, steel-clad Mars,*

whom Rome once conquered, and now worshiped; all of which old Victorinus had with thundering eloquence defended for so many years—despite all this, he did not blush to become a child of your Christ, a babe at your font, bowing his neck to the yoke of humility and submitting his forehead to the ignominy of the cross.[2]

[8.2.4] Lord, lord, who "bowed the heavens and descended, who touched the mountains and they smoked,"* by what means did you find your way into that breast? He used to read the holy scriptures, as Simplicianus said, and thought out and studied all the Christian writings most studiously. He said to Simplicianus—not openly but secretly as a friend—"You must know that I am a Christian." To which Simplicianus replied, "I shall not believe it, nor shall I count you among the Christians, until I see you in the church of Christ." Victorinus then asked, with mild mockery, "Is it then the walls that make Christians?" Thus he often would affirm that he was already a Christian, and as often Simplicianus made the same answer, and just as often his jest about the walls was repeated. He was fearful of offending his friends, proud demon worshipers, from the height of whose Babylonian dignity, as from the tops of the cedars of Lebanon which the lord had not yet broken down, he feared that a storm of enmity would descend upon him. But he steadily gained strength from reading and inquiry, and came to fear lest he should be denied by Christ before

---

* Psalms 144:5.

the holy angels if he now was afraid to confess him before men.* Thus
he came to appear to himself guilty of a great fault, in being ashamed of the
sacraments of the humility of your word, when he was not ashamed of the
sacrilegious rites of those proud demons, whose pride he had imitated
and whose rites he had shared. From this he became bold-faced against
vanity and shamefaced toward the truth. Thus, suddenly and unexpectedly, he said to Simplicianus—as he himself told me—"Let us go to the
church; I wish to become a Christian." Simplicianus went with him,
scarcely able to contain himself for joy. He was admitted to the first
sacraments of instruction, and not long afterward gave in his name that
he might receive the baptism of regeneration. At this Rome marveled
and the church rejoiced. The proud saw and were enraged; they gnashed
their teeth and melted away! But the lord god was your servant's hope
and he paid no attention to their vanity and lying madness.

[8.2.5] Finally, when the hour arrived for him to make a public profession of his faith—which at Rome those who are about to enter into your
grace make from a platform in the full sight of the faithful people, in a set
form of words learned by heart—the presbyters offered Victorinus the
chance to make his profession more privately, for this was the custom for
some who were likely to be nervous from embarrassment. But Victorinus
chose rather to profess his salvation in the presence of the holy congregation. For there was no salvation in the rhetoric which he taught, yet he
had professed that openly. Why, then, should he shrink from naming your
word before the sheep of your flock, when he had not shrunk from utter-
ing his own words before the mad multitude? So, then, when he ascended
the platform to make his profession, everyone, as they recognized him,
whispered his name one to the other, in tones of jubilation. Who was
there among them that did not know him? And a low murmur ran
through the mouths of all the rejoicing multitude: "Victorinus! Victorinus!" There was a sudden burst of exaltation at the sight of him, and suddenly they were hushed that they might hear him. He pronounced the
true faith with an excellent boldness, and all desired to take him to their
very heart—indeed, by their love and joy they did take him to their heart:
love and joy were the hands with which they took hold of him.

[8.3.6] Good god, what happens in a man to make him rejoice more at
the salvation of a soul that has been despaired of and then delivered from
greater danger than over one who has never lost hope, or never been in

---

* Luke 12:8–9.

such imminent danger? For you also, most merciful father, "rejoice more over one that repents than over ninety and nine just persons that need no repentance."* And we listen with much delight whenever we hear how the lost sheep is brought home again on the shepherd's shoulders while the angels rejoice; or when the piece of money is restored to its place in the treasury and the neighbors rejoice with the woman who found it. And the joy of the solemn festival of your house constrains us to tears when the story is read in your house about the younger son who "was dead and is alive again, was lost and is found."† For it is you who rejoice both in us and in your angels, who are holy through holy love. For you are ever the same because you know unchangeably all things which remain neither the same nor forever. What, then, happens in the soul when it takes more delight at finding or having restored to it the things it loves than if it had always possessed them? Indeed, many other things bear witness that this is so—all things are full of witnesses, crying out, "So it is." The commander triumphs in victory, yet he could not have conquered if he had not fought; and the greater the peril of the battle, the more the joy of the triumph. The storm tosses the voyagers, threatens shipwreck, and everyone turns pale in the presence of death. Then the sky and sea grow calm, and they rejoice as much as they had feared. A loved one is sick and his pulse indicates danger; all who desire his safety are themselves sick at heart; he recovers, though not able as yet to walk with his former strength; and there is more joy now than there was before when he walked sound and strong. Indeed, the very pleasures of human life—not only those which rush upon us unexpectedly and involuntarily, but also those which are voluntary and planned—are obtained by difficulties. There is no pleasure in caring and drinking unless the pains of hunger and thirst have preceded. Drunkards even eat certain salt meats in order to create a painful thirst—and when the drink allays this, it causes pleasure. It is also the custom that the affianced bride should not be immediately given in marriage so that the husband may not esteem her any less, whom as his betrothed he longed for.

This can be seen in the case of base and dishonorable pleasure. But it is also apparent in pleasures that are permitted and lawful: in the sincerity of honest friendship; and in him who was dead and lived again, who had been lost and was found. The greater joy is everywhere preceded by

---

* Luke 15:7.
† Luke 15:32.

the greater pain. What does this mean, lord my god, when you are an everlasting joy to yourself, and some creatures about you are ever rejoicing in you? What does it mean that this portion of creation thus ebbs and flows, alternately in want and satiety? Is this their mode of being and is this all you have allotted to them: that, from the highest heaven to the lowest earth, from the beginning of the world to the end, from the angels to the worm, from the first movement to the last, you were assigning to all their proper places and their proper seasons—to all the kinds of good things and to all your just works? What can I say? How high you are in the highest and how deep in the deepest! You never depart from us, and yet only with difficulty do we return to you.

[8.4.9] Go on, lord, and act: stir us up and call us back; inflame us and draw us to you; stir us up and grow sweet to us; let us now love you, let us run to you. Are there not many men who, out of a deeper pit of darkness than that of Victorinus, return to you—who draw near to you and are illuminated by that light which gives those who receive it power from you to become your sons? But if they are less well-known, even those who know them rejoice less for them. For when many rejoice together the joy of each one is fuller, in that they warm one another, catch fire from each other; moreover, those who are well-known influence many toward salvation and take the lead with many to follow them. Therefore, even those who took the way before them rejoice over them greatly, because they do not rejoice over them alone. But it ought never to be that in your tabernacle the persons of the rich should be welcome before the poor, or the nobly born before the rest—since "you have rather chosen the weak things of the world to confound the strong; and have chosen the base things of the world and things that are despised, and the things that are not, in order to bring to nought the things that are."* And indeed it was "the least of the apostles," by whose tongue you sounded forth these words, who by combat made Paulus the proconsul overcome his pride and pass under the easy yoke of your Christ and became an officer of the great king, whereupon the apostle himself also desired to be called Paul instead of Saul, his former name, in testimony to such a great victory.† For the enemy is more overcome in one on whom he has a greater hold, and whom he has hold of more completely. But the proud he controls more readily through their concern about their rank and, through them,

---

* 1 Corinthians 1:27–28.
† Acts 13:4–12.

he controls more by means of their influence. The more, therefore, the world prized the heart of Victorinus (which the devil had held in an impregnable stronghold) and the tongue of Victorinus (that sharp, strong weapon with which the devil had slain so many), all the more exultingly did your sons rejoice because our king had bound the strong man,* and they saw his vessels taken from him and cleansed, and made fit for your honor and "profitable to the Lord for every good work."†

[**8.5.10**] Now when this man of yours, Simplicianus, told me the story of Victorinus, I was eager to imitate him. Indeed, this was Simplicianus' purpose in telling it to me. But when he went on to tell how, in the reign of the Emperor Julian, there was a law passed by which Christians were forbidden to teach literature and rhetoric;[3] and how Victorinus, in ready obedience to the law, chose to abandon his school of words rather than your word, by which you make eloquent the tongues of the dumb—he appeared to me not so much brave as happy, because he had found a reason for giving his time wholly to you. For this was what I was longing to do, but as yet I was bound by the iron chain of my own will. The enemy held fast my will, and had made of it a chain, and had bound me tight with it. For out of the perverse will came lust, and the service of lust ended in habit, and habit, not resisted, became necessity. By these links, as it were, forged together—which is why I called it a chain—a hard bondage held me in slavery. But that new will which had begun to spring up in me freely to worship you and to enjoy you, my god, the only certain joy, was not able as yet to overcome my former willfulness, made strong by long indulgence. Thus my two wills—the old and the new, the carnal and the spiritual—were in conflict within me, and by their discord they tore my soul apart.

[**8.5.11**] Thus I came to understand from my own experience what I had read, how "the flesh lusts against the spirit, and the spirit against the flesh."‡ I truly lusted both ways, yet more in that which I approved in myself than in that which I disapproved in myself. For in the latter it was not now really I that was involved, because here I was rather an unwilling sufferer than a willing actor. And yet it was through me that habit had become an armed enemy against me, because I had willingly come to be what I unwillingly found myself to be. Who, then, can with any justice

---

* Matthew 12:29.

† 2 Timothy 2:21.

‡ Galatians 5:17.

speak against it, when just punishment follows the sinner? I had now no longer my accustomed excuse that, as yet, I hesitated to give up the world and serve you because my perception of the truth was uncertain. For now it was certain. But, still bound to the earth, I refused to be your soldier; and was as much afraid of being freed from all entanglements as we ought to fear to be entangled.

[8.5.12] Thus with the baggage of the world I was sweetly burdened, as one in slumber, and my musings on you were like the efforts of those who desire to awake, but who are still overpowered with drowsiness and fall back into deep slumber. And as no one wishes to sleep forever (for all men rightly count waking better)—yet a man will usually defer shaking off his drowsiness when there is a heavy lethargy in his limbs, and he is glad to sleep on even when his reason disapproves, and the hour for rising has struck—so was I assured that it was much better for me to give myself up to your love than to go on yielding myself to my own lust. Your love satisfied and vanquished me, my lust pleased and fettered me. I had no answer to your calling to me, "Awake, you who sleep, and arise from the dead, and Christ shall give you light."* On all sides, you showed me that your words are true, and I, convicted by the truth, had nothing at all to reply but the drawling and drowsy words: "Presently; see, presently. Leave me alone a little while." But "presently, presently," had no present and my "leave me alone a little while" went on for a long while. In vain did I "delight in your law in the inner man" while "another law in my members warred against the law of my mind and brought me into captivity to the law of sin which is in my members." For the law of sin is the tyranny of habit, by which the mind is drawn and held, even against its will. Yet it deserves to be so held because it so willingly falls into the habit. "Wretched man that I am! Who shall deliver me from the body of this death" but your grace alone, through Jesus Christ our lord?†

[8.6.13] And now I will tell and confess to your name, lord, my helper and my redeemer, how you delivered me from the chain of sexual desire by which I was so tightly held, and from the slavery of worldly business. With increasing anxiety I was going about my usual affairs, and daily sighing to you. I attended your church as frequently as my business, under the burden of which I groaned, left me free to do so. Alypius was with me, disengaged at last from his legal post, after a third term as assessor, and

---

* Ephesians 5:14.
† Romans 7:22–25.

now waiting for private clients to whom he might sell his legal advice as I sold the power of speaking (as if it could be supplied by teaching). But Nebridius had consented, for the sake of our friendship, to teach under Verecundus—a citizen of Milan and professor of grammar, and a very intimate friend of us all—who ardently desired, and by right of friendship demanded from us, the faithful aid he greatly needed.[4] Nebridius was not drawn to this by any desire of gain—for he could have made much more out of his learning had he been so inclined—but as he was a most sweet and kindly friend, he was unwilling, out of respect for the duties of friendship, to slight our request. But in this he acted very discreetly, taking care not to become known to those persons who had great reputations in the world. Thus he avoided all distractions of mind, and reserved as many hours as possible to pursue or read or listen to discussions about wisdom.

[8.6.14] On a certain day, then, when Nebridius was away—for some reason I cannot remember—there came to visit Alypius and me at our house one Ponticianus, a fellow countryman of ours from Africa, who held high office in the emperor's court. What he wanted with us I do not know; but we sat down to talk together, and it chanced that he noticed a book on a game table before us. He took it up, opened it, and, contrary to his expectation, found it to be the apostle Paul, for he imagined that it was one of my wearisome rhetoric textbooks.[5] At this, he looked up at me with a smile and expressed his delight and wonder that he had so unexpectedly found this book and only this one, lying before my eyes; for he was indeed a Christian and a faithful one at that, and often he prostrated himself before you, our god, in the church in constant daily prayer. When I had told him that I had given much attention to these writings, a conversation followed in which he spoke of Anthony, the Egyptian monk, whose name was in high repute among your servants, although up to that time not familiar to me.[6] When he learned this, he lingered on the topic, giving us an account of this eminent man, and marveling at our ignorance. We in turn were amazed to hear of your wonderful works so fully manifested in recent times—almost in our own—occurring in the true faith and the catholic church. We all wondered—we, that these things were so great, and he, that we had never heard of them.

[8.6.15] From this, his conversation turned to the multitudes in the monasteries and their manners so fragrant to you, and to the teeming solitudes of the wilderness, of which we knew nothing at all. There was even a monastery at Milan, outside the city's walls, full of good brothers under the fostering care of Ambrose—and we were ignorant of it. He went on with his story, and we listened intently and in silence. He then told us how,

on a certain afternoon, at Trier, when the emperor was occupied watching
the gladiatorial games, he and three comrades went out for a walk in the
gardens close to the city walls. There, as they chanced to walk two by two,
one strolled away with him, while the other two went on by themselves. As
they rambled, these first two came upon a certain cottage where lived
some of your servants, some of the "poor in spirit" (of such is the kingdom
of heaven*) where they found the book in which was written the life of
Anthony! One of them began to read it, to marvel and to be inflamed by
it. While reading, he meditated on embracing just such a life, giving up his
worldly employment to seek you alone. These two belonged to the group
of officials called "special agents."[7] Then, suddenly being overwhelmed
with a holy love and a sober shame and as if in anger with himself, he fixed
his eyes on his friend, exclaiming: "Tell me, I beg you, what goal are we
seeking in all these toils of ours? What is it that we desire? What is our motive in public service? Can our hopes in the court rise higher than to be
'friends of the emperor'? But how frail, how beset with peril, is that pride!
Through what dangers must we climb to a greater danger? And when
shall we succeed? But if I chose to become a friend of god, see, I can become one now." Thus he spoke, and in the pangs of the travail of the new
life he turned his eyes again onto the page and continued reading; he was
inwardly changed, as you saw, and the world dropped away from his
mind, as soon became plain to others. For as he read with a heart like a
stormy sea, more than once he groaned. Finally he saw the better course,
and resolved on it. Then, having become your servant, he said to his
friend: "Now I have broken loose from those hopes we had, and I am determined to serve god; and I enter into that service from this hour in this
place. If you are reluctant to imitate me, do not oppose me." The other
replied that he would continue bound in his friendship, to share in so
great a service for so great a prize. So both became yours, and began to
"build a tower," counting the cost—namely, giving up all that they had
and following you.[†] Shortly after, Ponticianus and his companion, who
had walked with him in the other part of the garden, came in search of
them to the same place, and having found them reminded them to return,
as the day was declining. But the first two, making known to Ponticianus
their resolution and purpose, and how a resolve had sprung up and become confirmed in them, entreated them not to take it ill if they refused

---

* Matthew 5:3.
† Luke 14:28–33.

to join themselves with them. But Ponticianus and his friend, although not changed from their former course, did nevertheless (as he told us) bewail themselves and congratulated their friends on their godliness, recommending themselves to their prayers. And with hearts inclining again toward earthly things, they returned to the palace. But the other two, setting their affections on heavenly things, remained in the cottage. Both of them had affianced brides who, when they heard of this, likewise dedicated their virginity to you.

[8.7.16] Such was the story Ponticianus told. But while he was speaking, you, lord, turned me toward myself, taking me from behind my back, where I had put myself while unwilling to exercise self-scrutiny. And now you set me face to face with myself, so that I might see how ugly I was, and how crooked and sordid, bespotted and ulcerous. And I looked and I loathed myself; but where to fly from myself I could not discover. And if I sought to turn my gaze away from myself, he would continue his narrative, and you would oppose me to myself and thrust me before my own eyes so that I might discover my iniquity and hate it. I had known it, but acted as though I knew it not—I winked at it and forgot it.

[8.7.17] But now, the more ardently I loved those whose wholesome affections I heard reported—that they had given themselves up wholly to you to be cured—the more I abhorred myself when compared with them. For many of my years—perhaps twelve—had passed away since my nineteenth, when, upon the reading of Cicero's *Hortensius,* I was roused to a desire for wisdom. And here I was, still postponing the abandonment of this world's happiness to devote myself to the search. For not just the finding alone, but also the bare search for it, ought to have been preferred above the treasures and kingdoms of this world; better than all bodily pleasures, though they were to be had for the taking. But, wretched youth that I was—supremely wretched even in the very outset of my youth—I had entreated chastity of you and had prayed, "Grant me chastity and continence, but not yet." For I was afraid that you might hear me too soon, and too soon cure me of my disease of lust which I desired to have satisfied rather than extinguished. And I had wandered through perverse ways of godless superstition—not really sure of it, either, but preferring it to the other, which I did not seek in piety, but opposed in malice.

[8.7.18] And I had thought that I delayed from day to day in rejecting those worldly hopes and following you alone because there did not appear anything certain by which I could direct my course. And now the day had arrived in which I was laid bare to myself and my conscience was to chide me: "Where are you, my tongue? You said indeed that you were not willing to cast off the baggage of vanity for uncertain truth. But see, now it is certain, and still that burden oppresses you. At the same time those who have not worn themselves out with searching for it as you have, nor spent ten years and more in thinking about it, have had their shoulders unburdened and have received wings to fly away." Thus was I inwardly confused, and mightily confounded with a horrible shame, while Ponticianus went ahead speaking such things. And when he had finished his story and the business he came for, he went his way. And then what did I not say to myself, within myself? With what scourges of rebuke did I not lash my soul to make it follow me, as I was struggling to go after you? Yet it drew back. It refused. It would not make an effort. All its arguments were exhausted and confuted. Yet it resisted in sullen disquiet, fearing the cutting off of that habit by which it was being wasted to death, as if that were death itself.

[8.8.19] Then, as this vehement quarrel, which I waged with my soul in the chamber of my heart, was raging inside my inner dwelling, agitated both in mind and countenance, I seized upon Alypius and exclaimed: "What is the matter with us? What is this? What did you hear? The uninstructed start up and take heaven, and we—with all our learning but so little heart—see where we wallow in flesh and blood! Because others have gone before us, are we ashamed to follow, and not rather ashamed at our not following?" I scarcely knew what I said, and in my excitement I flung away from him, while he gazed at me in silent astonishment. For I did not sound like myself: my face, eyes, color, tone expressed my meaning more clearly than my words. There was a little garden belonging to our lodging, of which we had the use—as of the whole house—for the master, our landlord, did not live there. The tempest in my breast hurried me out into this garden, where no one might interrupt the fiery struggle in which I was engaged with myself, until it came to the outcome that you knew though I did not. But I was mad for health, and dying for life; knowing what evil thing I was, but not knowing what good thing I was so shortly to become.

I fled into the garden, with Alypius following step by step; for I had no secret in which he did not share, and how could he leave me in such distress? We sat down, as far from the house as possible. I was greatly disturbed in spirit, angry at myself with a turbulent indignation because I had not entered your will and covenant, my god, while all my bones cried out to me to enter, extolling it to the skies. The way there is not by ships or chariots or feet—indeed it was not as far as I had come from the house to the place where we were seated. For to go along that road and indeed to reach the goal is nothing else but the will to go. But it must be a strong and single will, not staggering and swaying about this way and that—a changeable, twisting, fluctuating will, wrestling with itself while one part falls as another rises.

[8.8.20] Finally, in the very fever of my indecision, I made many motions with my body; like men do when they will to act but cannot, either because they do not have the limbs or because their limbs are bound or weakened by disease, or incapacitated in some other way. Thus if I tore my hair, struck my forehead, or, entwining my fingers, clasped my knee, these I did because I willed it. But I might have willed it and still not have done it, if the nerves had not obeyed my will. Many things then I did, in which the will and power to do were not the same. Yet I did not do that one thing which seemed to me infinitely more desirable, which before long I should have power to will because shortly when I willed, I would will with a single will. For in this, the power of willing is the power of doing; and as yet I could not do it. Thus my body more readily obeyed the slightest wish of the soul in moving its limbs at the order of my mind than my soul obeyed itself to accomplish in the will alone its great resolve.

[8.9.21] How can there be such a strange anomaly? And why is it? Let your mercy shine on me, so that I may inquire and find an answer, amid the dark labyrinth of human punishment and in the darkest contritions of the sons of Adam. What is the source of such an anomaly? And why should it be? The mind commands the body, and the body obeys. The mind commands itself and is resisted. The mind commands the hand to be moved and there is such readiness that the command is scarcely distinguished from the obedience in act. Yet the mind is mind, and the hand is body. The mind commands the mind to will, and yet though it be itself it does not obey itself. What is the source of this strange anomaly and why should it be? I repeat: the will commands itself to will, and could not give the command unless it wills; yet what is commanded is not done. But actually the will does not will entirely; therefore it does not command entirely. For as far as it wills, it commands. And as far as it does not will, the thing commanded is not done. For the will commands that there be an act of will—not another, but itself. But it does not command entirely. Therefore, what is commanded does not happen; for if the will were whole and entire, it would not even command it to be, because it would already be. It is, therefore, no strange anomaly partly to will and partly to be unwilling. This is actually an infirmity of mind, which cannot wholly rise, while pressed down by habit, even though it is supported by the truth. And so there are two wills, because one of them is not whole, and what is present in this one is lacking in the other.

[8.10.22] Let them perish from your presence, god, as vain talkers, and deceivers of the soul perish, who, when they observe that there are two wills in the act of deliberation, go on to affirm that there are two kinds of minds in us: one good, the other evil. They are indeed themselves evil when they hold these evil opinions—and they shall become good only when they come to hold the truth and consent to the truth that your apostle may say to them: "You were formerly in darkness, but now are you in the light in the lord."* But they desired to be light, not in the lord, but in themselves. They conceived the nature of the soul to be the same as what god is, and thus have become a thicker darkness than they were; for in their dread arrogance they have gone farther away from you, from you "the true light, that lights every man that comes into the world."† Mark what you say and blush for shame; draw near to him and be enlightened, and your faces shall not be ashamed.‡ While I was deliberating whether I would serve the lord my god now, as I had long purposed to do, it was I who willed and it was also I who was unwilling. In either case, it was I. I neither willed with my whole will nor was I wholly unwilling. And so I was at war with myself and torn apart by myself. And this strife was against my will; yet it did not show the presence of another mind, but the punishment of my own. Thus it was no more I who did it, but the sin that dwelt in me—the punishment of a sin freely committed by Adam, and I was a son of Adam.

[8.10.23] For if there are as many opposing natures as there are opposing wills, there will not be two but many more. If any man is trying to decide whether he should go to their conventicle or to the theater, the Manicheans at once cry out, "See, here are two natures—one good, drawing this way, another bad, drawing back that way; for how else can you explain this indecision between conflicting wills?" But I reply that both impulses are bad—that which draws to them and that which draws back to the theater. But they do not believe that the will which draws to them can be anything but good. Suppose, then, that one of us should try to decide, and through the conflict of his two wills should waver whether he should go to the theater or to our church. Would not those also waver

---

* Ephesians 5:8.

† John 1:9.

‡ Psalms 34:5.

about the answer here? For either they must confess, which they are un-willing to do, that the will that leads to our church is as good as that which carries their own adherents and those captivated by their mysteries; or else they must imagine that there are two evil natures and two evil minds in one man, both at war with each other, and then it will not be true what they say, that there is one good and another bad. Else they must be con-verted to the truth, and no longer deny that when anyone deliberates there is one soul fluctuating between conflicting wills.

[8.10.24] Let them no longer maintain that when they perceive two wills to be contending with each other in the same man the contest is be-tween two opposing minds, of two opposing substances, from two opposing principles, the one good and the other bad. Thus, true god, you reprove and confute and convict them. For both wills may be bad: as when a man tries to decide whether he should kill a man by poison or by the sword; whether he should take possession of this field or that one belonging to someone else, when he cannot get both; whether he should squander his money to buy pleasure or hold onto his money through the motive of cov-etousness; whether he should go to the circus or to the theater, if both are open on the same day; or, whether he should take a third course, open at the same time, and rob another man's house; or, a fourth option, whether he should commit adultery, if he has the opportunity—all these things concurring in the same space of time and all being equally longed for, al-though impossible to do at one time. For the mind is pulled four ways by four antagonistic wills—or even more, in view of the vast range of human desires—but even the Manicheans do not affirm that there are these many different substances. The same principle applies as in the action of good wills. For I ask them, "Is it a good thing to have delight in reading the apostle, or is it a good thing to delight in a sober psalm, or is it a good thing to discourse on the gospel?" To each of these, they will answer, "It is good." But what, then, if all delight us equally and all at the same time? Do not different wills distract the mind when a man is trying to decide what he should choose? Yet they are all good, and are at variance with each other until one is chosen. When this is done the whole united will may go forward on a single track instead of remaining as it was before, di-vided in many ways. So also, when eternity attracts us from above, and the pleasure of earthly delight pulls us down from below, the soul does not will either the one or the other with all its force, but still it is the same soul that does not will this or that with a united will, and is therefore pulled apart with grievous perplexities, because for truth's sake it prefers this, but for custom's sake it does not lay that aside.

[8.11.25] Thus I was sick and tormented, reproaching myself more bitterly than ever, rolling and writhing in my chain till it should be utterly broken. By now I was held but slightly, but still was held. And you, lord, pressed upon me in my inmost heart with a severe mercy, redoubling the lashes of fear and shame; lest I should again give way and that same slender remaining tie not be broken off, but recover strength and enchain me yet more securely. I kept saying to myself, "See, let it be done now; let it be done now." And as I said this I all but came to a firm decision. I all but did it—yet I did not quite. Still I did not fall back to my old condition, but stood aside for a moment and drew breath. And I tried again, and lacked only a very little of reaching the resolve—and then somewhat less, and then all but touched and grasped it. Yet I still did not quite reach or touch or grasp the goal, because I hesitated to die to death and to live to life. And the worse way, to which I was habituated, was stronger in me than the better, which I had not tried. And up to the very moment in which I was to become another man, the nearer the moment approached, the greater horror did it strike in me. But it did not strike me back, nor turn me aside, but held me in suspense.

[8.11.26] It was, in fact, my old mistresses, trifles of trifles and vanities of vanities, who still enthralled me. They tugged at my fleshly garments and softly whispered: "Are you going to part with us? And from that moment will we never be with you any more? And from that moment will not this and that be forbidden you forever?" What were they suggesting to me in those words "this or that"? What is it they suggested, my god? Let your mercy guard the soul of your servant from the vileness and the shame they suggested! And now I scarcely heard them, for they were not openly showing themselves and opposing me face to face; but muttering, as it were, behind my back; and furtively plucking at me as I was leaving, trying to make me look back at them. Still they delayed me, so that I hesitated to break loose and shake myself free of them and leap over to the place to which I was being called—for unruly habit kept saying to me, "Do you think you can live without them?"

[8.11.27] But now it said this very faintly; for in the direction I had set my face, and yet toward which I still trembled to go, the chaste dignity of Continence appeared to me—cheerful but not wanton, modestly alluring me to come and doubt nothing, extending her holy hands, full of a multitude of good examples—to receive and embrace me. There were there so many young men and maidens, a multitude of youth and every age, grave widows and ancient virgins; and Continence herself in their midst: not barren, but a fruitful mother of children—her joys—by you, lord, her husband. And she smiled on me with a challenging smile as if to say: "Can you not do what these young men and maidens can? Or can any of them do it of themselves, and not rather in the lord their god? The lord their god gave me to them. Why do you stand in your own strength, and so stand not? Cast yourself on him; fear not. He will not flinch and you will not fall. Cast yourself on him without fear, for he will receive and heal you." And I blushed violently, for I still heard the muttering of those trifles and hung suspended. Again she seemed to speak: "Stop your ears against those unclean members of yours, so that they may be mortified. They tell you of delights, but not according to the law of the lord your god." This struggle raging in my heart was nothing but the contest of self against self. And Alypius kept close beside me, and awaited in silence the outcome of my extraordinary agitation.

[8.12.28] Now when deep reflection had drawn up out of the secret depths of my soul all my misery and had heaped it up before the sight of my heart, there arose a mighty storm, accompanied by a mighty rain of tears. That I might give way fully to my tears and lamentations, I stole away from Alypius, for it seemed to me that solitude was more appropriate for the business of weeping. I went far enough away that I could feel that even his presence was no restraint upon me. This was the way I felt at the time, and he realized it. I suppose I had said something before I started up and he noticed that the sound of my voice was choked with weeping. And so he stayed alone, where we had been sitting together, greatly astonished. I flung myself down under a fig tree—how I know not—and gave free course to my tears.[8] The streams of my eyes gushed out an acceptable sacrifice to you. And, not indeed in these words, but to this effect, I cried to you: "And you, lord, how long? How long, lord? Will you be angry forever? Do not remember against us our former iniquities."* For I felt that I was still enthralled by them. I sent up these sorrowful cries: "How long, how long? Tomorrow and tomorrow? Why not now? Why not this very hour make an end to my uncleanness?"

[8.12.29] I was saying these things and weeping in the most bitter contrition of my heart, when suddenly I heard the voice of a boy or a girl—I know not which—coming from the neighboring house, chanting over and over again, "Pick up, read; pick up, read" [*Tolle, lege; tolle, lege*]. Immediately I ceased weeping and began most earnestly to think whether it was usual for children in some kind of game to sing such a song, but I could

---

* Psalms 6:3; 79:8.

not remember ever having heard the like. So, damming the torrent of my tears, I got to my feet, for I could only think that this was a divine command to open the book and read the first passage I should light upon. For I had heard how Anthony, accidentally coming into church while the gospel was being read, received the admonition as if what was read had been addressed to him: "Go and sell what you have and give it to the poor, and you shall have treasure in heaven; and come and follow me."* By such an oracle he was immediately converted to you. So I quickly returned to the bench where Alypius was sitting, for there I had put down the apostle's book when I had left. I snatched it up, opened it, and in silence read the paragraph on which my eyes first fell: "Not in rioting and drunkenness, not in chambering and wantonness, not in strife and envying, but put on the lord Jesus Christ, and make no provision for the flesh to fulfill the lusts thereof."† I wanted to read no further, nor did I need to. For instantly, as the sentence ended, there was infused in my heart something like the light of full certainty and all the gloom of doubt vanished away.⁹

[8.12.30] Closing the book, then, and putting my finger or something else for a mark I began—now with a tranquil countenance—to tell it all to Alypius. And he in turn disclosed to me what had been going on in himself, of which I knew nothing. He asked to see what I had read. I showed him, and he looked on even further than I had read. I had not known what followed. But indeed it was this, "Him that is weak in the faith, receive."‡ This he applied to himself, and told me so. By these words of warning he was strengthened, and by exercising his good resolution and purpose—all very much in keeping with his character, in which, in these respects, he was always far different from and better than I—he joined me in full commitment without any restless hesitation. Then we went in to my mother, and told her what happened, to her great joy. We explained to her how it had occurred, and she leaped for joy triumphant, and she blessed you, who are "able to do exceedingly abundantly above all that we ask or think."§ For she saw that you had granted her far more than she had ever asked for in all her pitiful and doleful lamentations. For you so converted me to you that I sought neither a wife nor any other of this

---

* Matthew 19:21.

† Romans 13:13.

‡ Romans 14:1.

§ Ephesians 3:20.

world's hopes, but set my feet on that rule of faith which so many years before you had showed her in her dream about me. And so you turned her grief into gladness more plentiful than she had ventured to desire, and dearer and purer than the desire she used to cherish of having grand-children of my flesh.

BOOK 9

[**9.1.1**] "Lord, I am your servant; I am your servant and the son of your handmaid. You have loosed my bonds. I will offer to you the sacrifice of thanksgiving."* Let my heart and my tongue praise you, and let all my bones say, "Lord, who is like you?" Let them say so, and you answer me and say to my soul, "I am your salvation."† Who am I, and what is my nature? What evil is there not in me and my deeds; or if not in my deeds, my words; or if not in my words, my will? But you, lord, are good and merciful, and your right hand reached into the depth of my death and emptied out the abyss of corruption from the bottom of my heart. And this was the result: now I did not will to do what I willed, and began to will to do what you did will. But where was my free will during all those years and from what deep and secret retreat was it called forth in a single moment, whereby I gave my neck to your easy yoke and my shoulders to your light burden, Christ Jesus, my strength and my redeemer? How sweet did it suddenly become to me to be without the sweetness of trifles! And it was now a joy to put away what I formerly feared to lose. For you cast them away from me, true and highest sweetness. You cast them away, and in their place you entered in yourself—sweeter than all pleasure, though not to flesh and blood; brighter than all light, but more veiled than all mystery; more exalted than all honor, though not to them that are exalted in their own eyes. Now was my soul free from the gnawing cares of seeking and getting, of wallowing in the mire and scratching the itch of lust. And I prattled like a child to you, lord my god—my light, my riches, and my salvation.

[**9.2.2**] And it seemed right to me, in your sight, not to snatch my tongue's service abruptly out of the speech market, but to withdraw quietly, so that the young men who were not concerned about your law or your peace, but with mendacious follies and forensic strifes, might no longer purchase from my mouth weapons for their frenzy. Fortunately, there were only a few days before the vintage vacation; and I determined to endure them, so that I might resign in due form and, now bought by you, return for sale no more. My plan was known to you, but, except for

---

* Psalms 116:16–17.
† Psalms 35:10, 3.

my own friends, it was not known to other men. For we had agreed that it should not be made public; although, in our ascent from the valley of tears and our singing of "the song of degrees," you had given us sharp arrows and hot burning coals to stop that deceitful tongue which opposes under the guise of good counsel, and devours what it loves as though it were food.[1]

[9.2.3] You had pierced our heart with your love, and we carried your words, as it were, skewered through our inmost parts. The examples of your servants whom you had changed from black to shining white, and from death to life, crowded into the bosom of our thoughts and burned and consumed our sluggish temper, to prevent us from toppling back into the abyss. And they fired us exceedingly, so that every breath of the deceitful tongue of our detractors might fan the flame and not blow it out. Though this vow and purpose of ours should find those who would loudly praise it—for the sake of your name, which you have sanctified throughout the earth—it nevertheless looked like a self-vaunting not to wait until the vacation time now so near. For if I had left such a public office ahead of time, and had made the break in the eye of the general public, all who took notice of this act of mine and observed how near was the vintage time that I wished to anticipate would have talked about me a great deal, as if I were trying to appear a great person. And what purpose would it serve that people should consider and dispute about my conversion so that my good should be evil spoken of?

[9.2.4] Furthermore, this same summer my lungs had begun to be weak from too much lecturing in class. Breathing was difficult; the pains in my chest showed that the lungs were affected and were soon fatigued by too loud or prolonged speaking. This had at first been a trial to me, for it would have compelled me almost of necessity to lay down that burden of teaching; or, if I was to be cured and become strong again, at least to take a leave for a while. But as soon as the full desire to be still so that I might know that you are the lord arose and was confirmed in me, you know, my god, that I began to rejoice that I had this excuse ready—and not a feigned one, either—which might somewhat temper the displeasure of those who for their sons' freedom wished me never to have any freedom of my own. Full of joy, then, I bore it until my time ran out—it was perhaps some twenty days—yet it was some strain to go through with it, for the greediness which helped to support the drudgery had gone, and I would have been overwhelmed had not its place been taken by patience. Some of your servants, my brethren, may say that I sinned in this, since having once fully and from my heart enlisted in your service, I permitted myself to sit a single hour in the chair of falsehood. I will not dispute it. But have you not, most merciful lord, pardoned and forgiven this sin in the holy water also, along with all the others, horrible and deadly as they were?

[9.3.5] Verecundus was severely disturbed by this new happiness of mine, since he was still firmly held by his bonds and saw that he would lose my companionship. For he was not yet a Christian, though his wife was; and, indeed, he was more firmly enchained by her than by anything else, and held back from that journey on which we had set out. Furthermore, he declared he did not wish to be a Christian on any terms except those that were impossible. However, he invited us most courteously to make use of his country house so long as we would stay there. Lord, you will recompense him for this "in the resurrection of the just,"* seeing that you have already given him "the lot of the righteous."† For while we were absent at Rome, he was overtaken with bodily sickness, and during it he was made a Christian and departed this life as one of the faithful. Thus you had mercy on him, and not on him only, but on us as well; lest, remembering the exceeding kindness of our friend to us and not able to count him in your flock, we should be tortured with intolerable grief. Thanks be to you, our god; we are yours. Your exhortations, consolations, and faithful promises assure us that you will repay Verecundus for that country house at Cassiciacum—where we found rest in you from the fever of the world—with the perpetual freshness of your paradise in which you have forgiven him his earthly sins, in that mountain flowing with milk, that fruitful mountain—your own.[2]

[9.3.6] Thus Verecundus was full of grief; but Nebridius was joyous. For he was not yet a Christian, and had fallen into the pit of deadly error, believing that the flesh of your son, the truth, was a phantom. Yet he had come up out of that pit and now held the same belief that we did. And though he was not as yet initiated in any of the sacraments of your church, he was a most earnest inquirer after truth. Not long after our conversion and regeneration by your baptism, he also became a faithful member of the catholic church, serving you in perfect chastity and continence among his own people in Africa, and bringing his whole household with him to Christianity. Then you released him from the flesh, and now he lives in

---

* Luke 14:14.
† Psalms 125:3.

Abraham's bosom.* Whatever is signified by that term "bosom," there lives my Nebridius, my sweet friend, your son by adoption, lord, and not a freedman any longer. There he lives; for what other place could there be for such a soul? There he lives in that abode about which he used to ask me so many questions—poor ignorant one that I was. Now he does not put his ear up to my mouth, but his spiritual mouth to your fountain, and drinks wisdom as he desires and as he is able, happy without end. But I do not believe that he is so inebriated by that draught as to forget me; since you, lord, who are the draught, art mindful of us. Thus, then, we were comforting the unhappy Verecundus—our friendship touched—reconciling him to our conversion and exhorting him to a faith fit for his condition (that is, to his being married). We tarried for Nebridius to follow us, since he was so close, and this he was just about to do when at last the interim ended. The days had seemed long and many because of my eagerness for leisure and liberty in which I might sing to you from my inmost part, "My heart has said to you, I have sought your face; your face, lord, will I seek."†

[9.4.7] Finally the day came on which I was actually to be relieved from the professorship of rhetoric, from which I had already been released in intention. And it was done. And you delivered my tongue as you had already delivered my heart; and I blessed you for it with great joy, and retired with my friends to the villa. My books testify to what I got done there in writing, which was now hopefully devoted to your service; though in this pause it was still as if I were panting from my exertions in the school of pride. These were the books in which I engaged in dialogue with my friends, and also those in soliloquy before you alone. And there are my letters to Nebridius, who was still absent.[3] When would there be enough time to recount all your great blessings which you bestowed on us in that time, especially as I am hastening on to still greater mercies? For my memory recalls them to me and it is pleasant to confess them to you, lord: the inward goads by which you subdued me and how you brought me low, leveling the mountains and hills of my thoughts, straightening my crookedness, and smoothing my rough ways. And I remember by what means you also subdued Alypius, my heart's brother, to the name of your only son, our lord and saviour Jesus Christ, which he at first refused to have inserted in our writings. For at first he

---

* Luke 16:22.
† Psalms 27:8.

preferred that they should smell of the cedars of the schools which the lord has now broken down, rather than of the wholesome herbs of the church, hostile to serpents.[4]

[9.4.8] My god, how I cried to you when I read the psalms of David, those hymns of faith, those paeans of devotion which leave no room for swelling pride! I was still a novice in your true love, a catechumen keeping holiday at the villa, with Alypius, a catechumen like myself. My mother was also with us—in woman's garb, but with a man's faith, with the peacefulness of age and the fullness of motherly love and Christian piety. What cries I used to send up to you in those songs, and how I was enkindled toward you by them! I burned to sing them if possible, throughout the whole world, against the pride of the human race. And yet, indeed, they are sung throughout the whole world, and none can hide himself from your heat. With what strong and bitter regret was I indignant at the Manicheans! Yet I also pitied them; for they were ignorant of those sacraments, those medicines, and raved insanely against the cure that might have made them sane! I wished they could have been somewhere close by, and—without my knowledge—could have seen my face and heard my words when, in that time of leisure, I pored over the Fourth Psalm. And I wish they could have seen how that psalm affected me. "When I called upon you, god of my righteousness, you heard me; you enlarged me when I was in distress. Have mercy upon me and hear my prayer." I wish they might have heard what I said in comment on those words, without my knowing that they heard, lest they should think that I was speaking it just on their account. For, indeed, I should not have said quite the same things, nor quite in the same way, if I had known that I was heard and seen by them. And if I had so spoken, they would not have meant the same things to them as they did to me when I spoke by and for myself before you, out of the private affections of my soul.[5]

[9.4.9] By turns I trembled with fear and warmed with hope and rejoiced in your mercy, father. And all these feelings showed forth in my eyes and voice when your good spirit turned to us and said, "O sons of men, how long will you be slow of heart, how long will you love vanity, and seek after falsehood?" For I had loved vanity and sought after falsehood. And you, lord, had already magnified your holy one, raising him from the dead and setting him at your right hand, that thence he should send forth from on high his promised paraclete, the spirit of truth. Already he had sent him, and I knew it not. He had sent him because he was now magnified, rising from the dead and ascending into heaven. For till then "the holy spirit was not yet given, because Jesus was not yet glorified."* And the prophet cried out: "How long will you be slow of heart? How long will you love vanity, and seek after falsehood? Know this, that the lord has magnified his holy one." He cries, "How long?" He cries, "Know this," and I, so long loving vanity, and seeking after falsehood, heard and trembled, because these words were spoken to such a one as I remembered that I myself had been. For in those phantoms which I once held for truth there was vanity and falsehood. And I spoke many things loudly and earnestly in the contrition of my memory which I wish they had heard, who still love vanity and seek after falsehood. Perhaps they would have been troubled, and have vomited up their error, and you would have heard them when they cried to you, for by a real death in the flesh he died for us who now makes intercession for us with you.

[9.4.10] I read on further, "Be angry, and sin not." And how deeply was I touched, my god; for I had now learned to be angry with myself for the things past, so that in the future I might not sin. Yes, to be angry with good cause, for it was not another nature out of the race of darkness that had sinned for me, as they affirm who are not angry with themselves, and who store up for themselves dire wrath against the day of wrath and the revelation of your righteous judgment. Nor were the good things I saw now outside me, nor were they to be seen with the eyes of flesh in the light of the earthly sun. For they that have their joys from without sink easily into emptiness and are spilled out on those things that are visible and temporal, and in their starving thoughts they lick their very shadows. If only they would grow weary with their hunger and would say, "Who will show us any good?" And we would answer, and they would hear, "Lord, the light of your countenance shines bright upon us." For we are not that light that enlightens every man, but we are enlightened by you, so that we who were formerly in darkness may now be alight in you. If only they could behold the inner light eternal which, now that I had tasted it, I gnashed my teeth because I could not show it to them unless they brought me their heart in their eyes—their roving eyes—and said, "Who will show us any good?" But even there, in the inner chamber of my soul where I was angry with myself, where I was inwardly pricked, where I had offered my sacrifice, slaying the old man in me, and hoping in you with the new resolve of a new life with my trust laid in you—even there you had begun to grow sweet to me and to "put gladness in my heart." And thus as I read all this, I cried aloud and felt its inward meaning. Nor did I

---

* John 7:39.

wish to be increased in worldly goods which are wasted by time, for now I possessed, in your eternal simplicity, other corn and wine and oil.

[9.4.11] And with a loud cry from my heart, I read the following verse: "Oh, in peace! Oh, in the selfsame!" See how he says it: "I will lay me down and take my rest." For who shall withstand us when the truth of this saying that is written is made manifest: "Death is swallowed up in victory"?* For surely you, who do not change, art the selfsame, and in you is rest and oblivion to all distress. There is none other beside you, nor are we to toil for those many things which are not you, for "only you, lord, make me to dwell in hope." These things I read and I was enkindled, but still I could not discover what to do with those deaf and dead Manicheans to whom I myself had belonged; for I had been a bitter and blind reviler against these writings, honeyed with the honey of heaven and luminous with your light. And I was sorely grieved at these enemies of this scripture.

[9.4.12] When shall I call to mind all that happened during those holidays? I have not forgotten them, nor will I be silent about the severity of your scourge, and the amazing quickness of your mercy. During that time you tortured me with a toothache; and when it had become so acute that I was not able to speak, it came into my heart to urge all my friends who were present to pray for me to you, the god of all health. And I wrote it down on the tablet and gave it to them to read. Presently, as we bowed our knees in supplication, the pain was gone. But what pain? How did it go? I confess that I was terrified, lord my god, because from my earliest years I had never experienced such pain. And your purposes were profoundly impressed upon me; and rejoicing in faith, I praised your name. But that faith allowed me no rest in respect of my past sins, which were not yet forgiven me through your baptism.

[9.5.13] Now that the vintage vacation was ended, I gave notice to the citizens of Milan that they might provide their scholars with another word-merchant. I gave as my reasons my determination to serve you and also my insufficiency for the task, because of the difficulty in breathing and the pain in my chest. And by letters I notified your bishop, the holy man Ambrose, of my former errors and my present resolution. And I asked his advice as to which of your books it was best for me to read so that I might be the more ready and fit for the reception of so great a grace. He recommended Isaiah the prophet; and I believe it was because

---

* 1 Corinthians 15:54.

Isaiah foreshows more clearly than others the gospel, and the calling of the gentiles. But because I could not understand the first part and because I imagined the rest to be like it, I laid it aside with the intention of taking it up again later, when better practiced in our lord's words.

[9.6.14] When the time arrived for me to give in my name, we left the country and returned to Milan. Alypius also resolved to be born again in you at the same time. He was already clothed with the humility that befits your sacraments, and was so brave a tamer of his body that he would walk the frozen Italian soil with his naked feet, which called for unusual fortitude. We took with us the boy Adeodatus, my son after the flesh, the offspring of my sin. You had made of him a noble lad. He was barely fifteen years old, but his intelligence excelled that of many grave and learned men. I confess to you your gifts, lord my god, creator of all, who have power to reform our deformities—for there was nothing of me in that boy but the sin. For it was you who inspired us to foster him in your discipline, and none other—your gifts I confess to you. There is a book of mine, entitled *The Teacher*. It is a dialogue between Adeodatus and me, and you know that all things there put into the mouth of my interlocutor are his, though he was then only in his sixteenth year.[6] Many other gifts even more wonderful I found in him. His talent was a source of awe to me. And who but you could be the worker of such marvels? And you quickly removed his life from the earth, and even now I recall him to mind with a sense of security, because I fear nothing for his childhood or youth, nor for his whole career. We took him for our companion, as if he were the same age in grace with ourselves, to be trained with ourselves in your discipline. And so we were baptized and the anxiety about our past life left us. Nor did I ever have enough in those days of the wondrous sweetness of meditating on the depth of your counsels concerning the salvation of the human race. How freely I wept in your hymns and canticles; how deeply was I moved by the voices of your sweet-speaking church! The voices flowed into my ears and the truth was poured forth into my heart, where the tide of my devotion overflowed, and my tears ran down, and I was happy in all these things.

[9.7.15] The church of Milan had only recently begun to employ this mode of consolation and exaltation with all the brethren singing together with great earnestness of voice and heart. For it was only about a year, not much more, since Justina, the mother of the boy-emperor Valentinian, had persecuted your servant Ambrose on behalf of her heresy, in which she had been seduced by the Arians. The devoted people kept guard in the church, prepared to die with their bishop, your servant. Among them my mother, your handmaid, taking a leading part in those anxieties and vigils, lived there in prayer. And even though we were still not wholly melted by the heat of your spirit, we were nevertheless excited by the alarmed and disturbed city. This was the time that the custom began, after the manner of the eastern church, that hymns and psalms should be sung, so that the people would not be worn out with the tedium of lamentation. This custom, retained from then till now, has been imitated by many, indeed, by almost all your congregations throughout the rest of the world.[7]

[9.7.16] Then by a vision you made known to your renowned bishop the spot where lay the bodies of Gervasius and Protasius, the martyrs, whom you had preserved uncorrupted for so many years in your secret storehouse, so that you might produce them at a fit time to check a woman's fury—a woman indeed, but also a queen! When they were discovered and dug up and brought with due honor to the basilica of Ambrose, as they were borne along the road many who were troubled by unclean spirits—the devils confessing themselves—were healed.[8] And there was also a certain man, a well-known citizen of the city, blind many years, who, when he had asked and learned the reason for the people's tumultuous joy, rushed out and begged his guide to lead him to the place. When he arrived there, he begged to be permitted to touch with his handkerchief the bier of your saints, whose death is precious in your sight. When he had done this, and put it to his eyes, they were immediately opened. The fame of all this spread abroad, from this your glory shone more brightly. And also from this the mind of that angry woman, though not enlarged to the sanity of a full faith, was nevertheless restrained from the fury of persecution.

Thanks to you, my god. Whence and whither have you led my memory, that I should confess such things as these to you? For great as they were, I had forgetfully passed them over. And yet at that time, when the sweet savor of your ointment was so fragrant, I did not run after you.* Therefore, I wept more bitterly as I listened to your hymns, having so long panted after you. And now at length I could breathe as much as the space allows in this our straw house.

[9.8.17] You, lord, who make those of one mind to dwell in a single house, also brought Evodius to join our company. He was a young man of our city, who, while serving as a special agent, was converted to you and baptized before us. He had relinquished his secular service, and prepared

---

* Song of Solomon 1:3–4.

himself for yours.[9] We were together, and we were resolved to live together in our devout purpose. We cast about for some place where we might be most useful in our service to you, and had planned on going back together to Africa. And when we had got as far as Ostia on the Tiber, my mother died.[10]

I am passing over many things, for I must hasten. Receive, my god, my confessions and thanksgiving for the unnumbered things about which I am silent. But I will not omit anything my mind has brought back concerning your handmaid who brought me forth in her flesh, so that I might be born into this world's light, and in her heart, so that I might be born to life eternal. I will not speak of her gifts, but of your gift in her; for she neither made herself nor trained herself. You created her, and neither her father nor her mother knew what kind of being was to come forth from them. And it was the rod of your Christ, the discipline of your only son, that trained her in your fear, in the house of one of your faithful ones who was a sound member of your church. Yet my mother did not attribute this good training of hers as much to the diligence of her own mother as to that of a certain elderly maidservant who had nursed her father, carrying him around on her back, as big girls carried babies. Because of her long-time service and also because of her extreme age and excellent character, she was much respected by the heads of that Christian household. The care of her master's daughters was also committed to her, and she performed her task with diligence. She was quite earnest in restraining them with a holy severity when necessary and instructing them with a sober sagacity. Thus, except at mealtimes at their parents' table—when they were fed very temperately—she would not allow them to drink even water, however parched they were with thirst. In this way she took precautions against an evil custom and added the wholesome advice: "You drink water now only because you don't control the wine; but when you are married and mistresses of pantry and cellar, you may not care for water, but the habit of drinking will be fixed." By such a method of instruction, and her authority, she restrained the longing of their tender age, and regulated even the thirst of the girls to such a decorous control that they no longer wanted what they ought not to have.

[9.8.18] And yet, as your handmaid related to me, her son, there had stolen upon her a love of wine. For, in the ordinary course of things, when her parents sent her as a sober maiden to draw wine from the cask, she would hold a cup under the tap; and then, before she poured the wine into the bottle, she would wet the tips of her lips with a little of it, for more than this her taste refused. She did not do this out of any craving for drink, but out of the overflowing buoyancy of her time of life, which bubbles up with sportiveness and youthful spirits, but is usually borne down by the gravity of the old folks. And so, adding daily a little to that little — for "he that condemns small things shall fall by a little here and a little there"* — she slipped into such a habit as to drink off eagerly her little cup nearly full of wine. Where now was that wise old woman and her strict prohibition? Could anything prevail against our secret disease if your medicine, lord, did not watch over us? Though father and mother and nurturers are absent, you are present, who create, who call, and who also work some good for our salvation, through those who are set over us. What did you do at that time, my god? How did you heal her? How did you make her whole? Did you not bring forth from another woman's soul a hard and bitter insult, like a surgeon's knife from your secret store, and with one thrust drain off all that putrefaction? For the slave girl who used to accompany her to the cellar fell to quarreling with her little mistress, as it sometimes happened when she was alone with her, and cast in her teeth this vice of hers, along with a very bitter insult, calling her a drunkard. Stung by this taunt, my mother saw her own vileness and immediately condemned and renounced it.

As the flattery of friends corrupts, so often do the taunts of enemies instruct. Yet you repay them, not for the good you work through their means, but for the malice they intended. That angry slave girl wanted to infuriate her young mistress, not to cure her, and that is why she spoke up when they were alone. Or perhaps it was because their quarrel just happened to break out at that time and place, or perhaps she was afraid of punishment for having told of it so late. But you, lord, ruler of heaven and earth, who change to your purposes the deepest floods and control the turbulent tide of the ages, you heal one soul by the unsoundness of another; so that no one, when he hears of such a happening, should attribute it to his own power if another person whom he wishes to reform is reformed through a word of his.

[9.9.19] Thus modestly and soberly brought up, she was made subject to her parents by you, rather more than by her parents to you. She arrived at a marriageable age, and she was given to a husband whom she served as her lord. And she busied herself to gain him to you, preaching you to him by her behavior, in which you made her fair and reverently amiable, and admirable to her husband. For she endured with patience his infidelity and never had any dissension with her husband on this account.

---

* Ecclesiasticus 19:1.

For she waited for your mercy upon him until, by believing in you, he might become chaste. Moreover, even though he was earnest in friendship, he was also violent in anger; but she had learned that an angry husband should not be resisted, either in deed or in word. But as soon as he had grown calm and was tranquil, and she saw a fitting moment, she would give him a reason for her conduct, if he had been excited unreasonably. As a result, while many matrons whose husbands were more gentle than hers bore the marks of blows on their disfigured faces, and would in private talk blame the behavior of their husbands, she would blame their tongues, admonishing them seriously—though in a jesting manner—that from the hour they heard what are called the matrimonial tablets read to them, they should think of them as instruments by which they were made servants. So, always being mindful of their condition, they ought not to set themselves up in opposition to their lords. And, knowing what a furious, bad-tempered husband she endured, they marveled that it had never been rumored, nor was there any mark to show, that Patricius had ever beaten his wife, or that there had been any domestic strife between them, even for a day. And when they asked her confidentially the reason for this, she taught them the rule I have mentioned. Those who observed it confirmed the wisdom of it and rejoiced; those who did not observe it were bullied and vexed.

[9.9.20] Even her mother-in-law, who was at first prejudiced against her by the whisperings of malicious servants, she conquered by submission, persevering in it with patience and meekness; with the result that the mother-in-law told her son of the tales of the meddling servants which had disturbed the domestic peace between herself and her daughter-in-law and begged him to punish them for it. In conformity with his mother's wish, and in the interest of family discipline to ensure the future harmony of its members, he had those servants beaten who were pointed out by her who had discovered them; and she promised a similar reward to anyone else who, thinking to please her, should say anything evil of her daughter-in-law. After this no one dared to do so, and they lived together with a wonderful sweetness of mutual good will.

[9.9.21] This other great gift you also bestowed, my god, my mercy, upon that good handmaid of yours, in whose womb you created me. It was that whenever she could she acted as a peacemaker between any differing and discordant spirits, and when she heard very bitter things on either side of a controversy—the kind of bloated and undigested discord which often belches forth bitter words, when crude malice is breathed out by sharp tongues to a present friend against an absent enemy—she would disclose nothing about the one to the other except what might serve toward their reconciliation. This might seem a small good to me if I did not know to my sorrow countless persons who, through the horrid and far-spreading infection of sin, not only repeat to enemies mutually enraged things said in passion against each other, but also add some things that were never said at all. It ought not to be enough in a truly humane person merely not to incite or increase the enmities of people by evil-speaking; one ought likewise to endeavor by kind words to extinguish them. Such a one was she—and you, her most intimate instructor, taught her in the school of her heart.

[9.9.22] Finally, her own husband, now toward the end of his earthly existence, she won over to you. Henceforth, she had no cause to complain of unfaithfulness in him, which she had endured before he became one of the faithful. She was also the servant of your servants. All those who knew her greatly praised, honored, and loved you in her because, through the witness of the fruits of a holy life, they recognized you present in her heart. For she had "been the wife of one man,"* had honored her parents, had guided her house in piety, was highly reputed for good works, and brought up her children, travailing in labor with them as often as she saw them swerving from you. Lastly, to all of us, lord—since of your favor you allow your servants to speak—to all of us who lived together in that association before her death in you she devoted such care as she might have if she had been mother of us all, while she served us as if she had been the daughter of us all.

[9.10.23] As the day now approached on which she was to depart this life—a day which you knew, but which we did not—it happened (though I believe it was by your secret ways arranged) that she and I stood alone, leaning in a certain window from which the garden of the house we occupied at Ostia could be seen. Here in this place, removed from the crowd, we were resting ourselves for the voyage after the fatigues of a long journey. We were conversing alone very pleasantly and "forgetting those things which are past, and reaching forward toward those things which are future."† We were in the present, and in the presence of truth (which you are), discussing together what is the nature of the eternal life of the saints, "which eye has not seen, nor ear heard, neither has entered into the heart of man."‡ We opened wide the mouth of our heart, thirsting for those

---

* 1 Timothy 5:9.
† Philippians 3:13.
‡ 1 Corinthians 2:9.

supernal streams of your fountain, the fountain of life which is with you, so that we might be sprinkled with its waters according to our capacity and might in some measure weigh the truth of so profound a mystery.

[9.10.24] And when our conversation had brought us to the point where the very highest of physical sense and the most intense illumination of physical light seemed, in comparison with the sweetness of that life to come, not worthy of comparison, nor even of mention, we lifted ourselves with a more ardent love toward the "selfsame,"* and we gradually passed through all the levels of bodily objects, and even through the heaven itself, where the sun and moon and stars shine on the earth. Indeed, we soared higher yet by an inner musing, speaking and marveling at your works. And we came at last to our own minds and went beyond them, in order that we might climb as high as that region of unfailing plenty where you feed Israel forever with the food of truth, where life is that wisdom by whom all things are made, both which have been and which are to be. Wisdom is not made, but is as it has been and forever shall be, for "to have been" and "to be hereafter" do not apply to it, but only "to be," because it is eternal and "to have been" and "to be hereafter" are not eternal. And while we were thus speaking and straining after it, we just barely touched it with the whole effort of our hearts. Then with a sigh, leaving the first fruits of the spirit bound to that ecstasy, we returned to the sounds of our own tongue, where the spoken word had both beginning and end. But what is like to your word, our lord, which remains in itself without becoming old, and makes all things new?

[9.10.25] What we said went something like this: "If to any man the tumult of the flesh were silenced; and the phantoms of earth and waters and air were silenced; and the poles were silent as well; indeed, if the very soul grew silent to itself, and went beyond itself by not thinking of itself; if fancies and imaginary revelations were silenced; if every tongue and every sign and every transient thing—for actually if anyone could hear them, all these would say, 'We did not create ourselves, but were created by him who abides forever'—and if, having uttered this, they too should be silent, having stirred our ears to hear him who created them; and if then he alone spoke, not through them but by himself, so that we might hear his word, not in fleshly tongue or angelic voice, nor sound of thunder, nor the obscurity of a parable, but might hear him—him for whose sake we love these things—if we could hear him without these, as we two now

---

* Psalms 4:9 (not in all modern versions).

strained ourselves to do, we then with rapid thought might touch on that eternal wisdom which abides over all. And if this could be sustained, and other visions of a far different kind be taken away, and this one should so ravish and absorb and envelop its beholder in these inward joys that his life might be eternally like that one moment of knowledge which we now sighed after—would not this be the reality of the saying, 'Enter into the joy of your lord'?* But when shall such a thing be? Shall it not be 'when we all shall rise again,' and shall it not be that 'all things will be changed'?"†

[9.10.26] Such a thought I was expressing, and if not in this manner and in these words, still, lord, you know that on that day we were talking thus and that this world, with all its joys, seemed cheap to us even as we spoke. Then my mother said: "Son, for myself I have no longer any pleasure in anything in this life. Now that my hopes in this world are satisfied, I do not know what more I want here or why I am here. There was indeed one thing for which I wished to tarry a little in this life, and that was that I might see you a catholic Christian before I died. My god has answered this more than abundantly, so that I see you now made his servant and spurning all earthly happiness. What more am I to do here?"

[9.11.27] I do not well remember what reply I made to her about this. However, it was scarcely five days later, certainly not much more, that she was prostrated by fever. While she was sick, she fainted one day and was for a short time quite unconscious. We hurried to her, and when she soon regained her senses, she looked at me and my brother[11] as we stood by her, and said, in inquiry, "Where was I?" Then looking intently at us, dumb in our grief, she said, "Here in this place shall you bury your mother." I was silent and held back my tears but my brother said something, wishing her the happier lot of dying in her own country and not abroad. When she heard this, she fixed him with her eye and an anxious countenance, because he savored of such earthly concerns, and then gazing at me she said, "See how he speaks." Soon after, she said to us both: "Lay this body anywhere, and do not let the care of it be a trouble to you at all. Only this I ask: that you will remember me at the lord's altar, wherever you are." And when she had expressed her wish in such words as she could, she fell silent, in heavy pain with her increasing sickness.

[9.11.28] But as I thought about your gifts, invisible god, which you

---

* Matthew 25:21.
† 1 Corinthians 15:51.

plant in the heart of your faithful ones, from which such marvelous fruits spring up, I rejoiced and gave thanks to you, remembering what I had known of how she had always been much concerned about her burial place, which she had provided and prepared for herself by the body of her husband. For as they had lived very peacefully together, her desire had always been—so little is the human mind capable of grasping things divine—that this last should be added to all that happiness, and commented on by others: that, after her travels beyond the sea, it would be granted her that the two of them, so united on earth, should lie in the same grave. When this vanity, through the bounty of your goodness, had begun to be no longer in her heart, I do not know; but I joyfully marveled at what she had thus disclosed to me—though indeed in our conversation in the window, when she said, "What is there here for me to do any more?" she appeared not to desire to die in her own country. I heard later on that, during our stay in Ostia, she had been talking in maternal confidence to some of my friends about her contempt of this life and the blessing of death. When they were amazed at the courage which was given her, a woman, and had asked her whether she did not dread having her body buried so far from her own city, she replied: "Nothing is far from god. I do not fear that, at the end of time, he should not know the place from which he is to resurrect me." And so on the ninth day of her sickness, in the fifty-sixth year of her life and the thirty-third of mine, that religious and devout soul was set loose from the body.

[9.12.29] I closed her eyes, and there flowed in a great sadness on my heart and it was passing into tears, when at the strong behest of my mind my eyes sucked back the fountain dry, and sorrow was in me like a convulsion. As soon as she breathed her last, the boy Adeodatus burst out wailing; but he was checked by us all, and became quiet. Likewise, my own childish feeling which was, through the youthful voice of my heart, seeking escape in tears, was held back and silenced. For we did not consider it fitting to celebrate that death with tearful wails and groanings. This is the way those who die unhappy or are altogether dead are usually mourned. But she neither died unhappy nor did she altogether die. For of this we were assured by the witness of her good life, her unfeigned faith, and other manifest evidence.

[9.12.30] What was it, then, that hurt me so grievously in my heart except the newly made wound, caused from having the sweet and dear habit of living together with her suddenly broken? I was full of joy because of her testimony in her last illness, when she praised my dutiful attention and called me kind, and recalled with great affection of love that she had never heard any harsh or reproachful sound from my mouth against her. But yet, my god who made us, how can that honor I paid her be compared with her service to me? I was then left destitute of a great comfort in her, and my soul was stricken; and that life was torn apart, as it were, which had been made but one out of hers and mine together.

[9.12.31] When the boy was restrained from weeping, Evodius took up the psalter and began to sing, with the whole household responding, the psalm, "I will sing of mercy and judgment to you, lord."* And when they heard what we were doing, many of the brethren and religious women came together. And while those whose office it was to prepare for the funeral went about their task according to custom, I discoursed in another part of the house, with those who thought I should not be left alone, on what was appropriate to the occasion. By this balm of truth, I softened the anguish known to you. They were unconscious of it and listened intently and thought me free of any sense of sorrow. But in your ears, where none of them heard, I reproached myself for the mildness of my feelings, and restrained the flow of my grief which bowed a little to my will. The paroxysm returned again, and I knew what I repressed in my heart, even though it did not make me burst forth into tears or even change my countenance; and I was greatly annoyed that these human things had such power over me, which in the due order and destiny of our natural condition must of necessity happen. And so with a new sorrow I sorrowed for my sorrow and was wasted with a twofold sadness.

[9.12.32] So, when the body was carried forth, we both went and returned without tears. For neither in those prayers which we poured forth to you, when the sacrifice of our redemption was offered up to you for her—with the body placed by the side of the grave as the custom is there, before it is lowered down into it—neither in those prayers did I weep. But I was most grievously sad in secret all the day, and with a troubled mind entreated you, as I could, to heal my sorrow; but you did not. I now believe that you were fixing in my memory, by this one lesson, the power of the bonds of all habit, even on a mind which now no longer feeds upon deception. It then occurred to me that it would be a good thing to go and bathe, for I had heard that the word for bath [*balneum*] derives from the Greek *balaneion*, because it throws grief out of the mind.[12] Now see, this also I confess to your mercy, "father of the fatherless":† I bathed and felt

---

* Psalms 101:1.

† Psalms 68:5.

the same as I had done before. For the bitterness of my grief was not sweated from my heart. Then I slept, and when I awoke I found my grief not a little assuaged. And as I lay there on my bed, those true verses of Ambrose came to my mind, for you are truly,

> Deus, creator omnium,
> Polique rector, vestiens
> Diem decoro lumine,
> Noctem sopora gratia;

> Artus solutos ut quies
> Reddat laboris usui
> Mentesque fessas allevet,
> Luctusque solvat anxios.

> *God, creator of all,*
> *Ruler of the heavens,*
> *You dress the day in lovely light,*
> *And the night with gracious sleep,*

> *So rest restores wearied limbs*
> *To useful work,*
> *Eases tired minds*
> *And undoes heavy griefs.*[13]

[9.12.33] And then, little by little, there came back to me my former memories of your handmaid: her devout life toward you, her holy tenderness and attentiveness toward us, which had suddenly been taken away from me—and it was a solace for me to weep in your sight, for her and for myself, about her and about myself. Thus I set free the tears which before I repressed, so that they might flow at will, spreading them out as a pillow beneath my heart. And it rested on them, for your ears were near me—not those of a man, who would have made a scornful comment about my weeping. But now in writing I confess it to you, lord! Read it those who will, and comment how they will, and if they find me to have sinned in weeping for my mother for part of an hour—that mother who was for a while dead to my eyes, who had for many years wept for me so that I might live in your eyes—let them not laugh at me; but if they are persons of generous love, let them weep for my sins against you, the father of all the brethren of your Christ.

[9.13.34] Now that my heart is healed of that wound—so far as it can be charged against me as a carnal affection—I pour out to you, our god, on behalf of your handmaid, tears of a very different sort: those which flow from a spirit broken by the thoughts of the dangers of every soul that dies in Adam. And while she had been made alive in Christ even before she was freed from the flesh, and had so lived as to praise your name both by her faith and by her life, yet I would not dare say that from the time you regenerated her by baptism no word came out of her mouth against your precepts. But it has been declared by your son, the truth, that "whosoever shall say to his brother, You fool, shall be in danger of hell-fire."* And there would be doom even for the life of a praiseworthy man if you judged it with your mercy set aside. But since you do not so stringently inquire after our sins, we hope with confidence to find some place in your presence. But whoever recounts his actual and true merits to you, what is he doing but recounting to you your own gifts? If only human beings would know themselves as but human, then "he that glories would glory in the Lord"!†

[9.13.35] Thus now, my praise and my life, god of my heart, forgetting for a little her good deeds for which I give joyful thanks to you, I now beseech you for the sins of my mother. Hearken to me, through that medicine of our wounds, who hung upon the tree and who sits at your right hand making intercession for us. I know that she acted in mercy, and from the heart forgave her debtors their debts. I beseech you also to forgive her debts, whatever she contracted during so many years since the water of salvation. Forgive her, lord, forgive her, I beseech you; enter not into judgment with her. Let your mercy be exalted above your justice, for your words are true and you have promised mercy to the merciful, that the merciful shall obtain mercy.‡ This is your gift, who "have mercy on whom you will have mercy and who will have compassion on whom you have compassion."§

[9.13.36] Indeed, I believe you have already done what I ask of you, but "accept the freewill offerings of my mouth, lord."‖ For when the day of her dissolution was so close, she took no thought to have her body sumptuously

---

* Matthew 5:22.

† 2 Corinthians 10:17.

‡ Matthew 5:7.

§ Romans 9:15.

‖ Psalms 119:108.

wrapped or embalmed with spices. Nor did she covet a handsome monument, or even care to be buried in her own country.[14] About these things she gave no commands at all, but only desired to have her name remembered at your altar, where she had served without the omission of a single day, and where she knew that the holy sacrifice was dispensed by which that handwriting that was against us is blotted out;* and that enemy vanquished who, when he summed up our offenses and searched for something to bring against us, could find nothing in him, in whom we conquer. Who will restore to him the innocent blood? Who will repay him the price with which he bought us, so as to take us from him? Thus to the sacrament of our redemption did your handmaid bind her soul by the bond of faith. Let none separate her from your protection. Let not the lion and dragon bar her way by force or fraud. For she will not reply that she owes nothing, lest she be convicted and duped by that cunning deceiver. Rather, she will answer that her sins are forgiven by him to whom no one is able to repay the price which he, who owed us nothing, laid down for us all.

[9.13.37] Therefore, let her rest in peace with her husband, before and after whom she was married to no other man, whom she obeyed with patience, bringing fruit to you that she might also win him for you. And inspire, my lord my god, inspire your servants, my brothers, your sons, my masters, who with voice and heart and writings I serve, that as many of them as shall read these confessions may also at your altar remember Monica, your handmaid, together with Patricius, once her husband, by whose flesh you did bring me into this life, in a manner I know not. May they with pious affection remember my parents in this transitory life, and remember my brothers under you our father in our catholic mother, and remember my fellow citizens in the eternal Jerusalem, for which your people sigh in their travel abroad from birth until their return. So be fulfilled what my mother desired of me, more richly in the prayers of so many gained for her through these confessions of mine than by my prayers alone.

---

* Colossians 2:14.

BOOK 10

[10.1.1] Let me know you, my knower; let me know you even as I am known. Strength of my soul, enter it and prepare it for yourself so that you may have and hold it, without spot or blemish. This is my hope, therefore have I spoken; and in this hope I rejoice whenever I rejoice aright. But as for the other things of this life, they deserve our lamentations less, the more we lament them; and some should be lamented all the more, the less men care for them. For see, "You desire truth"* and "he who does the truth comes to the light."† This is what I wish to do through confession in my heart before you, and in my writings before many witnesses.

[10.2.2] And what is there in me that could be hidden from you, lord, to whose eyes the abysses of man's conscience are naked, even if I were unwilling to confess it to you? In doing so I would only hide you from myself, not myself from you. But now that my groaning is witness to the fact that I am dissatisfied with myself, you shine forth and satisfy. You are beloved and desired; so that I blush for myself, and renounce myself and choose you, for I can neither please you nor myself except in you. To you, then, lord, I am laid bare, whatever I am, and I have already said with what profit I may confess to you. I do not do it with words and sounds of the flesh but with the words of the soul, and with the sound of my thoughts, which your ear knows. For when I am wicked, to confess to you means nothing less than to be dissatisfied with myself, but when I am truly devout, it means nothing less than not to attribute my virtue to myself; because you, lord, bless the righteous, but first you justify him while he is yet ungodly. My confession therefore, my god, is made to you silently in your sight—and yet not silently. As far as sound is concerned, it is silent. But in strong affection it cries aloud. For neither do I give voice to something that sounds right to human beings, which you have not heard from me before, nor do you hear anything of the kind from me which you did not first say to me.

[10.3.3] What is it to me that men should hear my confessions as if it were they who were going to cure all my infirmities? People are curious

---

* Psalms 51:6.

† John 3:21.

to know the lives of others, but slow to correct their own. Why are they anxious to hear from me what I am, when they are unwilling to hear from you what they are? And how can they tell when they hear what I say about myself whether I speak the truth, since no man knows what is in a man "except the spirit of man which is in him"?* But if they were to hear from you something concerning themselves, they would not be able to say, "The lord is lying." For what does it mean to hear from you about themselves but to know themselves? And who is he that knows himself and says, "This is false," unless he himself is lying? But, because "love believes all things"†—at least among those who are bound together in love by its bonds—I confess to you, lord, so that men may also hear; for if I cannot prove to them that I confess the truth, yet those whose ears love opens to me will believe me.

[10.3.4] But will you, my inner physician, make clear to me what profit I am to gain in doing this? For the confessions of my past sins (which you have forgiven and covered so that you might make me blessed in you, transforming my soul by faith and your sacrament), when they are read and heard, may stir up the heart so that it will stop dozing along in despair, saying, "I cannot," but will instead awake in the love of your mercy and the sweetness of your grace, by which he that is weak is strong, provided he is made conscious of his own weakness. And it will please those who are good to hear about the past errors of those who are now freed from them. And they will take delight, not because they are errors, but because they were and are so no longer. What profit, then, lord my god—to whom my conscience makes its daily confession, far more confident in the hope of your mercy than in its own innocence—what profit is there, I ask you, in confessing to human beings in your presence, through this book, both what I am now as well as what I have been? For I have seen and spoken of my harvest of things past. But what am I now, at this very moment of making my confessions? Many different people desire to know, both those who know me and those who do not know me. Some have heard about me or from me, but their ear is not close to my heart, where I am whatever it is that I am. They have the desire to hear me confess what I am within, where they can neither extend eye nor ear nor mind. They desire as those willing to believe—but will they understand? For the love by which they are good tells them that I am not lying in my confessions, and the love in them believes me.

---

* 1 Corinthians 2:11.
† 1 Corinthians 13:7.

[**10.4.5**] But for what profit do they desire this? Will they wish me happiness when they learn how near I have approached you, by your gifts? And will they pray for me when they learn how much I am still kept back by my own weight? To such as these I will declare myself. For it is no small profit, lord my god, that many people should give thanks to you on my account and that many should entreat you for my sake. Let the brotherly soul love in me what you teach him should be loved, and let him lament in me what you teach him should be lamented. Let it be the soul of a brother that does this, and not a stranger—not one of those "strange children, whose mouth speaks vanity, and whose right hand is the right hand of falsehood."* But let my brother do it who, when he approves of me, rejoices for me, but when he disapproves of me is sorry for me; because whether he approves or disapproves, he loves me. To such I will declare myself. Let them be refreshed by my good deeds and sigh over my evil ones. My good deeds are your acts and your gifts; my evil ones are my own faults and your judgment. Let them breathe expansively at the one and sigh over the other. And let hymns and tears ascend in your sight out of their brotherly hearts—which are your censers. And, lord, who take delight in the incense of your holy temple, have mercy upon me according to your great mercy, for your name's sake. And do not, on any account whatever, abandon what you have begun in me. Go on, rather, to complete what is yet imperfect in me.

[**10.4.6**] This, then, is the fruit of my confessions (not of what I was, but of what I am), that I may not confess this before you alone, in a secret exultation with trembling and a secret sorrow with hope, but also in the ears of the believing sons of men—who are the companions of my joy and sharers of my mortality, my fellow citizens and fellow travelers—those who have gone before and those who are to follow after, as well as the comrades of my present way. These are your servants, my brothers, whom you desire to be your sons. They are my masters, whom you have commanded me to serve if I desire to live with and in you. But this your word would mean little to me if it commanded in words alone, without your prevenient action. I do this, then, both in act and word. I do this under your wings, in a danger too great to risk if it were not that under your wings my soul is subject to you, and my weakness known to you. I am insufficient, but my father lives forever, and my defender is sufficient for

---

* Psalms 144:7–8.

me. For he is the selfsame who begot me and who watches over me; you are the selfsame who are all my good. You are the omnipotent, who are with me, even before I am with you. To those, therefore, whom you command me to serve, I will declare, not what I was, but what I now am and what I will continue to be. But I do not judge myself. Thus, therefore, let me be heard.

[10.5.7] For it is you, lord, who judge me. For although no man "knows the things of a man, except the spirit of the man which is in him,"* yet there is something of man which the spirit of the man which is in him does not know itself. But you, lord, who made him, know him completely. And even I — though in your sight I despise myself and count myself but dust and ashes — even I know something about you which I do not know about myself. And it is certain that "now we see through a glass darkly, not yet face to face."† Therefore, as long as I journey away from you, I am more present with myself than with you. I know that you cannot suffer violence, but I myself do not know what temptations I can resist, and what I cannot. But there is hope, because you are faithful and you will not allow us to be tempted beyond our ability to resist, but will with the temptation also make a way of escape so that we may be able to bear it. I would therefore confess what I know about myself; I will also confess what I do not know about myself. What I do know of myself, I know from your enlightening of me; and what I do not know of myself, I will continue not to know until the time when my "darkness is as the noonday"‡ in your sight.

[10.6.8] It is not with a doubtful consciousness, but one fully certain that I love you, lord. You have smitten my heart with your word, and I have loved you. And see also the heaven, and earth, and all that is in them — on every side they tell me to love you, and they do not cease to tell this to all human beings, "so that they are without excuse."§ Wherefore, still more deeply will you have mercy on whom you will have mercy, and compassion on whom you will have compassion. For otherwise, both heaven and earth would tell abroad your praises to deaf ears. But what is it that I love in loving you?[1] Not physical beauty, nor the splendor of time, nor the radiance of the light — so pleasant to our eyes — nor the

---

* 1 Corinthians 2:11.

† 1 Corinthians 13:12.

‡ Isaiah 58:10.

§ Romans 1:20.

sweet melodies of the various kinds of songs, nor the fragrant smell of flowers and ointments and spices; not manna and honey, not the limbs embraced in physical love—it is not these I love when I love my god. Yet it is true that I love a certain kind of light and sound and fragrance and food and embrace in loving my god, who is the light and sound and fragrance and food and embracement of my inner being—where that light shines into my soul which no place can contain, where time does not snatch away the lovely sound, where no breeze disperses the sweet fragrance, where no eating diminishes the food there provided, and where there is an embrace that no satiety comes to sunder. This is what I love when I love my god.

[**10.6.9**] And what is this god? I asked the earth, and it answered, "I am not he"; and everything in the earth made the same confession. I asked the sea and the deeps and the creeping things, and they replied, "We are not your god; seek above us." I asked the fleeting winds, and the whole air with its inhabitants answered, "Anaximenes was deceived; I am not god."[2] I asked the heavens, the sun, moon, and stars; and they answered, "Neither are we the god whom you seek." And I replied to all these things which stand around the door of my flesh: "You have told me about my god, that you are not he. Tell me something about him." And with a loud voice they all cried out, "He made us." My question had come from my observation of them, and their reply came from their beauty of order. And I turned my thoughts into myself and said, "Who are you?" And I answered, "A human being." For see, there is in me both a body and a soul; the one without, the other within. In which of these should I have sought my god, whom I had already sought with my body from earth to heaven, as far as I was able to send those messengers—the beams of my eyes? But the inner part is the better part; for to it, as both ruler and judge, all these messengers of the senses report the answers of heaven and earth and all the things therein, who said, "We are not god, but he made us." My inner being knew these things through the ministry of the outer being, and I, the inner being, knew all this—I, the soul, through the senses of my body. I asked the whole frame of earth about my god, and it answered, "I am not he, but he made me."

[**10.6.10**] Is not this beauty of form visible to all whose senses are unimpaired? Why, then, does it not say the same things to all? Animals, both small and great, see it but they are unable to interrogate its meaning, because their senses are not endowed with the reason that would enable them to judge the evidence which the senses report. But a human being can interrogate it, so that "the invisible things of him are clearly seen, being understood by the things that are made."* But human beings love these created things too much; they are brought into subjection to them—and, as subjects, are not able to judge. None of these created things reply to their questioners unless they can make rational judgments. The creatures will not alter their voice—that is, their beauty of form—if one person simply sees what another both sees and questions, so that the world appears one way to this person and another to that. It appears the same way to both; but it is mute to this one and it speaks to that one. Indeed, it actually speaks to all, but only they understand it who compare the voice received from without with the truth within. For the truth says to me, "Neither heaven nor earth nor anybody is your god." Their very nature tells this to the one who beholds them. They are a mass, less in part than the whole. Now, my soul, you are my better part, and to you I speak; since you animate the whole mass of your body, giving it life, whereas no body furnishes life to a body. But your god is the life of your life.

[**10.7.11**] What is it, then, that I love when I love my god? Who is he that is beyond the topmost point of my soul? Yet by this very soul will I mount up to him. I will soar beyond that power of mine by which I am united to the body, and by which the whole structure of it is filled with life. Yet it is not by that vital power that I find my god. For then "the horse and the mule, that have no understanding,"† also might find him, since they have the same vital power, by which their bodies also live. But there is, besides the power by which I animate my body, another by which I endow my flesh with sense—a power that the lord has provided for me; commanding that the eye is not to hear and the ear is not to see, but that I am to see by the eye and to hear by the ear; and giving to each of the other senses its own proper place and function, through the diversity of which I, the single mind, act. I will soar also beyond this power of mine, for the horse and mule have this too, for they also perceive through their bodily senses.

[**10.8.12**] I will soar, then, beyond this power of my nature also, still rising by degrees toward him who made me. And I enter the fields and spacious halls of memory, where are stored as treasures the countless images that have been brought into them from all manner of things by the senses. There, in the memory, is likewise stored what we cogitate, either by enlarging or reducing our perceptions, or by altering one way or another

---

* Romans 1:20.
† Psalms 32:9.

those things which the senses have made contact with; and everything else that has been entrusted to it and stored up in it, which oblivion has not yet swallowed up and buried. When I go into this storehouse, I ask that what I want should be brought forth. Some things appear immediately, but others require to be searched for longer, and then dragged out, as it were, from some hidden recess. Other things hurry forth in crowds, on the other hand, and while something else is sought and inquired for, they leap into view as if to say, "Is it not we, perhaps?" These I brush away with the hand of my heart from the face of my memory, until finally the thing I want makes its appearance out of its secret cell. Some things suggest themselves without effort, and in continuous order, just as they are called for—the things that come first give place to those that follow, and in so doing are treasured up again to be forthcoming when I want them. All of this happens when I repeat a thing from memory.

[10.8.13] All these things, each one of which came into memory in its own particular way, are stored up separately and under the general categories of understanding. For example, light and all colors and forms of bodies came in through the eyes; sounds of all kinds by the ears; all smells by the passages of the nostrils; all flavors by the gate of the mouth; by the sensation of the whole body, there is brought in what is hard or soft, hot or cold, smooth or rough, heavy or light, whether external or internal to the body. The vast cave of memory, with its numerous and mysterious recesses, receives all these things and stores them up, to be recalled and brought forth when required. Each experience enters by its own door, and is stored up in the memory. And yet the things themselves do not enter it, but only the images of the things perceived are there for thought to remember. And who can tell how these images are formed, even if it is evident which of the senses brought which perception in and stored it up? For even when I am in darkness and silence I can bring out colors in my memory if I wish, and discern between black and white and the other shades as I wish; and at the same time, sounds do not break in and disturb what is drawn in by my eyes, and which I am considering, because the sounds which are also there are stored up, as it were, apart. And these too I can summon if I please and they are immediately present in memory. And though my tongue is at rest and my throat silent, yet I can sing as I will; and those images of color, which are as truly present as before, do not interpose themselves or interrupt while another treasure which had flowed in through the ears is being thought about. Similarly all the other things that were brought in and heaped up by all the other senses, I can recall at my pleasure. And I distinguish the scent of lilies from that of violets while actually smelling nothing; and I prefer honey to mead, a smooth thing to a rough, even though I am neither tasting nor handling them, but only remembering them.

[**10.8.14**] All this I do within myself, in that huge hall of my memory. For in it, heaven, earth, and sea are present to me, and whatever I can cogitate about them—except what I have forgotten. There also I meet myself and recall myself—what, when, or where I did a thing, and how I felt when I did it. There are all the things that I remember, either having experienced them myself or been told about them by others. Out of the same storehouse, with these past impressions, I can construct now this, now that, image of things that I either have experienced or have believed on the basis of experience—and from these I can further construct future actions, events, and hopes; and I can meditate on all these things as if they were present.[3] "I will do this or that"—I say to myself in that vast recess of my mind, with its full store of so many and such great images—"and this or that will follow upon it." "O that this or that could happen!" "God prevent this or that." I speak to myself in this way; and when I speak, the images of what I am speaking about are present out of the same store of memory; and if the images were absent I could say nothing at all about them.

[**10.8.15**] Great is this power of memory, exceedingly great, my god—a large and boundless inner hall! Who has plumbed the depths of it? Yet it is a power of my mind, and it belongs to my nature. But I do not myself grasp all that I am. Thus the mind is far too narrow to contain itself. But where can that part of it be which it does not contain? Is it outside and not in itself? How can it be, then, that the mind cannot grasp itself? A great marvel rises in me; astonishment seizes me. Men go forth to marvel at the heights of mountains and the huge waves of the sea, the broad flow of the rivers, the vastness of the ocean, the orbits of the stars, and yet they neglect to marvel at themselves.[4] Nor do they wonder how it is that, when I spoke of all these things, I was not looking at them with my eyes—and yet I could not have spoken about them had it not been that I was actually seeing within, in my memory, those mountains and waves and rivers and stars which I have seen, and that ocean which I believe in—and with the same vast spaces between them as when I saw them outside me. But when I saw them outside me, I did not take them into me by seeing them; and the things themselves are not inside me, but only their images. And yet I knew through which physical sense each experience had made an impression on me.

[**10.9.16**] And yet this is not all that the unlimited capacity of my memory stores up. In memory, there are also all that one has learned of the liberal sciences, and has not forgotten—removed still further, so to say, into an inner place which is not a place. Of these things it is not the images that are retained, but the things themselves. For what grammar and logic are, and what I know about how many different kinds of questions there are—all these are stored in my memory as they are, so that I have not taken in the image and left the thing outside. It is not as though a sound had sounded and passed away like a voice heard by the ear which leaves a trace by which it can be called into memory again, as if it were still sounding in mind while it did so no longer outside. Nor is it the same as an odor which, even after it has passed and vanished into the wind, affects the sense of smell—which then conveys into the memory the image of the smell which is what we recall and re-create; or like food which, once in the belly, surely now has no taste and yet does have a kind of taste in the memory; or like anything that is felt by the body through the sense of touch, which still remains as an image in the memory after the external object is removed. For these things themselves are not put into the memory. Only the images of them are gathered with a marvelous quickness and stored, as it were, in the most wonderful filing system, and are thence produced in a marvelous way by the act of remembering.

[**10.10.17**] But now when I hear that there are three kinds of questions—"Whether a thing is? What it is? Of what kind it is?"—I do indeed retain the images of the sounds of which these words are composed and I know that those sounds pass through the air with a noise and now no longer exist. But the things themselves which were signified by those sounds I never could reach by any sense of the body nor see them at all except by my mind. And what I have stored in my memory was not their signs, but the things signified. How they got into me, let them tell who can. For I examine all the gates of my flesh, but I cannot find the door by which any of them entered. For the eyes say, "If they were colored, we reported that." The ears say, "If they gave any sound, we gave notice of that." The nostrils say, "If they smell, they passed in by us." The sense of taste says, "If they have no flavor, don't ask me about them." The sense of touch says, "If it had no bodily mass, I did not touch it, and if I never touched it, I gave no report about it." Whence and how did these things enter into my memory? I do not know. For when I first learned them, it was not that I believed them on the credit of another man's mind, but I recognized them in my own; and I saw them as true, took them into my mind and laid them up, so to say, where I could get at them again whenever I willed. There they were, then, even before I learned them, but they were not in my memory. Where were they, then? How does it come about that when they were spoken of, I could acknowledge them and say, "So it is, it is true," unless they were already in the memory, though far back and hidden, as it were, in the more secret caves, so that unless they had been drawn out by the teaching of another person, I should perhaps never have been able to think of them at all?

[**10.11.18**] Thus we find that learning those things whose images we do not take in by our senses, but which we intuit within ourselves without images and as they actually are, is nothing else except the gathering together of those same things which the memory already contains—but in an indiscriminate and confused manner—and putting them together by careful observation as they are at hand in the memory; so that whereas they formerly lay hidden, scattered, or neglected, they now come easily to present themselves to the mind which is now familiar with them. And how many things of this sort my memory has stored up, which have already been discovered and, as I said, laid up for ready reference! These are the things we may be said to have learned and to know. Yet, if I cease to recall them even for short intervals of time, they are again so submerged—and slide back, as it were, into the further reaches of the memory—that they must be drawn out again as if new from the same place (for there is nowhere else for them to have gone) and must be collected [*cogenda*] so that they can become known. In other words, they must be gathered up [*colligenda*] from their dispersion. This is where we get the word cogitate [*cogitare*]. For *cogo* [collect] and *cogito* [to go on collecting] have the same relation to each other as *ago* [do] and *agito* [do frequently], and *facio* [make] and *factito* [make frequently]. But the mind has properly laid claim to this word [cogitate] so that not everything that is gathered together anywhere, but only what is collected and gathered together in the mind, is properly said to be "cogitated."

[**10.12.19**] The memory also contains the principles and the unnumbered laws of numbers and dimensions. None of these has been impressed on the memory by a physical sense, because they have neither color nor sound, nor taste, nor sense of touch. I have heard the sound of the words by which these things are signified when they are discussed: but the sounds are one thing, the things another. For the sounds are one thing in Greek, another in Latin; but the things themselves are neither Greek nor Latin nor any other language. I have seen the lines of the craftsmen, the finest of which are like a spider's web, but mathematical lines are different. They are not the images of such things as the eye of my body has showed me. The man who knows them does so without any cogitation of physical objects whatever, but intuits them within himself. I have perceived with all the senses of my body the numbers we use in counting; but the numbers by which we count are far different from these. They are not the images of these; they simply are. Let the man who does not see these things mock me for saying them; and I will pity him while he laughs at me.

[10.13.20] All these things I hold in my memory, and I remember how I learned them. I also remember many things that I have heard quite falsely urged against them, which, even if they are false, yet it is not false that I have remembered them. And I also remember that I have distinguished between the truths and the false objections, and now I see that it is one thing to distinguish these things and another to remember that I did distinguish them when I have cogitated on them. I remember, then, both that I have often understood these things and also that I am now storing away in my memory what I distinguish and comprehend of them so that later on I may remember just as I understand them now. Therefore, I remember that I remembered, so that if afterward I call to mind that I once was able to remember these things it will be through the power of memory that I recall it.

[10.14.21] This same memory also contains the feelings of my mind; not in the manner in which the mind itself experienced them, but very differently according to a power peculiar to memory. For without being joyous now, I can remember that I once was joyous, and without being sad, I can recall my past sadness. I can remember past fears without fear, and former desires without desire. Again, the contrary happens. Sometimes when I am joyous I remember my past sadness, and when sad, remember past joy. This is not to be marveled at as far as the body is concerned; for the mind is one thing and the body another. If, therefore, when I am happy, I recall some past bodily pain, it is not so strange. But even as this memory is experienced, it is identical with the mind—as when we tell someone to remember something we say, "See that you bear this in mind"; and when we forget a thing, we say, "It did not enter my mind" or "It slipped my mind." Thus we call memory itself mind. Since this is so, how does it happen that when I am joyful I can still remember past sorrow? Thus the mind has joy, and the memory has sorrow; and the mind is joyful from the joy that is in it, yet the memory is not sad from the sadness that is in it. Is it possible that the memory does not belong to the mind? Who will say so? The memory doubtless is, so to say, the belly of the mind, and joy and sadness are like sweet and bitter food, which when they are committed to the memory are, so to say, passed into the belly where they can be stored but no longer tasted. It is ridiculous to consider this an analogy; yet they are not utterly unlike.

[10.14.22] But look, it is from my memory that I produce it when I say that there are four basic emotions of the mind: desire, joy, fear, sadness. Whatever kind of analysis I may be able to make of these, by dividing each into its particular species, and by defining it, I still find what to say in my memory and it is from my memory that I draw it out. Yet I am not moved by any of these emotions when I call them to mind by remembering them. Moreover, before I recalled them and thought about them, they were there in the memory; and this is how they could be brought forth in remembrance. Perhaps, therefore, just as food is brought up out of the belly by rumination, so also these things are drawn up out of the memory by recall. But why, then, does not the man who is thinking about the emotions, and is thus recalling them, feel in the mouth of his reflection the sweetness of joy or the bitterness of sadness? Is the comparison unlike in this because it is not complete at every point? For who would willingly speak on these subjects, if as often as we used the term sadness or fear, we should thereby be compelled to be sad or fearful? And yet we could never speak of them if we did not find them in our memories, not merely as the sounds of the names, as their images are impressed on it by the physical senses, but also the notions of the things themselves—which we did not receive by any gate of the flesh, but which the mind itself recognizes by the experience of its own passions, and has entrusted to the memory; or else which the memory itself has retained without their being entrusted to it.

[10.15.23] Now whether all this is by means of images or not, who can rightly affirm? For I name a stone, I name the sun, and those things themselves are not present to my senses, but their images are present in my memory. I name some pain of the body, yet it is not present when there is no pain; yet if there were not some such image of it in my memory, I could not even speak of it, nor should I be able to distinguish it from pleasure. I name bodily health when I am sound in body, and the thing itself is indeed present in me. At the same time, unless there were some image of it in my memory, I could not possibly call to mind what the sound of this name signified. Nor would sick people know what was meant when health was named, unless the same image were preserved by the power of memory, even though the thing itself is absent from the body. I can name the numbers we use in counting, and it is not their images but themselves that are in my memory. I name the image of the sun, and this too is in my memory. For I do not recall the image of that image, but that image itself, for the image itself is present when I remember it. I name memory and I know what I name. But where do I know it, except in the memory itself? Is it also present to itself by its image, and not by itself?

[10.16.24] When I name forgetfulness, and understand what I mean by the name, how could I understand it if I did not remember it? And if I refer not to the sound of the name, but to the thing which the term signifies, how could I know what that sound signified if I had forgotten what the name means? When, therefore, I remember memory, then memory is present to itself by itself, but when I remember forgetfulness then both memory and forgetfulness are present together—the memory by which I remember the forgetfulness which I remember. But what is forgetfulness except the privation of memory? How, then, is that present to my memory which, when it controls my mind, I cannot remember? But if what we remember we store up in our memory; and if, unless we remembered forgetfulness, we could never know the thing signified by the term when we heard it—then, forgetfulness is contained in the memory. It is present so that we do not forget it, but since it is present, we do forget. From this it is to be inferred that when we remember forgetfulness, it is not present to the memory through itself, but through its image; because if forgetfulness were present through itself, it would not lead us to remember, but only to forget. Now who will someday work this out? Who can understand how it is?

[10.16.25] Truly, lord, I toil with this and labor in myself. I have become a troublesome field that requires hard labor and heavy sweat. For we are not now searching out the tracts of heaven, or measuring the distances of the stars or inquiring about the weight of the earth. It is I myself—I, the mind—who remember. This is not much to marvel at, if what I myself am is not far from me. And what is nearer to me than myself? For see, I am not able to comprehend the force of my own memory, though I could not even call my own name without it. But what shall I say, when it is clear to me that I remember forgetfulness? Should I affirm that what I remember is not in my memory? Or should I say that forgetfulness is in my memory to the end that I should not forget? Both of these views are most absurd. But what third view is there? How can I say that the image of forgetfulness is retained by my memory, and not forgetfulness itself, when I remember it? How can I say this, since for the image of anything to be imprinted on the memory the thing itself must necessarily have been present first by which the image could have been imprinted? Thus I remember Carthage; thus, also, I remember all the other places where I have been. And I remember the faces of men whom I have seen and things reported by the other senses. I remember the health or sickness of the body. And when these objects were present, my memory received images from them so that they remain present in order for me to see them and reflect upon them in my mind, if I choose to remember them in their absence. If, therefore, forgetfulness is retained in the memory through its image and not through itself, then this means that it itself was once present, so that its image might have been imprinted. But when it was present, how did it write its image on the memory, since forgetfulness, by its presence, blots out even what it finds already written there? And yet in some way or other, even though it is incomprehensible and inexplicable, I am still quite certain that I also remember forgetfulness, by which we remember that something is blotted out.

[10.17.26] Great is the power of memory. It is a true marvel, my god, a profound and infinite multiplicity! And this is the mind, and this I myself am. What, then, am I, my god? Of what nature am I? A life various, and manifold, and exceedingly vast. Look in the numberless halls and caves, in the innumerable fields and dens and caverns of my memory, full without measure of numberless kinds of things—present there either through images as all bodies are; or present in the things themselves as are our thoughts; or by some notion or observation as our emotions are, which the memory retains even though the mind feels them no longer, as long as whatever is in the memory is also in the mind—through all these I run and fly to and fro. I penetrate into them on this side and that as far as I can and yet there is nowhere any end.

So great is the power of memory, so great the power of life in man whose life is mortal! What, then, shall I do, my true life, my god? I will pass even beyond this power of mine that is called memory—I will pass beyond it, that I may come to you, lovely light. And what are you saying to me? See, I soar by my mind toward you, who remain above me. I will also pass beyond this power of mine that is called memory, desiring to reach you where you can be reached, and wishing to cleave to you where it is possible to cleave to you. For even beasts and birds possess memory, or else they could never find their lairs and nests again, nor display many other things they know and do by habit. Indeed, they could not even form their habits except by their memories. I will therefore pass even beyond memory so that I may reach him who has differentiated me from the four-footed beasts and the fowls of the air by making me a wiser creature. Thus I will pass beyond memory; but where shall I find you, who are the true good and the steadfast sweetness? But where shall I find you? If I find you without memory, then I shall have no memory of you; and how could I find you at all, if I do not remember you?

[**10.18.27**] For the woman who lost her small coin* and searched for it with a light would never have found it unless she had remembered it. For when it was found, how could she have known whether it was the same coin, if she had not remembered it? I remember having lost and found many things, and I have learned this from that experience: that when I was searching for any of them and was asked: "Is this it? Is that it?" I answered, "No," until finally what I was seeking was shown to me. But if I had not remembered it—whatever it was—even though it was shown to me, I still would not have found it because I could not have recognized it. And this is the way it always is when we search for and find anything that is lost. Still, if anything is accidentally lost from sight—not from memory, as a visible body might be—its image is retained within, and the thing is searched for until it is restored to sight. And when the thing is found, it is recognized by the image of it which is within. And we do not say that we have found what we have lost unless we can recognize it, and we cannot recognize it unless we remember it. But all the while the thing lost to the sight was retained in the memory.

[**10.19.28**] But what happens when the memory itself loses something, as when we forget anything and try to recall it? Where, finally, do we search, but in the memory itself? And there, if by chance one thing is offered for another, we refuse it until we meet with what we are looking for; and when we do, we recognize that this is it. But we could not do this unless we recognized it, nor could we have recognized it unless we remembered it. Yet we had indeed forgotten it. Perhaps the whole of it had not slipped out of our memory; but a part was retained by which the other lost part was sought for, because the memory realized that it was not operating as smoothly as usual and was being held up by the crippling of its habitual working; hence, it demanded the restoration of what was lacking. For example, if we see or think of some man we know, and, having forgotten his name, try to recall it—if some other thing presents itself, we cannot tie it into the effort to remember, because it was not habitually thought of in association with him. It is consequently rejected, until something comes into the mind on which our knowledge can rightly rest as the familiar and sought-for object. And where does this name come back from, except from the memory itself? For even when we recognize it by another's reminding us of it, still it is from the memory that this comes, for we do not believe it as something new; but when we recall it, we admit

---

* Luke 15:8.

that what was said was correct. But if the name had been entirely blotted out of the mind, we should not be able to recollect it even when reminded of it. For we have not entirely forgotten anything if we can remember that we have forgotten it. For a lost notion, one that we have entirely forgotten, we cannot even search for.

[10.20.29] How, then, do I seek you, lord? For when I seek you, my god, I seek a happy life.[5] I will seek you in order that my soul may live. For my body lives by my soul, and my soul lives by you. How, then, do I seek a happy life, since happiness is not mine till I can rightly say: "It is enough. This is it." How do I seek it? Is it by remembering, as though I had forgotten it and still knew that I had forgotten it? Do I seek it in longing to learn of it as though it were something unknown, which either I had never known or had so completely forgotten as not even to remember that I had forgotten it? Is not the happy life the thing that all desire, and is there anyone who does not desire it at all? But where would they have got the knowledge of it, that they should so desire it? Where have they seen it that they should so love it? It is somehow true that we have it, but how I do not know.

There is, indeed, a sense in which when anyone has his desire he is happy. And then there are some who are happy in hope. These are happy in an inferior degree to those that are actually happy; yet they are better off than those who are happy neither in actuality nor in hope. But even these, if they had not known happiness in some degree, would not then desire to be happy. And yet it is most certain that they do so desire. How they come to know happiness, I cannot tell, but they have it by some kind of knowledge unknown to me, for I am very much in doubt as to whether it is in the memory. For if it is in there, then we have been happy once upon a time—either each of us individually or all of us in that man who first sinned and in whom also we all died and from whom we are all born in misery. How this is, I do not now ask; but I do ask whether the happy life is in the memory. For if we did not know it, we should not love it. We hear the name of it, and we all acknowledge that we desire the thing, for we are not delighted with the name only. For when a Greek hears it spoken in Latin, he does not feel delighted, for he does not know what has been spoken. But we are as delighted as he would be in turn if he heard it in Greek, because the thing itself is neither Greek nor Latin, this happiness which Greeks and Latins and people of all the other tongues long so earnestly to obtain. It is, then, known to all; and if all could with one voice be asked whether they wished to be happy, there is no doubt they would all answer that they would. And this would not be possible unless the thing itself, which we name "happiness," were held in the memory.

[10.21.30] But is it the same kind of memory as that of one who, having seen Carthage, remembers it? No, for the happy life is not visible to the eye, since it is not a physical object. Is it the sort of memory we have for numbers? No, for the man who has these in his understanding does not keep striving to attain more. Now we know something about the happy life and therefore we love it, but still we wish to go on striving for it so that we may be happy. Is the memory of happiness, then, something like the memory of eloquence? No, for although some, when they hear the term eloquence, call the thing to mind, even if they are not themselves eloquent—and further, there are many people who would like to be eloquent, from which it follows that they must know something about it—nevertheless, these people have noticed through their senses that others are eloquent and have been delighted to observe this and long to be this way themselves. But they would not be delighted if it were not some interior knowledge; and they would not desire to be delighted unless they had been delighted. But as for a happy life, there is no physical perception by which we experience it in others.

Do we remember happiness, then, as we remember joy? It may be so, for I remember my joy even when I am sad, just as I remember a happy life when I am miserable. And I have never, through physical perception, either seen, heard, smelled, tasted, or touched my joy. But I have experienced it in my mind when I rejoiced; and the knowledge of it clung to my memory so that I can call it to mind, sometimes with disdain and at other times with longing, depending on the different kinds of things I now remember that I rejoiced in. For I have been bathed with a certain joy even by unclean things, which I now detest and execrate as I call them to mind. At other times, I call to mind with longing good and honest things, which are not any longer near at hand, and I am therefore saddened when I recall my former joy.

[10.21.31] Where and when did I ever experience my happy life so that I can call it to mind and love it and long for it? It is not I alone or even a few others who wish to be happy, but absolutely everybody. Unless we knew happiness by a knowledge that is certain, we should not wish for it with a will which is so certain. Take this example. If two men were asked whether they wished to serve as soldiers, one of them might reply that he would, and the other that he would not; but if they were asked whether they wished to be happy, both of them would unhesitatingly say that they would. But the first one would wish to serve as a soldier and the other would not wish to serve, both from no other motive than to be happy. Is it, perhaps, that one finds his joy in this and another in that? Thus they agree in their wish for happiness just as they would also agree, if asked, in wishing for joy. Is this joy what they call a happy life? Although one could choose his joy in this way and another in that, all have one goal which they strive to attain, namely, to have joy. This joy, then, being something that no one can say he has not experienced, is therefore found in the memory and it is recognized whenever the phrase "a happy life" is heard.

[10.22.32] Forbid it, lord, put it far from the heart of your servant, who confesses to you—far be it from me to think I am happy because of any and all the joy I have. For there is a joy not granted to the wicked but only to those who worship you thankfully—and this joy you yourself are. The happy life is this—to rejoice to you, in you, and for you. This it is and there is no other. But those who think there is another follow after other joys, and not the true one. But their will is still not moved except by some image or shadow of joy.

[10.23.33] Is it, then, uncertain that all men wish to be happy, since those who do not wish to find their joy in you—which is alone the happy life—do not actually desire the happy life? Or, is it rather that all desire this, but because "the flesh lusts against the spirit and the spirit against the flesh," so that they "prevent you from doing what you would,"* you fall to doing what you are able to do and are content with that. For you do not want to do what you cannot do urgently enough to make you able to do it. Now I ask all men whether they would rather rejoice in truth or in falsehood. They will no more hesitate to answer, "In truth," than to say that they wish to be happy. For a happy life is joy in the truth. Yet this is joy in you, who are the truth, god my light, "the health of my countenance and my god."† All wish for this happy life; all wish for this life which is the only happy one: joy in the truth is what all men wish.

I have had experience with many who wished to deceive, but not one who wished to be deceived. Where, then, did they ever know about this happy life, except where they knew also what the truth is? For they love it, too, since they are not willing to be deceived. And when they love the happy life, which is nothing else but joy in the truth, then certainly they also love the truth. And yet they would not love it if there were not some knowledge of it in the memory. Why, then, do they not rejoice in it? Why are they not happy? Because they are so fully preoccupied with other things which do more to make them miserable than those which would

---

* Galatians 5:17.

† Psalms 42:11.

make them happy, which they remember so little about. Yet there is a little light in men. Let them walk—let them walk in it, lest the darkness
overtake them.

[10.23.34] Why, then, does truth generate hatred, and why does your
servant who preaches the truth come to be an enemy to them who also
love the happy life, which is nothing else than joy in the truth—unless it
be that truth is loved in such a way that those who love something else besides its wish that to be the truth which they do love. Since they are unwilling to be deceived, they are unwilling to be convinced that they have
been deceived. Therefore, they hate the truth for the sake of whatever it
is that they love in place of the truth. They love truth when it shines on
them; and hate it when it rebukes them. And since they are not willing to
be deceived, but do wish to deceive, they love truth when it reveals itself
and hate it when it reveals them. On this account, it will so repay them
that those who are unwilling to be exposed by it, it will indeed expose
against their will, and yet will not disclose itself to them.

So indeed it is, so it is: the human mind so blind and sick, so base and ill-
mannered, desires to lie hidden, but does not wish that anything should be
hidden from it. And yet the opposite is what happens—the mind itself is
not hidden from the truth, but the truth is hidden from it. Yet even so, for
all its wretchedness, it still prefers to rejoice in truth rather than in known
falsehoods. It will, then, be happy only when without other distractions it
comes to rejoice in that single truth through which all things else are true.

[10.24.35] Behold how great a territory I have explored in my memory
seeking you, lord! And in it all I have still not found you. Nor have I
found anything about you, except what I had already retained in my
memory from the time I learned of you. For where I found truth, there
found I my god, who is the truth. From the time I learned this I have not
forgotten. And thus since the time I learned of you, you have dwelt in my
memory, and it is there that I find you whenever I call you to remembrance, and delight in you. These are my holy delights, which you have
bestowed on me in your mercy, mindful of my poverty.

[10.25.36] But where in my memory do you abide, lord? Where do you
dwell there? What sort of lodging have you made for yourself there?
What kind of sanctuary have you built for yourself? You have done this
honor to my memory to take up your abode in it, but I must consider further in what part of it you do abide. For in calling you to mind, I soared
beyond those parts of memory which the beasts also possess, because I
did not find you there among the images of corporeal things. From there
I went on to those parts where I had stored the remembered affections of

my mind, and I did not find you there. And I entered into the inmost seat of my mind, which is in my memory, since the mind remembers itself also—and you were not there. For just as you are not a bodily image, nor the emotion of a living creature (such as we feel when we rejoice or are grief-stricken, when we desire, or fear, or remember, or forget, or anything of that kind), so neither are you the mind itself. For you are the lord god of the mind and of all these things that are mutable; but you abide immutable over all. Yet you have elected to dwell in my memory from the time I learned of you. But why do I now inquire about the part of my memory you dwell in, as if indeed there were separate parts in it? Assuredly, you dwell in it, since I have remembered you from the time I learned of you, and I find you in my memory when I call you to mind.

[10.26.37] Where, then, did I find you so as to be able to learn of you? For you were not in my memory before I learned of you. Where, then, did I find you so as to be able to learn of you—save in yourself beyond me. Place there is none. We go "backward" and "forward" and there is no place. Everywhere and at once, truth, you guide all who consult you, and simultaneously answer all even though they consult you on quite different things. You answer clearly, though all do not hear in clarity. All take counsel of you on whatever point they wish, though they do not always hear what they wish. He is your best servant who does not look to hear from you what he himself wills, but who wills rather to will what he hears from you.

[10.27.38] Belatedly I loved you, beauty so ancient and so new, belatedly I loved you. For see, you were within and I was without, and I sought you out there. Unlovely, I rushed heedlessly among the lovely things you have made. You were with me, but I was not with you. These things kept me far from you, even though they were not at all unless they were in you. You called and cried aloud, and forced open my deafness. You gleamed and shined, and chased away my blindness. You breathed fragrant odors and I drew in my breath; and now I pant for you. I tasted, and now I hunger and thirst. You touched me, and I burned for your peace.

[10.28.39] When I come to be united to you with all my being, then there will be no more pain and toil for me, and my life shall be a real life, being wholly filled by you. But since he whom you fill is the one you lift up, I am still a burden to myself because I am not yet filled by you. Joys of sorrow contend with sorrows of joy, and on which side the victory lies I do not know. What a state to be in! Lord, have pity on me; my evil sorrows contend with my good joys, and on which side the victory lies I do not know. Lord, have pity on me. See, I do not hide my wounds. You are the physician, I am the sick man; you are merciful, I need mercy. Is not human life on earth an ordeal? Who wishes for vexations and difficulties? You command them to be endured, not to be loved. For no one loves what he endures, though he may love to endure. Yet even if he rejoices to endure, he would prefer that there were nothing for him to endure. In adversity, I desire prosperity; in prosperity, I fear adversity. What middle place is there, then, between these two, where human life is not an ordeal? There is woe in the prosperity of this world; there is woe in the fear of misfortune; there is woe in the distortion of joy. There is woe in the adversities of this world—a second woe, and a third, from the desire of prosperity—because adversity itself is a hard thing to bear and makes shipwreck of endurance. Is not human life on earth an ordeal, and that without surcease?

[10.29.40] My whole hope is in your exceeding great mercy and that alone. Give what you command and command what you will.[6] You command continence from us, and when I knew, as it is said, that no one could be continent unless god gave it to him, even this was a point of wisdom to know whose gift it was. For by continence we are bound up and brought back together in the one, whereas before we were scattered abroad among the many. For he loves you too little who loves along with you anything else that he does not love for your sake, love, who burn forever and are never quenched. Love, my god, enkindle me! You command continence; give what you command, and command what you will.

[10.30.41] Obviously you command that I should be continent from "the lust of the flesh, and the lust of the eyes, and the pride of life."*[7] You command me to abstain from fornication, and as for marriage itself, you have counseled something better than what you allow. And since you gave it, it was done—even before I became a minister of your sacrament. But there still exist in my memory—of which I have spoken so much—the images of such things as my habits had fixed there. These things rush into my thoughts with no power when I am awake; but in sleep they rush in not only so as to give pleasure, but even to obtain consent and what very closely resembles the deed itself. Indeed, the illusion of the image prevails to such an extent, in both my soul and my flesh, that the illusion persuades me when sleeping to what the reality cannot do when I am awake. Am I not myself at such a time, lord my god? And is there so much of a difference between myself awake and myself in the moment when I pass from waking to sleeping, or return from sleeping to waking?

Where, then, is the power of reason which resists such suggestions when

---

* 1 John 2:16.

I am awake—for even if the things themselves be forced upon it I remain unmoved? Does reason cease when the eyes close? Is it put to sleep with the bodily senses? But in that case how does it come to pass that even in slumber we often resist, and with our conscious purposes in mind, continue most chastely in them, and yield no assent to such allurements? Yet there is at least this much difference: that when it happens otherwise in dreams, when we wake up, we return to peace of conscience. And it is by this difference between sleeping and waking that we discover that it was not we who did it, while we still feel sorry that in some way it was done in us.

[**10.30.42**] Is not your hand, almighty god, able to heal all the diseases of my soul and, by your more and more abundant grace, to quench even the lascivious motions of my sleep? You will increase your gifts in me more and more, lord, so that my soul may follow me to you, wrenched free from the sticky glue of lust so that it is no longer in rebellion against itself, even in dreams; so that it neither commits nor consents to these debasing corruptions which come through sensual images and which result in the pollution of the flesh. For it is no great thing for the almighty, who is "able to do more than we can ask or think,"* to bring it about that no such influence—not even one so slight that a nod might restrain it—should afford gratification to the feelings of a chaste person even when sleeping. This could come to pass not only in this life but even at my present age. But what I am still in this way of wickedness I have confessed to my good lord, rejoicing with trembling in what you have given me and grieving in myself for that in which I am still imperfect. I am trusting that you will perfect your mercies in me, to the fullness of that peace which both my inner and outward being shall have with you when death is swallowed up in victory.†

[**10.31.43**] There is yet another "evil of the day"‡ to which I wish I were sufficient. By eating and drinking we restore the daily losses of the body until that day when you destroy both food and stomach, when you will destroy this emptiness with an amazing fullness and will clothe this corruptible thing with an eternal incorruption. But now the necessity of habit is sweet to me, and against this sweetness must I fight, lest I be enthralled by it. Thus I carry on a daily war by fasting, constantly "bringing my body into subjection,"§ after which my pains are banished by pleasure. For

---

* Ephesians 3:20.

† 1 Corinthians 15:54.

‡ Matthew 6:34.

§ 1 Corinthians 9:27.

hunger and thirst are actual pain. They consume and destroy like fever does, unless the medicine of food is at hand to relieve us. And since this medicine at hand comes from the comfort we receive in your gifts (by means of which land and water and air serve our infirmity), even our calamity is called pleasure.

[10.31.44] This much you have taught me: that I should learn to take food as medicine. But during that time when I pass from the pinch of emptiness to the contentment of fullness, it is in that very moment that the snare of appetite lies baited for me. For the passage itself is pleasant; there is no other way of passing thither, and necessity compels us to pass. And while health is the reason for our eating and drinking, yet a perilous delight joins itself to them as a handmaid; and indeed, it tries to take precedence in order that I may want to do for its sake what I say I want to do for health's sake. They do not both have the same limit either. What is sufficient for health is not enough for pleasure. And it is often a matter of doubt whether it is the needful care of the body that still calls for food or whether it is the sensual snare of desire still wanting to be served. In this uncertainty my unhappy soul rejoices, and uses it to prepare an excuse as a defense. It is glad that it is not clear as to what is sufficient for the moderation of health, so that under the pretense of health it may conceal its projects for pleasure. These temptations I daily endeavor to resist and I summon your right hand to my help and cast my perplexities onto you, for I have not yet reached a firm conclusion in this matter.

[10.31.45] I hear the voice of my god commanding: "Let not your heart be overcharged with surfeiting and drunkenness."* Drunkenness is far from me. You will have mercy so that it does not come near me. But surfeiting sometimes creeps upon your servant. You will have mercy so that it may be put far from me. For no man can be continent unless you give it. Many things that we pray for you give us, and whatever good we receive before we prayed for it, we receive it from you, so that we might afterward know that we received it from you. I never was a drunkard, but I have known drunkards made into sober men by you. It was also your doing that those who never were drunkards have not been—and likewise, it was from you that those who have been might not remain so always. And it was likewise from you that both might know from whom all this came.

I heard another voice of yours: "Do not follow your lusts and refrain

---

* Luke 21:34.

yourself from your pleasures."* And by your favor I have also heard this saying in which I have taken much delight: "Neither if we eat are we the better; nor if we eat not are we the worse."† This is to say that neither shall the one make me to abound, nor the other to be wretched. I heard still another voice: "For I have learned, in whatsoever state I am, therewith to be content. I know how to be abased and I know how to abound. I can do all things through Christ who strengthens me."‡ See here a soldier of the heavenly army; not the sort of dust we are. But remember, lord, that we are dust and that you created man out of the dust, and that he was lost, and is found. Of course, he [the apostle Paul] could not do all this by his own power. He was of the same dust—he whom I loved so much and who spoke of these things through the breath of your inspiration: "I can," he said, "do all things through him who strengthens me." Strengthen me, that I too may be able. Give what you command, and command what you will. This man [Paul] confesses that he received the gift of grace and that, when he glories, he glories in the Lord. I have heard yet another voice praying that he might receive. "Take from me," he said, "the greediness of the belly."§ And from this it appears, my holy god, that you do give it, when what you command to be done is done.

[**10.31.46**] You have taught me, good father, that "to the pure all things are pure";‖ but "it is evil for that man who gives offense in eating";# and that "every creature of yours is good, and nothing is to be refused if it is received with thanksgiving";** and that "meat does not commend us to god";†† and that "no man should judge us in meat or in drink."‡‡ "Let not him who eats despise him who eats not, and let him that does not eat judge not him who does eat."§§ These things I have learned, thanks and praise be to you, my god and master, who knock at my ears and enlighten my heart. Deliver me from all temptation!

---

* Ecclesiasticus 18:30.

† 1 Corinthians 8:8.

‡ Philippians 4:11–13.

§ Ecclesiasticus 23:6.

‖ Titus 1:15.

Romans 14:20.

** 1 Timothy 4:4.

†† 1 Corinthians 8:8.

‡‡ Colossians 2:16.

§§ Romans 14:3.

It is not the uncleanness of meat that I fear, but the uncleanness of an incontinent appetite. I know that permission was granted Noah to eat every kind of flesh that was good for food;* that Elijah was fed with flesh;† that John, blessed with a wonderful abstinence, was not polluted by the living creatures (that is, the locusts) on which he fed.‡ And I also know that Esau was deceived by his hungering after lentils§ and that David blamed himself for desiring water,‖ and that our king was tempted not by flesh but by bread.# And, thus, the people in the wilderness truly deserved their reproof, not because they desired meat, but because in their desire for food they murmured against the lord.**

[10.31.47] Set down, then, in the midst of these temptations, I strive daily against my appetite for food and drink. For it is not the kind of appetite I am able to deal with by cutting it off once for all, and thereafter not touching it, as I was able to do with fornication. The bridle of the throat, therefore, must be held in the mean between slackness and tightness. And who, lord, is he who is not in some degree carried away beyond the bounds of necessity? Whoever he is, he is great; let him magnify your name. But I am not such a one, for I am a sinful man. Yet I too magnify your name, for he who has overcome the world intercedes with you for my sins, numbering me among the weak members of his body; for "your eyes saw what was imperfect in it, and in your book all shall be written down."††

[10.32.48] I am not much troubled by the allurement of odors. When they are absent, I do not seek them; when they are present, I do not refuse them; and I am always prepared to go without them. At any rate, I appear thus to myself; it is quite possible that I am deceived. For there is a lamentable darkness in which my capabilities are concealed, so that when my mind inquires into itself concerning its own powers, it does not readily venture to believe itself, because what already is in it is largely concealed unless experience brings it to light. Thus no man ought to feel

---

* Genesis 9:3.

† 1 Kings 17:6.

‡ Matthew 3:4.

§ Genesis 25:34.

‖ 2 Samuel 23:15–17.

Matthew 4:3.

** Numbers 11:1.

†† Psalms 139:16.

secure in this life, the whole of which is called an ordeal, ordered so that the person who could be made better from having been worse may not also from having been better become worse. Our sole hope, our sole confidence, our only assured promise, is your mercy.

[**10.33.49**] The delights of the ear drew and held me much more powerfully, but you unbound and liberated me. In those melodies which your words inspire when sung with a sweet and trained voice, I still find repose; yet not so as to cling to them, but always so as to be able to free myself as I wish. But it is because of the words which are their life that they gain entry into me and strive for a place of proper honor in my heart; and I can hardly assign them a fitting one. Sometimes, I seem to myself to give them more respect than is fitting, when I see that our minds are more devoutly and earnestly inflamed in piety by the holy words when they are sung than when they are not. And I recognize that all the diverse affections of our spirits have their appropriate measures in the voice and song, to which they are stimulated by I know not what secret correlation. But the pleasures of my flesh—to which the mind ought never to be surrendered nor by them enervated—often beguile me while physical sense does not attend on reason, to follow it patiently, but having once gained entry to help the reason, it strives to run on before it and be its leader. Thus in these things I sin unknowingly, but I come to know it afterward.

[**10.33.50**] On the other hand, when I avoid very earnestly this kind of deception, I err out of too great austerity. Sometimes I go to the point of wishing that all the melodies of the pleasant songs to which David's psalter is adapted should be banished both from my ears and from those of the church itself. In this mood, the safer way seemed to me the one I remember was once related to me concerning Athanasius, bishop of Alexandria, who required the readers of the psalm to use so slight an inflection of the voice that it was more like speaking than singing.[8] However, when I call to mind the tears I shed at the songs of your church at the outset of my recovered faith, and how even now I am moved, not by the singing but by what is sung (when they are sung with a clear and skillfully modulated voice), I then come to acknowledge the great utility of this custom. Thus I vacillate between dangerous pleasure and healthful exercise. I am inclined—though I pronounce no irrevocable opinion on the subject—to approve of the use of singing in the church, so that by the delights of the ear the weaker minds may be stimulated to a devotional mood. Yet when it happens that I am more moved by the singing than by what is sung, I confess myself to have sinned wickedly, and then I would rather not have heard the singing. See now what a condition I am in!

Weep with me, and weep for me, those of you who can so control your inward feelings that good results always come forth. As for you who do not act this way at all, such things do not concern you. But you, lord, my god, give ear; look and see, and have mercy upon me; and heal me—you, in whose sight I am become an enigma to myself; this itself is my weakness.

[10.34.51] There remain the delights of these eyes of my flesh, about which I must make my confession in the hearing of the ears of your temple, brotherly and pious ears. Thus I will finish the list of the temptations of carnal appetite which still assail me—groaning and desiring as I am to be "clothed with my house from heaven."* The eyes delight in fair and varied forms, and bright and pleasing colors. Let these not take possession of my soul! Rather let god possess it, he who made all these things very good indeed. He is still my good, and not these. The pleasures of sight affect me all the time I am awake. There is no rest from them given me, as there is from the voices of melody, which I can occasionally find in silence. For daylight, that queen of the colors, floods all that we look upon everywhere I go during the day. It flits about me in manifold forms and soothes me even when I am busy about other things, not noticing it. And it presents itself so forcibly that if it is suddenly withdrawn it is looked for with longing, and if it is long absent the mind is saddened.

[10.34.52] Light, which Tobit saw even with his eyes closed in blindness, when he taught his son the way of life—and went before him himself in the steps of love and never went astray;† or that light which Isaac saw when his fleshly eyes were dim, so that he could not see because of old age, and it was permitted him unknowingly to bless his sons, but in the blessing of them to know them;‡ or that light which Jacob saw, when he too, blind in old age yet with an enlightened heart, threw light on the nation of men yet to come—presignified in the persons of his own sons—and laid his hands mystically crossed upon his grandchildren by Joseph (not as their father, who saw them from without, but as though he were within them), and distinguished them aright:§ this is the true light; it is one, and all are one who see and love it.

But that corporeal light, of which I was speaking, seasons the life of the world for its blind lovers with a tempting and fatal sweetness. Those

---

* 2 Corinthians 5:2.
† Tobit 2–4.
‡ Genesis 27.
§ Genesis 48.

who know how to praise you for it, "God, creator of all," take it up in your hymn,[9] and are not taken over by it in their sleep. Such a one I desire to be. I resist the seductions of my eyes, lest my feet be entangled as I go forward in your way; and I raise my invisible eyes to you, so that you would be pleased to "pluck my feet out of the net."* You continually pluck them out, for they are easily ensnared. You cease not to pluck them out, but I constantly remain fast in the snares set all around me. However, you who "keep Israel shall neither slumber nor sleep."†

[10.34.53] What numberless things there are: products of the various arts and manufactures in our clothes, shoes, vessels, and all such things, as well as pictures and images of various kinds—and all these far beyond the necessary and moderate use of them or their significance for the life of piety—which human beings have added for the delight of the eye, copying the outward forms of the things they make but inwardly forsaking him by whom they were made and destroying what they themselves have been made to be![10] And I, my god and my joy, I also raise a hymn to you for all these things, and offer a sacrifice of praise to my sanctifier, because those beautiful forms which pass through the medium of the human soul into the artist's hands come from that beauty which is above our minds, which my soul sighs for day and night. But the craftsmen and devotees of these outward beauties discover the norm by which they judge them from that higher beauty, but not the measure of their use. Still, even if they do not see it, it is there nevertheless, to guard them from wandering astray, and to keep their strength for you, and not dissipate it in delights that pass into boredom. And for myself, though I can see and understand this, I am still entangled in my own course with such beauty, but you will rescue me, lord, you will rescue me, "for your loving-kindness is before my eyes."‡ For I am captivated in my weakness but you in your mercy rescue me: sometimes without my knowing it, because I had only lightly fallen; at other times, the rescue is painful because I was stuck fast.

[10.35.54] Besides this there is yet another form of temptation still more complex in its peril. For in addition to the fleshly appetite which strives for the gratification of all senses and pleasures—in which its slaves perish because they separate themselves from you—there is also a certain

---

* Psalms 25:15.

† Psalms 121:4.

‡ Psalms 26:3.

vain and curious longing in the soul, rooted in the same bodily senses, which is cloaked under the name of knowledge and learning; not having pleasure in the flesh, but striving for new experiences through the flesh. This longing—since its origin is our appetite for learning, and since the sight is the chief of our senses in the acquisition of knowledge—is called in the divine language "the lust of the eyes."* For seeing is a function of the eyes; yet we also use this word for the other senses as well, when we exercise them in the search for knowledge. We do not say, "Listen how it glows," "Smell how it glistens," "Taste how it shines," or "Feel how it flashes," since all of these are said to be seen. And we do not simply say, "See how it shines," which only the eyes can perceive; but we also say, "See how it sounds, see how it smells, see how it tastes, see how hard it is." Thus, as we said before, the whole round of sensory experience is called "the lust of the eyes" because the function of seeing, in which the eyes have the principal role, is applied by analogy to the other senses when they are seeking after any kind of knowledge.

[**10.35.55**] From this, then, one can the more clearly distinguish whether it is pleasure or curiosity that is being pursued by the senses. For pleasure pursues objects that are beautiful, melodious, fragrant, savory, soft. But curiosity, seeking new experiences, will even seek out the contrary of these, not with the purpose of experiencing the discomfort that often accompanies them, but out of a passion for experimenting and knowledge. For what pleasure is there in the sight of a lacerated corpse, which makes you shudder? And yet if there is one lying close by we flock to it, as if to be made sad and pale. People fear lest they should see such a thing even in sleep, just as they would if, when awake, someone compelled them to go and see it or if some rumor of its beauty had attracted them.

This is also the case with the other senses; it would be tedious to pursue a complete analysis of it. This malady of curiosity is the reason for all those strange sights exhibited in the theater. It is also the reason why we proceed to search out the secret powers of nature—those which have nothing to do with our destiny—which do not profit us to know about, and concerning which men desire to know only for the sake of knowing. And it is with this same motive of perverted curiosity for knowledge that we consult the magical arts. Even in religion itself, this prompting drives us to make trial of god when signs and wonders are eagerly asked of him—not desired for any saving end, but only to make trial of him.

---

* 1 John 2:16.

[10.35.56] In such a wilderness so vast, crammed with snares and dangers, see how many of them I have lopped off and cast from my heart, as you, god of my salvation, have enabled me to do. And yet, when would I dare to say, since so many things of this sort still buzz around our daily lives—when would I dare to say that no such motive prompts my seeing or creates a vain curiosity in me? It is true that now the theaters never attract me, nor do I now care to inquire about the courses of the stars, and my soul has never sought answers from the departed spirits. All sacrilegious oaths I abhor. And yet, lord my god, to whom I owe all humble and singlehearted service, with what subtle suggestion the enemy still influences me to require some sign from you! But by our king, and by Jerusalem, our pure and chaste homeland, I beseech you that where any consenting to such thoughts is now far from me, so may it always be farther and farther. And when I entreat you for the salvation of any man, the end I aim at is something quite different: let it be that as you do what you will, you do also give me the grace willingly to follow your lead.

[10.35.57] Now, really, in how many of the most minute and trivial things my curiosity is still daily tempted, and who can keep the tally on how often I succumb? How often, when people are telling idle tales, we begin by tolerating them lest we should give offense to the sensitive, and then gradually we come to listen willingly! I do not nowadays go to the circus to see a dog chase a rabbit, but if by chance I pass such a race in the fields, it quite easily distracts me even from some serious thought and draws me after it—not that I turn aside with my horse, but with the inclination of my mind. And unless, by showing me my weakness, you speedily warn me to rise above such a sight to you by a deliberate act of thought—or else to despise the whole thing and pass it by—then I become absorbed in the sight, vain creature that I am.

How is it that when I am sitting at home a lizard catching flies, or a spider entangling them as they fly into her webs, often arrests me? Is the feeling of curiosity not the same just because these are such tiny creatures? From them I proceed to praise you, the wonderful creator and disposer of all things; but it is not this that first attracts my attention. It is one thing to get up quickly and another thing not to fall—and of both such things my life is full and my only hope is in your exceeding great mercy. For when this heart of ours is made the depot of such things and is overrun by the throng of these abounding vanities, then our prayers are often interrupted and disturbed by them. Even while we are in your presence and direct the voice of our hearts to your ears, such a great business as this is broken off by the inroads of I know not what idle thoughts.

[**10.36.58**] Shall we, then, also reckon this vain curiosity among the things that are to be but lightly esteemed? Shall anything restore us to hope except your complete mercy since you have begun to change us? You know to what extent you have already changed me, for first of all you healed me of the lust for vindicating myself, so that you might then forgive all my remaining iniquities and heal all my diseases, and "redeem my life from corruption and crown me with loving-kindness and tender mercies, and satisfy my desires with good things."* It was you who restrained my pride with your fear, and bowed my neck to your yoke. And now I bear the yoke and it is light to me, because you promised it to be so, and have made it to be so.† And so in truth it was, though I knew it not when I feared to take it up.

[**10.36.59**] But, lord—you who alone reign without pride, because you alone are the true lord, who have no lord—has this third kind of temptation left me, or can it leave me during this life: the desire to be feared and loved of men, with no other view than that I may find in it a joy that is no joy? It is, rather, a wretched life and an unseemly ostentation. It is a special reason why we do not love you, nor devotedly fear you. Therefore "you resist the proud but give grace to the humble."‡ You thunder down on the ambitious designs of the world, and the foundations of the hills tremble.§

And yet certain offices in human society require the officeholder to be loved and feared of men, and through this the adversary of our true blessedness presses hard upon us, scattering everywhere his snares of "well done, well done"; so that while we are eagerly picking them up, we may be caught unawares and split off our joy from your truth and fix it on the deceits of men. In this way we come to take pleasure in being loved and feared, not for your sake but in your stead. By such means as this, the adversary makes men like himself, so that he may have them as his own, not in the harmony of love, but in the fellowship of punishment— the one who aspired to exalt his throne in the north,‖ so that in the darkness and the cold men might have to serve him, mimicking you in perverse and distorted ways.

---

* Psalms 103:3–5.
† Matthew 11:30.
‡ 1 Peter 5:5.
§ Psalms 18:7, 13.
‖ Isaiah 14:12–14.

But see, lord, we are your little flock. Possess us, stretch your wings above us, and let us take refuge under them. Be you our glory; let us be loved for your sake, and let your word be feared in us. Those who desire to be commended by the men whom you condemn will not be defended by men when you judge, nor will they be delivered when you condemn them. But when—not as a sinner is praised in the wicked desires of his soul nor when the unrighteous man is blessed in his unrighteousness—a man is praised for some gift that you have given him, and he is more gratified at the praise for himself than because he possesses the gift for which he is praised, such a one is praised while you condemn him. In such a case the one who praised is truly better than the one who was praised. For the gift of god in man was pleasing to the one, while the other was better pleased with the gift of man than with the gift of god.

[10.37.60] By these temptations we are daily tried, lord; we are tried unceasingly. Our daily furnace is the human tongue.* And also in this respect you command us to be continent. Give what you command and command what you will. In this matter, you know the groans of my heart and the rivers of my eyes, for I am not able to know for certain how far I am clean of this plague; and I stand in great fear of my secret faults, which your eyes perceive, though mine do not. For in respect of the pleasures of my flesh and of idle curiosity, I see how far I have been able to hold my mind in check when I abstain from them either by voluntary act of the will or because they simply are not at hand; for then I can inquire of myself how much more or less frustrating it is to me not to have them. This is also true about riches, which are sought for in order that they may minister to one of these three lusts, or two, or the whole complex of them. The mind is able to see clearly if, when it has them, it despises them so that they may be cast aside and it may prove itself.

But if we desire to test our power of doing without praise, must we then live wickedly or lead a life so atrocious and abandoned that everyone who knows us will detest us? What greater madness than this can be either said or conceived? And yet if praise, both by custom and right, is the companion of a good life and of good works, we should as little forgo its companionship as the good life itself. But unless a thing is absent I do not know whether I should be contented or troubled at having to do without it.

[10.37.61] What is it, then, that I am confessing to you, lord, concerning

---

* Proverbs 27:21.

this sort of temptation? What else, than that I am delighted with praise, but more with the truth itself than with praise. For if I were to have any choice whether, if I were mad or utterly in the wrong, I would prefer to be praised by all men or, if I were steadily and fully confident in the truth, would prefer to be blamed by all, I see which I should choose. Yet I wish I were unwilling that the approval of others should add anything to my joy for any good I have. Yet I admit that it does increase it; and, more than that, dispraise diminishes it. Then, when I am disturbed over this wretchedness of mine, an excuse presents itself to me, the value of which you know, god, for it renders me uncertain. For since it is not only continence that you have enjoined on us—that is, what things to hold back our love from—but righteousness as well—that is, what to bestow our love upon—and have wished us to love not only you, but also our neighbor, it often turns out that when I am gratified by intelligent praise I seem to myself to be gratified by the competence or insight of my neighbor; or, on the other hand, I am sorry for the defect in him when I hear him dispraise either what he does not understand or what is good. For I am sometimes grieved at the praise I get, either when those things that displease me in myself are praised in me, or when lesser and trifling goods are valued more highly than they should be. But, again, how do I know whether I feel this way because I am unwilling that he who praises me should differ from me concerning myself not because I am moved with any consideration for him, but because the good things that please me in myself are more pleasing to me when they also please another? For in a way, I am not praised when my judgment of myself is not praised, since either those things which are displeasing to me are praised, or those things which are less pleasing to me are more praised. Am I not, then, quite uncertain of myself in this respect?

[**10.37.62**] Behold, truth, it is in you that I see that I ought not to be moved at my own praises for my own sake, but for the sake of my neighbor's good. And whether this is actually my way, I truly do not know. On this score I know less of myself than you do. I beseech you now, my god, to reveal myself to me also, so that I may confess to my brethren, who are to pray for me in those matters where I find myself weak.

Let me once again examine myself the more diligently. If, in my own praise, I am moved with concern for my neighbor, why am I less moved if some other man is unjustly dispraised than when it happens to me? Why am I more irritated at that reproach which is cast on me than at one which is, with equal injustice, cast upon another in my presence? Am I ignorant of this also? Or is it still true that I am deceiving myself, and do not keep the truth before you in my heart and tongue? Put such madness far from me, lord, lest my mouth be to me "the oil of sinners, to anoint my head."*

[10.38.63] "I am needy and poor."† Still, I am better when in secret groanings I displease myself and seek your mercy until what is lacking in me is renewed and made complete for that peace which the eye of the proud does not know. The reports that come from the mouth and from actions known to men have in them a most perilous temptation to the love of praise. This love builds up a certain complacency in one's own excellency, and then goes around collecting solicited compliments. It tempts me, even when I inwardly reprove myself for it, and this precisely because it is reproved. For a person may often glory vainly in the very scorn of vainglory—and in this case it is not any longer the scorn of vainglory in which he glories, for he does not truly despise it when he inwardly glories in it.

[10.39.64] Within us there is yet another evil arising from the same sort of temptation. By it they become empty who please themselves in themselves, although they do not please or displease or aim at pleasing others. But in pleasing themselves they displease you very much, not merely taking pleasure in things that are not good as if they were good, but taking pleasure in your good things as if they were their own; or even as if they were yours but still as if they had received them through their own merit; or even as if they had them through your grace, still without this grace with their friends, but as if they envied that grace to others. In all these and similar perils and labors, you perceive the agitation of my heart, and I would rather feel my wounds being cured by you than not inflicted by me on myself.

[10.40.65] Where have you not accompanied me, truth, teaching me both what to avoid and what to desire, when I have submitted to you what I could understand about matters here below, and have sought your counsel about them? With my external senses I have viewed the world as I was able and have noticed the life which my body derives from me and from these senses of mine. From that stage I advanced inwardly into the recesses of my memory—the manifold chambers of my mind, marvelously full of unmeasured wealth. And I reflected on this and was afraid, and could understand none of these things without you and found you to be none of them. Nor did I myself discover these things—I who went over them all and labored to distinguish and to value everything according to

---

* Psalms 141:5.

† Psalms 109:22.

its dignity, accepting some things upon the report of my senses and questioning about others which I thought to be related to my inner self, distinguishing and numbering the reporters themselves; and in that vast storehouse of my memory, investigating some things, depositing other things, taking out still others. Neither was I myself when I did this—that is, that ability of mine by which I did it—nor was it you, for you are that never-failing light from which I took counsel about them all; whether they were what they were, and what was their real value. In all this I heard you teaching and commanding me. And this I often do—and this is a delight to me—and as far as I can get relief from my necessary duties, I resort to this kind of pleasure. But in all these things which I review when I consult you, I still do not find a secure place for my soul except in you, in whom my scattered members may be gathered together and nothing of me escape from you. And sometimes you introduce me to a most rare and inward feeling, an inexplicable sweetness. If this were to come to perfection in me I do not know to what point life might not then arrive. But still, by these wretched weights of mine, I relapse into these common things, and am sucked in by my old customs and am held. I sorrow much, yet I am still closely held. To this extent, then, the burden of habit presses us down. I can exist in this fashion but I do not wish to do so. In that other way I wish I were, but cannot be—in both ways I am wretched.

[10.41.66] And now I have thus considered the infirmities of my sins, under the headings of the three major lusts, and I have called your right hand to my aid. For with a wounded heart I have seen your brightness, and having been beaten back I cried: "Who can attain to it? I am cut off from before your eyes."* You are the truth, who preside over all things, but I, because of my greed, did not wish to lose you. But still, along with you, I wished also to possess a lie—just as no one wishes to lie in such a way as to be ignorant of what is true. By this I lost you, for you will not condescend to be enjoyed along with a lie.

[10.42.67] Whom could I find to reconcile me to you? Should I have approached the angels? What kind of prayer? What kind of rites? Many who were striving to return to you and were not able of themselves have, I am told, tried this and have fallen into a longing for curious visions and deserved to be deceived. Being exalted, they sought you in their pride of learning, and they thrust themselves forward rather than beating their breasts. And so by a likeness of heart, they drew to themselves the princes

---

* Psalms 31:22.

of the air, their conspirators and companions in pride, by whom they were deceived by the power of magic. Thus they sought a mediator by whom they might be cleansed, but there was none. For the mediator they sought was the devil, disguising himself as an angel of light.* And he allured their proud flesh the more because he had no fleshly body.[11]

They were mortal and sinful, but you, lord, to whom they arrogantly sought to be reconciled, are immortal and sinless. But a mediator between god and man ought to have something in him like god and something in him like man, lest in being like man he should be far from god, or if only like god he should be far from man, and so should not be a mediator. That deceitful mediator, then, by whom, by your secret judgment, human pride deserves to be deceived, had one thing in common with man, that is, his sin. In another respect, he would seem to have something in common with god, for not being clothed with the mortality of the flesh, he could boast that he was immortal. But since "the wages of sin is death,"[†] what he really has in common with men is that, together with them, he is condemned to death.

[10.43.68] But the true mediator, whom you in your secret mercy have revealed to the humble, and have sent to them so that through his example they also might learn the same humility—that "mediator between god and man, the man Christ Jesus,"[‡] appeared between mortal sinners and the immortal just one. He was mortal as men are mortal; he was righteous as god is righteous; and because the reward of righteousness is life and peace, he could, through his righteousness united with god, cancel the death of justified sinners, which he was willing to have in common with them. Hence he was manifested to holy men of old, to the end that they might be saved through faith in his passion to come, even as we are through faith in his passion which is past. As man he was mediator, but as the word he was not something in between the two; because he was equal to god, and god with god, and, with the holy spirit, one god.

[10.43.69] How have you loved us, good father, who did not spare your only son, but delivered him up for us wicked ones! How have you loved us, for whom he who did not count it robbery to be equal with you "became obedient to death, even the death of the cross"![§] He alone was free among the dead. He alone had power to lay down his life and power to

---

* 2 Corinthians 11:14.

† Romans 6:23.

‡ 1 Timothy 2:5.

§ Philippians 2:6–8.

take it up again, and for us he became to you both victor and victim; and victor because he was the victim. For us, he was to you both priest and sacrifice, and priest because he was the sacrifice. Out of slaves, he makes us your sons, because he was born of you and did serve us. Rightly, then, is my hope fixed strongly on him, that you will heal all my diseases through him, who sits at your right hand and makes intercession for us. Otherwise I should utterly despair. For my infirmities are many and great; indeed, they are very many and very great. But your medicine is still greater. Otherwise, we might think that your word was removed from union with man, and despair of ourselves, if it had not been that he was "made flesh and dwelt among us."*

Terrified by my sins and the load of my misery, I had resolved in my heart and considered flight into the wilderness.[12] But you forbade me, and you strengthened me, saying that "since Christ died for all, they who live should not henceforth live to themselves, but to him who died for them."† See, lord, how I cast all my care on you, so that I may live and "behold wondrous things out of your law."‡ You know my incompetence and my infirmities; teach me and heal me. Your only son—he "in whom are hid all the treasures of wisdom and knowledge"§—has redeemed me with his blood. Let not the proud speak evil of me, because I keep my ransom before my mind, and eat and drink and share my food and drink. For, being poor, I desire to be satisfied from him, together with those who eat and are satisfied: "and they shall praise the lord that seek him."‖

---

* John 1:14.
† 2 Corinthians 5:15.
‡ Psalms 119:18.
§ Colossians 2:3.
‖ Psalms 22:26.

BOOK 11

[11.1.1] Is it possible, lord, that, since you are in eternity, you are ignorant of what I am saying to you? Or, do you see in time an event at the time it occurs? If not, then why am I recounting such a tale of things to you? Certainly not in order to acquaint you with them through me; but, instead, that through them I may stir up my own love and the love of my readers toward you, so that all may say, "Great is the lord and greatly to be praised." I have said this before and will say it again.[1] For love of your love I do it. So also we pray—and yet truth tells us, "Your father knows what things you need before you ask him."* Consequently, we lay bare our feelings before you, so that, through our confessing to you our plight and your mercies toward us, you may go on to free us altogether, as you have already begun; and so that we may cease to be wretched in ourselves and blessed in you—since you have called us to be poor in spirit, meek, mourners, hungering and athirst for righteousness, merciful and pure in heart.† Thus I have told you many things, as I could find ability and will to do so, since it was your will in the first place that I should confess to you, lord my god—for "you are good and your mercy endureth forever."‡

[11.2.2] But how long would it take for the voice of my pen to tell enough of your exhortations and of all your terrors and comforts and leadings by which you brought me to preach your word and to administer your sacraments to your people? And even if I could do this sufficiently, the drops of time are very precious to me and I have for a long time been burning with the desire to meditate on your law, and to confess in your presence my knowledge and ignorance of it—from the first streaks of your light in my mind and the remaining darkness, until my weakness shall be swallowed up in your strength. And I do not wish to see drained into anything else those hours which I can find free from the necessary care of the body, the exercise of the mind, and the service we owe to our fellow human beings—and what we give even if we do not owe it.[2]

---

* Matthew 6:8.
† Matthew 5:1–11.
‡ Psalms 118:1.

[**11.2.3**] Lord my god, hear my prayer and let your mercy attend my longing. It does not burn for itself alone but longs as well to serve the cause of fraternal love. You see in my heart that this is so. Let me offer the service of my mind and my tongue—and give me what I may in turn offer back to you. For I am needy and poor; you are rich to all who call upon you—you who, in your freedom from care, care for us. Trim away from my lips, inwardly and outwardly, all rashness and lying. Let your scriptures be my chaste delight. Let me not be deceived in them, nor deceive others from them. Lord, hear and pity! Lord my god, light of the blind, strength of the weak—and also the light of those who see and the strength of the strong—hearken to my soul and hear it crying from the depths.* Unless your ears attend us even in the depths, where should we go? To whom should we cry?

"Yours is the day and the night is yours as well."† At your bidding the moments fly by. Grant me in them, then, an interval for my meditations on the hidden things of your law, nor close the door of your law against us who knock. You have not willed that the deep secrets of all those pages should have been written in vain. Those forests are not without their stags which keep retired within them, ranging and walking and feeding, lying down and ruminating. Perfect me, lord, and reveal their secrets to me. Behold, your voice is my joy; your voice surpasses in abundance of delights. Give me what I love, for I do love it. And this too is your gift. Abandon not your gifts and despise not your grass which thirsts for you. Let me confess to you everything that I shall have found in your books and "let me hear the voice of your praise."‡ Let me drink from you and "consider the wondrous things out of your law"§—from the very beginning, when you made heaven and earth, and thenceforward to the everlasting reign of your holy city with you.³

[**11.2.4**] Lord, have mercy on me and hear my petition. For my prayer is not for earthly things, neither gold nor silver and precious stones, nor gorgeous apparel, nor honors and power, nor fleshly pleasures, nor for bodily necessities in this life of our journeying: all of these things are added to those who seek your kingdom and your righteousness.‖ Observe,

---

* Psalms 130:1.

† Psalms 74:16.

‡ Psalms 26:7.

§ Psalms 119:18.

‖ Matthew 6:33.

god, from whence comes my desire. The unrighteous have told me of delights but not such as those in your law, lord. See, this is the spring of my desire. See, father, look and see—and approve! Let it be pleasing in your mercy's sight that I should find favor with you—that the secret things of your word may be opened to me when I knock. I beg this of you by our lord Jesus Christ, your son, the man of your right hand, the son of man; whom you made strong for your purpose as mediator between you and us; through whom you sought us when we were not seeking you, but sought us so that we might seek you; your word, through whom you made all things, and me among them; your only son, through whom you have called your faithful people to adoption, and me among them. I beseech it of you through him who sits at your right hand and makes intercession for us, "in whom are hid all treasures of wisdom and knowledge."* It is he I seek in your books. Moses wrote of him. He tells us so himself; the truth tells us so.

[11.3.5] Let me hear and understand how in the beginning you made heaven and earth. Moses wrote of this; he wrote and passed on—moving from you to you—and he is now no longer before me. If he were, I would lay hold on him and ask him and entreat him solemnly that in your name he would open out these things to me, and I would lend my bodily ears to the sounds that came forth out of his mouth. If, however, he spoke in the Hebrew language, the sounds would beat on my senses in vain, and nothing would touch my mind; but if he spoke in Latin, I would understand what he said. But how should I then know whether what he said was true? If I knew even this much, would it be that I knew it from him? Indeed, within me, deep inside the chambers of my thought, truth itself—neither Hebrew, nor Greek, nor Latin, nor barbarian, without any organs of voice and tongue, without the sound of syllables—would say, "He speaks the truth," and I should be assured by this. Then I would confidently say to that man of yours, "You speak the truth." However, since I cannot inquire of Moses, I beseech you, truth, from whose fullness he spoke truth; I beseech you, my god, forgive my sins, and as you gave your servant the gift to speak these things, grant me also the gift to understand them.[4]

[11.4.6] Look around; there are the heaven and the earth. They cry aloud that they were made, for they change and vary. Whatever there is that has not been made, and yet has being, has nothing in it that was not there before. This having something not already existent is what it

* Colossians 2:3.

means to be changed and varied. Heaven and earth thus speak plainly that they did not make themselves: "We are, because we have been made; we did not exist before we came to be so that we could have made ourselves!" And the voice with which they speak is simply their visible presence. It was you, lord, who made these things. You are beautiful; thus they are beautiful. You are good, thus they are good. You are; thus they are. But they are not as beautiful, nor as good, nor as truly real as you their creator are. Compared with you, they are neither beautiful nor good, nor do they even exist. These things we know, thanks be to you. Yet our knowledge is ignorance when it is compared with your knowledge.[5]

[11.5.7] But how did you make the heaven and the earth, and what was the tool of such a mighty work as yours? For it was not like a human worker fashioning body from body, according to the fancy of his mind, able somehow or other to impose on it a form which the mind perceived in itself by its inner eye (yet how should even he be able to do this, if you had not made that mind?). He imposes the form on something already existing and having some sort of being, such as clay, or stone or wood or gold or such like (and where would these things come from if you had not furnished them?). For you made his body for the artisan, and you made the mind which directs the limbs; you made the matter from which he makes anything; you created the capacity by which he understands his art and sees within his mind what he may do with the things before him; you gave him his bodily sense by which, as if he had an interpreter, he may communicate from mind to matter what he proposes to do and report back to his mind what has been done, so that the mind may consult with the truth which presideth over it as to whether what is done is well done.

All these things praise you, the creator of them all. But how did you make them? How, god, did you make the heaven and earth? For truly, neither in heaven nor on earth did you make heaven and earth—nor in the air nor in the waters, since all of these also belong to the heaven and the earth. Nowhere in the whole world did you make the whole world, because there was no place where it could be made before it was made. And you did not hold anything in your hand from which to fashion the heaven and the earth, for where could you have got what you had not made in order to make something with it? Is there, indeed, anything at all except because you are? Thus you spoke and they were made, and by your word you made them all.

[11.6.8] But how did you speak? Was it in the same manner in which the voice came from the cloud saying, "This is my beloved son"?* For that voice sounded forth and died away; it began and ended. The syllables sounded and passed away, the second after the first, the third after the second, and thence in order, till the very last after all the rest; and silence after the last. From this it is clear and plain that it was the action of a creature, itself in time, which sounded that voice, obeying your eternal will. And what these words were which were formed at that time the outer ear conveyed to the conscious mind, whose inner ear lay attentively open to your eternal word. But it compared those words which sounded in time with your eternal word sounding in silence and said: "This is different; quite different! These words are far below me; they are not even real, for they fly away and pass, but the word of my god remains above me forever." If, then, in words that sound and fade away you said that heaven and earth should be made, and thus made heaven and earth, then there was already some kind of corporeal creature before heaven and earth by whose motions in time that voice might have had its occurrence in time. But there was nothing corporeal before the heaven and the earth; or if there was, then it is certain that already, without a time-bound voice, you had created whatever it was out of which you made the time-bound voice by which you said, "Let the heaven and the earth be made!" For whatever it was out of which such a voice was made simply did not exist at all until it was made by you. Was it decreed by your word that a body might be made from which such words might come?

[11.7.9] You call us, then, to understand the word—the god who is god with you—which is spoken eternally and by which all things are spoken eternally. For what was first spoken was not finished, and then something else spoken until the whole series was spoken; but all things, at the same time and forever. For, otherwise, we should have time and change and not a true eternity, nor a true immortality. This I know, my god, and I give thanks. I know, I confess to you, lord, and whoever is not ungrateful for certain truths knows and blesses you along with me. We know, lord, this much we know: that in the same proportion as anything is not what it was, and is what it was not, in that very same proportion it passes away or comes to be. But there is nothing in your word that passes away or returns to its place; for it is truly immortal and eternal. And, therefore, to the word coeternal with you, at the same time and always you say all that you say. And whatever you say shall be made is made, and you make

---

* Matthew 3:17.

nothing otherwise than by speaking. Still, not all the things that you make by speaking are made at the same time and always.

[**11.8.10**] Why is this, I ask of you, lord my god? I see it after a fashion, but I do not know how to express it, unless I say that everything that begins to be and then ceases to be begins and ceases when it is known in your eternal reason that it ought to begin or cease—in your eternal reason where nothing begins or ceases. And this is your word, which is also "the beginning," because it also speaks to us.* Thus, in the gospel, he spoke through the flesh; and this sounded in the outward ears of men so that it might be believed and sought for within, and so that it might be found in the eternal truth, in which the good and only master teacheth all his disciples. There, lord, I hear your voice, the voice of one speaking to me, since he who teaches us speaks to us. But he who does not teach us does not really speak to us even when he speaks. Yet who is it that teaches us unless it be the truth immutable? For even when we are instructed by means of the mutable creation, we are thereby led to the truth immutable. There we learn truly as we stand and hear him, and we rejoice greatly "because of the bridegroom's voice,"† restoring us to the source whence our being comes. And therefore, unless the beginning remained immutable, there would then not be a place to which we might return when we had wandered away. But when we return from error, it is through our gaining knowledge that we return. In order for us to gain knowledge he teaches us, since he is the beginning, and speaks to us.

[**11.9.11**] In this beginning, god, you have made heaven and earth— through your word, your son, your power, your wisdom, your truth: all wondrously speaking and wondrously creating. Who shall comprehend such things and who shall tell of it? What is it that shines through me and strikes my heart without injury, so that I both shudder and burn? I shudder because I am unlike it; I burn because I am like it. It is wisdom itself that shines through me, clearing away my fog, which so readily overwhelms me so that I faint in it, in the darkness and burden of my punishment. For my strength is brought down in neediness, so that I cannot endure even my blessings until you, lord, who have been gracious to all my iniquities, also heal all my infirmities—for it is you who "shall redeem my life from corruption, and crown me with loving-kindness and tender mercy, and shall satisfy my desire with good things so that my youth shall

---

* John 8:25.
† John 3:29.

be renewed like the eagle's."* For by this hope we are saved, and through patience we await your promises. Let him that is able hear you speaking to his inner mind. I will cry out with confidence because of your own oracle, "How wonderful are your works, lord; in wisdom you have made them all."† And this wisdom is the beginning, and in that beginning you have made heaven and earth.

[11.10.12] Now, are not those still full of their old carnal nature who ask us: "What was god doing before he made heaven and earth? For if he was idle," they say, "and doing nothing, then why did he not continue in that state forever—doing nothing, as he had always done? If any new motion has arisen in god, and a new will to form a creature, which he had never before formed, how can that be a true eternity in which an act of will occurs that was not there before? For the will of god is not a created thing, but comes before the creation—and this is true because nothing could be created unless the will of the creator came before it. The will of god, therefore, pertains to his very essence. Yet if anything has arisen in the essence of god that was not there before, then that essence cannot truly be called eternal. But if it was the eternal will of god that the creation should come to be, why, then, is not the creation itself also from eternity?"⁶

[11.11.13] Those who say these things do not yet understand you, wisdom of god, light of souls. They do not yet understand how the things are made that are made by and in you. They endeavor to comprehend eternal things, but their heart still flies about in the past and future motions of created things, and is still unstable. Who shall hold and fix such a heart so that it may come to rest for a little; and then, by degrees, glimpse the glory of that eternity which abides forever; and then, comparing eternity with the temporal process in which nothing abides, may see that they are incommensurable? It would see that a long time does not become long, except from the many separate events that occur in its passage, which cannot be simultaneous. In the eternal, on the other hand, nothing passes away, but the whole is simultaneously present. But no temporal process is wholly simultaneous. Therefore, let the heart see that all time past is forced to move on by the incoming future; that all the future follows from the past; and that all, past and future, is created and issues out of that which is forever present. Who will hold the heart of man that it may stand

---

* Psalms 103:4–5.
† Psalms 104:24.

still and see how the eternity which always stands still is itself neither future nor past but expresses itself in the times that are future and past? Can my hand do this, or can the hand of my mouth bring about so difficult a thing even by persuasion?

[**11.12.14**] How, then, shall I respond to the person who asks, "What was god doing before he made heaven and earth?" I do not answer, as a certain one is reported to have done facetiously, shrugging off the force of the question. "He was preparing hell," he said, "for those who pry too deep." It is one thing to see the answer; it is another to laugh at the questioner—and for myself I do not answer these things thus. More willingly would I have answered, "I do not know what I do not know," than cause one who asked a deep question to be ridiculed—and by such tactics gain praise for a worthless answer. Rather, I say that you, our god, are the creator of every creature. And if in the term "heaven and earth" every creature is included, I make bold to say further: before god made heaven and earth, he did not make anything at all. For if he did, what did he make unless it were a creature? I do indeed wish that I knew all that I desire to know to my profit as surely as I know that no creature was made before any creature was made.

[**11.13.15**] But if the roving thought of someone should wander over the images of past time, and wonder that you, the almighty god, the all-creating and all-sustaining, the architect of heaven and earth, did for ages unnumbered abstain from so great a work before you actually did it, let him awake and consider that he wonders at illusions. For in what temporal medium could the unnumbered ages that you did not make pass by, since you are the author and creator of all the ages? Or what periods of time would those be that were not made by you? Or how could they have already passed away if they had not already been? Since, therefore, you are the creator of all times, if there was any time before you made heaven and earth, why is it said that you were abstaining from working? For you made that very time itself, and periods could not pass by before you made the whole temporal procession. But if there was no time before heaven and earth, how, then, can it be asked, "What were you doing then?" For there was no "then" when there was no time.

[**11.13.16**] Nor do you precede any given period of time by another period of time. Else you would not precede all periods of time. In the eminence of your ever-present eternity, you precede all times past, and extend beyond all future times, for they are still to come—and when they have come, they will be past. But "you are always the selfsame and your years shall have no end."* Your years neither go nor come; but ours both go and come in order that all separate moments may come to pass. All your years stand together as one, since they are abiding. Nor do your years past exclude the years to come because your years do not pass away. All these years of ours shall be with you, when all of them shall have ceased to be. Your years are but a day, and your day is not recurrent, but always today. Your today yields not to tomorrow and does not follow yesterday. Your today is eternity. Therefore, you generated the coeternal one, to whom you said, "This day I have begotten you."† You made all time and before all times you are, and there was never a time when there was no time.

[11.14.17] There was no time, therefore, when you had not made anything, because you had made time itself. And there are no times that are coeternal with you, because you abide forever; but if times should abide, they would not be times. For what is time?[7] Who can easily and briefly explain it? Who can even comprehend it in thought or put the answer into words? Yet is it not true that in conversation we refer to nothing more familiarly or knowingly than time? And surely we understand it when we speak of it; we understand it also when we hear another speak of it. What, then, is time? If no one asks me, I know what it is. If I wish to explain it to one who asks me, I do not know. Yet I say with confidence that I know that if nothing passed away, there would be no past time; and if nothing were still coming, there would be no future time; and if there were nothing at all, there would be no present time. But, then, how is it that there are the two times, past and future, when even the past is now no longer and the future is now not yet? But if the present were always present, and did not pass into past time, it obviously would not be time but eternity. If, then, time present—if it be time—comes into existence only because it passes into time past, how can we say that even this is, since the cause of its being is that it will cease to be? Thus, can we not truly say that time *is* only as it tends toward nonbeing?

[11.15.18] And yet we speak of a long time and a short time, but never speak this way except of time past and future. We call a hundred years ago, for example, a long time past. In like manner, we should call a hundred years hence a long time to come. But we call ten days ago a short time past; and ten days hence a short time to come. But in what sense is

---

* Psalms 102:27.

† Psalms 2:7.

something long or short that is nonexistent? For the past is not now, and the future is not yet. Therefore, let us not say, "It is long"; instead, let us say of the past, "It was long," and of the future, "It will be long." And yet, lord, my light, shall not your truth make mockery of man even here? For that long time past: was it long when it was already past, or when it was still present? For it might have been long when there was a period that could be long, but when it was past, it no longer was. In that case, that which was not at all could not be long. Let us not, therefore, say, "Time past was long," for we shall not discover what it was that was long because, since it is past, it no longer exists. Rather, let us say that "time present was long, because when it was present it was long." For then it had not yet passed on so as not to be, and therefore it still was in a state that could be called long. But after it passed, it ceased to be long simply because it ceased to be.

[11.15.19] Let us, therefore, human soul, see whether present time can be long, for it has been given you to feel and measure the periods of time. How, then, will you answer me? Is a hundred years when present a long time? But, first, see whether a hundred years can be present at once. For if the first year in the century is current, then it is present time, and the other ninety and nine are still future. Therefore, they are not yet. But, then, if the second year is current, one year is already past, the second present, and all the rest are future. And thus, if we fix on any middle year of this century as present, those before it are past, those after it are future. Therefore, a hundred years cannot be present all at once. Let us see, then, whether the year that is now current can be present. For if its first month is current, then the rest are future; if the second, the first is already past, and the remainder are not yet. Therefore, the current year is not present all at once. And if it is not present as a whole, then the year is not present. For it takes twelve months to make the year, from which each individual month which is current is itself present one at a time, but the rest are either past or future.

[11.15.20] Thus it comes out that time present, which we found was the only time that could be called long, has been cut down to the space of scarcely a single day. But let us examine even that, for one day is never present as a whole. For it is made up of twenty-four hours, divided between night and day. The first of these hours has the rest of them as future, and the last of them has the rest as past; but any of those between has those that preceded it as past and those that succeed it as future. And that one hour itself passes away in fleeting fractions. The part of it that has fled is past; what remains is still future. If any fraction of time be conceived that cannot now be divided even into the most minute momentary point, this alone is what we may call time present. But this flies so rapidly from future to past that it cannot be extended by any delay. For if it is extended, it is then divided into past and future. But the present has no extension whatever.

Where, therefore, is that time which we may call long? Is it future? Actually we do not say of the future, "It is long," for it has not yet come to be, so as to be long. Instead, we say, "It will be long." When will it be? For since it is future, it will not be long, for what may be long is not yet. It will be long only when it passes from the future which is not as yet, and will have begun to be present, so that there can be something that may be long. But in that case, time present cries aloud, in the words we have already heard, that it cannot be long.

[11.16.21] And yet, lord, we do perceive intervals of time, and we compare them with each other, and we say that some are longer and others are shorter. We even measure how much longer or shorter this time may be than that time. And we say that this time is twice as long, or three times as long, while this other time is only just as long as that other. But we measure the passage of time when we measure the intervals of perception. But who can measure times past which now are no longer, or times future which are not yet—unless perhaps someone will dare to say that what does not exist can be measured? Therefore, while time is passing, it can be perceived and measured; but when it is past, it cannot, since it is not.

[11.17.22] I am seeking the truth, father; I am not affirming it. My god, direct and rule me. Who is there who will tell me that there are not three times—as we learned when boys and as we have also taught boys—time past, time present, and time future? Who can say that there is only time present because the other two do not exist? Or do they also exist; but when, from the future, time becomes present, it proceeds from some secret place; and when, from times present, it becomes past, it recedes into some secret place? For where have those men who have foretold the future seen the things foretold, if then they were not yet existing? For what does not exist cannot be seen. And those who tell of things past could not speak of them as if they were true, if they did not see them in their minds. These things could in no way be discerned if they did not exist. There are therefore times present and times past.

[11.18.23] Give me leave, lord, to seek still further. My hope, let not my purpose be confounded. For if there are times past and future, I wish to know where they are. But if I have not yet succeeded in this, I still know that wherever they are, they are not there as future or past, but as present. For if they are there as future, they are there as "not yet"; if they are there as past, they are there as "no longer." Wherever they are and whatever they are they exist therefore only as present. Although we tell of past things as true, they are drawn out of the memory—not the things themselves, which have already passed, but words constructed from the images of the perceptions which were formed in the mind, like footprints in their passage through the senses. My childhood, for instance, which is no longer, still exists in time past, which does not now exist. But when I call to mind its image and speak of it, I see it in the present because it is still in my memory.[8] Whether there is a similar explanation for the foretelling of future events—that is, of the images of things which are not yet seen as if they were already existing—I confess, my god, I do not know. But this I certainly do know: that we generally think ahead about our future actions, and this premeditation is in time present; but that the action which we premeditate is not yet, because it is still future. When we shall have started the action and have begun to do what we were premeditating, then that action will be in time present, because then it is no longer in time future.

[11.18.24] Whatever may be the manner of this secret foreseeing of future things, nothing can be seen except what exists. But what exists now is not future, but present. When, therefore, they say that future events are seen, it is not the events themselves, for they do not exist as yet (that is, they are still in time future), but perhaps, instead, their causes and their signs are seen, which already do exist. Therefore, to those already beholding these causes and signs, they are not future, but present, and from them future things are predicted because they are conceived in the mind. These conceptions, however, exist now, and those who predict those things see these conceptions before them in time present.

Let me take an example from the vast multitude and variety of such things. I see the dawn; I predict that the sun is about to rise. What I see is in time present, what I predict is in time future—not that the sun is future, for it already exists; but its rising is future, because it is not yet. Yet I could not predict even its rising, unless I had an image of it in my mind; as, indeed, I do even now as I speak. But that dawn which I see in the sky is not the rising of the sun (though it does precede it), nor is it a conception in my mind. These two are seen in time present, in order that the event which is in time future may be predicted. Future events, therefore, are not yet. And if they are not yet, they do not exist. And if they do not exist, they cannot be seen at all, but they can be predicted from things present, which now are and are seen.

[**11.19.25**] Now, therefore, ruler of your creatures, what is the mode by which you teach souls those things which are still future? For you have taught your prophets. How do you, to whom nothing is future, teach future things—or rather teach things present from the signs of things future? For what does not exist certainly cannot be taught. This way of yours is too far from my sight; it is too great for me, I cannot attain to it. But I shall be enabled by you, when you will grant it, sweet light of my secret eyes.

[**11.20.26**] But even now it is manifest and clear that there are neither times future nor times past. Thus it is not properly said that there are three times, past, present, and future. Perhaps it might be said rightly that there are three times: a time present of things past; a time present of things present; and a time present of things future. For these three do coexist somehow in the soul, for otherwise I could not see them. The time present of things past is memory; the time present of things present is direct experience; the time present of things future is expectation. If we are allowed to speak of these things so, I see three times, and I grant that there are three. Let it still be said, then, as our misapplied custom has it: "There are three times, past, present, and future." I shall not be troubled by it, nor argue, nor object—always provided that what is said is understood, so that neither the future nor the past is said to exist now. There are but few things about which we speak properly—and many more about which we speak improperly—though we understand one another's meaning.

[**11.21.27**] I have said, then, that we measure periods of time as they pass so that we can say that this time is twice as long as that one or that this is just as long as that, and so on for the other fractions of time which we can count by measuring. So, then, as I was saying, we measure periods of time as they pass. And if anyone asks me, "How do you know this?", I can answer: "I know because we measure. We could not measure things that do not exist, and things past and future do not exist." But how do we measure present time since it has no extension? It is measured while it passes, but when it has passed it is not measured; for then there is nothing that could be measured. But whence, and how, and whither does it pass while it is being measured? Whence, but from the future? Which way, save through the present? Whither, but into the past? Therefore, from what is not yet, through what has no length, it passes into what is now no longer. But what do we measure, unless it is a time of some length? For we cannot speak of single, and double, and triple, and equal, and all the other ways in which we speak of time, except in terms of the length of the periods of time. But in what "length," then, do we measure passing time? Is it in the future, from which it passes over? But what does not yet exist cannot be measured. Or, is it in the present, through which it passes? But what has no length we cannot measure. Or is it in the past into which it passes? But what is no longer we cannot measure.

[**11.22.28**] My soul burns ardently to understand this most intricate enigma. Lord my god, good father, I beseech you through Christ, do not close off these things, both the familiar and the obscure, from my desire. Do not bar it from entering into them, but let their light dawn by your enlightening mercy, lord. Of whom shall I inquire about these things? And to whom shall I confess my ignorance of them with greater profit than to you, to whom these studies of mine (ardently longing to understand your scriptures) are not a bore? Give me what I love, for I do love it; and this you have given me. Father, who truly know how to give good gifts to your children, give this to me. Grant it, since I have undertaken to understand it, and hard labor is my lot until you open it. I beseech you, through Christ and in his name, the holy of holies, let no man interrupt me. "For I have believed, and therefore do I speak."* This is my hope; for this I live: in order that I may contemplate the joys of my lord. See, you have made my days grow old, and they pass away—and how I do not know.

We speak of this time and that time, and these times and those times: "How long ago since he said this?" "How long ago since he did this?" "How long ago since I saw that?" "This syllable is twice as long as that single short syllable." These words we say and hear, and we are understood and we understand. They are quite commonplace and ordinary, and still the meaning of these very same things lies deeply hid and its discovery is still to come.

[**11.23.29**] I once heard a learned man say that the motions of the sun, moon, and stars constituted time; and I did not agree. For why should not the motions of all bodies constitute time? What if the lights of heaven should cease, and a potter's wheel still turn round: would there be no time by which we might measure those rotations and say either that it turned at equal intervals, or, if it moved now more slowly and now more quickly, that some rotations were longer and others shorter? And while we were saying this, would we not also be speaking in time? Or would there not be in our words some syllables that were long and others short, because

---

* Psalms 116:10.

the first took a longer time to sound, and the others a shorter time? God, grant men to see in a small thing the notions that are common to all things, both great and small. Both the stars and the lights of heaven are "for signs and seasons, and for days and years."* This is doubtless the case, but just as I should not say that the circuit of that wooden wheel was a day, neither would that learned man say that there was, therefore, no time.

[11.23.30] I thirst to know the power and the nature of time, by which we measure the motions of bodies, and say, for example, that this motion is twice as long as that. For I ask, since the word "day" refers not only to the length of time that the sun is above the earth (which separates day from night), but also refers to the sun's entire circuit from east all the way around to east—on account of which we can say, "So many days have passed" (the nights being included when we say, "So many days," and their lengths not counted separately)—since, then, the day is ended by the motion of the sun and by his passage from east to east, I ask whether the motion itself is the day, or whether the day is the period in which that motion is completed, or both? For if the sun's passage is the day, then there would be a day even if the sun should finish its course in as short a period as an hour. If the motion itself is the day, then it would not be a day if from one sunrise to another there were a period no longer than an hour. But the sun would have to go round twenty-four times to make just one day. If it is both, then that could not be called a day if the sun ran its entire course in the period of an hour; nor would it be a day if, while the sun stood still, as much time passed as the sun usually covered during its whole course, from morning to morning. I shall, therefore, not ask any more what it is that is called a day, but rather what time is, for it is by time that we measure the circuit of the sun, and would be able to say that it was finished in half the period of time that it customarily takes if it were completed in a period of only twelve hours. If, then, we compare these periods, we could call one of them a single and the other a double period, as if the sun might run its course from east to east sometimes in a single period and sometimes in a double period.

Let no one tell me, therefore, that the motions of the heavenly bodies constitute time. For when the sun stood still at the prayer of a certain man in order that he might gain his victory in battle, the sun stood still but time

---

* Genesis 1:14.

went on. For in as long a span of time as was sufficient the battle was fought and ended.*

I see, then, that time is a certain kind of extension. But do I see it, or do I only seem to? You, light and truth, will show me.

[**11.24.31**] Do you command that I should agree if anyone says that time is the motion of a body? You do not so command. For I hear that no body is moved but in time; this you tell me. But that the motion of a body itself is time I do not hear; you do not say so. For when a body is moved, I measure by time how long it was moving from the time when it began to be moved until it stopped. And if I did not see when it began to be moved, and if it continued to move so that I could not see when it stopped, I could not measure the movement, except from the time when I began to see it until I stopped. But if I look at it for a long time, I can affirm only that the time is long but not how long it may be. This is because when we say, "How long?", we are speaking comparatively as: "This is as long as that," or, "This is twice as long as that"; or other such similar ratios. But if we were able to observe the point in space where and from which the body, which is moved, comes and the point to which it is moved; or if we can observe its parts moving as in a wheel, we can say how long the movement of the body took or the movement of its parts from this place to that. Since, therefore, the motion of a body is one thing, and the norm by which we measure how long it takes is another thing, we cannot see which of these two is to be called time. For, although a body is sometimes moved and sometimes stands still, we measure not only its motion but also its rest as well—and both by time! Thus we say, "It stood still as long as it moved," or, "It stood still twice or three times as long as it moved," or any other ratio which our measuring has either determined or imagined, either roughly or precisely, according to our custom. Therefore, time is not the motion of a body.

[**11.25.32**] And I confess to you, lord, that I am still ignorant as to what time is. And again I confess to you, lord, that I know that I am speaking all these things in time, and that I have already spoken of time a long time, and that "very long" is not long except when measured by the duration of time. How, then, do I know this, when I do not know what time is? Or, is it possible that I do not know how I can express what I do know? Alas for me! I do not even know the extent of my own

---

* Joshua 10:12–14.

ignorance. See, my god, in your presence I do not lie. As my heart is, so I speak. You will light my candle; you, lord my god, wilt enlighten my darkness.*

[11.26.33] Does not my soul most truly confess to you that I do measure intervals of time? But what is it that I thus measure, my god, and how is it that I do not know what I measure? I measure the motion of a body by time, but the time itself I do not measure. But, truly, could I measure the motion of a body—how long it takes, how long it is in motion from this place to that—unless I could measure the time in which it is moving? How, then, do I measure this time itself? Do we measure a longer time by a shorter time, as we measure the length of a crossbeam in terms of cubits? Thus, we can say that the length of a long syllable is measured by the length of a short syllable and thus say that the long syllable is double. So also we measure the length of poems by the length of the lines, and the length of the line by the length of the feet, and the length of the feet by the length of the syllable, and the length of the long syllables by the length of the short ones. We do not measure by pages—for in that way we would measure space rather than time—but when we speak the words as they pass by we say: "It is a long stanza, because it is made up of so many verses; they are long verses because they consist of so many feet; they are long feet because they extend over so many syllables; this is a long syllable because it is twice the length of a short one."

But no certain measure of time is obtained this way; since it is possible that if a shorter verse is pronounced slowly, it may take up more time than a longer one if it is pronounced hurriedly. The same would hold for a stanza, or a foot, or a syllable. From this it appears to me that time is nothing other than extendedness; but extendedness of what I do not know. This is a marvel to me. The extendedness may be of the mind itself. For what is it I measure, I ask you, my god, when I say either, roughly, "This time is longer than that," or, more precisely, "This is *twice* as long as that." I know that I am measuring time. But I am not measuring the future, for it is not yet; and I am not measuring the present because it is extended by no length; and I am not measuring the past because it no longer is. What is it, therefore, that I am measuring? Is it time in its passage, but not time past? This is what I have been saying.

[11.27.34] Press on, my mind, and attend with all your power. God is

---

* Psalms 18:28.

our helper: "it is he that hath made us and not we ourselves."* Give heed
where the truth begins to dawn. Suppose now that a bodily voice begins to
sound, and continues to sound—on and on—and then ceases. Now there
is silence. The voice is past, and there is no longer a sound. It was future
before it sounded, and could not be measured because it was not yet, and
now it cannot be measured because it is no longer. Therefore, while it was
sounding, it might have been measured because then there was something
that could be measured. But even then it did not stand still, for it was in
motion and was passing away. Could it, on that account, be any more readily measured? For while it was passing away, it was being extended into
some interval of time in which it might be measured, since the present has
no length. Supposing, though, that it might have been measured—then
also suppose that another voice had begun to sound and is still sounding
without any interruption to break its continued flow. We can measure it
only while it is sounding, for when it has ceased to sound it will be already
past and there will not be anything there that can be measured. Let us
measure it exactly, and let us say how much it is. But while it is sounding,
it cannot be measured except from the instant when it began to sound,
down to the final moment when it left off. For we measure the time interval itself from some beginning point to some end. This is why a voice that
has not yet ended cannot be measured, so that one could say how long or
how briefly it will continue. Nor can it be said to be equal to another voice
or single or double in comparison to it or anything like this. But when it is
ended, it is no longer. How, therefore, may it be measured? And yet we
measure times; not those which are not yet, nor those which no longer are,
nor those which are stretched out by some delay, nor those which have no
limit. Therefore, we measure neither times future nor times past, nor times
present, nor times passing by; and yet we do measure times.

[11.27.35] *Deus creator omnium*: this verse of eight syllables alternates
between short and long syllables.[9] The four short ones—that is, the first,
third, fifth, and seventh—are single in relation to the four long ones—that
is, the second, fourth, sixth, and eighth. Each of the long ones is double
the length of each of the short ones. I affirm this and report it, and common sense perceives that this indeed is the case. By common sense, then,
I measure a long syllable by a short one, and I find that it is twice as long.
But when one sounds after another, if the first be short and the latter long,
how can I hold the short one and how can I apply it to the long one as a

---

* Psalms 100:3.

measure, so that I can discover that the long one is twice as long, when, in fact, the long one does not begin to sound until the short one leaves off sounding? That same long syllable I do not measure as present, since I cannot measure it until it is ended; but its ending is its passing away.

What is it, then, that I can measure? Where is the short syllable by which I measure? Where is the long one that I am measuring? Both have sounded, have flown away, have passed on, and are no longer. And still I measure, and I confidently answer—as far as a trained ear can be trusted—that this syllable is single and that syllable double. And I could not do this unless they both had passed and were ended. Therefore I do not measure them, for they do not exist any more. But I measure something in my memory which remains fixed.

[11.27.36] It is in you, mind of mine, that I measure the periods of time. Do not shout me down that it exists otherwise; do not overwhelm yourself with the turbulent flood of your impressions. In you, as I have said, I measure the periods of time. I measure as time present the impression that things make on you as they pass by and what remains after they have passed by—I do not measure the things themselves which have passed by and left their impression on you. This is what I measure when I measure periods of time. Either, then, these are the periods of time or else I do not measure time at all.

What are we doing when we measure silence, and say that this silence has lasted as long as that voice lasts? Do we not project our thought to the measure of a sound, as if it were then sounding, so that we can say something concerning the intervals of silence in a given span of time? For, even when both the voice and the tongue are still, we review—in thought—poems and verses, and discourse of various kinds or various measures of motions, and we specify their time spans—how long this is in relation to that—just as if we were speaking them aloud. If anyone wishes to utter a prolonged sound, and if, in forethought, has decided how long it should be, that person has already in silence gone through a span of time, and committed sound to memory. Thus he begins to speak and his voice sounds until it reaches the predetermined end. It has truly sounded and will go on sounding. But what is already finished has already sounded and what remains will still sound. Thus it passes on, until the present intention carries the future over into the past. The past increases by the diminution of the future until by the consumption of all the future all is past.

[11.28.37] But how is the future diminished or consumed when it does not yet exist? Or how does the past, which exists no longer, increase, unless it is that in the mind in which all this happens there are three functions? For the mind expects, it attends, and it remembers; so that what it expects passes into what it remembers by way of what it attends to. Who denies that future things do not exist as yet? But still there is already in the mind the expectation of things still future. And who denies that past things now exist no longer? Still there is in the mind the memory of things past. Who denies that time present has no length, since it passes away in a moment? Yet, our attention has a continuity and it is through this that what is present may proceed to become absent. Therefore, future time, which is nonexistent, is not long; but a long future is a long expectation of the future. Nor is time past, which is now no longer, long; a long past is a long memory of the past.

[11.28.38] I am about to repeat a psalm that I know.[10] Before I begin, my attention encompasses the whole, but once I have begun, as much of it as becomes past while I speak is still stretched out in my memory. The span of my action is divided between my memory, which contains what I have repeated, and my expectation, which contains what I am about to repeat. Yet my attention is continually present with me, and through it what was future is carried over so that it becomes past. The more this is done and repeated, the more the memory is enlarged—and expectation is shortened—until the whole expectation is exhausted. Then the whole action is ended and passed into memory. And what takes place in the entire psalm takes place also in each individual part of it and in each individual syllable. This also holds in the even longer action of which that psalm is only a portion. The same holds in the whole of human life, of which all the actions of human beings are parts. The same holds in the whole age of the "sons of men," of which all human lives are parts.

[11.29.39] But "since your loving-kindness is better than life itself,"* observe how my life is but a stretching out, and how your right hand has upheld me in my lord, the son of man, the mediator between you, the one, and us, the many—in so many ways and by so many means. Thus through him I may lay hold upon him in whom I am also laid hold upon; and I may be gathered up from my old way of life to follow that one and to forget that which is behind, no longer stretched out but now pulled together again—stretching forth not to what shall be and shall pass away but to those things that are before me. Not distractedly now, but intently, I follow on for the prize of my heavenly calling,† where I may hear the sound of your praise and contemplate your delights, which neither come to be nor pass away.

---

* Psalms 63:3.

† Philippians 3:12–14.

But now my years are spent in mourning.* And you, lord, are my comfort, my eternal father. But I have been torn between the times, the order of which I do not know, and my thoughts, even the inmost and deepest places of my soul, are mangled by various commotions until I shall flow together into you, purged and molten in the fire of your love.

[11.30.40] And I will be immovable and fixed in you, and your truth will be my mold. And I shall not have to endure the questions of those people who, as if in a morbid disease, thirst for more than they can hold and say, "What did god make before he made heaven and earth?" or, "How did it come into his mind to make something when he had never before made anything?" Grant them, lord, to consider well what they are saying; and grant them to see that where there is no time they cannot say "never." When, therefore, he is said never to have made something—what is this but to say that it was made in no time at all? Let them therefore see that there could be no time without a created world, and let them cease to speak vanity of this kind. Let them also be stretched out to those things which are before them, and understand that you, the eternal creator of all times, are before all times and that no times are coeternal with you; nor is any creature, even if there is a creature above time.

[11.31.41] Lord my god, what a chasm there is in your deep secret! How far short of it have the consequences of my sins cast me? Heal my eyes, so that I may enjoy your light. Surely, if there is a mind that so greatly abounds in knowledge and foreknowledge, to which all things past and future are as well known as one psalm is well known to me, that mind would be an exceeding marvel and altogether astonishing. For whatever is past and whatever is yet to come would be no more concealed from him than the past and future of that psalm were hidden from me when I was chanting it: how much of it had been sung from the beginning and what and how much still remained till the end. But far be it from you, creator of the universe, and creator of our souls and bodies—far be it from you that you should merely know all things past and future. Far, far more wonderfully, and far more mysteriously you know them. For it is not as the feelings of one singing familiar songs, or hearing a familiar song in which, because of his expectation of words still to come and his remembrance of those that are past, his feelings are varied and his senses are divided. This is not the way that anything happens to you, who are unchangeably eternal, that is, the truly eternal creator of minds. As in the beginning you knew both the heaven and the

---

* Psalms 31:10.

earth without any change in your knowledge, so you made heaven and earth in their beginnings without any division in your action. Let him who understands this confess to you, and let him who does not understand also confess to you! Exalted as you are, still the humble in heart are your dwelling place! For you lift them who are cast down and they fall not for whom you are the most high.

BOOK 12

[**12.1.1**] My heart is deeply stirred, lord, when in this poor life of mine the words of your holy scripture strike upon it. This is why the poverty of the human intellect expresses itself in an abundance of language. Inquiry is more loquacious than discovery. Demanding takes longer than obtaining and the hand that knocks is more active than the hand that receives. But we have the promise, and who shall break it? "If god be for us, who can be against us?"* "Ask, and you shall receive; seek, and you shall find; knock, and it shall be opened to you; for everyone that asks receives, and he who seeks finds, and to him that knocks, it shall be opened."† These are your own promises, and who need fear to be deceived when truth promises?

[**12.2.2**] In lowliness my tongue confesses to your exaltation, for you made heaven and earth. This heaven which I see, and this earth on which I walk—from which came this earth that I carry about me—you did make. But where is that heaven of heavens, lord, of which we hear in the words of the psalm, "The heaven of heavens is the lord's, but the earth he has given to the children of men"?‡ Where is the heaven that we cannot see, in relation to which all that we can see is earth? For this whole corporeal creation has been beautifully formed—though not everywhere in its entirety—and our earth is the lowest of these levels. Still, compared with that heaven of heavens, even the heaven of our own earth is only earth. Indeed, it is not absurd to call each of those two great bodies earth in comparison with that ineffable heaven which is the lord's, and not for the sons of men.[1]

[**12.3.3**] And truly this earth was "invisible and unformed," and there was an inexpressibly profound abyss above which there was no light since it had no form. You commanded it written that "darkness was on the face of the deep."§ What else is darkness except the absence of light? For if there had been light, where would it have been except by being over all, showing itself rising aloft and giving light? Therefore, where there was no

---

* Romans 8:31.
† Matthew 7:7–8.
‡ Psalms 115:16.
§ Genesis 1:2.

light as yet, why was it that darkness was present, unless it was that light was absent? Darkness, then, was heavy upon it, because the light from above was absent; just as there is silence where there is no sound. And what is it to have silence anywhere but simply not to have sound? Have you not, lord, taught this soul which confesses to you? Have you not thus taught me, lord, that before you formed and separated this formless matter there was nothing: neither color, nor figure, nor body, nor spirit? Yet it was not absolutely nothing; it was a certain formlessness without any shape.

[12.4.4] What, then, should that formlessness be called so that somehow it might be indicated to those of sluggish mind, unless we use some word in common speech? But what can be found anywhere in the world nearer to a total formlessness than the earth and the abyss? Because of their being on the lowest level, they are less beautiful than are the other and higher parts, all translucent and shining. Therefore, why may I not consider the formlessness of matter—which you created without shapely form, from which to make this shapely world—as fittingly indicated to human beings by the phrase, "the earth invisible and unformed"?

[12.5.5] When our thought seeks something for our sense to fasten to and when it says to itself, "It is not an intelligible form, such as life or justice, since it is the material for bodies; and it is not a former perception, for there is nothing in the invisible and unformed which can be seen and felt"—while human thought says such things to itself, it may be attempting either to know by being ignorant or by knowing how not to know.

[12.6.6] But if, lord, I am to confess to you, by my mouth and my pen, the whole of what you have taught me concerning this unformed matter, I must say first of all that when I first heard of such matter and did not understand it—and those who told me of it could not understand it either—I conceived of it as having countless and varied forms. Thus, I did not think about it rightly. My mind in its agitation used to turn up all sorts of foul and horrible forms, but still they were forms. And still I called it formless, not because it was unformed, but because it had what seemed to me a kind of form that my mind turned away from, as bizarre and incongruous, before which my human weakness was confused. And even what I did conceive of as unformed was so, not because it was deprived of all form, but only as it compared with more beautiful forms. Right reason, then, persuaded me that I ought to remove altogether all vestiges of form whatever if I wished to conceive matter that was wholly unformed; and this I could not do. For I could more readily imagine that what was deprived of all form simply did not exist than I could conceive of anything between form and nothing—something which was neither formed nor nothing, something that was unformed and nearly nothing. Thus my mind ceased to question my spirit—filled as it was with the images of formed bodies, changing and varying them according to its will. And so I applied myself to the bodies themselves and looked more deeply into their mutability, by which they cease to be what they had been and begin to be what they were not. This transition from form to form I had regarded as involving something like a formless condition, though not actual nothingness.

But I desired to know, not to guess. And, if my voice and my pen were to confess to you all the various knots you have untied for me about this question, who among my readers could endure to grasp the whole of the account? Still, despite this, my heart will not cease to give honor to you or to sing your praises concerning those things which it is not able to express. For the mutability of mutable things carries with it the possibility of all those forms into which mutable things can be changed. But this mutability—what is it? Is it soul? Is it body? Is it the external appearance of soul or body? Could it be said, "Nothing was something," and "That which is, is not"? If this were possible, I would say that this was it, and in some such manner it must have been in order to receive these visible and composite forms.

[12.7.7] Whence and how was this, unless it came from you, from whom all things are, in so far as they are? But the farther something is from you, the more unlike you it is—and this is not a matter of distance or place. Thus it was that you, lord, who are not one thing in one place and another thing in another place but the selfsame, and the selfsame, and the selfsame— "holy, holy, holy, lord god almighty"*—thus it was that in the beginning, and through your wisdom which is from you and born of your substance, you created something and that out of nothing.[2] For you created the heaven and the earth—not out of yourself, for then they would be equal to your only son and thereby to you. And there is no sense in which it would be right that anything should be equal to you that was not of you. But what else besides you was there out of which you might create these things, god, one trinity, and trine unity? And, therefore, it was out of nothing at all that you created the heaven and earth—something great and something small—for you are almighty and good, and able to make all things good: even the great heaven and the small earth. You were, and there was nothing else from which you created heaven and earth: these two things, one near you, the other near to

---

* Isaiah 6:3.

nothing; the one to which only you are superior, the other to which nothing else is inferior.

[12.8.8] That heaven of heavens was yours, lord, but the earth which you gave to the sons of men to be seen and touched was not then in the same form as that in which we now see it and touch it. For then it was invisible and unformed and there was an abyss over which there was no light. The darkness was truly over the abyss, that is, more than just in the abyss. For this abyss of waters which now is visible has even in its depths a certain light appropriate to its nature, perceptible in some fashion to fishes and the things that creep about on the bottom of it. But then the entire abyss was almost nothing, since it was still altogether unformed. Yet even there, there was something that had the possibility of being formed. For you, lord, had made the world out of unformed matter, and this you made out of nothing and made it into almost nothing. From it you have then made these great things which we, the sons of men, marvel at. For this corporeal heaven is truly marvelous, this firmament between the water and the waters which you made on the second day after the creation of light, saying, "Let it be done," and it was done.* This firmament you called heaven, that is, the heaven of this earth and sea which you made on the third day, giving a visible shape to the unformed matter which you had made before all the days. For even before any day you had already made a heaven, but that was the heaven of this heaven: for in the beginning you had made heaven and earth.

But this earth itself which you had made was unformed matter; it was invisible and unformed, and darkness was over the abyss. Out of this invisible and unformed earth, out of this formlessness which is almost nothing, you then made all these things of which the changeable world consists—and yet does not fully consist in itself—for its very changeableness appears in this, that its times and seasons can be observed and numbered. The periods of time are measured by the changes of things, while the forms, whose matter is the invisible earth of which we have spoken, are varied and altered.

[12.9.9] And therefore the spirit, the teacher of your servant [Moses], when he mentions that "in the beginning you made heaven and earth," says nothing about times and is silent as to the days. For, clearly, that heaven of heavens which you created in the beginning is in some way an intellectual creature, although in no way coeternal with the trinity that

---

* Genesis 1:6.

you are. Yet it is nonetheless a partaker in your eternity. Because of the sweetness of its most happy contemplation of you, it is greatly restrained in its own mutability and cleaves to you without any lapse from the time in which it was created, surpassing all the rolling change of time. But this shapelessness—this earth invisible and unformed—was not numbered among the days itself. For where there is no shape or order there is nothing that either comes or goes, and where this does not occur there certainly are no days, nor any vicissitude of periods of time.

[12.10.10] Truth, light of my heart, let not my own darkness speak to me! I had fallen into that darkness and was darkened thereby. But in it, even in its depths, I came to love you. I went astray and still I remembered you. I heard your voice behind me, bidding me return, though I could scarcely hear it for the tumults of my boisterous passions. And now, look, I am returning, burning and thirsting after your fountain. Let no one hinder me; here will I drink and so have life. Let me not be my own life, for of myself I have lived badly. I was death to myself; in you I have revived. Speak to me, converse with me. I have believed your books, and their words are very deep.[3]

[12.11.11] You have told me already, lord, with a strong voice in my inner ear, that you are eternal and alone have immortality. You are not changed by any shape or motion, and your will is not altered by temporal process, because no will that changes is immortal. This is clear to me, in your sight; let it become clearer and clearer, I beseech you. In that light let me abide soberly under your wings.

You have also told me, lord, with a strong voice in my inner ear, that you have created all natures and all substances, which are not what you are yourself; and yet they do exist. Only that which is nothing at all is not from you, and that motion of the will away from you, who are, toward something that exists only in a lesser degree—such a motion is an offense and a sin. No one's sin either hurts you or disturbs the order of your rule, either first or last. All this, in your sight, is clear to me. Let it become clearer and clearer, I beseech you, and in that light let me abide soberly under your wings.

[12.11.12] Likewise, you have told me, with a strong voice in my inner ear, that this creation—whose delight you alone are—is not coeternal with you. With a most persevering purity it draws its support from you and nowhere and never betrays its own mutability, for you are ever present with it, and it cleaves to you with its entire affection, having no future to expect and no past that it remembers; it is varied by no change and is extended by no time. Blessed one—if such there be—clinging to your blessedness! It is blest in you, its everlasting inhabitant and its light. I cannot find a term that I would judge more fitting for "the heaven of the heavens of the lord" than "your house"—which contemplates your delights without any declination toward anything else and which, with a pure mind in most harmonious stability, joins all together in the peace of those saintly spirits who are citizens of your city in those heavens that are above this visible heaven.

[**12.11.13**] From this let the soul that has journeyed far away from you understand—if now it thirsts for you; if now its tears have become its bread, while daily it is asked, "Where is your god?";* if now it requests of you just one thing and seeks after this: that it may dwell in your house all the days of its life (and what is its life but you? And what are your days but your eternity, like your years which do not fail, since you are the selfsame?)—from this, I say, let the soul understand (as far as it can) how far above all times you are in your eternity; and how your house has never journeyed away from you; and, although it is not coeternal with you, it continually and unfailingly clings to you and suffers no vicissitudes of time. This, in your sight, is clear to me; may it become clearer and clearer to me, I beseech you, and in this light may I abide soberly under your wings.

[**12.11.14**] Now I do not know what kind of formlessness there is in these mutations of these last and lowest creatures. Yet who will tell me, unless it is someone who, in the emptiness of his own heart, wanders about and begins to be dizzy in his own fancies? Who except such a one would tell me whether, if all form were diminished and consumed, formlessness alone would remain, through which a thing was changed and turned from one species into another, so that sheer formlessness would then be characterized by temporal change? And surely this could not be, because without motion there is no time, and where there is no form there is no change.

[**12.12.15**] These things I have considered as you have given me ability, my god, as you have excited me to knock, and as you have opened to me when I knock. Two things I find which you have made, not within intervals of time, although neither is coeternal with you. One of them is so formed that, without any wavering in its contemplation, without any interval of change—mutable but not changed—it may fully enjoy your eternity and immutability. The other is so formless that it could not change

---

* Psalms 42:3, 10.

from one form to another (either of motion or of rest), and so time has no hold upon it. But you did not leave this formless, for, before any "day" in the beginning, you created heaven and earth—these are the two things of which I spoke. But "the earth was invisible and unformed, and darkness was over the abyss." By these words its formlessness is indicated to us—so that by degrees they may be led forward who cannot wholly conceive of the privation of all form without arriving at nothing. From this formlessness a second heaven might be created and a second earth—visible and well formed, with the ordered beauty of the waters, and whatever else is recorded as created (though not without days) in the formation of this world. And all this because such things are so ordered that in them the changes of time may take place through the ordered processes of motion and form.

[12.13.16] Meanwhile this is what I understand, my god, when I hear your scripture saying, "In the beginning god made the heaven and the earth, but the earth was invisible and unformed, and darkness was over the abyss." It does not say on what day you created these things. Thus, for the time being I understand that "heaven of heavens" to mean the intelligible heaven, where to understand is to know all at once—not "in part," not "darkly," not "through a glass"—but as a simultaneous whole, in full sight, "face to face."* It is not this thing now and then another thing, but (as we said) knowledge all at once without any temporal change. And by the invisible and unformed earth, I understand that which suffers no temporal vicissitude. Temporal change customarily means having one thing now and another later; but where there is no form there can be no distinction between this or that. It is, then, by means of these two—one thing well formed in the beginning and another thing wholly unformed, the one heaven (that is, the heaven of heavens) and the other one earth (but the earth invisible and unformed)—it is by means of these two notions that I am able to understand why your scripture said, without mention of days, "In the beginning god created the heaven and the earth." For it immediately indicated which earth it was speaking about. When, on the second day, the firmament is recorded as having been created and called heaven, this suggests to us which heaven it was that he was speaking about earlier, without specifying a day.

[12.14.17] Marvelous is the depth of your oracles. Their surface is before us, inviting the little ones; and yet wonderful is their depth, my god,

---

* 1 Corinthians 13:12.

marvelous is their depth! It is a fearful thing to look into them: an awe of
honor and a tremor of love.[4] Their enemies I hate vehemently. If only you
would slay them with your two-edged sword, so that they should not be enemies! For I would prefer that they should be slain to themselves, that they
might live to you. But see, there are others who are not critics but praisers
of the book of Genesis; they say: "The spirit of god who wrote these things
by his servant Moses did not wish these words to be understood like this.
He did not wish to have it understood as you say, but as we say." To them,
god of us all, yourself being the judge, I give answer.

[**12.15.18**] Will you say that these things are false which truth tells me,
with a loud voice in my inner ear, about the very eternity of the creator:
that his essence is changed in no respect by time and that his will is not
distinct from his essence? Thus, he does not will one thing now and another thing later, but he wills once and for all everything that he wills—
not again and again; and not now this and now that. Nor does he will
afterward what he did not will before, nor does he cease to will what he
had willed before. Such a will would be mutable and no mutable thing is
eternal. But our god is eternal.

Again, he tells me in my inner ear that the expectation of future things
is turned to sight when they have come to pass. And this same sight is
turned into memory when they have passed. Moreover, all thought that
varies thus is mutable, and nothing mutable is eternal. But our god is eternal. These things I sum up and put together, and I conclude that my god,
the eternal god, has not made any creature by any new will, and his
knowledge does not admit anything transitory.

[**12.15.19**] What, then, will you say to this, you objectors? Are these
things false? "No," they say. What then? Is it false that every entity already
formed and all matter capable of receiving form is from him alone who is
supremely good, because he is supreme? "We do not deny this, either,"
they say. What then? Do you deny this: that there is a certain sublime created order which cleaves with such a chaste love to the true and truly eternal god that, although it is not coeternal with him, yet it does not separate
itself from him, and does not flow away into any mutation of change or
process but abides in true contemplation of him alone? If you, god, show
yourself to him who loves you as you have commanded—and are sufficient
for him—then, such a one will neither turn himself away from you nor turn
away toward himself. This is the house of god. It is not an earthly house
and it is not made from any celestial matter, but it is a spiritual house, and
it partakes in your eternity because it is without blemish forever. For you
have made it steadfast forever and ever; you have given it a law which will

not be removed. Still, it is not coeternal with you, god, since it is not without beginning—it was created.

[**12.15.20**] For, although we can find no time before it (for wisdom was created before all things),* this is certainly not that wisdom which is absolutely coeternal and equal with you, our god, its father, the wisdom through whom all things were created and in whom, in the beginning, you created the heaven and earth. This is truly the created wisdom, namely, the intelligible nature which, in its contemplation of light, is light. For this is also called wisdom, even if it is a created wisdom. But the difference between the light that lightens and that which is enlightened is as great as is the difference between the wisdom that creates and that which is created. So also is the difference between the righteousness that justifies and the righteousness that is made by justification. For we also are called your righteousness, for a certain servant of yours says, "that we might be made the righteousness of god in him."† Therefore, there is a certain created wisdom that was created before all things: the rational and intelligible mind of that chaste city of yours. It is our mother which is above and is free and "eternal in the heavens"‡—but in what heavens except those which praise you, the heaven of heavens? This also is the heaven of heavens which is the lord's, although we find no time before it, since what has been created before all things also precedes the creation of time. Still, the eternity of the creator himself is before it, from whom it took its beginning as created, though not in time (since time as yet was not), even though time belongs to its created nature.

[**12.15.21**] Thus it is that the intelligible heaven came to be from you, our god, but in such a way that it is quite another being than you are; it is not the selfsame. Yet we find that time is not only not before it, but not even in it, thus making it able to behold your face forever and not ever be turned aside. Thus, it is varied by no change at all. But there is still in it that mutability in virtue of which it could become dark and cold, if it did not, by cleaving to you with a supernal love, shine and glow from you like a perpetual noon. House full of light and splendor! "I have loved your beauty and the place of the habitation of the glory of my lord,"§ your builder and possessor. In my journeying let me sigh for you; this I ask of

---

* Ecclesiasticus 1:4.

† 2 Corinthians 5:21.

‡ 2 Corinthians 5:1.

§ Psalms 26:8.

him who made you, that he should also possess me in you, seeing that he has also made me. "I have gone astray like a lost sheep";* yet upon the shoulders of my shepherd, who is your builder, I have hoped that I may be brought back to you.

[12.15.22] What will you say to me now, you objectors to whom I spoke, who still believe that Moses was the holy servant of god, and that his books were the oracles of the holy spirit? Is it not in this house of god — not coeternal with god, yet in its own mode eternal in the heavens — that you vainly seek for temporal change? You will not find it there. It rises above all extension and every revolving temporal period, and it rises to what is forever good and cleaves fast to god.

"It is so," they reply. What, then, about those things which my heart cried out to my god, when it heard, within, the voice of his praise? What, then, do you contend is false in them? Is it because matter was unformed, and since there was no form there was no order? But where there was no order there could have been no temporal change. Yet even this "almost nothing," since it was not altogether nothing, was truly from him from whom everything that exists is in whatever state it is. "This also," they say, "we do not deny."

[12.16.23] Now, I would like to discuss a little further, in your presence, my god, with those who admit that all these things are true that your truth has indicated to my mind. Let those who deny these things bark and drown their own voices with as much clamor as they please. I will endeavor to persuade them to be quiet and to permit your word to reach them. But if they are unwilling, and if they repel me, I ask of you, my god, that you should not be silent to me. Speak truly in my heart; if only you would speak thus, I would send them away, blowing up the dust and raising it in their own eyes. As for myself I will enter into my chamber and there sing to you the songs of love, groaning with groanings that are unutterable now in my journeying, and remembering Jerusalem with my heart uplifted to Jerusalem my country, Jerusalem my mother; and to you yourself, the ruler of the source of light, its father, guardian, husband; its chaste and strong delight, its solid joy and all its goods ineffable — and all of this at the same time, since you are the one supreme and true good! And I will not be turned away until you have brought back together all that I am from this dispersion and deformity to the peace of that dearest mother, where the first fruits of my spirit are to be found and from which all these things are promised

---

* Psalms 119:176.

me which you conform and confirm forever, my god, my mercy. But as for those who do not say that all these things which are true are false, who still honor your scripture set before us by the holy Moses, who join us in placing it on the summit of authority for us to follow, and yet who oppose us in some particulars, I say this: may you, god, be the judge between my confessions and their gainsaying.

[12.17.24] For they say: "Even if these things are true, still Moses did not refer to these two things when he said, by divine revelation, 'In the beginning god created the heaven and the earth.' By the term 'heaven' he did not mean that spiritual or intelligible created order which always beholds the face of god. And by the term 'earth' he was not referring to unformed matter."

What then do these terms mean?

They reply, "That man [Moses] meant what we mean; this is what he was saying in those terms."

What is that?

"By the terms of heaven and earth," they say, "he wished first to indicate universally and briefly this whole visible world; then after this, by an enumeration of the days, he could point out, one by one, all the things that it has pleased the holy spirit to reveal in this way. For the people to whom he spoke were rude and carnal, so that he judged it prudent that only those works of god which were visible should be mentioned to them."

But they do agree that the phrases, "the earth was invisible and unformed," and "the darkened abyss," may not inappropriately be understood to refer to this unformed matter—and that out of this, as it is subsequently related, all the visible things which are known to all were made and set in order during those specified "days."

But now, what if another one should say, "This same formlessness and chaos of matter was first mentioned by the name of heaven and earth because, out of it, this visible world—with all its entities which clearly appear in it and which we are accustomed to be called by the name of heaven and earth—was created and perfected"? And what if still another should say: "The invisible and visible nature is quite fittingly called heaven and earth. Thus, the whole creation which god has made in his wisdom—that is, in the beginning—was included under these two terms. Yet, since all things have been made, not from the essence of god, but from nothing; and because they are not the same reality that god is; and because there is in them all a certain mutability, whether they abide as the eternal house of god abides or whether they are changed as the soul and body of man are changed—then the common matter of all things invisible

and visible (still formless but capable of receiving form) from which
heaven and earth were to be created (that is, the creature already fashioned, invisible as well as visible)—all this was spoken of in the same
terms by which the invisible and unformed earth and the darkness over
the abyss would be called. There was this difference, however: that the invisible and unformed earth is to be understood as having corporeal matter before it had any manner of form; but the darkness over the abyss was
spiritual matter, before its unlimited fluidity was harnessed, and before it
was enlightened by wisdom."

And if anyone wished, he might also say, "The entities already perfected and formed, invisible and visible, are not signified by the terms
'heaven and earth,' when it reads, 'In the beginning god created the
heaven and the earth'; instead, the unformed beginning of things, the matter capable of receiving form and being made was called by these terms—
because the chaos was contained in it and was not yet distinguished by
qualities and forms, which have now been arranged in their own orders
and are called heaven and earth: the former a spiritual creation, the latter a physical creation."

[12.18.27] When all these things have been said and considered, I am
unwilling to contend about words, for such contention is profitable for
nothing but the subverting of the hearer.* But the law is profitable for edification if a man use it lawfully: for the end of the law "is love out of a
pure heart, and a good conscience, and faith unfeigned."† And our master knew it well, for it was on these two commandments that he hung all
the Law and the Prophets.[5] And how would it harm me, my god, you light
of my eyes in secret, if while I am ardently confessing these things—since
many different things may be understood from these words, all of which
may be true—what harm would be done if I should interpret the meaning of the sacred writer differently from the way some other man interprets? Indeed, all of us who read are trying to trace out and understand
what our author wished to convey, and since we believe that he speaks
truly we dare not suppose that he has spoken anything that we either
know or suppose to be false. Therefore, since every person tries to understand in the holy scripture what the writer understood, what harm is
done if a man understands what you, the light of all truth-speaking minds,
show him to be true, although the author he reads did not understand this

---

* 2 Timothy 2:14.
† 1 Timothy 1:5.

aspect of the truth even though he did understand the truth in a different meaning?

[12.19.28] For it is certainly true, lord, that you created the heaven and the earth. It is also true that "the beginning" is your wisdom in which you created all things. It is likewise true that this visible world has its own great division (the heaven and the earth) and these two terms include all entities that have been made and created. It is further true that everything mutable confronts our minds with a certain lack of form, whereby it receives form, or whereby it is capable of taking form. It is true, yet again, that what cleaves to the changeless form so closely that even though it is mutable it is not changed is not subject to temporal process. It is true that the formlessness which is almost nothing cannot have temporal change in it. It is true that that from which something is made can, in a manner of speaking, be called by the same name as the thing that is made from it. Thus that formlessness of which heaven and earth were made might be called "heaven and earth." It is true that of all things having form nothing is nearer to the unformed than the earth and the abyss. It is true that not only every created and formed thing but also everything capable of creation and of form were created by you, from whom all things are. It is true, finally, that everything that is formed from what is formless was formless before it was formed.

[12.20.29] From all these truths, which are not doubted by those to whom you have granted insight in such things in their inner eye and who believe unshakably that your servant Moses spoke in the spirit of truth—from all these truths, then, one person takes the sense of "In the beginning god created the heaven and the earth" to mean, "In his word, coeternal with himself, god made both the intelligible and the tangible, the spiritual and the corporeal creation." Another takes it in a different sense, that "In the beginning god created the heaven and the earth" means, "In his word, coeternal with himself, god made the universal mass of this corporeal world, with all the observable and known entities that it contains." Still another finds a different meaning, that "In the beginning god created the heaven and the earth" means, "In his word, coeternal with himself, god made the unformed matter of the spiritual and corporeal creation." Another can take the sense that "In the beginning god created the heaven and the earth" means, "In his word, coeternal with himself, god made the unformed matter of the physical creation, in which heaven and earth were as yet indistinguished; but now that they have come to be separated and formed, we can now perceive them both in the mighty mass of this world." Another takes still a further meaning, that

"In the beginning god created heaven and earth" means, "In the very beginning of creating and working, god made that unformed matter which contained, undifferentiated, heaven and earth, from which both of them were formed, and both now stand out and are observable with all the things that are in them."

[**12.21.30**] Again, regarding the interpretation of the following words, one person selects, from all the various truths, the interpretation that "the earth was invisible and unformed and darkness was over the abyss" means, "that corporeal entity which god made was as yet the formless matter of physical things without order and without light." Another takes it in a different sense, that "but the earth was invisible and unformed, and darkness was over the abyss" means, "this totality called heaven and earth was as yet unformed and lightless matter, out of which the corporeal heaven and the corporeal earth were to be made, with all the things in them that are known to our physical senses." Another takes it still differently and says that "but the earth was invisible and unformed, and darkness was over the abyss" means, "this totality called heaven and earth was as yet an unformed and lightless matter, from which were to be made that intelligible heaven (which is also called 'the heaven of heavens') and the earth (which refers to the whole physical entity, under which term may be included this corporeal heaven)—that is, he made the intelligible heaven from which every invisible and visible creature would be created." A person takes it in yet another sense who says that "but the earth was invisible and unformed, and darkness was over the abyss" means, "the scripture does not refer to that formlessness by the term 'heaven and earth'; that formlessness itself already existed. This it called the invisible 'earth' and the unformed and lightless 'abyss,' from which—as it had said before—god made the heaven and the earth (namely, the spiritual and the corporeal creation)." Still another says that "but the earth was invisible and formless, and darkness was over the abyss" means, "there was already an unformed matter from which, as the scripture had already said, god made heaven and earth, namely, the entire corporeal mass of the world, divided into two very great parts, one superior, the other inferior, with all those familiar and known creatures that are in them."

[**12.22.31**] Now suppose that someone tried to argue against these last two opinions as follows: "If you will not admit that this formlessness of matter appears to be called by the term 'heaven and earth,' then there was something that god had not made out of which he did make heaven and earth. And scripture has not told us that god made *this* matter, unless we understand that it is implied in the term 'heaven and earth' (or the term 'earth' alone) when it is said, 'In the beginning god created the heaven and earth.' Thus, in what follows—'the earth was invisible and unformed'— even though it pleased Moses thus to refer to unformed matter, yet we can only understand by it that which god himself has made, as it stands written in the previous verse, 'god made heaven and earth.' " Those who maintain either one or the other of these two opinions which we have set out above will answer to such objections: "We do not deny at all that this unformed matter was created by god, from whom all things are, and are very good—because we hold that what is created and endowed with form is a higher good; and we also hold that what is made capable of being created and endowed with form, though it is a lesser good, is still a good. But the scripture has not said specifically that god made this formlessness—any more than it has said it specifically of many other things, such as the orders of 'cherubim' and 'seraphim' and those others of which the apostle distinctly speaks: 'thrones,' 'dominions,' 'principalities,' 'powers'*—yet it is clear that god made all of these. If in the phrase 'he made heaven and earth' all things are included, what are we to say about the waters upon which the spirit of god moved? For if they are understood as included in the term 'earth,' then how can unformed matter be meant by the term 'earth' when we see the waters so beautifully formed? Or, if it be taken thus, why, then, is it written that out of the same formlessness the firmament was made and called heaven, and yet is it not specifically written that the waters were made? For these waters, which we perceive flowing in so beautiful a fashion, are not formless and invisible. But if they received that beauty at the time god said of them, 'Let the waters which are under the firmament be gathered together,'† thus indicating that their gathering together was the same thing as their reception of form, what, then, is to be said about the waters that are above the firmament? Because if they are unformed, they do not deserve to have a seat so honorable, and yet it is not written by what specific word they were formed. If, then, Genesis is silent about anything that god has made, which neither sound faith nor unerring understanding doubts that god has made, let not any sober teaching dare to say that these waters were coeternal with god because we find them mentioned in the book of Genesis and do not find it mentioned when they were created. If truth instructs us, why may we not interpret that unformed

---

* Colossians 1:16.
† Genesis 1:9.

matter which the scripture calls the earth—invisible and unformed—and the lightless abyss as having been made by god from nothing; and thus understand that they are not coeternal with him, although the narrative fails to tell us precisely when they were made?"

[12.23.32] I have heard and considered these theories as well as my weak apprehension allows, and I confess my weakness to you, lord, though already you know it. Thus I see that two sorts of disagreements may arise when anything is related by signs, even by trustworthy reporters. There is one disagreement about the truth of the things involved; the other concerns the meaning of the one who reports them. It is one thing to inquire as to what is true about the formation of the creation. It is another thing, however, to ask what that excellent servant of your faith, Moses, would have wished for the reader and hearer to understand from these words. As for the first question, let all those depart from me who imagine that Moses spoke things that are false. But let me be united with them in you, lord, and delight myself in you with those who feed on your truth in the bond of love. Let us approach together the words of your book and make diligent inquiry in them for your meaning through the meaning of your servant by whose pen you have given them to us.

[12.24.33] But in the midst of so many truths which occur to the interpreters of these words (understood as they can be in different ways), which one of us can discover that single interpretation which warrants our saying confidently that Moses thought thus and that in this narrative he wishes this to be understood, as confidently as he would say that this is true, whether Moses thought the one or the other. For see, my god, I am your servant, and I have vowed in this book an offering of confession to you, and I beseech you that by your mercy I may pay my vow to you. Now, see, could I assert that Moses meant nothing else than this when he wrote, "In the beginning god created the heaven and the earth," as confidently as I can assert that you in your immutable word have created all things, invisible and visible?[6] No, I cannot do this because it is not as clear to me that this was in his mind when he wrote these things, as I see it to be certain in your truth. For his thoughts might be set upon the very beginning of the creation when he said, "In the beginning"; and he might have wished it understood that, in this passage, "heaven and earth" refers to no formed and perfect entity, whether spiritual or corporeal, but each of them only newly begun and still formless. Whichever of these possibilities has been mentioned I can see that it might have been said truly. But which of them he did actually intend to express in these words I do not clearly see. However, whether it was one of these or some other meaning which I have not mentioned that this great man saw in his mind when he used these words I have no doubt whatever that he saw it truly and expressed it suitably.

[12.25.34] Let no man fret me now by saying, "Moses did not mean what you say, but what I say." Now if he asks me, "How do you know that Moses meant what you deduce from his words?", I ought to respond calmly and reply as I have already done, or even more fully if he happens to be untrained. But when he says, "Moses did not mean what you say, but what I say," and then does not deny what either of us says but allows that both are true—then, my god, life of the poor, in whose breast there is no contradiction, pour your soothing balm into my heart that I may patiently bear with people who talk like this! It is not because they are godly men and have seen in the heart of your servant what they say, but rather they are proud men and have not considered Moses' meaning, but only love their own—not because it is true but because it is their own. Otherwise they could equally love another true opinion, as I love what they say when what they speak is true—not because it is theirs but because it is true, and therefore not theirs but true. And if they love an opinion because it is true, it becomes both theirs and mine, since it is the common property of all lovers of the truth. But I neither accept nor approve of it when they contend that Moses did not mean what I say but what they say—and this because, even if it were so, such rashness is born not of knowledge, but of impudence. It comes not from vision but from vanity.

And therefore, lord, your judgments should be held in awe, because your truth is neither mine nor his nor anyone else's; but it belongs to all of us whom you have openly called to have it in common; and you have warned us not to hold on to it as our own special property, for if we do we lose it. For if anyone arrogates to himself what you have bestowed on all to enjoy, and if he desires something for his own that belongs to all, he is forced away from what is common to all to what is, indeed, his very own—that is, from truth to falsehood. For he who tells a lie speaks of his own thought.*

[12.25.35] Hear, god, best judge of all! Truth itself, hear what I say to this disputant. Hear it, because I say it in your presence and before my brethren who use the law rightly to the end of love. Hear and give heed to what I shall say to him, if it pleases you. For I would return this brotherly and peaceful word to him: if we both see that what you say is true,

---

* John 8:44.

and if we both say that what I say is true, where is it, I ask you, that we see this? Certainly, I do not see it in you, and you do not see it in me, but both of us see it in the unchangeable truth itself, which is above our minds. If, then, we do not disagree about the true light of the lord our god, why do we disagree about the thoughts of our neighbor, which we cannot see as clearly as the immutable truth is seen? If Moses himself had appeared to us and said, "This is what I meant," it would not be in order that we should see it but that we should believe him. Let us not, then, "go beyond what is written and be puffed up for the one against the other."* Let us, instead, "love the lord our god with all our heart, with all our soul, and with all our mind, and our neighbor as ourself."† Unless we believe that whatever Moses meant in these books he meant to be ordered by these two precepts of love, we shall make god a liar, if we judge of the soul of his servant in any other way than as he has taught us. See now, how foolish it is, in the face of so great an abundance of true opinions which can be elicited from these words, rashly to affirm that Moses especially intended only one of these interpretations; and then, with destructive contention, to violate love itself, on behalf of which he had said all the things we are endeavoring to explain!

[12.26.36] And yet, my god, you exaltation of my humility and rest of my toil, who hear my confessions and forgive my sins, since you command me to love my neighbor as myself, I cannot believe that you gave your most faithful servant Moses a lesser gift than I should wish and desire for myself from you, if I had been born in his time, and if you had placed me in the position where, by the use of my heart and my tongue, those books might be produced which so long after were to profit all nations throughout the whole world—from such a great pinnacle of authority—and were to surmount the words of all false and proud teachings. If I had been Moses—and we all come from the same mass,‡ and what is man that you are mindful of him?§—if I had been Moses at the time that he was, and if I had been ordered by you to write the book of Genesis, I would surely have wished for such a power of expression and such an art of arrangement to be given me, that those who cannot as yet understand how god creates would still not reject my words as surpassing their

* 1 Corinthians 4:6.
† Matthew 22:37–39.
‡ Romans 9:21.
§ Psalms 8:4.

powers of understanding. And I would have wished that those who are already able to do this would find fully contained in the laconic speech of your servant whatever truths they had arrived at in their own thought; and if, in the light of the truth, some other man saw some further meaning, that too would be found congruent to my words.[7]

[12.27.37] For just as a spring dammed up is more plentiful and affords a larger supply of water for more streams over wider fields than any single stream led off from the same spring over a long course—so also is the narration of your minister: it is intended to benefit many who are likely to discourse about it and, with an economy of language, it overflows into various streams of clear truth, from which each one may draw out for himself that particular truth which he can about these topics—this one that truth, that one another truth, by the broader survey of various interpretations. For some people, when they read or hear these words [at the beginning of Genesis], think that god, like some sort of human being or some sort of huge body, by some new and sudden decision, produced outside himself and at a certain distance two great bodies: one above, the other below, within which all created things were to be contained. And when they hear, "God said, 'Let such and such be done,' and it was done," they think of words begun and ended, sounding in time and then passing away, followed by the coming into being of what was commanded. They think of other things of the same sort which their familiarity with the world suggests to them. In these people, who are still little children and whose weakness is borne up by this humble language as if on a mother's breast, their faith is built up healthfully and they come to possess and to hold as certain the conviction that god made all entities that their senses perceive all around them in such marvelous variety. And if one despises these words as if they were trivial, and with proud weakness stretches himself beyond his fostering cradle, he will, alas, fall away wretchedly. Have pity, lord god, lest those who pass by trample on the unfledged bird, and send your angel who may restore it to its nest, that it may live until it can fly.

[12.28.38] But others, to whom these words are no longer a nest but, rather, a shady thicket, spy the fruits concealed in them and fly around rejoicing and search among them and pluck them with cheerful chirpings. For when they read or hear these words, god, they see that all times past and times future are transcended by your eternal and stable permanence, and they see also that there is no temporal creature that is not of your making. By your will, since it is the same as your being, you have created all things, not by any mutation of will and not by any will that previously was nonexistent—and not out of yourself, but in your own likeness, you did make from nothing the form of all things. This was an unlikeness which was capable of being formed by your likeness through its relation to you, the one, as each thing has been given form appropriate to its kind according to its preordained capacity. Thus, all things were made very good, whether they remain around you or whether, removed in time and place by various degrees, they cause or undergo the beautiful changes of natural process. Such people see these things and they rejoice in the light of your truth to whatever degree they can.

[12.28.39] Again, one of these directs his attention to the verse, "In the beginning god made the heaven and the earth," and beholds wisdom as the true beginning, because it also speaks to us. Another directs his attention to the same words, and by "beginning" understands simply the commencement of creation, and interprets it thus: "In the beginning he made," as if it were the same thing as to say, "At the first moment, god made ..." And among those who interpret "In the beginning" to mean that in your wisdom you have created the heaven and earth, one believes that the matter out of which heaven and earth were to be created is what is referred to by the phrase "heaven and earth." But another believes that these entities were already formed and distinct. Still another will understand it to refer to one formed entity—a spiritual one, designated by the term "heaven"—and to another unformed entity of corporeal matter, designated by the term "earth." But those who understand the phrase "heaven and earth" to mean the yet unformed matter from which the heaven and the earth were to be formed do not take it in a simple sense: one regards it as that from which the intelligible and tangible creations are both produced; and another only as that from which the tangible, corporeal world is produced, containing in its vast bosom these visible and observable entities. Nor are they in simple accord who believe that "heaven and earth" refers to the created things already set in order and arranged. One believes that it refers to the invisible and visible world; another, only to the visible world, in which we admire the luminous heavens and the darkened earth and all the things that they contain.

[12.29.40] But one who understands "In the beginning he made" as if it meant, "At first he made," can truly interpret the phrase "heaven and earth" as referring only to the "matter" of heaven and earth, namely, of the prior universal, which is the intelligible and corporeal creation. For if he would try to interpret the phrase as applying to the universe already formed, it then might rightly be asked of him, "If god first made this, what then did he do afterward?" And, after the universe, he will find nothing.

But then he must, however unwillingly, face the question, How is this the first if there is nothing afterward? But when he said that god made matter first formless and then formed, he is not being absurd if he is able to discern what precedes by eternity, and what proceeds in time; what comes from choice, and what comes from origin. In eternity, god is before all things; in the temporal process, the flower is before the fruit; in the act of choice, the fruit is before the flower; in the case of origin, sound is before the tune. Of these four relations, the first and last that I have referred to are understood with much difficulty. The second and third are very easily understood. For it is an uncommon and lofty vision, lord, to behold your eternity immutably making mutable things, and thereby standing always before them. Whose mind is acute enough to be able, without great labor, to discover how the sound comes before the tune? For a tune is a formed sound, and an unformed thing may exist, but a thing that does not exist cannot be formed. In the same way, matter is prior to what is made from it. It is not prior because it makes its product, for it is itself made; and its priority is not that of a time interval. For in time we do not first utter formless sounds without singing and then adapt or fashion them into the form of a song, as wood or silver from which a chest or vessel is made. Such materials precede in time the forms of the things which are made from them. But in singing this is not so. For when a song is sung, its sound is heard at the same time. There is not first a formless sound, which afterward is formed into a song; but just as soon as it has sounded it passes away, and you cannot find anything of it which you could gather up and shape. Therefore, the song is absorbed in its own sound and the "sound" of the song is its "matter." But the sound is formed in order that it may be a tune. This is why, as I was saying, the matter of the sound is prior to the form of the tune. It is not "before" in the sense that it has any power of making a sound or tune. Nor is the sound itself the composer of the tune; rather, the sound is sent forth from the body and is ordered by the soul of the singer, so that from it he may form a tune. Nor is the sound first in time, for it is given forth together with the tune. Nor is it first in choice, because a sound is no better than a tune, since a tune is not merely a sound but a beautiful sound. But it is first in origin, because the tune is not formed in order that it may become a sound, but the sound is formed in order that it may become a tune.

From this example, let one who is able to understand see that the matter of things was first made and was called "heaven and earth" because out of it the heaven and earth were made. This primal formlessness was not made first in time, because the form of things gives rise to time; but now, in time, it is intuited together with its form. And yet nothing can be related of this unformed matter unless it is regarded as if it were the first in the time series though the last in value—because things formed are certainly superior to things unformed—and it is preceded by the eternity of the creator, so that from nothing there might be made that from which something might be made.

[12.30.41] In this discord of true opinions let truth itself bring concord, and may our god have mercy on us all, that we may use the law rightly to the end of the commandment which is pure love. Thus, if anyone asks me which of these opinions was the meaning of your servant Moses, these would not be my confessions did I not confess to you that I do not know. Yet I do know that those opinions are true—with the exception of the carnal ones—about which I have said what I thought was proper. Yet those little ones of good hope are not frightened by these words of your book, for they speak of high things in a lowly way and of a few basic things in many varied ways. But let all of us, whom I acknowledge to see and speak the truth in these words, love one another and also love you, our god, fountain of truth—as we will if we thirst not after vanity but for the fountain of truth. Indeed, let us so honor this servant of yours, the dispenser of this scripture, full of your spirit, so that we will believe that when you revealed yourself to him, and he wrote these things down, he intended through them what will chiefly minister both for the light of truth and to the increase of our fruitfulness.

[12.31.42] Thus, when one person says, "Moses meant what I mean," and another says, "No, he meant what I do," I think that I speak more faithfully when I say: Why could he not have meant both if both opinions are true? And if there should be still a third truth or a fourth one, and if anyone should seek a truth quite different in those words, why would it not be right to believe that Moses saw all these different truths, since through him the one god has tempered the holy scriptures to the understanding of many different people, who should see truths in it even if they are different? Certainly—and I say this fearlessly and from my heart—if I were to write anything that would have such a supreme authority, I would prefer to write it so that, whatever of truth anyone might apprehend from the matter under discussion, my words should re-echo in the several minds rather than that they should set down one true opinion so clearly on one point that I should exclude the rest, even though they contained no falsehood that offended me. Therefore, I am unwilling, my god, to be so headstrong as not to believe that this man [Moses] has received at least this much from you. Surely when he was writing these words, he saw fully and understood all the truth we have been able to find in them, and also much besides that we have not been able to discern, or are not yet able to find out, though it is there in them still to be found.

[12.32.43] Finally, lord—who are god and not flesh and blood—if anyone sees anything less, can anything lie hid from "your good spirit" who shall "lead me into the land of uprightness,"* which you yourself, through those words, was revealing to future readers, even though he through whom they were spoken fixed on only one among the many interpretations that might have been found? And if this is so, let it be agreed that the meaning he saw is more exalted than the others. But to us, lord, either point out the same meaning or any other true one, as it pleases you. Thus, whether you make known to us what you made known to that man of yours, or some other meaning by the agency of the same words, still may you feed us and may error not deceive us. See, lord, my god, how much we have written concerning these few words—how much, indeed! What strength of mind, what length of time, would suffice for all your books to be interpreted in this fashion? Allow me, therefore, in these concluding words to confess more briefly to you and select some one, true, certain, and good sense that you will inspire, although many meanings offer themselves and many indeed are possible. This is the faith of my confession, that if I could say what your servant meant, that is truest and best, and for that I must strive. Yet if I do not succeed, may it be that I shall say at least what your truth wished to say to me through its words, just as it said what it wished to Moses.

---

* Psalms 143:10.

BOOK 13

[13.1.1] I call on you, my god, my mercy, who made me and did not forget me, though I was forgetful of you. I call you into my soul, which you prepared for your reception by the desire which you inspire in it. Do not abandon me when I call on you, who anticipated me before I called and who repeatedly urged with many calls that I should hear you afar off and be turned and call upon you, who call me. For you, lord, have blotted out all my evil deserts, not punishing me for what my hands have done; and you have anticipated all my good deserts so as to recompense me for what your hands have done—the hands which made me. Before I was, you were, and I was not anything at all that you should grant me being. Yet, see how I exist by reason of your goodness, which made provision for all that you made me to be and all that you made me from. For you did not stand in need of me, nor am I the kind of good entity which could be a help to you, my lord and my god. It is not that I may serve you as if you were fatigued in working, or as if your power would be the less if it lacked my assistance. Nor is the cult I offer you like the cultivation of a field, so that you would go untended if I did not tend you. Instead, it is so that I may serve and worship you to the end that I may have my well-being from you, from whom comes my capacity for well-being.

[13.2.2] Indeed, it is from the fullness of your goodness that your creation exists at all: to the end that the created good might not fail to be, even though it can profit you nothing, and is nothing of you nor equal to you—since its created existence comes from you. For what did the heaven and earth, which you made in the beginning, ever deserve from you? Let them declare—these spiritual and corporeal entities, which you made in your wisdom—let them declare what they merited at your hands, so that the inchoate and the formless, whether spiritual or corporeal, would deserve to be held in being in spite of the fact that they tend toward disorder and extreme unlikeness to you? An unformed spiritual entity is more excellent than a formed corporeal entity; and the corporeal, even when unformed, is more excellent than if it were simply nothing at all. Still, these formless entities are held in their state of being by you, until they are recalled to your unity and receive form and being from you, the one sovereign good. What have they deserved of you, since they would not even be unformed entities except from you?

[13.2.3] What has corporeal matter deserved of you—even in its invisible and unformed state—since it would not exist even in this state if you had not made it? And, if it did not exist, it could not merit its existence from you. Or, what has that formless spiritual creation deserved of you—that it should flow lightlessly like the abyss—since it is so unlike you and would not exist at all if it had not been turned by the word which made it that same word, and, illumined by that word, had been made light although not as your equal but only as an image of that form [of light] which is equal to you? For, in the case of a body, its being is not the same thing as its being beautiful, else it could not then be a deformed body. Likewise, in the case of a created spirit, living is not the same state as living wisely, else it could then be immutably wise. But the true good of every created thing is always to cleave fast to you, lest, in turning away from you, it lose the light it had received in being turned by you, and so relapse into a life like that of the dark abyss. As for ourselves, who are a spiritual creation by virtue of our souls, when we turned away from you, our light, we were in that former life of darkness; and we toil amid the shadows of our darkness until—through your only son—we become your righteousness, like the mountains of god. For we, like the great abyss, have been the objects of your judgments.*

[13.3.4] Now what you said in the beginning of the creation—"Let there be light: and there was light"†—I interpret, not unfitly, as referring to the spiritual creation, because it already had a kind of life which you could illuminate. But, since it had not merited from you that it should be a life capable of enlightenment, so neither, when it already began to exist, did it merit from you that it should be enlightened. For neither could its formlessness please you until it became light—and it became light, not from the bare fact of existing, but by the act of turning its face to the light which enlightened it, and by cleaving to it. Thus it owed the fact that it lived, and lived happily, to nothing whatsoever but your grace, since it had been turned, by a change for the better, toward that which cannot be changed for either better or worse. You alone are, because you alone are without complication. For you it is not one thing to live and another thing to live in blessedness; for you are yourself your own blessedness.

[13.4.5] What, therefore, would there have been lacking in your good, which you yourself are, even if these things had never been made or had

---

* Psalms 36:6.
† Genesis 1:3.

remained unformed? You did not create them out of any lack but out of the plenitude of your goodness, ordering them and turning them toward form, but not because your joy had to be perfected by them. For you are perfect, and their imperfection is displeasing. Therefore were they perfected by you and became pleasing to you—but not as if you were before that imperfect and had to be perfected in their perfection. For your good spirit which moved over the face of the waters* was not borne up by them as if he rested on them. For those in whom your good spirit is said to rest he actually causes to rest in himself. But your incorruptible and immutable will—in itself all-sufficient for itself—moved over that life which you had made: in which living is not at all the same thing as living happily, since that life still lives even as it flows in its own darkness. But it remains to be turned to him by whom it was made and to live more and more like the fountain of life, and in his light to see light, and to be perfected, and enlightened, and made blessed.[1]

[13.5.6] See now, how the trinity appears to me in an enigma. And you are the trinity, my god, since you, father—in the beginning of our wisdom, that is, in your wisdom born of you, equal and coeternal with you, that is, your son—created the heaven and the earth. Many things we have said about the heaven of heavens, and about the earth invisible and unformed, and about the shadowy abyss—speaking of the aimless flux of its being spiritually deformed unless it is turned to him from whom it has its life (such as it is) and by his light comes to be a life suffused with beauty. Thus it would be a [lower] heaven of that [higher] heaven, which afterward was made between water and water.† And now I came to recognize, in the name of god, the father who made all these things, and in the term "the beginning" to recognize the son, through whom he made all these things; and since I did believe that my god was the trinity, I sought still further in his holy word, and, behold, "your spirit moved over the waters." Thus, see the trinity, my god: father, son, and holy spirit, the creator of all creation!

[13.6.7] But why, truth-speaking light? To you I lift up my heart—let it not teach me vain notions. Disperse its shadows and tell me, I beseech you, by that love which is our mother; tell me, I beseech you, the reason why—after the reference to heaven and to the invisible and unformed earth, and darkness over the abyss—your scripture should then at long

---

* Genesis 1:2.

† Genesis 1:6.

last refer to your spirit? Was it because it was appropriate that he should first be shown to us as "moving over"; and this could not have been said unless something had already been mentioned over which your spirit could be understood as moving? For he did not move over the father and the son, and he could not properly be said to be moving over if he were moving over nothing. Thus, what it was he was moving over had to be mentioned first and he whom it was not proper to mention otherwise than as moving over could then be mentioned. But why was it not fitting that he should have been introduced in some other way than in this context of moving over?

[13.7.8] Now let him who is able follow your apostle with his understanding when he says, "Your love is shed abroad in our hearts by the holy spirit, who is given to us"* and who teaches us about spiritual gifts† and shows us a more excellent way of love;‡ and who bows his knee to you for us, so that we may come to the surpassing knowledge of the love of Christ.§ Thus, from the beginning, he who is above all was "moving over" the waters.

To whom shall I tell this? How can I speak of the weight of concupiscence which drags us downward into the deep abyss, and of the love which lifts us up by your spirit who moved over the waters? To whom shall I tell this? How shall I tell it? For concupiscence and love are not certain places into which we are plunged and out of which we are lifted again. What could be more like, and yet what more unlike? They are both feelings; they are both loves. The uncleanness of our own spirit flows downward with the love of worldly care; and the sanctity of your spirit raises us upward by the love of release from anxiety—that we may lift our hearts to you where your spirit is "moving over the waters." Thus, we shall have come to that supreme rest where our souls shall have passed through the waters which give no standing ground.‖

[13.8.9] The angels fell, and the soul of man fell; thus they indicate to us the deep darkness of the abyss, which would have still contained the whole spiritual creation if you had not said, in the beginning, "Let there be light: and there was light"—and if every obedient mind in your heavenly

---

* Romans 5:5.

† 1 Corinthians 12:1.

‡ 1 Corinthians 12:31 ff.

§ Ephesians 3:14, 19.

‖ Psalms 124:4–5.

city had not adhered to you and had not reposed in your spirit, which moved immutable over all things mutable. Otherwise, even the heaven of heavens itself had been a dark shadow, instead of being, as it is now, light in the lord.* For even in the restless misery of the fallen spirits, who exhibit their own darkness when they are stripped of the garments of your light, you show clearly how noble you made the rational creation, for whose rest and beatitude nothing suffices save you yourself. And certainly it is not itself sufficient for its beatitude. For it is you, our god, who will enlighten our darkness; from you shall come our garments of light, and then our darkness shall be as the noonday.† Give yourself to me, my god, restore yourself to me! See, I love you; and if it be too little, let me love you still more strongly. I cannot measure my love so that I may come to know how much there is still lacking in me before my life can run to your embrace and not be turned away until it is hidden in "the covert of your presence."‡ Only this I know, that my existence is my woe except in you—not only in my outward life, but also within my inmost self—and all abundance I have which is not my god is poverty.

[**13.9.10**] But was neither the father nor the son "moving over the waters"? If we understand this as a motion in space, as a body moves, then not even the holy spirit "moved." But if we understand the changeless supereminence of the divine being above every changeable thing, then father, son, and holy spirit "moved over the waters." Why, then, is this said of your spirit alone? Why is it said of him only—as if he had been in a place that is not a place—about whom alone it is written that he is your gift?§ It is in your gift that we rest. It is there that we enjoy you. Our rest is our "place." Love lifts us up toward that place, and your good spirit lifts our lowliness from the gates of death.‖ Our peace rests in the goodness of will. The body tends toward its own place by its own gravity. A weight does not tend downward only, but moves to its own place. Fire tends upward; a stone tends downward. They are propelled by their own mass; they seek their own places. Oil poured under the water rises above the water; water poured on oil sinks under the oil. They are moved by their own mass; they seek their own places. If they are out of order, they are

---

* Ephesians 5:8.
† Isaiah 58:10.
‡ Psalms 31:20.
§ Acts 2:38.
‖ Psalms 9:13.

restless; when their order is restored, they are at rest. My weight is my love. By it I am carried wherever I am carried. By your gift, we are enkindled and are carried upward. We burn inwardly and move forward. We ascend your ladder which is in our heart, and we sing a canticle of degrees;* we glow inwardly with your fire—with your good fire—and we go forward because we go up to the peace of Jerusalem; for I was glad when they said to me, "Let us go into the house of the lord."† There your good pleasure will settle us so that we will desire nothing more than to dwell there forever.

[**13.10.11**] Happy would be that creature who, though it was in itself other than you, still had known no other state than this from the time it was made, so that it was never without your gift which moves over everything mutable—who had been borne up by the call in which you said, "Let there be light: and there was light." For in us there is a distinction between the time when we were darkness and the time when we were made light. But we are not told what would have been the case with that creature if the light had not been made. It is spoken of as though there had been something of flux and darkness in it beforehand so that the cause by which it was made to be otherwise might be evident. This is to say, by being turned to the unfailing light it might become light. Let the one who is able understand this; and let the one who is not ask of you. Why trouble me, as if *I* could "enlighten every man that comes into the world"?‡

[**13.11.12**] Who can understand the omnipotent trinity? And yet who does not speak about it, if indeed it is of it that such a person speaks? Rare is the soul which, when speaking of it, also knows of what it speaks. And all contend and strive, but no one sees the vision of it without peace. I could wish that human beings would consider three things which are within themselves. These three things are quite different from the trinity, but I mention them in order that people may exercise their minds and test themselves and come to realize how different from it they are. The three things I speak of are: to be, to know, and to will. For I am, and I know, and I will. I am a knowing and a willing being; I know that I am and that I will; and I will to be and to know. In these three functions, therefore, let anyone who can see how integral a life is; for there is one life, one mind, one essence. Finally, the distinction does not separate the things, and yet it is a distinction. Surely

---

* Psalms 119–33 (endnote 1 on book 9).

† Psalms 122:1.

‡ John 1:9.

a man has this distinction before his mind; let him look into himself and see, and tell me. But when he discovers and can say anything about any one of these, let him not think that he has thereby discovered what is immutable above them all, which is immutably and knows immutably and wills immutably. But whether there is a trinity there because these three functions exist in the one god, or whether all three are in each person so that they are each threefold, or whether both these notions are true and, in some mysterious manner, the infinite is in itself its own selfsame object—at once one and many, so that by itself it is and knows itself and suffices to itself without change, so that the selfsame is the abundant magnitude of its unity—who can readily conceive? Who can in any fashion express it plainly? Who can in any way rashly make a pronouncement about it?

[**13.12.13**] Go forward in your confession, my faith; say to the lord your god, "Holy, holy, holy, lord my god, in your name we have been baptized, in the name of the father, son, and holy spirit." In your name we baptize, in the name of the father, the son, and the holy spirit. For among us also god in his Christ made heaven and earth, namely, the spiritual and carnal members of his church. And true it is that before it received the form of doctrine, our earth [the church] was "invisible and unformed," and we were covered with the darkness of our ignorance; for you do correct man for his iniquity,* and "your judgments are a great abyss."† But because your spirit was moving over these waters, your mercy did not abandon our wretchedness, and you said, "Let there be light; repent, for the kingdom of heaven is at hand."‡ Repent, and let there be light. Because our soul was troubled within us, we remembered you, lord, from the land of Jordan, and from the mountain—and as we became displeased with our darkness we turned to you, and there was light. And see, we were formerly in darkness, but now we are light in the lord.²

[**13.13.14**] But even so, we still live by faith and not by sight, for we are saved by hope; but hope that is seen is not hope. Thus far deep calls to deep, but now in "the noise of your waterfalls."§ And thus far he who said, "I could not speak to you as if you were spiritual ones, but only as if you were carnal"‖—thus far even he does not count himself to have

---

* Psalms 39:11.

† Psalms 36:6.

‡ Matthew 3:2.

§ Psalms 42:7.

‖ 1 Corinthians 3:1.

apprehended, but forgetting the things that are behind and reaching forth to the things that are before, he presses on to those things that are ahead,* and he groans under his burden and his soul thirsts after the living god as the stag pants for the water brooks,† and says, "When shall I come?"‡—"desiring to be further clothed by his house which is from heaven."§ And he called to this lower deep, saying, "Be not conformed to this world, but be transformed by the renewing of your mind."‖ And "be not children in understanding, although in malice be children," in order that "in understanding you may become perfect."# "O foolish Galatians, who has bewitched you?"** But this is not now only in his own voice but in your voice, who sent your spirit from above through him who both "ascended up on high"†† and opened up the floodgates of his gifts, that the force of his streams might make glad the city of god.‡‡

For that city and for him sighs the bridegroom's friend,§§ who has now the first fruits of the spirit laid up with him, but who is still groaning within himself and waiting for adoption, that is, the redemption of his body. To him he sighs, for he is a member of the bride; for him he is jealous, not for himself, but because not in his own voice but in the voice of your waterfalls he calls on that other deep, of which he is jealous and in fear; for he fears lest, as the serpent seduced Eve by his subtlety, his mind should be corrupted from the purity which is in our bridegroom, your only son. What a light of beauty that will be when "we shall see him as he is"‖‖—and when these tears shall pass away which "have been my meat day and night, while they continually say to me, 'Where is your god?'"##

[13.14.15] And I myself say: "My god, where are you? See now, where are you?" In you I take my breath for a little while, when I pour out my soul beyond myself in the voice of joy and praise, in the voice of him that

---

* Philippians 3:13.

† Psalms 42:1.

‡ Psalms 42:2.

§ 2 Corinthians 5:1–4.

‖ Romans 12:2.

1 Corinthians 14:20.

** Galatians 3:1.

†† Ephesians 4:8–9.

‡‡ Psalms 46:4.

§§ John 3:29.

‖‖ 1 John 3:2.

Psalms 42:3.

keeps holyday.* And still it is cast down because it relapses and becomes
an abyss, or rather it feels that it still is an abyss. My faith speaks to my
soul—the faith that you kindle to light my path in the night: "Why are you
cast down, my soul, and why are you disquieted in me? Hope in god."†
For his word is a lamp to your feet.‡ Hope and persevere until the night
passes—that mother of the wicked; until the lord's wrath subsides—that
wrath whose children once we were, of whom we were beforehand in
darkness, whose residue we still bear about us in our bodies, dead because of sin.§ Hope and endure until the day breaks and the shadows flee
away.‖ Hope in the lord: in the morning I shall stand in his presence and
keep watch;# I shall forever give praise to him. In the morning I shall
stand and shall see my god, who is the health of my countenance,** who
also will quicken our mortal bodies by the spirit that dwells in us,†† because in mercy he was moving over our lightless and restless inner deep.
From this we have received an earnest, even now in this journeying, that
we are now in the light, since already we are saved by hope and are children of the light and children of the day—not children of the night, nor
of the darkness,‡‡ which we have been hitherto. Between those children
of the night and ourselves, in this still uncertain state of human knowledge, only you can rightly distinguish—you who test the heart and who
call the light day, and the darkness night.§§ For who can see us clearly but
you? What do we have that we have not received from you, who made
from the same lump some vessels to noble, and others to ignoble, use?‖‖

[13.15.16] Now who but you, our god, made for us that firmament of
the authority of your divine scripture to be over us? For "the heaven shall
be folded up like a scroll";## but now it is stretched over us like a skin.
Your divine scripture is of more sublime authority now that those mortal

---

* Psalms 42:4.

† Psalms 43:5.

‡ Psalms 119:105.

§ Romans 8:10.

‖ Song of Solomon 2:17.

Psalms 5:3.

** Psalms 43:5.

†† Romans 8:11.

‡‡ 1 Thessalonians 5:5.

§§ Genesis 1:5.

‖‖ Romans 9:21.

Isaiah 34:4.

men through whom you dispensed it to us have departed this life. And you know, lord, you know how you clothed men with skins when they became mortal because of sin.* In something of the same way, you have stretched out the firmament of your book as a skin—that is to say, you have spread your harmonious words over us through the ministry of mortal men. For by their very death that solid firmament of authority in your sayings, spoken forth by them, stretches high over all that now drift under it; whereas while they lived on earth their authority was not so widely extended. Then you had not yet spread out the heaven like a skin; you had not yet spread abroad everywhere the fame of their death.[3]

[13.15.17] Let us see, lord, "the heavens, the work of your fingers,"† and clear away from our eyes the fog with which you have covered them. In them is that testimony of yours which gives wisdom even to the little ones. Out of the mouth of babes and sucklings, my god, perfect your praise.‡ For we know no other books that so destroy man's pride, that so break down the adversary and the self-defender who resists your reconciliation by an effort to justify his own sins. I do not know, lord, I do not know any other such pure words that so persuade me to confession and make my neck submissive to your yoke, and invite me to serve you for nothing else than your own sake. Let me understand these things, good father. Grant this to me, since I am placed under them; for you have established these things for those placed under them.

[13.15.18] There are other waters that are above this firmament, and I believe that they are immortal and removed from earthly corruption. Let them praise your name—this super-celestial society, your angels, who have no need to look up at this firmament or to gain a knowledge of your word by reading it—let them praise you. For they always behold your face and read therein, without any syllables in time, what your eternal will intends. They read, they choose, they love. They are always reading, and what they read never passes away. For by choosing and by loving they read the very immutability of your counsel. Their book is never closed, nor is the scroll folded up, because you yourself are this to them, and are this to them eternally; because you ranged them above this firmament which you made firm over the infirmities of the people below the heavens, where they might look up and learn your mercy, which proclaims in time you who made all times.

---

*Genesis 3:21.

† Psalms 8:3.

‡ Psalms 8:2.

"For your mercy, lord, is in the heavens, and your faithfulness reaches to the clouds."* The clouds pass away, but the heavens remain. The preachers of your word pass away from this life into another, but your scripture is spread abroad over the people, even to the end of the world. Indeed, both heaven and earth shall pass away, but your words shall never pass away.† The scroll shall be rolled together, and the "grass" over which it was spread shall, with all its goodliness, pass away; but your word remains forever‡— your word which now appears to us in the dark image of the clouds and through the glass of heaven, and not as it really is. And even if we are the well-beloved of your son, it has not yet appeared what we shall be.§ He has seen us through the entanglement of our flesh, and he is fair-speaking, and he has enkindled us, and we run after his fragrance.‖ But "when he shall appear, then we shall be like him, for we shall see him as he is."# As he is, lord, we shall see him—although that time is not yet.

[13.16.19] For just as you are the utterly real, you alone fully know, since you are immutably, and you know immutably, and you will immutably. And your being knows and wills immutably. Your knowledge is and wills immutably. Your will is and knows immutably. And it does not seem right to you that the immutable light should be known by the enlightened but mutable creature in the same way as it knows itself. Therefore, to you my soul is as a land where no water is;** for, just as it cannot enlighten itself by itself, so it cannot satisfy itself by itself. Thus the fountain of life is with you, and "in your light shall we see light."††

[13.17.20] Who has gathered the embittered ones into a single society? For they all have the same end, which is temporal and earthly happiness. This is their motive for doing everything, although they may fluctuate within an innumerable diversity of concerns. Who but you, lord, gathered them together, you who said, "Let the waters be gathered together into one place and let the dry land appear"—athirst for you? For the sea also is yours, and you made it, and your hands formed the dry land.‡‡ For it is

---

* Psalms 36:5.
† Matthew 24:35.
‡ Isaiah 40:6–8.
§ 1 John 3:2.
‖ Song of Solomon 1:3–4.
1 John 3:2.
** Psalms 63:1.
†† Psalms 36:9.
‡‡ Psalms 95:5.

not the bitterness of men's wills but the gathering together of the waters which is called "the sea"; yet you curb the wicked lusts of human souls and fix their bounds: how far they are allowed to advance, and where their waves will be broken against each other—and thus you make it "a sea," by the providence of your governance of all things.[4]

[**13.17.21**] But as for the souls that thirst after you and who appear before you—separated from the society of the sea by reason of their different ends—you water them by a secret and sweet spring, so that the earth may bring forth her fruit and—you, lord, commanding it—our souls may bud forth in works of mercy after their kind.* Thus we shall love our neighbor in ministering to his bodily needs, for in this way the soul has seed in itself after its kind when in our own infirmity our compassion reaches out to the relief of the needy, helping them even as we would desire to be helped ourselves if we were in similar need. Thus we help, not only in easy problems (as is signified by "the herb yielding its seed") but also in the offering of our best strength in affording them the aid of protection (such as "the tree bearing its fruit"). This is to say, we seek to rescue him who is suffering injury from the hands of the powerful—furnishing him with the sheltering protection which comes from the strong arm of a righteous judgment.

[**13.18.22**] Thus, lord, thus I beseech you: let it happen as you have prepared it, as you give joy and the capacity for joy. Let truth spring up out of the earth, and let righteousness look down from heaven,[†] and let there be lights in the firmament.[‡] Let us break our bread with the hungry, let us bring the shelterless poor to our house; let us clothe the naked, and never despise those of our own flesh.[§] See from the fruits which spring forth from the earth how good it is. Thus let our temporal light break forth, and let us from even this lower level of fruitful action come to the joy of contemplation and hold on high the word of life. And let us at length appear like "lights in the world,"[‖] cleaving to the firmament of your scripture.

For in it you make it plain to us how we may distinguish between things intelligible and things tangible, as if between the day and the

---

* Genesis 1:10 ff.
† Psalms 85:11.
‡ Genesis 1:14.
§ Isaiah 58:7.
‖ Philippians 2:15.

night—and to distinguish between souls who give themselves to things of the mind and others absorbed in things of sense. Thus it is that now you are not alone in the secret of your judgment as you were before the firmament was made, and before you divided between the light and the darkness. But now also your spiritual children, placed and ranked in this same firmament—your grace being thus manifest throughout the world—may shed light upon the earth, and may divide between the day and night, and may be for the signs of the times;* because old things have passed away, and, see, all things are become new;† and because our salvation is nearer than when we believed; and because the night is far spent and the day is at hand;‡ and because you crown the year with blessing,§ sending the laborers into your harvest, in which others have labored in the sowing and sending laborers also to make new sowings whose harvest shall not be until the end of time. Thus you grant the prayers of one who seeks, and you bless the years of the one who is righteous. But you are always the selfsame, and in your years which fail not you prepare a granary for our transient years. For by an eternal design you spread the heavenly blessings on the earth in their proper seasons.

[13.18.23] For to one there is given by your spirit the word of wisdom‖ (which resembles the greater light—which is for those whose delight is in the clear light of truth—as the light which is given for the ruling of the day.# But to another the word of knowledge is given by the same spirit (as it were, the lesser light); to another, faith; to another, the gift of healing; to another, the power of working miracles; to another, the gift of prophecy; to another, the discerning of spirits; to another, other kinds of tongues—and all these gifts may be compared to the stars. For in them all the one and selfsame spirit is at work, dividing to everyone a portion, as he wills, and making stars to appear in their bright splendor for the profit of souls. But the word of knowledge, in which is contained all the mysteries which change in their seasons like the moon; and all the other promises of gifts, which when counted are like the stars—all of these fall short of that splendor of wisdom in which the day rejoices and are only for the ruling

---

* Genesis 1:14.

† 2 Corinthians 5:17.

‡ Romans 13:11–12.

§ Psalms 65:11.

‖ 1 Corinthians 12:7 ff.

Genesis 1:16.

of the night. Yet they are necessary for those to whom your most prudent servant could not speak as to the spiritually mature, but only as if to carnal men—even though he could speak wisdom among the perfect.* Still the natural man—as a babe in Christ, and a drinker of milk, until he is strong enough for solid meat, and his eye is able to look into the sun—do not leave him in a lightless night. Instead, let him be satisfied with the light of the moon and the stars. In your book you discuss these things with us wisely, our god—in your book, which is your firmament—in order that we may be able to view all things in admiring contemplation, although thus far we must do so through signs and seasons and in days and years.

[13.19.24] But, first, wash yourselves and make you clean; put away iniquity from your souls and from before my eyes†—so that the dry land may appear. Learn to do well, judge the fatherless, plead for the widow,‡ so that the earth may bring forth the green herb for food and fruit-bearing trees. "And come, let us reason together, says the lord,"§ so that there may be lights in the firmament of heaven and that they may shine upon the earth.

There was that rich man who asked of the good teacher what he should do to attain eternal life.‖5 Let the good teacher (whom the rich man thought a man and nothing more) give him an answer—he is good for he is god. Let him answer him that, if he would enter into life, he must keep the commandments: let him put away from himself the bitterness of malice and wickedness; let him not kill, nor commit adultery, nor steal, nor bear false witness, so that the dry land may appear and bring forth the honoring of fathers and mothers and the love of neighbor. "All these," he replied, "I have kept." Where do so many thorns come from, if the earth is really fruitful? Uproot the brier patch of avarice; sell what you have, and be filled with fruit by giving to the poor, and you shall have treasure in heaven; and follow the lord if you would be perfect and joined with those in whose midst he speaks wisdom—who know how to give rightly to the day and to the night—and you will also understand, so that for you also there may be lights in the firmament of heaven—which will not be

---

* 1 Corinthians 3:1, 2:6.

† Isaiah 1:16.

‡ Isaiah 1:17.

§ Isaiah 1:18.

‖ Matthew 19:16 ff.

there, however, unless your heart is there also. And your heart will not be there unless your treasure is there,* as you have heard from the good teacher. But the barren earth was grieved, and the briers choked the word.†

[**13.19.25**] But you, elect people, set in the firmament of the world, who have given up all so that you may follow the lord: follow him now, and confound the mighty! Follow him, beautiful feet,‡ and shine in the firmament, so that the heavens may declare his glory, dividing the light of the perfect ones—though not yet so perfect as the angels—from the darkness of the little ones—who are nevertheless not utterly despised. Shine over all the earth, and let the day be lighted by the sun, utter the word of wisdom to the day ("day to day utters speech"§) and let the night, lighted by the moon, display the word of knowledge to the night. The moon and the stars give light for the night; the night does not put them out, and they illumine in its proper mode. For see, it is as if god were saying, "Let there be lights in the firmament of the heaven": and suddenly there came a sound from heaven, as if it were a rushing mighty wind, and there appeared cloven tongues of fire, and they sat on each of them.‖ And then they were made to be lights in the firmament of heaven, having the word of life. Run to and fro everywhere, you holy fires, you lovely fires, for you are the light of the world and you are not to be hid under a peck measure.# He to whom you cleave is raised on high, and he has raised you on high. Run to and fro; make yourselves known among all the nations!

[**13.20.26**] Also let the sea conceive and bring forth your works, and let the waters bear the moving creatures that have life.** For by separating the precious from the vile you are made the mouth of god†† by whom he said, "Let the waters bring forth." This does not refer to the living creatures which the earth brings forth, but to the creeping creatures that have life and the fowls that fly over the earth. For, by the ministry of your holy ones, your mysteries have made their way amid the buffeting billows of the world, to instruct the nations in your name, in your baptism.

---

* Matthew 6:21.
† Matthew 13:7.
‡ Isaiah 52:7.
§ Psalms 19:2.
‖ Acts 2:2–3.
Matthew 5:14–15.
** Genesis 1:20.
†† Jeremiah 15:19.

And among these things many great and marvelous works have been wrought, which are analogous to the huge whales. The words of your messengers have gone flying over the earth, high in the firmament of your book which is spread over them as the authority beneath which they are to fly wheresoever they go. For there is no speech nor language where their voice is not heard, because their sound has gone out through all the earth, and their words to the end of the world*—and this because you, lord, have multiplied these things by your blessing.

[13.20.27] Am I speaking falsely? Am I mingling and confounding and not rightly distinguishing between the knowledge of these things in the firmament of heaven and those corporeal works in the swelling sea and beneath the firmament of heaven? For there are those things, the knowledge of which is solid and defined. It does not increase from generation to generation and thus they stand, as it were, as lights of wisdom and knowledge. But there are many and varied physical processes that manifest these selfsame principles. And thus one thing growing from another is multiplied by your blessing, god, who do so refresh our easily wearied mortal senses that in our mental cognition a single thing may be figured and signified in many different ways by different bodily motions. The waters have brought forth these mysteries, but only at your word. The needs of the people who were alien to the eternity of your truth have called them forth, but only in your gospel, since it was these waters which cast them up—the waters whose stagnant bitterness was the reason why they came forth through your word.

Now all the things that you have made are fair, and yet, see, you who made all things are inexpressibly fairer. And if Adam had not fallen away from you, that brackish sea—the human race—so deeply prying, so boisterously swelling, so restlessly moving, would never have flowed forth from his belly. Thus, there would have been no need for your ministers to use corporeal and tangible signs in the midst of many waters in order to show forth their mystical deeds and words. For this is the way I interpret the phrases "creeping creatures" and "flying fowl." Still, men who have been instructed and initiated and made dependent on your corporeal mysteries would not be able to profit from them if it were not that their soul has a higher life and unless, after the word of its admission, it did not look beyond toward its perfection.

[13.21.29] And thus, in your word, it was not the depth of the sea but

---

* Psalms 19:4.

the earth, separated from the brackishness of the water, that brought forth, not the creeping and the flying creature that has life, but the living soul itself! And now this soul no longer has need of baptism, as the heathen had, or as it did when it was covered with the waters—and there can be no other entrance into the kingdom of heaven, since you have appointed that baptism should be the entrance. Nor does it seek great, miraculous works by which to buttress faith. For such a soul does not refuse to believe unless it sees signs and marvels, now that the faithful earth is separated from the waters of the sea, which have been made bitter by infidelity. Thus, for them, tongues are for a sign, not to those who believe but to those who do not believe.*

And the earth which you have founded above the waters does not stand in need of those flying creatures which the waters brought forth at your word. Send forth your word into it by the agency of your messengers. For we only tell of their works, but it is you who do the works in them, so that they may bring forth a living soul in the earth.

The earth brings forth the living soul because the earth is the cause of such things being done by your messengers, just as the sea was the cause of the production of the creeping creatures having life and the flying fowl under the firmament of heaven. The earth no longer needs them, although it feeds on the fish which was taken out of the deep, set out on that table which you preparest in the presence of those who believe. To this end he was raised from the deep: so that he might feed the dry land. And the fowl, even though they were bred in the sea, will yet be multiplied on the earth. The preaching of the first evangelists was called forth by reason of human infidelity, but the faithful also are exhorted and blessed by them in manifold ways, day by day. The living soul has its origin from the earth, because only to the faithful is there any profit in restraining themselves from the love of this world, so that their soul may live to you. This soul was dead while it was living in pleasures—in pleasures that bear death in them—whereas you, lord, are the living delight of the pure heart.

[13.21.30] Now, therefore, let your ministers do their work on the earth—not as they did formerly in the waters of infidelity, when they had to preach and speak by miracles and mysteries and mystical expressions, in which ignorance—the mother of wonder—gives them an attentive ear because of its fear of occult and strange things. For this is the entry into

---

* 1 Corinthians 14:22.

faith for the sons of Adam who are forgetful of you, who hide themselves from your face, and who have become a darkened abyss. Instead, let your ministers work even as on the dry land, safe from the whirlpools of the abyss. Let them be an example to the faithful by living before them and stirring them up to imitation.

For in such a setting, people will heed, not with the mere intent to hear, but also to act. Seek the lord and your soul shall live* and the earth may bring forth the living soul. Be not conformed to this world;† separate yourselves from it. The soul lives by avoiding those things which bring death if they are loved. Restrain yourselves from the unbridled wildness of pride, from the indolent passions of luxury, and from what is falsely called knowledge.‡ Thus may the wild beast be tamed, the cattle subdued, and the serpent made harmless. For, in allegory, these figures are the motions of our mind: that is to say, the haughtiness of pride, the delight of lust, and the poison of curiosity are motions of the dead soul—not so dead that it has lost all motion, but dead because it has deserted the fountain of life, and so has been taken up by this transitory world and conformed to it.

[13.21.31] But your word, god, is a fountain of life eternal, and it does not pass away. Therefore, this desertion is restrained by your word when it says to us, "Be not conformed to this world," to the end that the earth may bring forth a living soul in the fountain of life—a soul disciplined by your word, by your evangelists, by the following of the followers of your Christ. For this is the meaning of "after his kind." A man tends to follow the example of his friend. Thus, he [Paul] says, "Become as I am, because I have become as you are."§

Thus, in this living soul there shall be good beasts, acting meekly. For you have commanded this, saying: "Do your work in meekness and you shall be loved by all men."‖ And the cattle will be good, for if they eat much they shall not suffer from satiety; and if they do not eat at all they will suffer no lack. And the serpents will be good, not poisonous to do harm, but only cunning in their watchfulness—exploring only as much of this temporal nature as is necessary in order that the eternal

---

* Psalms 69:32.

† Romans 12:2.

‡ 1 Timothy 6:20.

§ Galatians 4:12.

‖ Ecclesiasticus 3:19.

nature may "be clearly seen, understood through the things that have been made."* For all these animals will obey reason when, having been restrained from their death-dealing ways, they live and become good.

[13.22.32] Thus, lord, our god, our creator, when our affections have been turned from the love of the world, in which we died by living ill; and when we began to be a living soul by living well; and when the word, "Be not conformed to this world," which you spoke through your apostle, has been fulfilled in us, then will follow what you immediately added when you said, "but be transformed by the renewing of your mind."† This will not now be after their kind, as if we were following the neighbor who went before us, or as if we were living after the example of a better man— for you did not say, "Let man be made after his kind," but rather, "Let us make man in our own image and our own likeness,"‡ so that then we may be able to prove what your will is.

This is why your minister—begetting children by the gospel so that he might not always have them babes whom he would have to feed with milk and nurse as children—this is why he said, "Be transformed by the renewing of your minds, that you may prove what is the good and acceptable and perfect will of god."§ Therefore you did not say, "Let man be made," but rather, "Let us make man." And you did not say, "after his kind," but after "our image" and "likeness." Indeed, it is only when man has been renewed in his mind, and comes to behold and apprehend your truth, that he does not need another man as his director, to show him how to imitate human examples. Instead, by your guidance, he proves what is your good and acceptable and perfect will. And you teach him, now that he is able to understand, to see the trinity of the unity and the unity of the trinity.

This is why the statement in the plural, "Let us make man," is also connected with the statement in the singular, "and god made man." Thus it is said in the plural, "after our likeness," and then in the singular, "after the image of god." Man is thus transformed in the knowledge of god, according to the image of him who created him. And now, having been made spiritual, he judges all things—that is, all things that

---

* Romans 1:20.

† Romans 12:2.

‡ Genesis 1:26.

§ Romans 12:2.

are appropriate to be judged—and he himself is judged of no human being.*

[13.23.33] Now this phrase, "he judges all things," means that man has dominion over the fish of the sea, and over the fowl of the air, and over all cattle and wild beasts, and over all the earth, and over every creeping thing that creeps on the earth. And he does this by the power of reason in his mind by which he perceives "the things of the spirit of god."† But, when man was put in this high office, he did not understand what was involved and thus was reduced to the level of the brute beasts, and made like them.

Therefore in your church, our god, by the grace you have given us—since we are your workmanship, created in good works (not only those who are in spiritual authority but also those who are spiritually subject to them)—you made man male and female.‡ Here all are equal in your spiritual grace where, as far as sex is concerned, there is neither male nor female, just as there is neither Jew nor Greek, nor bond nor free.§ Spiritual men, therefore, whether those who are in authority or those who are subject to authority, judge spiritually. They do not judge by the light of that spiritual knowledge which shines in the firmament, for it is inappropriate for them to judge by so sublime an authority. Nor does it behoove them to judge concerning your book itself, although there are some things in it which are not clear. Instead, we submit our understanding to it and believe with certainty that what is hidden from our sight is still rightly and truly spoken. In this way, even though a man is now spiritual and renewed by the knowledge of god according to the image of him who created him, he must be a doer of the law rather than its judge.‖ Neither does the spiritual man judge concerning that division between spiritual and carnal men which is known to your eyes, god, and which may not, as yet, be made manifest to us by their external works, so that we may know them by their fruits; yet you, god, know them already and you have divided and called them secretly, before the firmament was made. Nor does a man, even though he is spiritual, judge the disordered state of society in this world. For what business of his is it to

---

* 1 Corinthians 2:15.
† 1 Corinthians 2:14.
‡ Genesis 1:27.
§ Galatians 3:28.
‖ James 4:11.

judge those who are without, since he cannot know which of them may later on come into the sweetness of your grace, and which of them may continue in the perpetual bitterness of their impiety?

[13.23.34] Man, then, even if he was made after your own image, did not receive the power of dominion over the lights of heaven, nor over the secret heaven, nor over the day and the night which you called forth before the creation of the heaven, nor over the gathering together of the waters which is the sea. Instead, he received dominion over the fish of the sea, and the fowls of the air; and over all cattle, and all the earth; and over all creeping things which creep on the earth. Indeed, he judges and approves what he finds right and disapproves what he finds amiss, whether in the celebration of those mysteries by which are initiated those whom your mercy has sought out in the midst of many waters; or in that sacrament in which is exhibited the fish itself which, being raised from the depths, the pious earth feeds upon; or, in the signs and symbols of words, which are subject to the authority of your book—such signs as burst forth and sound from the mouth, as if it were flying under the firmament, interpreting, expounding, discoursing, disputing, blessing, invoking you, so that the people may answer, "Amen."* The reason that all these words have to be pronounced vocally is because of the abyss of this world and the blindness of our flesh in which thoughts cannot be seen directly, but have to be spoken aloud in our ears. Thus, although the flying fowl are multiplied on the earth, they still take their origins from the waters.

The spiritual man also judges by approving what is right and reproving what he finds amiss in the works and morals of the faithful, such as in their almsgiving, which is signified by the phrase, "the earth bringing forth its fruit." And he judges of the living soul, which is then made to live by the disciplining of its affections in chastity, in fasting, and in holy meditation. And he also judges concerning all those things which are perceived by the bodily senses. For it can be said that he should judge in all matters about which he also has the power of correction.

[13.24.35] But what is this; what kind of mystery is this? See, lord, you bless men in order that they may be "fruitful and multiply, and replenish the earth."† In this are you not making a sign to us that we may understand something? Why did you not also bless the light, which you called the day,

---

* 1 Corinthians 14:16.

† Genesis 1:28.

nor the firmament of heaven, nor the lights, nor the stars, nor the earth, nor the sea? I might reply, our god, that you in creating us after your own image—I might reply that you wished to bestow this gift of blessing upon man alone, if you had not similarly blessed the fishes and the whales, so that they too should be fruitful and multiply and replenish the waters of the sea; and also the fowls, so that they should be multiplied on the earth. In like fashion, I might say that this blessing properly belonged only to such creatures as are propagated from their own kind, if I could find it given also as a blessing to trees, and plants, and the beasts of the earth. But this "increase and multiply" was not said to plants or trees or beasts or serpents—although all of these, along with fishes and birds and men, do actually increase by propagation and so preserve their species.

[13.24.36] What, then, shall I say, truth, my life: that it was idly and vainly said? Surely not this, father of piety; far be it from a servant of your word to say anything like this! But if I do not understand what you mean by that phrase, let those who are better than I—that is, those more intelligent than I—interpret it better, in the degree that you have given each of us the ability to understand. But let also my confession be pleasing in your eyes, for I confess to you that I believe, lord, that you have not spoken thus in vain. Nor will I be silent as to what my reading has suggested to me. For it is valid, and I do not see anything to prevent me from thus interpreting the figurative sayings in your books. For I know that a thing that is understood in only one way in the mind may be expressed in many different ways by the body; and I know that a thing that has only one manner of expression through the body may be understood in the mind in many different ways.[7] For consider this single example—the love of god and of our neighbor—by how many different mysteries and countless languages, and, in each language, by how many different ways of speaking, this is signified corporeally! In similar fashion, the young fish in the waters increase and multiply. On the other hand, whoever you are who read this, observe and behold what scripture declares, and how the voice pronounces it in only one way, "In the beginning god created heaven and earth." Is this not understood in many different ways by different kinds of true interpretations which do not involve the deceit of error? Thus the offspring of men are fruitful and do multiply.

[13.24.37] If, then, we consider the nature of things, in their strictly literal sense, and not allegorically, the phrase, "Be fruitful and multiply," applies to all things that are begotten by seed. But if we treat these words figuratively, as I judge that the scripture intended them to be—since it cannot be for nothing that this blessing is attributed only to the offspring of marine life and man—then we discover that the characteristic of fecundity belongs also to the spiritual and physical creations (which are signified by "heaven and earth"), and also in righteous and unrighteous souls (which are signified by "light and darkness") and in the sacred writers through whom the law is uttered (who are signified by "the firmament established between the waters and the waters"); and in the earthly commonwealth still steeped in their bitterness (which is signified by "the sea"); and in the zeal of holy souls (signified by "the dry land"); and the works of mercy done in this present life (signified by "the seed-bearing herbs and fruit-bearing trees"); and in spiritual gifts which shine out for our edification (signified by "the lights of heaven"); and to human affections ruled by temperance (signified by "the living soul"). In all these instances we meet with multiplicity and fertility and increase; but the particular way in which "Be fruitful and multiply" can be exemplified differs widely. Thus a single category may include many things, and we cannot discover them except through their signs displayed corporeally and by the things being excogitated by the mind.

We thus interpret the phrase, "the generation of the waters," as referring to the corporeally expressed signs [of fecundity], since they are made necessary by the degree of our involvement in the flesh. But the power of human generation refers to the process of mental conception; this we see in the fruitfulness of reason. Therefore, we believe that to both of these two kinds it has been said by you, lord, "Be fruitful and multiply." In this blessing, I recognize that you have granted us the faculty and power not only to express what we understand by a single idea in many different ways but also to understand in many ways what we find expressed obscurely in a single statement. Thus the waters of the sea are replenished, and their waves are symbols of diverse meanings. And thus also the earth is also replenished with human offspring. Its dryness is the symbol of its thirst for truth, and of the fact that reason rules over it.

[13.25.38] I also desire to say, my lord god, what the following scripture suggests to me. Indeed, I will speak without fear, for I will speak the truth, as you inspire me to know what you will that I should say concerning these words. For I do not believe I can speak the truth by any other inspiration than yours, since you are the truth, and every man a liar.* Hence, he that speaks a lie, speaks out of himself. Therefore, if I am to speak the truth, I must speak of your truth.

_____

* Romans 3:4.

See, you have given us for our food every seed-bearing herb on the face of the earth, and all trees that bear in themselves seed of their own kind; and not to us only, but to all the fowls of the air and the beasts of the field and all creeping things.* Still, you have not given these things to the fishes and great whales. We have said that by these fruits of the earth the works of mercy were signified and figured forth in an allegory: thus, from the fruitful earth, things are provided for the necessities of life. Such an earth was the godly Onesiphorus, to whose house you gave mercy because he often refreshed Paul and was not ashamed of his bonds.† This was also the way of the brethren from Macedonia, who bore such fruit and supplied to him what he lacked.‡ But notice how he grieves for certain trees, which did not give him the fruit that was due, when he said, "At my first answer no man stood with me, but all men forsook me: I pray god, that it be not laid up to their charge."§ For we owe fruits to those who minister spiritual doctrine to us through their understanding of the divine mysteries. We owe these to them as human beings. We owe these fruits, also, to the living souls since they offer themselves as examples for us in their own continence. And, finally, we owe them likewise to the flying creatures because of their blessings which are multiplied on the earth, for "their sound has gone forth into all the earth."‖

[13.26.39] Those who find their joy in it are fed by these fruits; but those whose god is their belly find no joy in them. For in those who offer these fruits, it is not the fruit itself that matters, but the spirit in which they give them. Therefore, he who serves god and not his own belly may rejoice in them, and I plainly see why. I see it, and I rejoice with him greatly. For he [Paul] had received from the Philippians the things they had sent by Epaphroditus; yet I see why he rejoiced. He was fed by what he found his joy in; for, speaking truly, he says, "I rejoice in the lord greatly, that now at the last your care of me has flourished again, in which you were once so careful, but it had become a weariness to you."# These Philippians, in their extended period of weariness in well-doing, had become weak and were, so to say, dried up; they were no longer bringing forth the fruits of good

---

* Genesis 1:29–30.

† 2 Timothy 1:16.

‡ 2 Corinthians 11:9.

§ 2 Timothy 4:16.

‖ Psalms 19:4.

Philippians 4:10.

works. And now Paul rejoices in them—and not just for himself alone—
because they were flourishing again in ministering to his needs. Therefore
he adds: "I do not speak in respect of my want, for I have learned in whatsoever state I am therewith to be content. I know both how to be abased
and how to abound; everywhere and in all things I am instructed both to
be full and to be hungry, both to abound and to suffer need. I can do all
things through Christ who strengthens me."*

[**13.26.40**] Where do you find joy in all things, great Paul? What is the
cause of your joy? On what do you feed, man, renewed now in the knowledge of god after the image of him who created you, living soul of such
great continence—tongue like a winged bird, speaking mysteries? What
food is owed such creatures; what is it that feeds you? It is joy! For hear
what follows: "Nevertheless, you have done well in that you have shared
with me in my affliction."† This is what he finds his joy in; this is what he
feeds on. They have done well, not merely because his need had been
relieved—for he says to them, "You have opened my heart when I was in
distress"—but because he knew both how to abound and how to suffer
need, in you who strengthened him. And so he said, "You [Philippians]
know also that in the beginning of the gospel, when I departed from
Macedonia, no church shared with me in regard to giving and receiving,
except you only. For even in Thessalonica you sent time and time again,
according to my need."‡ He now finds his joy in the fact that they have returned once again to these good works, and he is made glad that they are
flourishing again, as a fruitful field when it recovers its fertility.

[**13.26.41**] Was it on account of his own needs alone that he said, "You
have sent me gifts according to my needs?" Does he find joy in that? Certainly not for that alone. But how do we know this? We know it because
he himself adds, "Not because I desire a gift, but because I desire fruit."§
Now I have learned from you, my god, how to distinguish between the
terms "gift" and "fruit." A gift is the thing itself, given by one who be-
stows life's necessities on another—such as money, food, drink, clothing,
shelter, and aid. But the fruit is the good and right will of the giver. For
the good teacher not only said, "He that receives a prophet," but he
added, "in the name of a prophet." And he did not say only, "He who

---

* Philippians 4:11–13.

† Philippians 4:14.

‡ Philippians 4:15–17.

§ Philippians 4:17.

receives a righteous man," but added, "in the name of a righteous man."*
Thus, surely, the former shall receive the reward of a prophet; the latter,
that of a righteous man. Nor did he say only, "Whoever shall give a cup
of cold water to one of these little ones to drink," but added, "in the name
of a disciple"; and concluded, "Truly I tell you he shall not lose his reward." The gift involves receiving a prophet, receiving a righteous man,
handing a cup of cold water to a disciple: but the fruit is to do all this in
the name of a prophet, in the name of a righteous man, in the name of a
disciple. Elijah was fed by the widow with fruit, for she knew that she was
feeding a man of god and this is why she fed him. But he was fed by the
raven with a gift. The inner man of Elijah was not fed by this gift, but only
the outer man, which otherwise might have perished from the lack of such
food.†

[13.27.42] Therefore I will speak before you, lord, what is true, in order
that the uninstructed and the infidels, who require the mysteries of initiation and great works of miracles—which we believe are signified by the
phrase, "fishes and great whales"—may be helped in being gained [for the
church] when they endeavor to provide that your servants are refreshed in
body, or otherwise aided in this present life. For they do not really know
why this should be done, and to what end. Thus the former do not feed the
latter, and the latter do not feed the former; for neither do the former offer
their gifts through a holy and right intent, nor do the others rejoice in the
gifts of those who do not as yet see the fruit. For it is on the fruit that the
mind is fed, and by which it is gladdened. And, therefore, fishes and whales
are not fed on such food as the earth alone brings forth when they have
been separated and divided from the bitterness of the waters of the sea.

[13.28.43] And you, god, saw everything that you had made and, "behold, it was very good."‡ We also see the whole creation and, behold, it is
all very good. In each separate kind of your work, when you said, "Let
them be made," and they were made, you saw that it was good. I have
counted seven times where it is written that you saw what you had made
was good. And there is the eighth time when you saw all things that you
had made and, behold, they were not only good but also very good; for
they were now seen as a totality. Individually they were only good; but
taken as a totality they were both good and very good. Beautiful bodies

---

* Matthew 10:41–42.

† 1 Kings 17:4 ff.

‡ Genesis 1:31.

express this truth; for a body which consists of several parts, each of which is beautiful, is itself far more beautiful than any of its individual parts separately, by whose well-ordered union the whole is completed even though these parts are separately beautiful.

[**13.29.44**] And I looked attentively to find whether it was seven or eight times that you saw your works were good, when they were pleasing to you, but I found that there was no "time" in your seeing which would help me to understand in what sense you had looked so many times at what you had made. And I said: Lord, is not this your scripture true, since you are true, and your truth sets it forth? Why, then, do you say to me that in your seeing there are no times, while this scripture tells me that what you made each day you saw to be good; and when I counted them I found how many times? To these things, you replied to me, for you are my god, and you speak to your servant with a strong voice in his inner ear, my deafness, and crying: "Man, what my scripture says, I say. But it speaks in terms of time, whereas time does not affect my word—my word which exists coeternally with myself. Thus the things you see through my spirit, I see; just as what you say through my spirit, I say. But while you see those things in time, I do not see them in time; and when you speak those things in time, I do not speak them in time."

[**13.30.45**] And I heard this, lord my god, and drank up a drop of sweetness from your truth, and understood that there are some men to whom your works are displeasing, who say that many of them you made under the compulsion of necessity—such as the pattern of the heavens and the courses of the stars—and that you did not make them out of what was yours, but that they were already created elsewhere and from other sources. It was thus [they say] that you collected and fashioned and wove them together, as if from your conquered enemies you raised up the walls of the universe; so that, built into the ramparts of the building, they might not be able a second time to rebel against you. And, even of other things, they say that you neither made them nor arranged them—for example, all flesh and all the very small living creatures, and all things fastened to the earth by their roots. But [they say] a hostile mind and an alien nature—not created by you and in every way contrary to you—begot and framed all these things in the nether parts of the world. They who speak thus are out of their minds, since they do not see your works through your spirit, nor recognize you in them.[8]

[**13.31.46**] But for those who see these things through your spirit, it is you who see them in them. When, therefore, they see that these things are good, it is you who see that they are good; and whatsoever things are pleasing because of you, it is you who give us pleasure in those things. Those things which please us through your spirit are pleasing to you in us. "For what man knows the things of a man except the spirit of a man which is in him? Even so, no man knows the things of god, but the spirit of god. Now we have not received the spirit of the world, but the spirit of god, that we might know the things that are freely given to us from god."* And I am admonished to say: Yes, truly. No man knows the things of god, but the spirit of god: but how, then, do we also know what things are given us by god? The answer is given me: "Because we know these things by his spirit; for no one knows but the spirit of god." But just as it is truly said to those who were to speak through the spirit of god, "It is not you who speak," so it is also truly said to them who know through the spirit of god, "It is not you yourselves who know," and just as rightly it may be said to those who perceive through the spirit of god that a thing is good; it is not they who see, but god who sees that it is good.

It is, therefore, one thing to think like the people who judge something to be bad when it is good, as do those whom we have already mentioned. It is quite another thing that someone should see as good what is good— as is the case with many whom your creation pleases because it is good, yet what pleases them in it is not you, and so they would prefer to find their joy in your creatures rather than to find their joy in you. It is still another thing that when someone sees a thing to be good, god should see in him that it is good—that truly he may be loved in what he has made, he who cannot be loved except through the holy spirit which he has given us: "Because the love of god is shed abroad in our hearts by the holy spirit who is given to us."† It is by him that we see whatever we see to be good in any degree, since it is from him, who does not exist in any particular degree but who simply is what he is.

[13.32.47] Thanks be to you, lord! We see the heaven and the earth, either the corporeal part—higher and lower—or the spiritual and physical creation. And we see the light made and divided from the darkness for the adornment of these parts, from which the universal mass of the world or the universal creation is constituted. We see the firmament of heaven, either the original body of the world between the spiritual (higher) waters and the corporeal (lower) waters[9] or the expanse of air—which is also called heaven—through which the fowls of heaven wander, between the

---

* 1 Corinthians 2:11–12.

† Romans 5:5.

waters which move in clouds above them and which drop down in dew on clear nights, and those waters which are heavy and flow along the earth. We see the waters gathered together in the vast plains of the sea; and the dry land, first bare and then formed, so as to be visible and well-ordered; and the soil of herbs and trees. We see the light shining from above—the sun to serve the day, the moon and the stars to give cheer in the night; and we see by all these that the intervals of time are marked and noted. We see on every side the watery elements, fruitful with fishes, beasts, and birds—and we notice that the density of the atmosphere which supports the flights of birds is increased by the evaporation of the waters. We see the face of the earth, replete with earthly creatures; and man, created in your image and likeness, in the very image and likeness of you—that is, having the power of reason and understanding—by virtue of which he has been set over all irrational creatures. And just as there is in his soul one element which controls by its power of reflection and another which has been made subject so that it should obey, so also, physically, the woman was made for the man; for, although she had a like nature of rational intelligence in the mind, still in the sex of her body she should be similarly subject to the sex of her husband, as the appetite of action is subjected to the deliberation of the mind in order to conceive the rules of right action.[10] These things we see, and each of them is good; and the whole is very good!

[13.33.48] Let your works praise you, so that we may love you; and let us love you so that your works may praise you—those works which have a beginning and an end in time—a rising and a setting, a growth and a decay, a form and a privation. Thus, they have their successions of morning and evening, partly hidden, partly plain. For they were made from nothing by you, and not from yourself, and not from any matter that is not yours, or that was created beforehand. They were created from con-created matter—that is, matter that was created by you at the same time that you did form its formlessness, without any interval of time. Yet, since the matter of heaven and earth is one thing and the form of heaven and earth is another thing, you created matter out of absolutely nothing, but the form of the world you formed from formless matter. But both were done at the same time, so that form followed matter with no delaying interval.

[13.34.49] We have also explored the question of what you desired to figure forth, both in the creation and in the description of things in this particular order. And we have seen that things taken separately are good, and all things taken together are very good, both in heaven and earth.

And we have seen that this was wrought through your word, your only son, the head and the body of the church, and it signifies your predestination before all times, without morning and evening. But when, in time, you began to unfold the things destined before time, so that you might make hidden things manifest and might reorder our disorders—since our sins were over us and we had sunk into profound darkness away from you, and your good spirit was moving over us to help us in due season—you justified the ungodly and also divided them from the wicked; and you made the authority of your book a firmament between those above who would be amenable to you and those beneath who would be subject to them. And you gathered the society of unbelievers into a conspiracy, in order that the zeal of the faithful might become manifest and that they might bring forth works of mercy to you, giving their earthly riches to the poor to obtain heavenly riches. Then you kindled the lights in the firmament, which are your holy ones, who have the word of life and who shine with an exalted authority, warranted to them by their spiritual gifts. And then, for the instruction of the unbelieving nations, you did out of physical matter produce the mysteries and the visible miracles and the sounds of words in harmony with the firmament of your book, through which the faithful should be blessed. After this you formed the living soul of the faithful, through the ordering of their passions by the strength of continence. And then you renewed, after your image and likeness, the mind which is faithful to you alone, which needs to imitate no human authority. Thus, you subordinated rational action to the higher excellence of intelligence, as the woman is subordinate to the man. Finally, in all your ministries which were needed to perfect the faithful in this life, you willed that these same faithful ones should themselves bring forth good things, profitable for their temporal use and fruitful for the life to come. We see all these things, and they are very good, because you see them thus in us—you who have given us your spirit, by which we may see them so and love you in them.

[13.35.50] Lord god, grant us your peace—for you have given us all things. Grant us the peace of quietness, the peace of the sabbath, the peace without an evening. All this most beautiful array of things, all so very good, will pass away when all their courses are finished—for in them there is both morning and evening. But the seventh day is without an evening, and it has no setting, for you have sanctified it with an everlasting duration. After all your works of creation, which were very good, you rested on the seventh day, although you had created them all in unbroken rest—and this so that the voice of your book might speak to us with the prior assurance that after

our works—and they also are very good because you have given them to
us—we may find our rest in you in the sabbath of life eternal.

[**13.36.51**] For then also you shall so rest in us as now you work in us;
and, thus, that will be your rest through us, as these are your works
through us. But you, lord, work evermore and are always at rest. You
see not in time, you move not in time, you rest not in time. And yet you
make all those things which are seen in time—indeed, the very times
themselves—and everything that proceeds in and from time.

[**13.37.52**] We can see all those things which you have made because
they are—but they are because you see them. And we see with our eyes
that they are, and we see with our minds that they are good. But you saw
them as made when you saw that they would be made. And now, in this
present time, we have been moved to do well, now that our heart has been
quickened by your spirit; but in the former time, having abandoned you, we
were moved to do evil. But you, the one good god, have never ceased to do
good! And we have accomplished certain good works by your good gifts,
and even though they are not eternal, still we hope, after these things here,
to find our rest in your great sanctification. But you are the good, and need
no rest, and are always at rest, because you yourself are your own rest.

What man will teach men to understand this? And what angel will
teach the angels? Or what angels will teach men? We must ask it of you;
we must seek it in you; we must knock for it at your door. Only thus shall
we receive; only thus shall we find; only thus shall your door be opened.

ENDNOTES

Book 1

1. (pp. 9–10) *To this end I was sent to school... they were then a great and grievous ill to me:* The young Augustine's initiation in the formal language arts of the late Roman school system (grammar, logic, rhetoric) is set against his extracurricular acquisition of an alternative mode of speech: the direct address to god that is also the idiom of his *Confessions.* The attempt to distinguish a "divine" art of language from the routines of human eloquence is pursued to the end of the work.

2. (pp. 10–11) *the shows and sports of my elders.... able to give such shows:* Top-ranking civic officials in late Roman society were expected to lay on lavish entertainments for the urban populace: gladiatorial contests, theatrical performances, displays of wild animals, and so on. The privilege (and financial burden) of hosting such shows was thus a sign of high achievement.

3. (p. 11) *I was signed with the sign of his cross, and was seasoned with his salt even from the womb of my mother, who greatly trusted in you:* Infants of Christian families were sanctified with prayers, the sign of the cross, and the placing of salt on the tongue as exorcism. Baptism itself was often deferred, though the practice of baptizing infants was more prevalent in North Africa than elsewhere and contributed to the development of Augustine's theory of inherited or "original" sin, according to which even newborn children already shared in the guilt of Adam.

4. (p. 12) *But what were the causes for my strong dislike of Greek literature, which I studied from my boyhood?... in the midst of these things:* Although elite Roman culture in the western part of the empire was bilingual (Latin and Greek) in theory, in practice formal instruction in Greek was quite limited. Augustine never read Greek easily. Here he draws a line between lessons in elementary literacy, whether Greek or Latin, and the more advanced study of literary works, such as the poems of Homer or Virgil. Virgil's *Aeneid* was a central text of the school curriculum, serving as a virtual encyclopedia of Roman history and culture. It tells how Aeneas and other refugees from the sacked city of Troy came at length to Italy and there implanted the future race of Rome. Along the way Aeneas won the heart of Dido, queen of Carthage. Her suicide after his desertion forms the climax of book 4 of the *Aeneid*. The quotation in 1.13.21 below (*Aeneid* 6.457) is from Aeneas' speech to Dido in the underworld; she does not reply. The sword she had used to kill herself was Aeneas' own. Creusa (1.13.22) was the wife of Aeneas, left for dead in the ruins of Troy, who afterward appeared to him in a vision (*Aeneid* 2.736–795). See also Introduction, pp. xvi–xvii and xl–xlii.

5. (pp. 14–15) *But woe to you, torrent of human custom! . . . "whoever committed such crimes might appear to imitate the celestial gods and not abandoned men":* The licentious behavior of the deities in mythological poetry had made such literature suspect to ancient moralists long before Christians took issue with it. Augustine picks up one line of rationalizing explanation—these so-called "gods" were modeled after human beings—and uses it to mount a fresh attack.

6. (p. 15) *Of Jove's descending in a shower of gold . . . I've done it, and with all my heart, I'm glad:* The quotations are from Terence's play *The Eunuch*, lines 585 ff.

7. (p. 16) *The assignment was that I should declaim the words of Juno, as she raged and sorrowed that she could not "bar off Italy from all the approaches of the Teucrian king":* The passage is from Virgil's *Aeneid* 1.38. In the poem, Juno is the supporter of Carthage against Rome, vainly striving to prevent the fulfillment of Aeneas' destiny. The "declamation" was a standard exercise in the rhetorical schools. It required the student to compose a speech for a given occasion and in a given character, often taken from history or, as here, historical fiction.

8. (p. 16) *But it was no wonder that I was thus carried toward vanity and was estranged from you, my god, when men were held up . . . so long as they did it in a full and ornate oration of well-chosen words:* The complaint against those who are more tolerant of moral than of grammatical irregularity gives a new twist to a point already made by Augustine in his *Christian Teaching* (*De doctrina Christiana*) 3.3.7, in which he insisted that it was more important for the preacher to make himself understood by ordinary people, even at the cost of speaking "incorrectly," than to observe every nicety of Latin grammar and diction.

9. (p. 16) *That younger son did not charter horses or chariots, or ships, or fly away on visible wings, or journey by walking so that in the far country he might prodigally waste all that you gave him when he set* *out:* The gospel parable of the Prodigal Son underlies all the motifs of wandering or travel abroad on which the spiritual narrative of the *Confessions* is plotted. Allusions to it are usually combined with hints of the scheme of the human soul's journey away from, and return to, the divine One, as imprinted on Augustine's mind by the *Enneads* of Plotinus and related works of late Platonist—"Neoplatonic"—philosophy; see 7.9.13 for the "books of the Platonists." Intermittently, as here, the imagery of travel acquires a further, ironic dimension by being associated with the epic journey of the Roman hero Aeneas.

Book 2

1. (p. 19) *Thus you may gather me up out of those fragments in which I was torn to pieces, while I turned away from you who are one, and lost myself among the many:* The metaphor of dispersal and reintegration, like the metaphor of departure and return, is Neoplatonic in inspiration; see also note 9 to book 1. As the *Confessions* proceeds, the horizontal axis of travel and separation is complemented by a vertical axis of descent and ascent, likewise Neoplatonic but accommodated by Augustine to a biblically derived cosmology.

2. (p. 20) *This project was more a matter of my father's ambition than of his means, for he was only a poor citizen of Thagaste:* Augustine's father Patricius (named at 9.9.19) was evidently a small landowner of the tax-class known as "curial," meaning those who were financially and personally responsible for assuring the public services of the municipality. Such a man would naturally want his son to have a good education, but it is clear that Patricius and Monica were over-extending themselves in the hope that Augustine would get on in the world and raise the fortunes of the family. Getting on, in this case, meant first of all getting to Carthage. As mentioned already in passing at 1.16.26, schoolmasters charged fees to the parents, even if the best of them also drew a salary from the public purse. Only a tiny minority of young male Romans received a full training in the primary and secondary school subjects of grammar (language and literature) and rhetoric (composition, public speaking) that were the prerequisites for professional and civil service careers.

3. (p. 22) *See with what companions I walked the streets of Babylon!:* Babylon, the biblical place of the captivity of the Israelites, serves as a topographical metaphor for the allurements of the world and the senses, and is opposed to the (heavenly) city of Jerusalem as the goal of properly spiritual desire. This particular pairing of place names, which was traditional in Christian exegesis and ideology by Augustine's time, would be enshrined by him in the *City of God* as a division between the "earthly city" and the "city of god," twin communities intermingled in history but separated at the Last Judgment.

4. (p. 24) *So it seems that even Catiline himself loved not his own villainies, but something else, and it was this that gave him the motive for his crimes:* Catiline was a famously corrupt governor of Africa who later tried to seize overall control of the Roman Republic, was vigorously opposed by Cicero, and was finally defeated and killed in battle by Mark Antony in 62 B.C. Augustine quotes from Sallust, *Catiline* 16.

5. (p. 27) *And I became a wasteland to myself:* "Wasteland" is A. C. Outler's unique translation of *regio egestatis* ("region of lack"). Augustine's phrase blends a reminiscence of the parable of the Prodigal Son (Luke 15:14) with a geography of spiritual alienation derived from Plotinus. Outler must have had in mind T. S. Eliot's poem *The Waste Land* (1922), which includes a direct quotation (line 307) of the opening of book 3 of the *Confessions*, as translated by Tobie Matthew (1620), "To Carthage then I came. . . ." See Introduction, pp. xv–xviii.

Book 3

1. (p. 30) *I dared, even while your solemn rites were being celebrated inside the walls of your church, to indulge my lust and to plan a project which merited death as its fruit:* A sermon of Augustine's confirms that church services were seen by some as god-given opportunities for beginning sexual conquests. For a countervailing emphasis on "the walls of the church" as bulwarks of salvation, rather than as cover for seduction, see 8.2.4–5.

2. (p. 30) *Still I was relatively sedate, lord, as you know, and had no share in the wreckings of the Wreckers . . . they amused themselves in jeering and horseplay at the expense of others:* Student discipline seems to have been more of a problem at Carthage than elsewhere; see also 5.8.14. Augustine's gang members are literally "overturners" (*eversores*). Hence he puns that they were themselves "overturned" (*eversi*) and "turned the wrong way" (*perversi*) by "demons," meaning—in his mythology—the angels who fell from heaven with Satan and who thereafter delight in coming between human beings and god (10.42.67). There is an implicit contrast with the process of *conversio* ("turning around"), by which Augustine himself will be brought back to god through the genuine mediation of Christ.

3. (p. 31) *In the ordinary course of study I came upon a certain book of Cicero's . . . what won me was not its style but its substance:* The *Hortensius* was a dialogue based on Aristotle's *Protrepticus*, designed as an exhortation to the study of philosophy, named after one of Cicero's great rivals as an orator, who was a character in it. Only fragments survive, and this reference in the *Confessions* is the only clue to the work's place in the Roman educational curriculum. Cicero's perfect orator was also a trained philosopher, an ideal rarely realized in practice and ignored by the standard rhetorical handbooks of Augustine's time. Although comparable narratives of philosophical "conversion" appear in both non-Christian and Christian texts that Augustine may be supposed to have known, his sense of philosophical vocation was unusual—as indeed, by the standards of the age, was the philosophical culture that he eventually managed to acquire. Adolescent readings aside, the main stimulus probably came from the Platonist circles to which he was introduced at Milan; see book 7.

4. (p. 32) *When I then turned toward the scriptures, they appeared to me to be quite unworthy to be compared with the dignity of Tully. . . . I looked upon myself as fully grown:* "Tully" is Marcus Tullius Cicero. The opposition of *style* to *substance* is one of Augustine's devices for thinking through the relations between human eloquence and the proper language(s) of conversation with and about god, especially in connection with the texts of the divinely authorized "scriptures" (that is, the books of the biblical canon, the Old and New Testaments). Since the style of the Latin translations of the scriptures used by Augustine and his contemporaries was far less polished than that of Cicero and other cherished classical models, the best arguments he can make are for the Bible's superior virtues of content and intelligibility. Here the emphasis is at once on the Bible's accessibility to novice readers, provided they are not too proud to appreciate such simplicity, and on the deeper meanings that it reserves for the more spiritually enlightened. See further 6.5.8, 12.14.17 ff.

5. (p. 32) *Thus I fell among men, delirious in their pride, carnal and voluble . . . the basic elements of this world, your creation:* Frustrated in his search for wisdom in the Bible, Augustine turns to the esoteric Christian philosophy of the Manicheans, a sect banned by Roman imperial law. See Introduction, pp. xxxi–xxxv. The next few paragraphs present a somewhat miscellaneous array of Manichean teachings, now considered by Augustine as erroneous: their cosmology; their rejection of certain Old Testament books on the grounds that they represented god in physical terms and the patriarchs as engaging in unlawful acts; their dietary rules. See also 4.1.1, 5.5.8. Anti-Manichean animus is the main driving force of books 3–7, and a potent factor throughout the *Confessions*.

6. (p. 33) *For how much better were the fables of the grammarians and poets than these snares! . . . though I sang about "the flying Medea" I never believed it, but those other things I did believe:* Augustine returns to the critique of pagan mythology launched in book 1, but with an important concession: However implausible they may be, the fictions of pagan poets can nonetheless be made to serve a useful purpose (for example, by allegorical interpretation in a moral sense). By contrast, the cosmological myths of the Manicheans are merely deceptive. The story of Medea in flight is found in Ovid, *Metamorphoses* 7.219–236 and was presumably a classroom standard.

7. (p. 37) *These are the major forms of iniquity that spring out of the lust of the flesh, and of the eye, and of power:* The threefold division of misdemeanors—excesses of the flesh, excesses of the gaze (including intellectual curiosity), excessive desire for prestige and power over other people—underpins much of the analysis in the *Confessions*. The scriptural root is 1 John 2:16: "For all that is in the world, the lust of the flesh, and the lust of the eyes, and the pride of life, is not of the father, but is of the world" (King James Version). The fullest development of the scheme comes at 10.30.41–10.39.64.

8. (p. 40) *"But let him alone for a time . . . what an error it is and how great its impiety is":* The anonymous bishop inadvertently anticipated one of the most striking features of Augustine's autobiographical narrative: its construction as a series of acts of reading. However this phenomenon is explained, it is hard to overlook the evidence that points to an exceptionally intelligent, sensitive, and inquisitive young man whose access to books and appetite for reading constantly outstripped the local supply of qualified mentors and conversation partners. The author who became famous for talking aloud and in writing to himself and to god was first and last a student in a class of his own.

Book 4

1. (pp. 41–42) *In those years I had one to whom I was not joined in lawful marriage. . . . compel our love:* This kind of common-law relation-

ship was not at all unusual in antiquity, and makes sense in the light
of Augustine's plans for social advancement by marrying up; see
6.13.23. The moralizing, dismissive tone of this passage fails, however, to capture the warmth of what was evidently a powerful af-
fective bond: Contrast 6.15.25, and 9.6.14 on the son born of this
union.

2. (p. 43) *There was at that time a wise man, very skillful and quite famous in medicine. . . . rhetorical contest:* Helvius Vindicianus (named
at 7.6.8) was governor of the province of Africa Proconsularis from
c.379 to 382; he was also known as an author of medical books. That
his contact with Augustine did not end with the ceremony of prize-
giving may be taken as a sign that the schoolmaster was now moving
comfortably in the best Carthaginian society.

3. (p. 43) *For when a man, by accident, opens the pages of some poet . . .
wondrously apposite to the reader's present business:* The habit of
drawing "lots" or "fortunes" by random consultation of a literary
work, such as Virgil's *Aeneid*, may have become more common as
books were increasingly produced in the form of spine-hinged codices
rather than as continuous scrolls; see Introduction, p. xviii. Biblical
texts could be used for the same purpose; see 8.12.29.

4. (pp. 43–44) *my most dear Nebridius—a splendid youth and most circumspect, who scoffed at the whole business of divination:* Nebridius,
the son of a well-off Carthaginian family, would later follow Augustine to Milan (6.10.17, 7.2.3). He shared his friend's intellectual and
religious interests, and Augustine made a point of preserving a set of
their letters. He "converted" soon after Augustine himself and died
not long after returning to Africa (9.3.6).

5. (p. 44) *thus far, I had come upon no certain proof . . . by which it could
be shown without doubt that what had been truly foretold by those
consulted came from accident or chance, and not from the art of the
stargazers:* This is the heart of the matter for Augustine. The diviners
claimed to practice an *art*—that is, to be in possession of a rule-based
science of prediction. As a Christian thinker, Augustine would determine that any success they had in their predictions must be the result of pure chance or, alternatively, the result of a deliberate deception
wrought by "demons" to further blind diviners and their clients to the
true ordinances of the Christian god. In both the *Confessions* and the
partly contemporary *Christian Teaching*, Augustine is at pains to es-
tablish the art of biblical interpretation as the only scientific way to
understand the course of individual human lives and of history as a

whole—though he is always careful not to claim predictive powers for the interpreter.

6. (p. 46) *the friendship of Orestes and Pylades; they would have gladly died for one another . . . worse than death to them:* Orestes, son of Agamemnon, is a leading figure in plays by Aeschylus and Euripides; Pylades appears as his faithful companion. Their names are routinely linked to exemplify perfect friendship. While granting that their story might be fiction, Augustine is willing to make use of it for his own purpose, thus demonstrating how pagan mythology can be recycled for Christian purposes, according to the principle stated at 3.6.11 (see also endnote 6 on book 3).

7. (p. 46) *"He was half of my soul" . . . perhaps I was also afraid to die, in case he should then die wholly whom I had so greatly loved:* The quoted saying appears in Ovid, *Tristia* 4.4.72, and elsewhere. In his *Revisions* (see Introduction, pp. xxxvii–xl) Augustine censures the last sentence of this paragraph as more suited to a declamation or scholastic exercise than to the seriousness of confession. In mitigation of his own fault, he notes that at least he had the grace to insert the word "perhaps."

8. (p. 48) *Let my soul praise you, in all these things, god, creator of all:* The phrase "god, creator of all" echoes the first line of a hymn by Ambrose of Milan that will return like a refrain later in the *Confessions* (9.12.32, 10.34.52, 11.27.35).

9. (p. 49) *The word itself calls you to return, and there there is a place of unperturbed rest, where love is not forsaken unless it first forsakes:* This "word" is otherwise known as the "only-begotten" son of god (as in John 1:1 ff.), second "person" of the Christian trinity (with the father and the holy spirit). It is the creative force behind the universe, assumes human flesh as Jesus Christ, and is also identified with the divine "word" of the scriptures. These theological coordinates had been established by Christian teachers and church councils by the time Augustine came to compose the *Confessions*. His own writing contributes to their naturalization in the language of (Latin) Christianity.

10. (p. 51) *Hierius, orator of the city of Rome . . . so wonderful a Latin orator and also so well versed in philosophy:* Nothing is known for certain of this Hierius besides what Augustine tells us here. Presumably some of his writings had reached Carthage. In any case, he held the kind of position that a fellow orator in a provincial capital was bound to envy. Augustine himself makes the connection explicit. In the course of the next few books, other contemporary figures will be introduced who will serve in similar fashion to model the life options to which Augustine was successively drawn. All of these characters are staged for a purpose, and it is the author's characterization of them, rather than any independently documented biographical profile, that counts most for the *Confessions*. Augustine's treatise *On the Beautiful and the Fitting* has never come to light; nor would he have wished it to. Only works composed after his "conversion" were catalogued in his *Revisions* and thereby guaranteed secure transmission to later ages.

11. (p. 54) *a book of Aristotle's entitled* The Ten Categories ... *under the chief category of substance:* The *Ten Categories* was the first text in the Aristotelian corpus of logic, dealing—as this summary indicates—with forms of predication or what can be said *about* something. Here it illustrates the difficulty that Augustine was having, and would continue to have, in saying anything reliable about god. It is not only logic that comes up short: The whole cycle of the "liberal arts," he says, was of no avail to him at this stage, at least from the point of view from which he now looks back.

Book 5

1. (p. 58) *a certain bishop of the Manicheans, Faustus by name, a great snare of the devil ... the charm of his eloquence:* Faustus was a man a few years older than Augustine himself, from the town of Milev in Numidia. He abandoned his wife and children on becoming a Manichean and was made a bishop of the sect by 382. A few years later he was denounced to the Roman authorities—Manicheism being illegal—and exiled to an island in the Mediterranean, but was released soon afterward. Before he died (c.390) he produced a treatise refuting objections made by catholic Christians against Manichean doctrine and attacking Christian belief in the divine inspiration of the Old Testament. Augustine answered this work at length in his *Against Faustus*, composed around the same time as the *Confessions*.

2. (p. 62) *He had, however, read some of Tully's orations, a very few books of Seneca, and some of the poets:* Faustus had the kind of intellectual equipment to be expected of someone who had been to school but not read far outside the curriculum. "Tully" is Cicero, the model orator and a favorite of Augustine's too. Seneca was either the philosopher of that name or possibly his father the rhetorician. The poets would have included Virgil and Horace. Augustine can be disdainful of such a limited repertoire, but few of the original audience of the *Confessions* would have been any better read.

3. (p. 65) *I lied to my mother—and such a mother!—and escaped. . . . That night I slipped away secretly, and she remained to pray and weep:* This is one of several places where the plotting of the *Confessions* ironically recalls Virgil's *Aeneid*. As Aeneas had put to sea without word to Dido (*Aeneid* 4.571–583), so Augustine gives his mother the slip. Cyprian was the bishop of Carthage, martyred in 258. See also Introduction, pp. xvi–xvii, xxii, xli–xlii.

4. (p. 66) *you had forgiven me none of these things in Christ, neither had he abolished by his cross the enmity that I had incurred from you through my sins. . . . appeared to me unreal:* Following Saint Paul (Romans 5), the author of the *Confessions* has the death of the "man" Christ lift the general death sentence passed on humankind as a penalty for the fault of the "first man," Adam; see also Colossians 2:14. The Augustine who lay sick at Rome in 383 was both intellectually and practically excluded from the benefit of this saving act: He still lacked a proper understanding of the humanity of Christ, and he had not yet been baptized into the community of professing Christians.

5. (p. 67) *I was now half inclined to believe that those philosophers whom they call Academics were wiser than the rest . . . just as they are commonly reputed to do:* The reference is to the Greek philosophical school known as the New Academy, of the mid-second century B.C., which developed the position known as Skepticism, summarized here by Augustine. His main source, at least until he came upon the more recent "books of the Platonists" (7.9.13), would have been dialogues of Cicero's, the *Academica*.

6. (pp. 69–70) *I used the influence of those same persons . . . to ensure that Symmachus, who was then prefect, after he had proved me by audition, should appoint me:* Quintus Aurelius Symmachus, prefect of the city of Rome in 384, was a prominent member of the traditionalist party that resisted the innovations brought about by the Christianization of Roman society and institutions in the second half of the fourth century. While prefect, he urged the emperor Valentinian II (whose merits Augustine would soon be proclaiming [6.6.9]), to restore the Altar of Victory—a symbol of Rome's greatness dating from the time of

Augustus—to the senate house at Rome. A collection of his letters survives, as do several speeches.

7. (p. 70) *Ambrose the bishop, famed through the whole world as one of the best of mortals, your devoted servant:* The son of a high-ranking imperial official, Ambrose had pursued a traditional administrative career path until 374 when, as governor of the province of Aemilia-Liguria, he was suddenly, and to his own evident surprise, made bishop of Milan by popular acclamation. As bishop he exercised notable influence over the emperors Gratian (367–383) and Valentinian II (375–392), and in 384 opposed Symmachus' campaign to restore the Altar of Victory; see previous note. A vigorous promoter of the ascetic ideals of consecrated virginity and clerical celibacy, skilled at applying Platonist concepts to Christian doctrine, champion of the Nicene dogma of the divine trinity in opposition to the Arians (see note 7 to book 9), prolific expositor of biblical texts, and an accomplished orator, he would have presented Augustine with the figure of a bishop such as he had never encountered before. In the *Confessions* Ambrose is credited above all with helping Augustine to see past Manichean objections to the Old Testament and to conceive of god as a spiritual being. Although Ambrose published a large number of works of controversial theology, ascetic direction, and biblical exegesis, Augustine seems not to have read many of them. Nor do his own writings before the *Confessions* give any hint that Ambrose was a formative influence for him. It is worth observing that the composition of the *Confessions* probably dates from 397, the year in which Ambrose died, and that Paulinus of Nola, with whom Augustine had begun corresponding a little earlier (see Introduction, pp. xxxi–xxxv), was a great admirer of the bishop of Milan. The one clear textual link between Ambrose and the *Confessions* is provided by Augustine's quotations of the hymn "Deus creator omnium" (see note 8 to book 4). In the story as Augustine will tell it here, it was his mother, Monica, who had the closer dealings with Ambrose.

Book 6

1. (p. 73) *So also my mother brought to certain oratories, erected in the memory of the saints, offerings of porridge, bread, and wine . . . question his prohibition:* Christian mortuary observances were only slowly differentiated from those otherwise customary in the Greco-Roman world. Festive eating and drinking at tombs was a routine feature of the "pagan" cult of the dead; see Introduction, p. xxxix. In this area, as in others, Ambrose seems to have been an innovator.

2. (p. 74) *Ambrose himself I esteemed a happy man. . . . Only his celibacy appeared to me a painful burden:* Ambrose's profession of celibacy was as much of a surprise to Augustine as was his prohibition of graveside picnics to Monica, and obviously far harder to reckon with. Here again the bishop of Milan was setting new standards. Not until the fifth century in the West did celibacy come to be widely regarded as a requirement for all higher ranks of clergy; even then, and for long afterward, the rule was not generally enforced. To make celibacy a condition for full Christian profession by one who did not expect to take holy orders was even more extreme. Augustine's vision of Continence personified at 8.11.27 (and see 6.11.20) can thus be numbered among the more special effects of the *Confessions*. Without ever promoting the merits of the celibate life to the detriment of procreative marital sexuality, as some of his contemporaries did, Augustine nonetheless contributed substantially to the Christian institutionalization of sexual abstinence.

3. (p. 74) *Now, as he read, his eyes glanced over the pages and his heart searched out the sense, but his voice and tongue were silent. . . . Whatever his motive was in so doing, it was doubtless, in such a man, a good one:* This is a celebrated passage in modern scholarly discussion. The practice of reading to oneself without vocalizing the text was less common in antiquity than it has since become. In a culture that set a high value on oratory and public performance of all kinds, in which the production of books was very labor-intensive, the majority of the population was illiterate, and where those with the leisure to enjoy literary works also had slaves to read to them, written texts were more likely to be seen as scripts for recitation than as vehicles of silent reflection. However, there is also abundant evidence that silent reading *did* occur in antiquity and that it was not usually regarded as freakish. Why then does Augustine linger over the figure of Ambrose as silent reader? Any answer to this question should probably take account of all the other passages in the *Confessions* in which the activity of reading is foregrounded and where our own readerly acts, alongside Augustine's or those of another character, are implicitly brought under consideration.

4. (p. 76) *"The letter kills, but the spirit gives life":* This was and remains a fundamental principle of Christian hermeneutics, not least—historically—because Augustine so insisted upon it; see especially book 3 of his *Christian Teaching*. In the first instance, such "spiritual" interpretation enabled Christian readers consistently to derive a sense from the Hebrew scriptures (Old Testament) that was compatible with the teaching of the New Testament, a project seen as impossible by the Manicheans, among others. While there is no sign in Ambrose's extant writings that 2 Corinthians 3:6 was a favorite text of his, the larger interpretive strategy had a long history before him, and he certainly relied on it in his own exegesis.

5. (p. 77) *I always believed both that you are and that you have a care for us . . . that through them your will may be believed in and that you might be sought:* Augustine's conviction of the supreme truthfulness and authority of the canonical books of scripture is based on the assumption that a god who cares for his human creatures would not allow them all to be misled on such a grand scale by false tradition. Thus, at a stroke, he severs the Gordian knot of problems of transmission, authenticity, and textual reliability that have preoccupied biblical philologists from before his time to the present day.

6. (p. 78) *the day on which I was preparing to recite a panegyric on the emperor:* As public orator in the imperial capital of Milan, Augustine was regularly called upon to deliver speeches on state occasions. These would have to purvey a version of the current official policy and burnish the figure of the emperor or one of his top officers. Praising the teenage Valentinian II, whose policy was directed by his mother, Justina, and a few courtiers, would have demanded special resources of tact and hyperbole. Other speeches from this period, by other orators, survive, allowing one to gain a sense of the atmosphere of such occasions. The nearest we come to Augustine's own imperial panegyric style may be in the *Confessions* itself, where at last he could invoke a lord and master worthy of his rhetorical powers.

7. (p. 79) *Alypius had been born in the same town as I; his parents were of the highest rank there, but he was a bit younger than I:* On Alypius, see Introduction, pp. xxviii–xxxv. By the time of the *Confessions*, he was bishop in Augustine's home town of Thagaste. A vivid figure in Augustine's narrative, and frequently named in official church documents of the time, he has left no significant writings of his own.

8. (p. 87) *Romanianus, my fellow townsman, an intimate friend from childhood days:* Other sources reveal that Romanianus acted as a patron to Augustine, beginning by helping to pay for his education at Carthage. The scheme of a philosophical commune would have depended in large measure on his wealth. Augustine would dedicate to

him his work *Against the Academics*, composed in circumstances to be recounted in book 9. A Manichean partly as a result of Augustine's influence, Romanianus was not baptized until the mid-390s.

Book 7

1. (p. 92) *Who was it that put this in me, and implanted in me the root of bitterness . . . since a good creator made him wholly a good angel?:* Having rejected the Manichean view of evil as a distinct entity or principle in the universe, Augustine has to account for the appearance of evil in a universe created by a god who is perfectly good. The question that resonates through the early part of this book is therefore: Where does evil come from? The language at this point anticipates interests that Augustine would only acquire a decade after the thought processes he is describing. Persuaded by his reading of Paul's Epistles in the 390s that evil in human beings arises from a weakness of the will, making us *actively* fail to do what is good, Augustine also inferred from Paul that such failure, though culpable in every case, was inescapable because of a universal genetic defect in the human will inherited from the "original sin" of Adam and Eve; see 8.8.19–8.10.24. Hence the ulterior question was: Why did Adam and Eve, created perfect by god, sin in the first place? Christian exegetes, going beyond the canonical narrative of Genesis, had already worked up the notion that Satan or the devil, identified both with the serpent of Genesis 3 and with Lucifer, the fallen angel of Isaiah 14:12–15, had precipitated the sin of Adam and Eve. How then, asks Augustine, did an angel, also part of god's perfect creation, develop the evil will that led to his own fall and then Adam's? This line of exegetical reasoning, firmly sketched in the *Confessions* (see especially 8.8.20 ff.) would be more fully developed in the tracts that Augustine later wrote against Pelagius (see note 6 to book 10 below) and others who, in his view, seriously overestimated the present power of the human will to do good without special help from god. (For the fall of the angels, see books 11 and 12 of the *City of God*.) The rest of the present discussion in book 7 has a more philosophical color, dictated by the readings announced at 7.9.13 and perhaps also by the Platonist strain in Ambrose's preaching.

2. (p. 95) *Vindicianus . . . Firminus:* Vindicianus has appeared already in this connection at 4.3.5. Of Firminus nothing else is known.

3. (p. 98) *certain books of the Platonists, translated from Greek into Latin:* At 8.2.3 Augustine attributes at least some of these Latin translations to Marius Victorinus (on whom see note 2 to book 8). Exactly which Platonist philosophers (apart from Plato, whose works he knew at best indirectly) Augustine read, in which versions, at this time in his life or later, are matters of scholarly debate. There is general agreement that in the 380s he became familiar with the *Enneads* of Plotinus (204/5–270), which Victorinus had translated, and probably also with certain works by Plotinus' disciple Porphyry (c.234–c.301). The strongly theological Neoplatonism of Plotinus and Porphyry offered a field of encounter between "pagan" intellectuals and highly educated Christians, and there was clearly a circle of people interested in this material in Milan at the time of Augustine's stay there. The "monstrously proud" provider of the books used by him is thought to have been Manlius Theodorus, a high-ranking imperial officer to whom he devoted his dialogue *The Happy Life* not long afterward, though he came to think less well of him in time (*Revisions* 2.1). In the passage that follows, Augustine measures the theological contents of the Platonist books against the biblical revelation of John 1 and other New Testament texts. In the *City of God* 10.29, he would recall once being told that a certain (Milanese?) Platonist used to say that the opening lines of John's gospel deserved to be set up in letters of gold in every church. Books 8–10 of the *City of God* provide a running commentary on the "Christian Platonist" content of the *Confessions*. By the time he composed them, however, Augustine had belatedly realized that Porphyry had been a trenchant critic of Christianity, and his tone is therefore less conciliatory than here.

4. (p. 100) *that Egyptian food for which Esau lost his birthright . . . that gold which you did allow your people to take from Egypt, since wherever it was it was yours:* Egypt, as a place of captivity for the ancient Israelites (like Babylon; see note 3 to book 2), provides another geographical metaphor for the condition of being "away from home" that Augustine sees as defining the life of the Christian community in the present world. The Platonist books, for all the useful teaching they contained, were nonetheless products of "Egypt," hence potentially dangerous to the Christian reader. Augustine claims to have extracted what was valuable in them, without being corrupted. The idea that Christians might appropriate the truthful (because god-given) elements of "pagan" philosophy and other disciplines, in the same way that the biblical Israelites carried off the gold and silver vessels and fine attire of their Egyptian captors, had been developed by earlier writers as part of a rationale for selective Christian use of

the intellectual amenities of their surrounding culture. The passage
that Augustine here cites from Acts (17.28) was regularly used to exemplify the principle. His own fullest statement of this policy of "de-
spoiling the Egyptians" is in *Christian Teaching* 2.40.60–61.

5. (p. 104) *And thus by degrees I was led upward from bodies to the
soul . . . was not yet able to eat:* This is the first of three places in the
Confessions in which Augustine narrates a mystical ascent toward
oneness with god, scripted on a Plotinian model with additional biblical touches. See also 9.10.23–25, 10.8.12 ff. While at Milan, he
planned a set of books on the liberal arts that would have "led by certain steps from corporeal to incorporeal things" (*Revisions* 1.6).

6. (p. 105) *I saw in our lord Christ only a man of eminent wisdom to
whom no other man could be compared . . . his divine care for us:* At
this point, Augustine sees Christ as an exceptional human being, not
as the divine "word" made human in the flesh. It was for such a belief that Photinus (named later in the section) was convicted of
heresy in 351. Alypius, he goes on to say, was subject to another erroneous opinion about Christ's nature, associated with a certain
Apollinaris. Ambrose of Milan had been instrumental in the official
condemnation of Apollinarianism in the West.

Book 8

1. (p. 109) *Simplicianus, who appeared to me a faithful servant of
yours . . . one who felt as I did to walk in your way:* Simplicianus was
also Augustine's informant on the Platonist enthusiast for John 1:1–5;
see note 3 to book 7. Despite his advanced age, he would succeed
Ambrose as bishop of Milan in 397. Shortly before embarking on the
Confessions, Augustine produced written answers to a set of questions posed to him by Simplicianus on passages in Romans 7 and 9. It
was in the course of discussion of the latter that he came to the radi-
cal conclusion that the human will was powerless to answer god's call
without god's special help or "grace." This was the basis for his subsequent teaching and controversial writing (for example, against
Pelagius) on grace, free will, and predestination (god's choice of those
he would reserve for a life of eternal bliss and those he would not).

2. (pp. 110–111) *he told me about Victorinus himself . . . submitting his
forehead to the ignomiy of the cross:* The orator Marius Victorinus,
an African émigré like Augustine at this time, was the author and
translator of important works of grammar, rhetoric, and Greek phi-

losophy; see also note 3 to book 7. Following his "conversion," he turned his talents to Christian theological and exegetical writings, some of which Augustine may conceivably have known at first hand. Augustine makes him a champion of "pagan" polytheism who saw the error of his ways. The verse quotation is from Virgil, *Aeneid* 8.698–700, referring to Egyptian deities once ranged by Cleopatra against the Roman pantheon and later adopted by the Romans themselves. The statue of Victorinus in the Forum is also mentioned by Jerome in his adaptation of Eusebius' *Chronicle*, and there is a chance that this and several other historical details in book 8 were suggested to Augustine by his reading of that work. Like the other "conversion" scenes related in the first part of this book, the one starring Victorinus is layered with foreshadowings of Augustine's own experience.

3. (p. 115) *in the reign of the Emperor Julian, there was a law passed by which Christians were forbidden to teach literature and rhetoric:* Julian, called "apostate" by ecclesiastical writers because he rejected his Christian upbringing and restored polytheistic cults, ruled as sole emperor from 361 to 363. One of his laws from that period banned Christians from teaching grammar and rhetoric, on the grounds that it was immoral for them to expound texts proclaiming gods in whom they themselves did not believe. The law was naturally resented by Christians and criticized even by such an admirer of Julian's as the historian Ammianus Marcellinus. How many teachers actually lost or resigned their jobs is not clear. For Augustine in the *Confessions*, like Jerome before him, the "pagan" intolerance of Julian supplied a model for a similarly hard-line attitude toward traditional high culture on the part of Christians.

4. (p. 117) *Verecundus—a citizen of Milan and professor of grammar, and a very intimate friend of us all ... he greatly needed:* Verecundus was better off than the ordinary run of grammarians; see 9.3.5 for his country estate.

5. (p. 117) *Ponticianus, a fellow countryman of ours from Africa, ... one of my wearisome rhetoric textbooks:* Ponticianus' surprise tells us that copies of Christian texts like Paul's Epistles in a single codex would not have differed outwardly from utilitarian works of classical culture such as schoolbooks. Literate Christianity depended on the same technology of "pocket" editions as literacy in general.

6. (p. 117) *Anthony, the Egyptian monk, whose name was in high repute among your servants, although up to that time not familiar to me:* This Antony was reputedly a propertied gentleman who, around 285, on hearing Christ's command to the rich man (Matthew 19:21) read in church, gave up all his possessions and retired into the Egyptian desert to live as a hermit. Nascent monastic legend made him the first Christian exponent of this radically asocial option for holiness. A *Life of Antony* written in Greek by Athanasius, bishop of Alexandria in the mid-fourth century, had wide circulation and was available in Latin translation by the time Augustine came to Milan. However, none of Augustine's references to Antony suggest that he had studied the *Life* closely, or even read it for himself. The *Confessions* participates in a contemporary fascination with life-writing, without being part of anything robust enough to count yet as a Christian biographical tradition.

7. (p. 118) *the group of officials called "special agents": Agentes in rebus* were official couriers often used for internal intelligence work and therefore regarded by many with suspicion bordering on dread. For these agents, success in the job could lead to promotion and imperial favor, reflected in the informal title "friend of the emperor."

8. (p. 125) *I flung myself down under a fig tree—how I know not—and gave free course to my tears:* The fig tree that provides cover for Augustine's anguish is already loaded with associations from Genesis 3:7 (the shame of Adam and Eve), Matthew 21:19–20 (Jesus' curse on the tree without fruit), and John 1:47–50 (Nathanael's acclamation of Jesus). Note also 3.10.18 for a Manichean echo. This scene, to an even greater degree than all the others staged in book 8, has raised questions about the balance between historical and symbolic truth in Augustine's narrative. There may be times when a fig tree is just a fig tree, but this is not one of them.

9. (p. 126) *I had heard how Anthony, accidentally coming into church while the gospel was being read, . . . all the gloom of doubt vanished away:* Antony was "converted" by a scriptural text read out loud by a member of the clergy in a public assembly of Christians, Augustine (in the *Confessions*) by one that he reads silently to himself *and* makes public in a book of his own. See also 9.4.8, where he explicitly considers the kind of private-yet-public performance of scriptural texts and readings that is the essence of "confession" in the sense he intends.

Book 9

1. (p. 129) *there were only a few days before the vintage vacation; . . . devours what it loves as though it were food:* The vintage school vacation ran from August 23 to October 15. The mention of the season is a cue for the clusters of imagery relating to harvest and wine-drinking that mark the book as a whole. Even the narrative of the young Monica's overindulgence in wine (9.8.17–18) fits the larger scheme, while also partly prefiguring—by parody—the mystical ascent to plenty at 9.10.24. In both cases, Augustine will emphasize progress by degrees. Here already he associates the coming of his freedom from teaching with Psalms 119–133, each of which was entitled *canticum graduum* ("song of degrees") in his Latin psalter, encouraging figurative interpretation in terms of a narrative of ascent.

2. (p. 130) *you will repay Verecundus for that country house at Cassiciacum— ... that fruitful mountain—your own:* The house party at Verecundus' country estate near Milan follows a pattern of genteel "philosophical" retreat that had been favored by the Roman nobility and their clients since the time of the late Republic, when Cicero composed the works that were to be Augustine's chief literary model for the dialogues of Cassiciacum; see following note.

3. (p. 131) *My books testify to what I got done there in writing, ... my letters to Nebridius, who was still absent:* Augustine's extant writings of this period are mainly listed at the beginning of his *Revisions*. There are dialogues titled *Against the Academics* (that is, against the school of philosophy discussed at 5.10.19), *The Happy Life*, and *Order* (about providence), and the first-ever experiment in the genre of what Augustine called *Soliloquies*, a conversation out loud with himself. A series of letters to and from Nebridius survives as numbers 3–14 in the modern collection of Augustine's correspondence, though most of those pieces are apparently of slightly later date. As a group, the works from Cassiciacum attest the philosophical concerns recorded in books 5–8 of the *Confessions*, but in a language that is far more classically sedate and far less vivid with scriptural allusion. For all that, they are remarkable essays in a new mode of Christian philosophy. Augustine's dialogues are staged with characters from his own immediate entourage, largely familiar to us from the *Confessions*. He presents the texts as transcripts of conversations that actually occurred, taken down by shorthand writers (but no doubt carefully reworked). Strikingly, Monica—a woman, without formal education—not only has a speaking part in this company but speaks with a powerful and distinctive voice.

4. (pp. 131–132) *For at first he preferred that they should smell of the cedars of the schools which the lord has now broken down, rather than of the wholesome herbs of the church, hostile to serpents:* Here Augustine combines a reference to the biblical "cedars of Lebanon" (Psalms 29:5) with an allusion to the practice of using cedar oil to preserve the coverings of books.

5. (p. 132) *I pored over the Fourth Psalm. . . . out of the private affections of my soul . . . :* The Psalms are Augustine's primer in the art of praising god, which is the art of the *Confessions*. However, individual psalms often speak in a variety of different voices or persons, presenting something like a play (or dialogue) and requiring the interpreter to decide who is speaking at each turn. Augustine was particularly sensitive to the dramatic quality of these texts, as his improvisation on Psalm 4 will demonstrate. Before launching into it, he stops to consider how his own performance as reader and commentator on a psalm would strike a spectator looking from the point of view that had once been his own. Even more than the earlier "scene" of Ambrose's silent reading (6.3.3), this one seems designed to catch a reader of the *Confessions* in the act. (Note that the Latin text of Psalm 4 used by Augustine does not correspond at all points to modern English versions.)

6. (p. 135) *the boy Adeodatus, my son after the flesh, the offspring of my sin. . . . he was then only in his sixteenth year:* Adeodatus (the name means "god-given") was Augustine's son by the woman he had cast off for the sake of the plan — since abandoned — of making a society marriage (6.15.25). Born in the early 370s, Adeodatus would have accompanied Augustine throughout his time in Italy. The dialogue *The Teacher*, in which Adeodatus debates with his father, was written in Africa in 389, not long before the young man's death. He is the only child of Augustine that the latter ever mentions.

7. (pp. 135–136) *The church of Milan had only recently begun to employ this mode of consolation and exaltation . . . almost all your congregations throughout the rest of the world:* In January 386 Valentinian II issued an edict of toleration for those, such as the Goths by then settled in Italy, who still resisted the definition of Christ as being "of the same substance" (in Greek, *homoousios*) as god the father; their opponents called them "Arians" after the Alexandrian presbyter Arius, whose opinions had originally provoked the debates leading up to the Council of Nicea in 325. Ambrose followed the Nicene, "homoousian" line endorsed by the Council of Constantinople in 381. In the face of Valentinian's demand that the bishop hand over his church for Easter Week of 386, he had his congregation occupy the basilica around the clock. Arius and his supporters had long before used

hymns as propaganda, and the practice of hymn singing in church seems to have become widespread in eastern, Greek-speaking Christian communities during the fourth century. Partly on the strength of this passage, Ambrose is credited with introducing it in the West. He himself composed a number of Latin hymns; see below, note 13.

8. (p. 136) *Then by a vision you made known to your renowned bishop the spot where lay the bodies of Gervasius and Protasius ... were healed:* A letter of Ambrose records how, when preparing to dedicate a new church in Milan in June 386, he was inspired to dig in a certain place, whereupon two skeletons were discovered with their heads severed, and duly identified as the remains of martyrs of an early persecution. As the era of Christian martyrdoms under the Roman Empire began to recede, the cult of such relics acquired new importance as a stimulus to piety and support for the idea of a Christian community extended through time; see Introduction, pp. xxv–xxviii. Though initially skeptical about miracle stories, Augustine later grew more convinced of their value (*City of God* 22.8–10). In the present case, he appears to have telescoped events in order to have the discovery of the saints' relics coincide with the contest between Ambrose and the empress Justina.

9. (pp. 136–137) *You, lord, who make those of one mind to dwell in a single house, also brought Evodius to join our company. . . . prepared himself for yours:* Evodius would be Augustine's interlocutor in two dialogues—*Free Will* (book 1) and *The Magnitude of the Soul*—composed at Rome shortly after the events related here. By the time the *Confessions* appeared he was bishop of Uzalis in North Africa, one of the new generation of well-educated African clerics with experience of the wider world, skills acquired in imperial service, and a sense of the power—and limits—of diplomacy.

10. (p. 137) *And when we had got as far as Ostia on the Tiber, my mother died:* For the importance of Monica's death in the conception of the *Confessions*, see Introduction, pp. xxxix–xl.

11. (p. 142) *my brother:* He is named as Navigius in the dialogues of Cassiciacum, and is Augustine's only known sibling.

12. (p. 144) *I had heard that the word for bath* [balneum] *derives from the Greek* balaneion, *because it throws grief out of the mind:* Augustine derives the Greek word for bath (*balaneion*) from the verb "to throw" (*ballein*) and the noun "grief" (*ania*). The etymology is no more or less fanciful than others commonly alleged throughout antiquity and the Middle Ages.

13. (p. 145) Deus, creator omnium, . . . *And undoes heavy griefs:* The lines are from a hymn of Ambrose to be sung at evening service. The first line has already been echoed at 4.10.15 (as well as less distinctly elsewhere) and will sound again in books 10 and 11.

14. (pp. 146–147) *For when the day of her dissolution was so close, she took no thought to have her body sumptuously wrapped . . . or even care to be buried in her own country:* Flouting this dying wish, Ancius Auchenius Bassus, consul for the year 431, had a monumental inscription placed at Monica's burial place. Part of the stone was discovered by boys digging a hole for a basketball hoop in 1945. The epitaph praised Monica as the chaste mother of a famous son. Her presumed remains were transferred to the church of San Agostino at Rome in 1430. Augustine gave his view of such matters in a treatise, *The Care of the Dead*, written around 422 in response to an inquiry from Paulinus of Nola, himself a notable impresario of the cult of saints; see Introduction, pp. xxix–xxxiii. As this passage of the *Confessions* indicates, Augustine believed that prayers for the dead could be beneficial to them, especially when offered at the mass. From hints such as this, later theologians would develop the doctrine of purgatory.

Book 10

1. (p. 151) *But what is it that I love in loving you?:* The question announces the master theme of the first half of book 10, to 10.27.38.

2. (p. 152) *"Anaximenes was deceived; I am not god":* Anaximenes of Miletus, a pre-Socratic philosopher, taught that air was the primitive matter of the whole cosmos, the substance from which other elements were derived. In one of his letters Augustine cites Anaximenes as an exemplar of the kind of vain quest after knowledge ("curiosity") that he will criticize at 10.35.54–57.

3. (p. 155) *All this I do within myself, in that huge hall of my memory. . . . I can meditate on all these things as if they were present:* The memory is the faculty that makes a work like the *Confessions* possible. The search for god and the comprehension of the self are strictly cognate processes.

4. (p. 155) *Men go forth to marvel . . . they neglect to marvel at themselves:* This is the passage to which Petrarch would claim to have turned by chance, in his famous account of a hike up Mount Ventoux, written in 1336 when he was the same age as Augustine had been at the moment of his enlightenment in the garden at Milan (8.12.29–30). Petrarch's sense of affinity with Augustine, partly the product of late-medieval spiritual readings of the *Confessions*, also heralds the modern appreciation of the *Confessions* as a master-text of individual self-consciousness.

5. (p. 163) *How, then, do I seek you, lord? For when I seek you, my god, I seek a happy life:* The Happy Life was among the dialogues composed by Augustine at Cassiciacum. There he concluded that a happy person was one who possessed or held fast to god. Happiness ("blessedness" in older English Bible translations) is a recurrent theme of the Psalms, beginning at Psalm 1:1, and the keyword of Matthew 5:3–11 (the "beatitudes"), as well as a standard topic of classical philosophy. The Latin word for "happy" (*beatus*) occurs almost forty times in this book of the *Confessions*.

6. (p. 168) *Give what you command and command what you will:* From a late work of Augustine's, *The Gift of Perseverance*, we know that this sentence caught the attention of Pelagius, a British monk living at Rome, who heard someone else quote it from the *Confessions*. To Pelagius' ears, the suggestion that god should be responsible for granting human beings the ability to perform his commands made nonsense of the idea of divine lawgiving. Without wishing to impugn god's justice, Augustine laid his main emphasis on divine grace (that is, god's free gift of salvation). Beginning, after Saint Paul, from a conviction of the inherent weakness of the human will caused by Adam's sin, he held that human beings were powerless to obey god's commands unless aided by god himself; see note 1 to book 7. The difference of opinion became public a decade after the *Confessions* was published, leading to a prolonged and ill-tempered contest between Augustine and those whom he called Pelagians. Here, in line with the narrative of book 8, sexual continence provides the primary test case for Augustine's theory. The literal sense of continence as self-containment is enriched by an (ultimately Neoplatonic) insistence on god as the principle of the reintegration of the fragmented human being.

7. (p. 168) *"the lust of the flesh, and the lust of the eyes, and the pride of life":* This is the biblical injunction motivating an anatomy of "lust" (in Latin, *concupiscentia*) that is fundamental to the *Confessions;* see note 7 to book 3. The second half of book 10 lays out the whole scheme: lust of the flesh (10.30.41–34.53), lust of the eyes or "curiosity" (10.35.54–57), and lust for power and prestige (10.36.58–39.64).

8. (p. 173) *Athanasius, bishop of Alexandria, who required the readers of the psalm to use so slight an inflection of the voice that it was more like*

speaking than singing: Athanasius (c.296–373) was a leading promoter of the Nicene cause during the fourth-century debates over the
relationship between the first two persons of the divine trinity; not
coincidentally, he was also a leading publicist for the new, ascetic, and
monastic style of dedicated Christian life; see note 6 to book 8 for his
Life of Antony. His *Letter to Marcellinus,* on how to make best use of
the Psalms, forms a fascinating parallel with Augustine's practice in
the *Confessions* and elsewhere, though it cannot have provided this
direction for liturgical reading.

9. (pp. 174–175) *Those who know how to praise you for it, "God, creator
of all," take it up in your hymn:* See 9.12.32 for this hymn of Ambrose.

10. (p. 175) *What numberless things there are: products of the various arts
and manufactures in our clothes, shoes, vessels, and all such things, as
well as pictures and images of various kinds—and all these far beyond
the necessary and moderate use of them or their significance for the life
of piety—which human beings have added for the delight of the eye,
copying the outward forms of the things they make but inwardly forsaking him by whom they were made and destroying what they themselves have been made to be!:* The distinction between useful human
artifacts and artworks designed purely to please the outer or inner
eye is a key feature of Augustine's discussion of the forms of human
culture in book 2 of the contemporary *Christian Teaching* (2.25.38–39).
Pictures, statues, theatrical performances, literary fictions and other
works of art that copy nature serve no useful purpose, since the
originals are already there to attest and praise the creator. Only
god is worth possessing, and human art cannot represent him; at
best—as in a hymn by Ambrose or in Augustine's *Confessions*—it
may declare him.

11. (p. 183) *For the mediator they sought was the devil, disguising himself
as an angel of light. And he allured their proud flesh the more because
he had no fleshly body:* Building on hints in the New Testament (for
example, 1 Corinthians 10:20, James 2:19), Augustine identifies Satan
and the fallen angels with the "demons" or incorporeal beings whom
Platonic philosophers and practitioners of theurgic rites treated as in-
termediaries between the gods and human beings; see especially *City
of God,* books 8–10. In his system, there is only one true mediator between humanity and god—namely, Christ, god in the flesh.

12. (p. 184) *Terrified by my sins and the load of my misery, I had resolved
in my heart and considered flight into the wilderness:* What actual moment in his life is Augustine recalling here? We know that he was

initially reluctant to take on the role of presbyter when ordained in the church at Hippo in 391. A recent hypothesis has him briefly contemplating a life of ascetic seclusion as an alternative to the burdens of pastoral office. The conjecture makes excellent sense of this passage of the *Confessions*, in which Augustine also cites Psalm 119:18 on the wonders of god's "law," thus announcing the biblical exegesis to follow in books 11–13. One of the ways Augustine appears to have made sense of his pastoral role was by preaching intensively on scripture. He began to do this as a presbyter, contrary to the normal practice of the African church, which reserved preaching for bishops. His sermons on biblical texts, transcribed and preserved at his behest, were to be a major resource for later preachers.

Book 11

1. (p. 185) *so that all may say, "Great is the lord and greatly to be praised." I have said this before and will say it again:* See 1.1.1. The deliberate echo signals both continuity of overall design and a new departure after the partly recapitulative book 10.

2. (p. 185) *But how long would it take for the voice of my pen to tell enough of your exhortations . . . what we give even if we do not owe it:* We hear the voice of the over-taxed bishop for whom "service" includes much besides the special activity of scriptural exegesis to which he now wishes to turn. Later in his career Augustine would appoint a surrogate to take care of routine business while he devoted himself to his literary labors.

3. (p. 186) *from the very beginning, when you made heaven and earth . . . thenceforward to the everlasting reign of your holy city with you:* The scope of the project anticipates books 11–22 of the *City of God*, which attempt to account for all history between termini given by the biblical Genesis and Revelation, respectively. For any reader looking for a sequel to the *Confessions*, those books of the *City of God* are an obvious choice, while books 1–10 expand on the cultural and philosophical concerns of the earlier work.

4. (p. 187) *Let me hear and understand how in the beginning you made heaven and earth. . . . grant me also the gift to understand them:* Here, as at several other points in the *Confessions*, it is possible to suspect a slightly polemical—or at least strategic—distancing of Augustine's position from that of his contemporary Jerome. Where the latter stressed the importance of returning to the Hebrew and Greek

originals of biblical texts in order to reach an accurate interpretation, Augustine, who had no Hebrew and little Greek, appeals to a criterion of truth beyond philology. The word and son of god who speaks in the scriptures speaks also to the inward sense of every believer.

5. (pp. 187–188) *Look around; there are the heaven and the earth. . . . our knowledge is ignorance when it is compared with your knowledge:* Augustine's double appeal to the scriptures and to the creatures as parallel declarations of god opened the way to medieval and later doctrines of god's two books, of Nature (or the World) and the Bible.

6. (p. 191) *Now, are not those still full of their old carnal nature who ask us: "What was god doing before he made heaven and earth?" . . . why, then, is not the creation itself also from eternity?":* The argument here is with the Manicheans and certain Neoplatonists who objected to the Genesis account of creation on the grounds that a god who set about something in this sudden fashion must have had a change of mind, and hence himself be subject to change. By ingeniously identifying the "beginning" of Genesis 1:1 with the "beginning" of John 8:25 (at 11.8.10–9.11), Augustine turns the first of these verses into a statement that god created the world through his son, the word, thereby removing the suspicion of temporal innovation. He now tries several other tacks. See further 12.20.29.

7. (p. 193) *There was no time, therefore, when you had not made anything, because you had made time itself. . . . For what is time?:* Augustine's treatment of the problem of time recalls longstanding debates among ancient philosophers. His particular contribution is to develop Aristotle's suggestion that time is subjective, an experience of the human soul, by linking it at once with the dynamics of memory (as already discussed in book 10) and with a Plotinian idea of human life in time as distracted and dispersed ("distended," he will say) until gathered into the eternal One.

8. (pp. 195–196) *Give me leave, lord, to seek still further. . . . I see it in the present because it is still in my memory:* The autobiographical reminiscences of the *Confessions* thus illustrate a more general point about the role of the memory in the perception of time. By the end of this book, the perspective will have been almost reversed: All experience of human life in time, we are there invited to think, is like the experience of a literary text. For the next paragraph or two, Augustine is concerned with the special class of "memories of the future" presented by biblical prophecy. Although he quickly abandons the problem as too difficult, the drift of his thought is toward a

theory of the biblical text as a linear unfolding of the eternal, atemporal "memory" of god (11.31.41).

9. (p. 202) Deus creator omnium: *this verse of eight syllables alternates between short and long syllables:* See 9.12.32 for the hymn of Ambrose of which Augustine here quotes the first line.

10. (p. 204) *I am about to repeat a psalm that I know:* Yet again this biblical genre provides Augustine with a paradigm for the "action" that the *Confessions* strives somehow to compress. The book that began with a reprise of the psalmist's praise of the creator will end with a vision of all creation encoded like a psalm.

Book 12

1. (p. 207) *But where is that heaven of heavens, lord, of which we hear in the words of the psalm . . . and not for the sons of men:* Augustine takes the psalmist's reference to a "heaven of heavens" to signify that there is another, purely intelligible sphere beyond the visible heaven or "sky" belonging to the material creation ("earth" in the largest sense). Taking up other hints from scripture apart from Genesis 1, he will subsequently describe this superior heaven as the "house of god," as created "wisdom," and as the realm in which spiritual beings—god and the angels, and ultimately all the blessed inhabitants of the heavenly "Jerusalem" or everlasting "city of god"—apprehend the total reality of creation without being subject to the constraints of temporality. The initial discussion runs to 12.13.16, after which Augustine turns to broader methodological issues raised by the problem of interpreting Genesis 1:1. His line-by-line exegesis then continues in book 13, to Genesis 2:3. This was not his first essay in expounding the biblical creation story, an interpretive genre with ample precedent in earlier Christian literature. He had already written a treatise *On Genesis against the Manicheans* (see also note 6 to book 11) and begun his *Literal Commentary on Genesis.* The interpretation offered in book 13 will be predominantly allegorical. There and in the present book the author constantly interweaves ideas derived from scripture with others suggested by his readings of Platonist philosophers such as Plotinus. It has been noticed that in quoting Psalm 115:16 here, Augustine (unusually for the *Confessions*) names a "psalm" as his source, a gesture which may underline the importance he attached to this particular text of scripture as a witness to the whole order of creation, and which in any case recalls his suggested analogy at the end of book 11 between human knowledge of a psalm and god's knowledge of everything.

2. (p. 209) *you created something and that out of nothing:* Augustine endorses an already widely accepted Christian view that god created the universe "out of nothing" (*ex nihilo*), rather than making use of pre-existing matter as the Platonists believed.

3. (p. 211) *Truth, light of my heart, let not my own darkness speak to me! . . . I have believed your books, and their words are very deep:* Despite its occasional *longueurs*, the whole discussion of Genesis 1 remains part of the single verbal performance of the *Confessions*, conceived from the outset as an encounter with god facilitated by the words of his scriptures and informed by the promptings of the inner voice of truth (Christ, the word).

4. (pp. 213–214) *Marvelous is the depth of your oracles. . . . It is a fearful thing to look into them: an awe of honor and a tremor of love:* Since 3.5.9, if somewhat intermittently in the ensuing books, Augustine has been sketching a theory of the special nature of the divine books that he and other Christians called simply "scripture(s)." In the remainder of this book, he will thrash out the problem in more detail, in a context enlivened by the prospect of stubborn contradiction by other parties. The major themes are those of all hermeneutics or interpretive theory: authorial intention, multiple meaning, the limits of legitimate interpretation. See also Introduction, pp. xxxii–xxxv.

5. (p. 218) *And our master knew it well, for it was on these two commandments that he hung all the Law and the Prophets:* Augustine alludes to the double command to love god and neighbor (Matthew 22:37–39, cited at 12.25.35). According to the hermeneutical "rule of love" propounded by Augustine, no legitimate interpretation of scripture can conflict with this injunction of Christ's. Conversely, no interpretation that tends to reinforce love for god and neighbor can be harmful, even if demonstrably false. The rule is laid down formally in *Christian Teaching* 1.36.40, 2.7.10. See also 13.24.36 below.

6. (p. 222) *But in the midst of so many truths which occur to the interpreters of these words . . . you in your immutable word have created all things, invisible and visible?:* The confidence with which Augustine asserts the second of these things is literally one of faith. Belief in god the father as creator of all things through his only-begotten, coeternal son was part of the creed-based consensus of Nicene Christianity that Augustine had accepted on returning to the church. The idea of a "rule of faith" consisting of the core doctrines of Christianity and normative for all scriptural exegesis can be traced back to the second century. This hermeneutical principle is stated formally in *Christian Teaching* 1.5–21.

7. (pp. 224–225) *I cannot believe that you gave your most faithful servant Moses a lesser gift . . . congruent to my words:* To lend psychological plausibility to his theory that the biblical text is miraculously designed by its (ultimate) divine author to be accessible in different ways to readers of different capacities, Augustine imagines what *he* would have wanted for a text of *his* composition, had he been Moses and known of the reception that was in store for his writings. He repeats the experiment at 12.31.42. Although it is tempting to read these passages as authorial warrant to regard the *Confessions* itself as providentially polysemic in the same way as Genesis when read by Augustine, we must note that in both places he stresses the unique authority (*auctoritas*) of the divinely inspired scriptures. Although Augustine understands his own ministry as a Christian teacher to be part of the same overall divine dispensation that provided for the canonical books of the Bible, he never blurs the boundary between what is "scripture" in the canonical sense and what is merely Christian writing, by him or anyone else. Even so, the psychological appeal of the argument depends on his and our being able to entertain for a moment the idea that god *could* have summoned Augustine as another (or instead of) Moses.

Book 13

1. (p. 232) *For your good spirit which moved over the face of the waters . . . and made blessed:* After rejecting as absurd any idea that the creation could have been merited by the creatures or needed by god, Augustine is ready to speak of the "spirit of god" of Genesis 1:2, whom he identifies as the third person of the Christian trinity and, in a scheme original to him, as the *will* of god. The full triadic structure of divine *being* (god the father), *knowing* (son), and *willing* (holy spirit) is explained briefly at 13.11.12 and in Augustine's work *The Trinity*, begun soon after the *Confessions*. The work of the holy spirit in the world is the matter of this book, presented as an allegorical exegesis of the six days of creation, beginning at 13.12.13.

2. (p. 236) *Go forward in your confession, my faith . . . we were formerly in darkness, but now we are light in the lord:* This last confession of the *Confessions* has as its grammatical subject the universal body of confessing believers, mystically identified with the body of Christ. Augustine is speaking from within the church into which he was baptized in Milan at Easter 387, but also on behalf of a longer-term community of the "city of god" (the elect) and with an eye too to those outside this godly society (the damned). The whole of human history is covered by his exegesis of the remaining verses of Genesis 1. Characteristically, the speech that he now begins to utter is one confected from the sayings of biblical authors, especially Paul and, as ever, the psalmist.

3. (pp. 238–239) *Now who but you, our god, made for us that firmament of the authority of your divine scripture to be over us? . . . the fame of their death:* This is a particularly clear instance of the way in which the exegetical narrative of book 13 is composed. An allegorical-ecclesial interpretation of Genesis 1:6–8 is made possible by the imported analogy of heaven and scroll from Isaiah 34:4, then deepened by a surprising inference from Genesis 3:21. Under cover of this reinvented "firmament," Augustine will descant upon the authority of scripture and the difference between human and angelic apprehension of god's "word." The proliferating scenarios of the rest of the book arise from similar processes of cross-fertilization between scriptural texts. For an authorial key to the emerging plot, see 13.24.37 and 13.34.49.

4. (pp. 240–241) *Who has gathered the embittered ones into a single society? . . . by the providence of your governance of all things:* Augustine interprets the bitter waters of the sea as an image of those who follow worldly ends instead of being turned to god. The separation of seas from the land (Genesis 1:9–10) thus symbolizes the division between the "city of god"—provisionally the church—and the "city of the world." However, human beings in this present life cannot know exactly who will be counted in each of those communities at the end of time. That is the judgment of god, who predestined their membership before the beginning of time; see the end of 13.23.33, the beginning of 13.34.49 and, for the full treatment, the *City of God*.

5. (p. 243) *There was that rich man who asked of the good teacher what he should do to attain eternal life:* This is a subliminal link back to the story of Antony at 8.6.15 and 8.12.29.

6. (p. 249) *Therefore in your church . . . just as there is neither Jew nor Greek, nor bond nor free:* For Augustine's understanding of differences in sex and gender, see note 10 below.

7. (p. 251) *What, then, shall I say, truth, my life: that it was idly and vainly said? . . . understood in the mind in many different ways:* This important hermeneutical principle is expounded at length in book 2 of *Christian Teaching*. Once again, the interpretive practice of the *Confessions* illustrates the theory of the slightly earlier work. It also expands it, since Augustine here makes hermeneutical activity part of god's design in the creation of humanity: The ability to construe more than one meaning in a single expression and to find more than one expression for a given teaching or truth is an aspect of the human "procreative" function announced at Genesis 1:28.

8. (p. 256) *And I heard this, lord my god, and drank up a drop of sweetness from your truth, . . . they do not see your works through your spirit, nor recognize you in them:* A final jibe at the Manicheans, who, failing to see that all creation was originally good, posited a separate evil power as the author of what was not.

9. (p. 257) *We see the firmament of heaven, either the original body of the world between the spiritual (higher) waters and the corporeal (lower) waters:* In *Revisions* 2.6 Augustine censures this remark as carelessly made, averring that "the matter is very obscure." As we have seen, his exposition of Genesis 1:7 at 13.15.16–16.19 avoids defining what is literally meant by the waters above and below the firmament, to focus instead on the allegory of the firmament as god's scripture.

10. (p. 258) *We see the face of the earth, replete with earthly creatures; and man, created in your image and likeness . . . subjected to the deliberation of the mind in order to conceive the rules of right action:* The equivalences "male = mind, spirit" and "female = body, fleshly appetite" were settled in (Platonist) Christian thought long before Augustine, and he does nothing to disturb them. Statements he makes elsewhere suggest that he believed that women shared in the "image of god" only as members of the human species, not in their femaleness. Such an understanding presumably underlies the present (concessive) statement about woman's "like nature of rational intelligence in the mind." Augustine's attitudes were normal for his time and culture. While his interpretations of Genesis 2–4 did much to propagate negative views of the female body and female sexuality, some of his thinking about gender roles appears contrastingly progressive. See note 3 to book 9 above on Monica's contribution to the philosophical dialogues of Cassiciacum. Augustine's theological correspondence with women displays a quiet confidence in their intellectual powers and capacity to influence public opinion. Although his own report on the impact of the *Confessions* refers only to its effect on certain "brothers," he surely envisaged a mixed audience from the start. The evidence of surviving manuscripts shows that when the work came into fashion in the later Middle Ages, it was appreciated as much by female as by male readers. The first abridged edition in English, at Paris in 1638 (based on Tobie Matthew's translation of 1620), was published by a woman, Françoise Blagaert.

INSPIRED BY AUGUSTINE
AND THE *CONFESSIONS*

Augustine was renowned in the Latin-speaking world as a founding father of Christian theology, but his influence proceeds far beyond that. In the *Confessions*, Augustine broke ground by exploring his chosen topic—faith in God—using a tool that had little precedent in prior scholarship: his own life. Equally important, Augustine found room in the young Christian religion for the highly evolved thought of the so-called pagan philosophers, particularly Plato. This may seem simple enough on its face, but, without exaggeration, Augustine was centuries ahead of his time. The personal nature of the *Confessions* gave everyday relevance to the more abstract elements of Platonic thought and Christian theology, bringing the rival philosophies into harmony and delivering them to millions of readers. Weaving together introspection, classical learning, and faith, Augustine outlined the underpinnings of the Renaissance in Europe, two centuries that followed the Middle Ages and were marked by a "rebirth" of classical values and humanism, the belief in the dignity of each member of the human race. The Renaissance, according to many scholars, began on the spring day in 1336 when a young poet named Petrarch opened a copy of the *Confessions* and found in it a justification for scanning his own consciousness rather than searching the world for answers to the great questions of life. In some ways the Renaissance never ended, as the innovations made during that period in art, science, commerce, and politics laid the basis for the world we recognize today. In many fundamental ways, in the *Confessions* Augustine articulated the soul of modern man.

The *Confessions* emerged from a perfect storm that had been brewing for hundreds of years. In the fourth century B.C.E., the Greek philosopher Plato advanced his theory of forms: the notion that any concept we can conceive of flows from an ideal of that concept that exists free from imperfection and beyond space and time; for instance, Plato calls the form of the good the ideal version of goodness that exists beyond the reach of man except through contemplation. In the third century C.E., after a long period of stagnation, the Roman philosopher Plotinus stimulated a resurgence of Platonic ideals. Plotinus took Plato's theory of forms one step further, positing that all forms emanate from a single entity, known as the One; his ideas became known as Neo-Platonism. Despite the similarities between Neo-Platonism and Christianity, members of the two belief systems were not in accord. One prominent Neo-Platonist remarked, "The gods have proclaimed Christ to have been most pious, but the Christians are a confused and vicious sect." Further, those who practiced the Christian religion were still subject to government-sanctioned persecution. Yet the Roman Empire was in decline, and as it weakened, Christianity became stronger.

That change, in fact, came swiftly. Four decades after the death of Plotinus, the Edict of Milan, signed in 313, decriminalized Christianity in the Roman Empire, and in 380 the leaders of the Empire declared Christianity the official religion of the land. Augustine, born in 354 to a Christian mother and a pagan father, at first embraced Manichaeism, then Neo-Platonism, but on Easter Sunday in 387, his thirty-third year, he was baptized and embraced Christianity. He died in 430, and in 476 the Heruli chieftain Odoacer deposed Romulus Augustus, ending Roman supremacy on the continent and clearing the way for the rise of the European states.

Despite the decline of the civilization that produced Augustine, his writings remained dominant throughout the West for the next several centuries. Alongside those of Ambrose and Jerome, the works of Augustine had a tremendous influence on the theological framework of the evolving Roman Catholic Church, which during the Middle Ages strengthened its grip on the former Roman Empire and beyond. The ideas of Plato and Plotinus, on the other hand, vanished from the common consciousness in the West, as knowledge of Ancient Greek was rare in the former Roman Empire until the fifteenth century. Latin translations of Greek philosophical texts all but disappeared, with the exception of some fragments from Aristotle, the most famous student of Plato. Among his many contributions to human thought, Aristotle turned away from Plato's belief-based theory of forms and instead emphasized directly observable fact, laying the foundation for the scientific method and the modern university system. Fragments of his works translated into Latin by Boethius in the sixth century were Europe's only direct access to classical philosophy for the next six hundred years. *Consolation of Philosophy*, Boethius' masterwork, has many parallels with the *Confessions*, yet without a trace Christian thought. It was Augustine's thoroughly Christian writings that carried the torch of ancient Greece during the intensely Christian Middle Ages. When the works of Plato and Aristotle re-entered the Western consciousness, Augustine's writings enabled members of the Roman Catholic

Church to recognize what they had in common with the great pagan thinkers.

Questions posed by the twelfth-century Andalusian-Arab philosopher Averroës helped spark the return of Greek thought to Europe. In trying to reconcile the works of Aristotle, which he read in Arabic, with Islam, Averroës created great controversy in the Roman Catholic Church regarding the relationship between reason and faith. Thomas Aquinas, the greatest thinker of the thirteenth century and perhaps the entire Middle Ages (his *Summa Theologiae* is arguably the most important document in the Roman Catholic Church after the Bible), both ended the debate and vindicated the pagan Aristotle. Deeply passionate about Augustine's writings, Aquinas was inspired equally by Averroës' attempts to reconcile a faith-based system such as Islam with the empirical thought of Aristotle. Yet Aquinas rejected arguments posed by both followers of Averroës, who contended that reason and faith were separate but equal powers, and followers of Augustine, who felt that faith was a precondition to reason. In a major innovation, Aquinas asserted that reason and faith need not be separate; instead, they ought properly to work hand in hand in all discourse. Aquinas applied this notion in his own rigorous Aristotelian proofs of the existence of God, wherein he demonstrated the power of pagan philosophy and effectively ended the sporadic papal bans that prevented such works from being taught at the early European universities, a development that forever changed academic life in the West. Petrarch was born soon after, in 1304, and, with renewed communication between Europe and the East, the Byzantine scholar Gemistus Pletho began teaching the work of Plato to the Florentines in 1438. The lofty proclamations of the idealistic Plato captured the imagination of the Italians and inspired them to brilliance, simultaneously ending the philosophical dominance of Aristotle, whose fastidiousness led to a reliance on outlines, details, and proofs that encumbered more transcendent expressions of creativity. The Renaissance had begun. Even after the Renaissance, however, those who have thought deeply about the human condition have never been content to let Augustine lie dormant. In the sixteenth century, his emphasis on subjectivity and one's personal relationship with God inspired Martin Luther and John Calvin to hold strong to their view that the Roman Catholic Church had become institutionally corrupt, partly through the sale of indulgences. At a time when the growing university system and the advent of the printing press were dramatically improving the circulation of information, the works of Augustine catalyzed another religious upheaval: the Protestant Reformation.

Secular philosophers equally found relevance in Augustine, particularly at the dawn of the seventeenth century and the next major period in European history: the Enlightenment. The most famous sentence in the history of philosophy—French thinker René Descartes' assertion "I think, therefore I am"—is a strikingly modern inversion of Book 1 of the *Confessions*, where Augustine lays out the dilemma of how to address God. Amid a raft of questions that probe the ineffability of the divine, Augustine presses forward, announcing, "I believe, and therefore I speak," demonstrating how, for some, faith in God is a precondition to all other action. Descartes' statement, on the other hand, justifies existence on the basis of faith in reason, a significant variation (some might say a paradigm shift) that became a defining characteristic of thought during the Age of Enlightenment, the Industrial Revolution, and the Internet era.

COMMENTS & QUESTIONS

In this section, we aim to provide the reader with an array of perspectives on the text, as well as questions that challenge those perspectives. The commentary has been culled from sources as diverse as reviews contemporaneous with the work, letters written by the author, literary criticism of later generations, and appreciations written throughout the work's history. Following the commentary, a series of questions seeks to filter the Confessions *through a variety of points of view and bring about a richer understanding of this enduring work.*

Comments

PETRARCH

While my thoughts were divided thus, now turning my attention to thoughts of some worldly object before me, now uplifting my soul, as I had done my body, to higher planes, it occurred to me to look at Augustine's *Confessions*, a gift of your love that I always keep with me in memory of the author and the giver. I opened the little volume, small in size but infinitely sweet, with the intention of reading whatever came to hand, for what else could I happen upon if not edifying and devout words. Now I happened by chance to open it to the tenth book. My brother stood attentively waiting to hear what St Augustine would say from my lips. As God is my witness and my brother too, the first words my eyes fell upon were: 'And men go about admiring the high mountains and the mighty waves of the sea and the wide sweep of rivers and the sound of the ocean and the movement of the stars, but they themselves they abandon.' I was ashamed, and asking my brother, who was anxious to hear more, not to bother me, I closed the book, angry with myself for continuing to admire the things of this world when I should have learned a long time ago from the pagan philosophers themselves that nothing is admirable but the soul beside whose greatness nothing can be as great. Then, having seen enough of the mountain I turned an inward eye upon myself, and from that moment on not a syllable passed my lips until we reached the bottom.

—from a letter to Dionisio da Borgo San Sepolcro
(April 26, 1336), as translated by Mark Musa

RENÉ DESCARTES

Augustine, whose remarks on the subject of God are as worthwhile and sublime as any that have appeared since the time of the sacred authors, frequently explains that in God there is no past or future but only eternally present existence. This makes it even clearer that the question of why God should continue in existence cannot be asked without absurdity, since the question manifestly involves the notions of 'before' and 'after', past and future, which should be excluded from the concept of an infinite being.

> —from *Objections and Replies* (1641), as translated by
> John Cottingham, Robert Stoothoff, and Dugald Murdoch

GOTTFRIED WILHELM LEIBNIZ

'It is better to doubt concerning what is hidden than to argue over what is uncertain' (Augustine, *De genesi ad litteram* VIII.5) .... If only all theologians, including St Augustine himself, had always acted on the maxim expressed in that passage! But men believe that a spirit of dogmatism is a sign of their zeal for the truth; when it is just the opposite—we truly love truth only in so far as we love to examine the proofs which make it known for what it is. And when someone jumps to a conclusion he is always impelled by less high-minded reasons.

> —from *New Essays on Human Understanding* (1765),
> as translated by Peter Remnant and Jonathan Bennett

SØREN KIERKEGAARD

For a long time mankind had despaired of making anything out of this existence, despaired of finding the truth—then came Christianity with divine authority. Augustine, for example, always turns the whole matter in such a way that the perfection in Christianity is precisely the authority, that Christianity has truth in its most perfect form, the authority, that if one could have the same truth without authority it would be less perfect, for it is precisely the authority which is the perfection. Alas, even Augustine had learned what it is men need: authority, which is precisely what the race, weary of philosophers' doubt and the wretchedness of life, had learned through the entry of Christianity into the world.

> —from notes composed circa 1854,
> as translated by Howard V. Hong and Edna H. Hong

FRIEDRICH NIETZSCHE

I have been reading, as relaxation, St. Augustine's *Confessions*, much regretting that you were not with me. O this old rhetorician! What false-ness, what rolling of eyes! How I laughed! (for example, concerning the "theft" of his youth, basically an undergraduate story). What psycho-logical falsity! (for example, when he talks about the death of his best friend, with whom he shared a *single soul*, he "resolved to go on living, so that in this way his friend would not wholly die." Such things are re-voltingly dishonest). Philosophical value zero! *vulgarized* Platonism—that is to say, a way of thinking which was invented for the highest aristocracy of soul, and which he adjusted to suit slave natures. More-over, one sees into the guts of Christianity in this book.

—from a letter to Franz Overbeck (March 31, 1885),
as translated by Christopher Middleton

WILLIAM JAMES

Now in all of us, however constituted, but to a degree the greater in proportion as we are intense and sensitive and subject to diversified temptations, and to the greatest possible degree if we are decidedly psychopathic, does the normal evolution of character chiefly consist in the straightening out and unifying of the inner self. The higher and lower feelings, the useful and the erring impulses, begin by being a comparative chaos within us—they must end by forming a stable sys-tem of functions in right subordination. Unhappiness is apt to charac-terize the period of order-making and struggle. If the individual be of tender conscience and religiously quickened, the unhappiness will take the form of moral remorse and compunction, of feeling inwardly vile and wrong, and of standing in false relations to the author of one's being and appointer of one's spiritual fate. This is the religious melan-choly and 'conviction of sin' that have played so large a part in the his-tory of Protestant Christianity. The man's interior is a battle-ground for what he feels to be two deadly hostile selves, one actual, the other ideal. . . . Wrong living, impotent aspirations; "What I would, that do I not; but what I hate, that do I," as Saint Paul says; self-loathing, self-despair; an unintelligible and intolerable burden to which one is mys-teriously the heir.

Let me quote from some typical cases of discordant personality, with melancholy in the form of self-condemnation and sense of sin. Saint Au-gustine's case is a classic example. You all remember his half-pagan, half-

Christian bringing up at Carthage, his emigration to Rome and Milan, his adoption of Manicheism and subsequent skepticism, and his restless search for truth and purity of life; and finally how, distracted by the struggle between the two souls in his breast, and ashamed of his own weakness of will, when so many others whom he knew and knew of had thrown off the shackles of sensuality and dedicated themselves to chastity and the higher life, he heard a voice in the garden say, "*Sume, lege*" (take and read), and opening the Bible at random, saw the text, "not in chambering and wantonness," etc., which seemed directly sent to his address, and laid the inner storm to rest forever. Augustine's psychological genius has given an account of the trouble of having a divided self which has never been surpassed. . . .

There could be no more perfect description of the divided will, when the higher wishes lack just that last acuteness, that touch of explosive intensity, of dynamogenic quality (to use the slang of the psychologists), that enables them to burst their shell, and make irruption efficaciously into life and quell the lower tendencies forever.

—from *The Varieties of Religious Experience* (1902)

ADOLPH HARNACK

The significance of the 'Confessions' is as great on the side of form as on that of content. Before all, they were a literary *achievement*. No poet, no philosopher before him undertook what he here performed; and I may add that almost a thousand years had to pass before a similar thing was done. It was the poets of the Renascence, who formed themselves on Augustine, that first gained from his example the daring to depict themselves and to present their personality to the world. For what do the 'Confessions' of Augustine contain? The portrait of a soul—not psychological disquisitions on the Understanding, the Will, and the Emotions in Man, not abstract investigations into the nature of the soul, not superficial reasonings and moralising introspections like the Meditations of Marcus Aurelius, but the most exact portraiture of a distinct human personality, in his development from childhood to full age, with all his propensities, feelings, aims, mistakes; a portrait of a soul, in fact, drawn with a perfection of observation that leaves on one side the mechanical devices of psychology, and pursues the method of the physician and the physiologist.

—from *The Confessions of St Augustine* (1911),
as translated by E. E. Kellett and F. H. Marseille

OLIVER WENDELL HOLMES

I had one sweet hour of repose when all my jobs were finished and divided it between another instalment of Marcel Proust—*Le côté de Guermantes*—and the *Confessions of St. Augustine.* . . . Of the two I would rather read St. Augustine. It is like a painting by Morland set over an altar. Rum thing to see a man making a mountain out of robbing a pear tree in his teens.

—from a letter to Harold Laski (January 5, 1921)

HAROLD LASKI

In the way of reading I have had little time for other than work—mainly St. Augustine. I wasn't very profoundly impressed, except by a certain unmistakable dexterity and fullness of mind—chiefly out of Plato and Cicero. He seemed to me to run away from all his real problems, and to lack altogether the ability to judge oneself that makes Spinoza so formidable an analyst.

—from a letter to Oliver Wendell Holmes (December 3, 1927)

LUDWIG WITTGENSTEIN

[Possibly] the most serious book ever written.

—Wittgenstein's view of the *Confessions*,
as recalled by M. O'C. Drury in
Acta Philosophica Fennica (1976)

Questions

1. Oliver Wendell Holmes wrote that it's a "Rum thing to see a man making a mountain out of robbing a pear tree in his teens." Do you agree? Or is Holmes being petty and disingenuous? Did he miss something important?

2. Do you, by the end of the *Confessions*, feel that Augustine truly came to understand himself? Could a skeptic make a plausible case that Augustine's Christianity led him not to self-knowledge but to a pretext for self-ignorance?

3. What does a sympathetic reader learn about himself or herself from reading the *Confessions*? Can Augustine's personal lessons be adapted universally—to anyone, even today?

4. What is Augustine's attitude to sex, as revealed in the *Confessions*? When these attitudes are seen clearly, would you describe them as healthy or rationally justified?

FOR FURTHER READING

Biographies and General Works on Augustine

Brown, Peter. *Augustine of Hippo: A Biography*. 1967. New edition with an epilogue. Berkeley and Los Angeles: University of California Press, 2000. The classic biography; presents a rounded view of Augustine as a man of the late Roman Empire.

Chadwick, Henry. *Augustine*. Oxford: Oxford University Press, 1986. Elegant introduction to the complex of Augustine's thought, including its theological intricacies.

Fitzgerald, Allan D., ed. *Augustine through the Ages: An Encyclopedia*. Grand Rapids, MI: William B. Eerdmans, 1999. Contains useful articles on Augustine's historical milieu, his theological and philosophical positions, his literary and intellectual sources, controversies in which he was involved, and the later reception of his work and ideas.

Lancel, Serge. *Saint Augustine*. Translated by Antonia Nevill. London: SCM Press, 2002. The most richly documented modern biography.

O'Donnell, James J. *Augustine: A New Biography*. New York: Harper-Collins, 2005. A subtle probing of what Augustine does and does not tell us about himself. O'Donnell maintains a valuable website on Augustine: http://ccat.sas.upenn.edu/jod/augustine.html.

Rist, John M. *Augustine: Ancient Thought Baptized*. Cambridge: Cambridge University Press, 1994. A full and lucid exposition of Augustine's philosophical thought.

Wills, Garry. *Saint Augustine*. New York: Viking, 1999. Stylish capsule biography by a Pulitzer Prize–winning historian. The author has also published several lively new translations of individual books of the *Confessions*.

Studies Especially Relevant to the Confessions

Bright, Pamela M., ed. and trans. *Augustine and the Bible*. Notre Dame, IN: University of Notre Dame Press, 1999. A collection of essays on Augustine's approach to and use of biblical texts, including a number directly on the *Confessions*.

Clark, Elizabeth A., ed. Saint Augustine on Marriage and Sexuality. Washington, DC: The Catholic University of America Press, 1996. Selected passages in translation from a range of Augustine's works, with illuminating commentary and bibliography.

Clark, Gillian. *Augustine: The Confessions.* Exeter: Bristol Phoenix Press, 2005. A clear and well-informed introduction to the work, with a guide to resources for further study.

Kermode, Frank. *The Classic: Literary Images of Permanence and Change.* Cambridge, MA: Harvard University Press, 1983. A study that provides the essential context for an understanding of the place of the *Confessions* in the long history of Western literature.

MacCormack, Sabine. *The Shadows of Poetry: Vergil in the Mind of Augustine.* Berkeley: University of California Press, 1998. A finely drawn portrait of the most important literary relationship in the *Confessions*.

Miles, Margaret R. *Desire and Delight: A New Reading of Augustine's* Confessions. New York: Crossroad, 1992. A stimulating account of Augustine's treatment of emotions, the body, sexuality, and human relationships.

O'Connell, Robert J. *St Augustine's Confessions: The Odyssey of Soul.* Cambridge, MA: Belknap Press of Harvard University Press, 1969. A strong reading of the Neoplatonic quest for unity in Augustine's work.

Paffenroth, Kim, and Robert P. Kennedy, eds. *A Reader's Companion to Augustine's* Confessions. Louisville, KY: Westminster John Knox Press, 2003. Thirteen essays, one on each book of the *Confessions* taken as an interpretive key to the whole.

Power, Kim. *Veiled Desire: Augustine on Women.* New York: Continuum, 1996. A careful and largely persuasive analysis of Augustine's attitudes.

Starnes, Colin. *Augustine's Conversion: A Guide to the Argument of* Confessions *I–IX*. Waterloo, Ontario: Wilfrid Laurier University Press, 1990. An accessible running commentary, drawing on extensive scholarship.

Stock, Brian. *Augustine the Reader: Meditation, Self-Knowledge, and the Ethics of Interpretation.* Cambridge, MA: Harvard University Press, 1996. Dense but illuminating study of a crucial dimension of Augustine's work, centered on the *Confessions*.

Look for the following titles, available now from
BARNES & NOBLE CLASSICS

Visit your local bookstore for these and more fine titles.
Or to order online go to: WWW.BN.COM/CLASSICS

Adventures of Huckleberry Finn	Mark Twain	1-59308-112-X	$5.95
The Adventures of Tom Sawyer	Mark Twain	1-59308-139-1	$5.95
The Aeneid	Vergil	1-59308-237-1	$8.95
Aesop's Fables		1-59308-062-X	$5.95
The Age of Innocence	Edith Wharton	1-59308-143-X	$5.95
Agnes Grey	Anne Brontë	1-59308-323-8	$6.95
Alice's Adventures in Wonderland and Through the Looking-Glass	Lewis Carroll	1-59308-015-8	$5.95
The Ambassadors	Henry James	1-59308-378-5	$8.95
Anna Karenina	Leo Tolstoy	1-59308-027-1	$8.95
The Arabian Nights	Anonymous	1-59308-281-9	$9.95
The Art of War	Sun Tzu	1-59308-017-4	$7.95
The Autobiography of an Ex-Colored Man and Other Writings	James Weldon Johnson	1-59308-289-4	$5.95
The Awakening and Selected Short Fiction	Kate Chopin	1-59308-113-8	$6.95
Babbitt	Sinclair Lewis	1-59308-267-3	$8.95
The Beautiful and Damned	F. Scott Fitzgerald	1-59308-245-2	$7.95
Beowulf	Anonymous	1-59308-266-5	$6.95
Billy Budd and The Piazza Tales	Herman Melville	1-59308-253-3	$6.95
Bleak House	Charles Dickens	1-59308-311-4	$9.95
The Bostonians	Henry James	1-59308-297-5	$8.95
The Brothers Karamazov	Fyodor Dostoevsky	1-59308-045-X	$9.95
Bulfinch's Mythology	Thomas Bulfinch	1-59308-273-8	$12.95
The Call of the Wild and White Fang	Jack London	1-59308-200-2	$5.95
Candide	Voltaire	1-59308-028-X	$4.95
The Canterbury Tales	Geoffrey Chaucer	1-59308-080-8	$9.95
A Christmas Carol, The Chimes and The Cricket on the Hearth	Charles Dickens	1-59308-033-6	$6.95
The Collected Oscar Wilde		1-59308-310-6	$9.95
The Collected Poems of Emily Dickinson		1-59308-050-6	$5.95
Common Sense and Other Writings	Thomas Paine	1-59308-209-6	$7.95
The Communist Manifesto and Other Writings	Karl Marx and Friedrich Engels	1-59308-100-6	$5.95
The Complete Sherlock Holmes, Vol. I	Sir Arthur Conan Doyle	1-59308-034-4	$7.95
The Complete Sherlock Holmes, Vol. II	Sir Arthur Conan Doyle	1-59308-040-9	$7.95
Confessions	Saint Augustine	1-59308-259-2	$6.95
A Connecticut Yankee in King Arthur's Court	Mark Twain	1-59308-210-X	$7.95
The Count of Monte Cristo	Alexandre Dumas	1-59308-151-0	$7.95
The Country of the Pointed Firs and Selected Short Fiction	Sarah Orne Jewett	1-59308-262-2	$7.95
Crime and Punishment	Fyodor Dostoevsky	1-59308-081-6	$9.95
Cyrano de Bergerac	Edmond Rostand	1-59308-387-4	$7.95
Daisy Miller and Washington Square	Henry James	1-59308-105-7	$5.95
Daniel Deronda	George Eliot	1-59308-290-8	$9.95

(continued)

Dead Souls	Nikolai Gogol	1-59308-092-1	$8.95
The Deerslayer	James Fenimore Cooper	1-59308-211-8	$10.95
Don Quixote	Miguel de Cervantes	1-59308-046-8	$9.95
Dracula	Bram Stoker	1-59308-114-6	$7.95
Emma	Jane Austen	1-59308-152-9	$6.95
Essays and Poems by Ralph Waldo Emerson		1-59308-076-X	$6.95
Essential Dialogues of Plato		1-59308-269-X	$10.95
The Essential Tales and Poems of Edgar Allan Poe		1-59308-064-6	$7.95
Ethan Frome and Selected Stories	Edith Wharton	1-59308-090-5	$5.95
Fairy Tales	Hans Christian Andersen	1-59308-260-6	$9.95
Far from the Madding Crowd	Thomas Hardy	1-59308-223-1	$7.95
The Federalist	Hamilton, Madison, Jay	1-59308-282-7	$7.95
Founding America: Documents from the Revolution to the Bill of Rights	Jefferson, et al.	1-59308-230-4	$10.95
Frankenstein	Mary Shelley	1-59308-115-4	$5.95
The Good Soldier	Ford Madox Ford	1-59308-268-1	$7.95
Great American Short Stories: From Hawthorne to Hemingway	Various	1-59308-086-7	$9.95
The Great Escapes: Four Slave Narratives	Various	1-59308-294-0	$6.95
Great Expectations	Charles Dickens	1-59308-116-2	$6.95
Grimm's Fairy Tales	Jacob and Wilhelm Grimm	1-59308-056-5	$9.95
Gulliver's Travels	Jonathan Swift	1-59308-132-4	$5.95
Hard Times	Charles Dickens	1-59308-156-1	$5.95
Heart of Darkness and Selected Short Fiction	Joseph Conrad	1-59308-123-5	$5.95
The History of the Peloponnesian War	Thucydides	1-59308-091-3	$11.95
The House of Mirth	Edith Wharton	1-59308-153-7	$7.95
The House of the Dead and Poor Folk	Fyodor Dostoevsky	1-59308-194-4	$9.95
The House of the Seven Gables	Nathaniel Hawthorne	1-59308-231-2	$7.95
The Hunchback of Notre Dame	Victor Hugo	1-59308-140-5	$7.95
The Idiot	Fyodor Dostoevsky	1-59308-058-1	$9.95
The Iliad	Homer	1-59308-232-0	$7.95
The Importance of Being Earnest and Four Other Plays	Oscar Wilde	1-59308-059-X	$6.95
Incidents in the Life of a Slave Girl	Harriet Jacobs	1-59308-283-5	$5.95
The Inferno	Dante Alighieri	1-59308-051-4	$7.95
The Interpretation of Dreams	Sigmund Freud	1-59308-298-3	$8.95
Ivanhoe	Sir Walter Scott	1-59308-246-0	$9.95
Jane Eyre	Charlotte Brontë	1-59308-117-0	$7.95
Journey to the Center of the Earth	Jules Verne	1-59308-252-5	$4.95
Jude the Obscure	Thomas Hardy	1-59308-035-2	$6.95
The Jungle Books	Rudyard Kipling	1-59308-109-X	$5.95
The Jungle	Upton Sinclair	1-59308-118-9	$6.95
King Solomon's Mines	H. Rider Haggard	1-59308-275-4	$7.95
Lady Chatterley's Lover	D. H. Lawrence	1-59308-239-8	$7.95
The Last of the Mohicans	James Fenimore Cooper	1-59308-137-5	$5.95
Leaves of Grass: First and "Death-bed" Editions	Walt Whitman	1-59308-083-2	$11.95
The Legend of Sleepy Hollow and Other Writings	Washington Irving	1-59308-225-8	$7.95
Les Misérables	Victor Hugo	1-59308-066-2	$9.95
Les Liaisons Dangereuses	Pierre Choderlos de Laclos	1-59308-240-1	$9.95
Little Women	Louisa May Alcott	1-59308-108-1	$6.95

(continued)

Lost Illusions	Honoré de Balzac	1-59308-315-7	$9.95
Madame Bovary	Gustave Flaubert	1-59308-052-2	$8.95
Maggie: A Girl of the Streets and Other Writings about New York	Stephen Crane	1-59308-248-7	$8.95
The Magnificent Ambersons	Booth Tarkington	1-59308-263-0	$8.95
Main Street	Sinclair Lewis	1-59308-386-6	$9.95
Man and Superman and Three Other Plays	George Bernard Shaw	1-59308-067-0	$7.95
The Man in the Iron Mask	Alexandre Dumas	1-59308-233-9	$10.95
Mansfield Park	Jane Austen	1-59308-154-5	$5.95
The Mayor of Casterbridge	Thomas Hardy	1-59308-309-2	$7.95
The Metamorphoses	Ovid	1-59308-276-2	$7.95
The Metamorphosis and Other Stories	Franz Kafka	1-59308-029-8	$6.95
Moby-Dick	Herman Melville	1-59308-018-2	$9.95
Moll Flanders	Daniel Defoe	1-59308-216-9	$8.95
My Ántonia	Willa Cather	1-59308-202-9	$5.95
My Bondage and My Freedom	Frederick Douglass	1-59308-301-7	$8.95
Narrative of Sojourner Truth		1-59308-293-2	$6.95
Narrative of the Life of Frederick Douglass, an American Slave		1-59308-041-7	$4.95
Nicholas Nickleby	Charles Dickens	1-59308-300-9	$8.95
Night and Day	Virginia Woolf	1-59308-212-6	$9.95
Nostromo	Joseph Conrad	1-59308-193-6	$9.95
Notes from Underground, The Double and Other Stories	Fyodor Dostoevsky	1-59308-124-3	$8.95
O Pioneers!	Willa Cather	1-59308-205-3	$7.95
The Odyssey	Homer	1-59308-009-3	$5.95
Of Human Bondage	W. Somerset Maugham	1-59308-238-X	$10.95
Oliver Twist	Charles Dickens	1-59308-206-1	$6.95
The Origin of Species	Charles Darwin	1-59308-077-8	$7.95
Paradise Lost	John Milton	1-59308-095-6	$7.95
The Paradiso	Dante Alighieri	1-59308-317-3	$9.95
Père Goriot	Honoré de Balzac	1-59308-285-1	$8.95
Persuasion	Jane Austen	1-59308-130-8	$5.95
Peter Pan	J. M. Barrie	1-59308-213-4	$6.95
The Phantom of the Opera	Gaston Leroux	1-59308-249-5	$7.95
The Picture of Dorian Gray	Oscar Wilde	1-59308-025-5	$4.95
The Pilgrim's Progress	John Bunyan	1-59308-254-1	$7.95
A Portrait of the Artist as a Young Man and Dubliners	James Joyce	1-59308-031-X	$6.95
The Possessed	Fyodor Dostoevsky	1-59308-250-9	$10.95
Pride and Prejudice	Jane Austen	1-59308-201-0	$6.95
The Prince and Other Writings	Niccolò Machiavelli	1-59308-060-3	$5.95
The Prince and the Pauper	Mark Twain	1-59308-218-5	$4.95
Pudd'nhead Wilson and Those Extraordinary Twins	Mark Twain	1-59308-255-X	$7.95
The Purgatorio	Dante Alighieri	1-59308-219-3	$9.95
Pygmalion and Three Other Plays	George Bernard Shaw	1-59308-078-6	$8.95
The Red Badge of Courage and Selected Short Fiction	Stephen Crane	1-59308-119-7	$4.95
Republic	Plato	1-59308-097-2	$6.95
The Return of the Native	Thomas Hardy	1-59308-220-7	$7.95
Robinson Crusoe	Daniel Defoe	1-59308-360-2	$5.95
A Room with a View	E. M. Forster	1-59308-288-6	$5.95
Scaramouche	Rafael Sabatini	1-59308-242-8	$9.95
The Scarlet Letter	Nathaniel Hawthorne	1-59308-207-X	$5.95

(continued)

The Scarlet Pimpernel	Baroness Orczy	1-59308-234-7	$5.95
The Secret Agent	Joseph Conrad	1-59308-305-X	$8.95
The Secret Garden	Frances Hodgson Burnett	1-59308-277-0	$5.95
Selected Stories of O. Henry		1-59308-042-5	$5.95
Sense and Sensibility	Jane Austen	1-59308-125-1	$5.95
Siddhartha	Hermann Hesse	1-59308-379-3	$5.95
Silas Marner and Two Short Stories	George Eliot	1-59308-251-7	$6.95
Sister Carrie	Theodore Dreiser	1-59308-226-6	$10.95
The Souls of Black Folk	W. E. B. Du Bois	1-59308-014-X	$7.95
The Strange Case of Dr. Jekyll and Mr. Hyde and Other Stories	Robert Louis Stevenson	1-59308-131-6	$4.95
Swann's Way	Marcel Proust	1-59308-295-9	$9.95
A Tale of Two Cities	Charles Dickens	1-59308-138-3	$5.95
Tarzan of the Apes	Edgar Rice Burroughs	1-59308-227-4	$7.95
Tess of d'Urbervilles	Thomas Hardy	1-59308-228-2	$7.95
This Side of Paradise	F. Scott Fitzgerald	1-59308-243-6	$6.95
Three Theban Plays	Sophocles	1-59308-235-5	$7.95
Thus Spoke Zarathustra	Friedrich Nietzsche	1-59308-278-9	$7.95
The Time Machine and The Invisible Man	H. G. Wells	1-59308-388-2	$6.95
Tom Jones	Henry Fielding	1-59308-070-0	$10.95
Treasure Island	Robert Louis Stevenson	1-59308-247-9	$4.95
The Turn of the Screw, The Aspern Papers and Two Stories	Henry James	1-59308-043-3	$5.95
Twenty Thousand Leagues Under the Sea	Jules Verne	1-59308-302-5	$5.95
Uncle Tom's Cabin	Harriet Beecher Stowe	1-59308-121-9	$7.95
Vanity Fair	William Makepeace Thackeray	1-59308-071-9	$7.95
The Varieties of Religious Experience	William James	1-59308-072-7	$7.95
Villette	Charlotte Brontë	1-59308-316-5	$9.95
The Virginian	Owen Wister	1-59308-236-3	$9.95
Walden and Civil Disobedience	Henry David Thoreau	1-59308-208-8	$5.95
War and Peace	Leo Tolstoy	1-59308-073-5	$12.95
The War of the Worlds	H. G. Wells	1-59308-362-9	$5.95
Ward No. 6 and Other Stories	Anton Chekhov	1-59308-003-4	$7.95
The Waste Land and Other Poems	T. S. Eliot	1-59308-279-7	$4.95
The Way We Live Now	Anthony Trollope	1-59308-304-1	$10.95
The Wind in the Willows	Kenneth Grahame	1-59308-265-7	$8.95
The Wings of the Dove	Henry James	1-59308-296-7	$9.95
Wives and Daughters	Elizabeth Gaskell	1-59308-257-6	$9.95
The Woman in White	Wilkie Collins	1-59308-280-0	$7.95
Women in Love	D. H. Lawrence	1-59308-258-4	$9.95
The Wonderful Wizard of Oz	L. Frank Baum	1-59308-221-5	$6.95
Wuthering Heights	Emily Brontë	1-59308-128-6	$5.95

BARNES & NOBLE CLASSICS

If you are an educator and would like to receive an
Examination or Desk Copy of a Barnes & Noble Classics edition,
please refer to Academic Resources on our website at
WWW.BN.COM/CLASSICS
or contact us at
BNCLASSICS@BN.COM

All prices are subject to change.